hale

A Single Dad Sports Romance

Hale Brothers
Book One

anastasija white

Edited by Caroline Knecht, https://reedsy.com/caroline-knecht

Cover Design © Leila @ Opulent Swag and Designs https://www.opulentswagand designs.com/

This book is intended for an 18+ audience.

For content warnings, please visit https://www.anastasijawhite.com

ISBN 978-609-08-0364-6 (ebook)

ISBN 978-609-08-0363-9 (paperback)

To anyone who ever had a crush on someone they shouldn't — this one's for you.
And now, be a good daddy's girl for Hunter Hale...and enjoy.

playlist

1. "bad idea right?" - Olivia Rodrigo
2. "Slow Down" - Chase Atlantic
3. "run for the hills" - Tate McRae
4. "Shape of You - Acoustic" - Ed Sheeran
5. "Wildest Dreams (Taylor's Version)" - Taylor Swift
6. "Sunshine" - OneRepublic
7. "Will you cry?" - Gracie Abrams
8. "Disaster" - Conan Gray
9. "Mentally Cheating" - Natalie Jane
10. "So Good" - Halsey
11. "Blinding Lights" - The Weeknd
12. "nasty" - Ariana Grande
13. "Power Over Me" - Dermot Kennedy
14. "uh oh" - Tate McRae
15. "A Thousand Years" - James Arthur

Find the rest of **HALE** playlist here:

1
friday night sucks
PIPER

THERE IS NOTHING I LOVE MORE THAN BEING ON THE beach alone.

Nothing feels better than sitting on the sand, watching as the waves reach the shore then retreat. The murmur of the ocean is the best lullaby, hypnotic and steady. I've been a complete mess these days, so coming to the beach has become my routine.

Sighing, I pull my legs into my chest and hug myself tight. It's almost the middle of August, and I feel lost. Taking a year off to work and cover my sister's medical bills wasn't something I expected to happen. I've got no plan or even the slightest idea of what I need to do next. Except for one: I desperately need to figure out a way to earn money so I can go back to school next year.

A burst of laughter bolts through the air, and I close my eyes. I love the quiet, but it's impossible to enjoy it when I have Hayden Hale as my best friend. He's the life of the party. The second he steps into any room, all eyes are on him. He's like a magnet, pulling everyone into his orbit. Some days I love him for that, but some days I want to stay away from him.

Hayden and I met when we were five and he and his mom moved back from Spain. We've been inseparable ever since. Boys at school couldn't understand why he preferred my company over theirs, while

1

girls wanted to be friends with me so they could get closer to him. No surprise we mostly kept to ourselves, spending time together and never getting bored. Nothing's changed, even now when we're twenty. *If I never meet my soulmate in a lover, I'll always have one in my best friend.*

"Pip!" Hayden yells.

Rolling my eyes, I hide my face in my knees. I hate being a mood-killer. It's one of the reasons I walked away from our group of friends.

"Piper," he calls out again.

Rule number one: the silent treatment won't work with Hayden. Rule number two: if I try it anyway, I need to be ready for his wrath. Tossing me over his shoulder, dragging me places I don't want to be, or just pushing me into the ocean—he's already tried plenty of options on me, and he'd be more than happy to repeat any of them.

Hayden lowers himself onto the sand beside me. Cold glass presses to my thigh, and I sit up straight. Glancing to my left, I meet his dark green eyes and smile. He has two beer bottles, and he's handing one of them to me.

"Thought this would cheer you up."

I take the beer and slowly take a sip, allowing the cold liquid to slide down my throat. "Friday night sucks, so I really needed this. Thanks, Hade."

"What can I do to help? I hate seeing you so bummed." He drapes an arm over my shoulders and pulls me to his side. "This isn't you, Pip."

"It's a new version of me: hopeless, jobless, degreeless." I shake my head at my bad attempt at a joke. "I'll get over it as soon as I find a job. Don't worry."

"Easier said than done." Hayden kisses my temple. "Do you want me to call my buddies again? Maybe they'll have something for you."

"Hade, you've already done enough." I sigh, putting my head on his shoulder. "Hopefully Mr. Russell hires me. My interview with him went well."

"Russell?"

"Yeah, the owner of the coffee shop. You know, at the corner of—"

"Like Joseph Russell?"

"Yeah, why?" I pull away and peer at Hayden. His green eyes are dark as he stares at me, his eyebrows drawn together.

"He's not a great dude, Pip. I don't want you around him."

"He was nothing but respectful to me. When I was at the shop, I talked to a girl who works there, Uma. She had only nice things to say about him." I nervously touch my necklace. Two years ago, Hayden asked me to help him pick out a gift for his mom's birthday. Eventually we ended up in the jewelry store, and I was mesmerized by a silver necklace with a little butterfly pendant. It was simple yet elegant. I wanted it so badly, but there was no way I could afford it since I was saving money for college. Hade caught me staring at it and gave it to me on my eighteenth birthday. I've barely taken it off since.

"She's his friend's daughter; of course he can't be an asshole to her." Hayden frowns. "He's bad news. I don't want you to work for him."

"I'm not even sure I'll get the job," I counter. "Do I need to remind you I've been looking for a job for a month? *A month*, Hayden. And all I hear is no. So many small businesses are struggling and can't hire extra staff. I'm slowly losing my shit. If I want to go back to school, I need a job so I can save money to pay for it."

"Why can't I pay for you?"

I've heard this question a million times. I know he means well, but I don't want to be his charity case.

"This conversation is over." I stand up and stomp away from him. Taking a swig of my beer, I head in the opposite direction of the bonfire and our friends.

"Piper." Hayden runs after me and grabs my hand, turning me around to face him. "I'm fucking confused. Why can't I pay for you?"

"Because I don't want your money. I'm fully capable of earning everything I need, just like I did when we were in high school. How can you—"

"It'll be a loan, okay? You'll pay me back."

"No."

"Why not?"

I throw my hands in the air, barely avoiding spilling my beer. "I'm not taking your money. That's final."

"But I want to help, Piper," he pleads, stepping closer and wrapping his arms around my waist. "You're my best friend, and I hate seeing you unhappy."

How can I ever be angry with him?

"Everything's going to be alright; I promise. I'll bounce back, and you'll see a smile on my face as usual. I'm your sunshine girl for a reason."

"You are." Hayden chuckles and kisses the tip of my nose. "Don't push me away. I hate it."

"I know."

His eyes roam over my face, and then he steps back. "Let's get back to our friends."

Hade takes my hand and makes me follow him. As soon as we get closer to the bonfire, I meet Kayla's glare. She's definitely not my number one fan.

I pull my hand out of Hayden's grip and go sit with Bo, as far from him and his groupie as possible. She's not even his girlfriend. Just another girl who follows him everywhere, hoping for a chance to hop into his bed. Hade can't even remember her name; he calls her "K." *Real boyfriend material, right there.*

"You okay?" I shift my gaze to Bo and smile. He's the drummer in Hayden's band, Sabotage, and also my friend.

"I'm good," I say. "I might start a job on Monday."

"Really? That's great." He smiles, and we clink our bottles together. "Where at?"

"I'll tell you more if I get the offer. I don't want to jinx it." And I don't want him to lecture me if he's heard anything about Mr. Russell too.

"Cool." Bo leans forward, resting his elbows on his knees. His deep brown eyes scrutinize me, and my cheeks warm. He likes me, and it's obvious to everyone, including Hade. Rule number three of being

4

best friends with Hayden Hale: sleeping with his buddies never ends well for me, so I stopped taking the risk right after my hookup with Bo.

"Do you need a ride home?" Bo asks.

"Thanks. I'll walk."

Bo sighs in exasperation. "Hade needs to let you breathe, Piper."

"It has nothing to do with him." I tsk and take a sip of my beer.

The problem with me getting involved with Hayden's friends is simple. He either claims the guys are bad for me or starts cheering for them, encouraging me to give them a chance. Sex with Bo was good, but Hayden following me around and telling me how much his friend likes me was horrible. There's no way I'll repeat that mistake again.

"Yo, Hade, how's your brother? I think I saw his car at your parents' yesterday," Jimmy, the guitarist, shouts, drawing everyone's attention to Hayden.

"Getting used to the city. He hasn't lived in the US for twenty-three years now, just visited here and there. He's having a blast." Hayden snickers, and everyone else laughs too, while I continue to sip my drink.

I look at the ocean again, racking my brain for something I remember about Hayden's brother. Hunter is thirteen years older than Hayden and me, and he's been living in Europe since he was ten. Of course, I saw him play soccer when Hade and I would watch his brother's games on TV, but the last time I saw him in person, I was barely fourteen. I never really talked to him, unless you count "hi" and "bye" as conversation. Hunter Hale is a mystery, one I'm not sure I'll ever solve. We have nothing in common, and we are from two different worlds.

"I'm sure he's having a great time," Kayla says, shoving her boobs in Hayden's face and sneaking a glance at me. "We're going to have a lot of fun too. As soon as *college* starts."

Her jab isn't even subtle. She knows I'm taking a year off, and she rubs it in every opportunity she gets.

"Speak for yourself." Hayden pushes her away a little and meets my gaze. "To have fun, I need my best friend with me. Only her."

Love you, I mouth to him, and he winks as he stands up.

"Sorry, guys, but your questions about my brother kinda reminded me of something." Hayden comes over and hauls me to my feet. "I promised to take my niece for a walk around town tomorrow morning. Show her my favorite places."

"And why do you need Piper with you?" Kayla asks through her teeth.

"Because Pip is coming with me." He shrugs and drags me away from the bonfire, waving over his shoulder. "See you at the rehearsal, guys."

"Bye," I yell, following him with no questions asked.

Once we're in Hayden's car, I squint at him. "Why the farce?"

"Farce? I promised to take Story for a walk around town, and you're coming with us." His eyes round, and he's staring at me like Puss in Boots. "Pretty please, Piper? I don't know anyone better than you to deal with Story."

"To *deal with* her?" My brows knit together as he starts the engine.

"Hunter is looking for a nanny for Story, and so far? He hates everyone," Hayden mutters. "He has two more interviews tomorrow, and asked me to look after her."

"What about her mom? Will she come live in the US as well?"

"Amelia's in Italy right now, filming another movie," he explains, chewing on his bottom lip. He's never liked his brother's wife, and nothing has changed since the divorce was finalized. "I have no idea what she plans to do next, but I hope she'll keep focusing on herself and her career. Hunter will be fine on his own."

"But he's not on his own; he has a daughter," I correct him, and Hayden snorts.

"That's exactly why I want you with me. You'll know what to do, and I'm sure you're gonna love Story. She's the cutest little girl in the world."

"Okay, I'll go with you."

"I love when you're on board with my plans," he says, and I smile.

"Well, usually your plans don't disappoint." I sigh in relief. "God,

I didn't realize I was so tired. But I'm still grateful to you for inviting me tonight."

"Looks like Friday night doesn't really suck, huh?" Hayden asks, and we both burst out laughing.

"Definitely not."

I look out the window; excitement builds inside me. I met his niece a long time ago, when she was just a year old. It's been six years, and I'm super curious about Story. Hayden doesn't give his love and attention to many people, but he adores this little girl to the moon and back. It'll be interesting to see her again. I just hope she likes me.

2
lost girls
PIPER

"RILEY, DAMMIT," I CURSE, STUMBLING OVER MY SISTER'S bag on the floor.

"What?" She stops in the doorway, watching me with amusement. "Why are you shouting?"

"I'm not shouting," I huff, massaging my ankle. "Your stuff is everywhere, and this isn't a freaking mansion."

"Well, Piper, if you were watching—"

"Nuh-uh." I shake my head, cutting her off. "We're not talking about me now. We're talking about you. You need to do better."

Riley sighs and leans against the doorframe, taking a bite of the apple she's holding in her hand. "It's just..." She hesitates; her eyes are locked on mine. "It's nothing, sorry."

"Is something bothering you? How do you feel? Did you sleep okay? Did you eat?" Questions fly out of my mouth at full speed, fueled by my worry for her. Images of Riley in her bed fill my mind in an instant, and I'm a mess all over again.

"Piper," Riley chuckles. She winds her hands around my waist; her big crystal blue eyes glimmer with happiness as she smiles at me. "You heard the doctor. We know what's wrong with me now, and I've been okay. My thyroid is under control, I promise."

"Memories are a bitch, baby." I tuck a strand of her long blonde hair behind her ear.

The only two attributes we got from our mother are our hair color and our full lips. All the rest, we got from our fathers. At least, I can say Riley has a father. Her dad, Garret, was our mother's husband the longest, for six years, until she got bored and kicked him out. He's still here, ready to help support Riley and me whenever and however he can. Unlike my father...who I've never seen. I have no idea who he is. He's the only man my mom doesn't want to talk about. It's as if he never existed.

"I know, Pip." Riley buries her face in my neck, hugging me tightly. She's fifteen already, but I often treat her as if she's still a child. Over the years, I've gotten used to taking care of her, and it's not easy to change my habits. "Sorry if I made you worried."

"Don't apologize." I cup her cheek with my palm, caressing it with my fingers. "But you better tell me what you're hiding from me. I'm all ears."

Riley chuckles, stepping back. "You're not letting me off the hook, are you?"

"Never." I wink, grab her hand, and drag her to the living room. Hayden and Story are going to pick me up in an hour, so I have time for a quick interrogation. "Is it a boy?"

"How did you know?" Her eyes widen, and I burst out laughing.

"Just a wild guess." I nudge her with my shoulder as we slump down onto the couch. "Start talking, little lady. Maybe I'll know what to do."

"I wanted to talk to you about it, I just wasn't sure how to start. Um...it's Josh, my dance partner. Yesterday he told me he likes me," she mutters, lowering her gaze to her feet. "It's all good, and I'm excited, but...Lola likes him too."

Snuggling in more comfortably, I peer at her face. Boy drama between two friends is the worst. Another reason I cherish my friendship with Hayden so much. Having a male best friend saves me a million troubles.

No boy will ever be worthy of ruining my relationship with Hayden Hale.

"HEY." I climb inside Hayden's Honda CR-V and glance in the backseat, instantly locking my gaze with a little girl's. Her big green eyes framed by thick black eyelashes twinkle with mischief, and the next thing I know, she's smiling from ear to ear.

"I'm Piper," I say.

"Hey, Piper," she murmurs. "I'm Story. It's very nice to meet you."

"You, too." I grin in return. "Actually, we've already met. But you've grown so much! You're such a beautiful girl."

"That's because I'm Mommy's copy," she says, and I register Hayden's eye roll. "Though I have my dad's eye color."

"You're a Hale, Story," Hayden chimes in, and the little girl giggles. "Green eyes are our thing."

I shake my head, looking out the window. Griffith Park is ahead of us. I should've guessed. Sometimes this guy is so boring and so predictable, especially for a true artist. There are tons of unique places in LA, and yet he chose an old classic.

"Any particular plans for our day in Griffith Park?" I ask sweetly.

Hayden glares at me, noticing my sarcasm. "We're going to have lots of fun, Evans. Trust the process."

"The process?" I lift an eyebrow, and he snorts. Last time I trusted his process, I ended up half naked, dancing on the table at the bar he was playing at. Some guy tried to give me five hundred bucks and something extra in a private room. "You and I both know nothing good comes from that."

"Everything is going to be alright, Pip. I won't let you down," he assures me. Story is with us, and Hayden is many things, but he's always responsible. His family would disown him if he let something happen to his brother's daughter.

Ten minutes later, Hayden parks, and we slowly climb out of the car. Story and I glance at each other, and she pads closer to me. Her long brown hair is collected into a high ponytail, and it bounces as she steps forward. Scrunching her little upturned nose, she smiles at me, and I grin in return.

Heading further into the park, we walk straight to the zoo. Story talks nonstop, telling Hayden and me about her life in London. I listen closely, and, for whatever reason, she's not sad to leave the city behind. She sounds excited when she talks about Los Angeles and her time with her dad. He's been focusing entirely on her since the day they moved here two weeks ago, and that's not something she experienced while living in England.

We've spent more than two hours at the zoo, going from one animal to the other. It's so fun, I often forget Story's just seven years old. Her thoughts, the questions she asks, and her behavior don't match her age at all. It makes me wonder what made her this way. Is it just because her parents were often absent? Or is it something else? She intrigues me, and her sunshiny energy fills me with happiness. I enjoy her company, a significant change from the days I've had this past month.

"Are you Hayden's girlfriend?" Story asks as we sit on a bench.

"Nope. He's my best friend," I tell her, watching her uncle from afar as he strolls away to buy us ice cream. "He's family."

"Okay." She giggles, playing with a strand of her hair. "I just thought—"

"We've been friends for fifteen years. I love him, but only as a friend."

Story becomes thoughtful, avoiding eye contact. This reaction is weird, but I decide not to push it. The last thing I want is for her to be afraid of me or think I'm trying to invade her privacy. I lean closer, bowing my head. "Want to see my favorite animal?"

"Your favorite animal?" Story's voice hitches in her throat, and she licks her lips. Her gaze darts to Hayden, who has his eyes glued to his phone while waiting for the ice cream.

"Fennecs. A fennec fox."

"Should we wait for my uncle?" she asks, and I shake my head no. For a moment, her pupils widen, and I think maybe I'm asking too much from this child. She basically just met me, so she has zero trust in me. Maybe—

"Cool!" Story jumps to her feet and grabs my hand.

"You sure about this?" I ask.

"Yes." She exhales. "I've never had as much fun as I am right now...with you and Uncle Hayden."

"Well..." I squeeze her hand and lead us away from the bench and Hade. "Get ready; we're going to become lost girls. Hayden will need to think *really* hard to remember what my favorite animal is."

3
bad news, hunter

HUNTER

I TAKE A SIP OF WATER, HIDING MY IRRITATION BEHIND THE glass. If someone told me it'd be this hard to find a nanny for my kid, I would've laughed in their faces. I'm not looking for someone with a PhD. I don't even need a highly skilled person. All I'm looking for is someone who loves kids, will be happy to spend time with my daughter, and won't flirt with me.

So far, it's been a disaster.

"You know, I never watched a soccer game before yesterday, it was pretty intense!" the candidate exclaims, grinning at me.

"Football is intense," I say, noticing her frown in confusion. "Sorry, it's a habit. After living in Europe for so many years, I can't bring myself to call it soccer. I've tried but I can't, it will always be football to me."

"Oh, I get it. How do you like being back home then?" she asks, tucking strands of her red hair behind her ears. Her big blue eyes are focused on me, and her lips curl in a pouty smile. *Nice, we're talking about me?* How about asking about Story? About what things she loves? About her favorite toys or movies? "I've never been to Europe, but I'm sure it's very different from the States."

"It is. But LA is my hometown, so it's all good." I shrug and set my glass on the table. "I honestly expected Story to struggle, but so far she loves everything here."

"Cool," she says, leaning forward. I'm very close to kicking her out, because her desire to impress me is becoming ridiculous. She hasn't asked a single question about Story. "What about the girl's mom? Will she be visiting?"

I set my jaw and huff through my nostrils. The reason I told the staffing agency to be honest about who I am is simple: I didn't want to hide anything from my future employee. I wanted them to understand what they were signing up for, especially since I'll need them to share the house with Story and me once I start playing. And yet, it's only brought me a horde of women vying for my attention, as if I'm the one who needs a babysitter.

There were two exceptions. Two very nice, very professional ladies who didn't cross boundaries. Why didn't I hire them? Because Story didn't like them, and I always listen to her.

"My ex-wife is a very busy person. She has her hands full with her current and future projects. She'll be visiting from time to time, but I genuinely don't understand what that has to do with being Story's nanny."

"Oh, sorry, I didn't mean to intrude. It's just..." She leans back and starts fiddling with her fingers, nervously looking around. She finally has figured out my mood, and she's trying to find a way to fix the situation. Unfortunately for her, I've already made my decision. There's no way I'm hiring someone who isn't interested in Story. "I just wanted to see the whole...er...picture."

"And? How do you find the whole picture?" I scowl. She's wasting my time, and I hate it.

"It's easy to see you love your daughter. You're going to be busy with your job, so you'll need someone who can live with the two of you." She flashes me an awkward smile. "Story will be going to elementary school, so the person you hire will be taking her to school and then picking her up later. They'll need to help her with homework, with any extracurricular activities, and also with food. Did I get that right?"

"You did," I confirm, taking a glass from the table and holding it between my palms.

She sighs and tilts her head. "You're definitely not going to choose me."

"Unfortunately," I say slowly, "I had a few candidates, but Story didn't like any of them. That's why I'm still looking."

"Do you think she won't like me?" Her brows pinch together, and I click my tongue. Life outside the US toughened me up. Some people might call me an asshole, but I can't pay any attention to them. I love to be straightforward, and I rarely sugarcoat anything.

"It's not about my daughter." I hold her gaze, lowering the glass back onto the table. "I'm not interested in a relationship."

"But I—" Her cheeks flame red, and her eyes widen in an instant.

"You were flirting with me the second I invited you inside. You barely listened to anything I had to say about Story, but you were more than keen to know about my ex-wife and my career," I bite out, folding my arms across my chest. "I just need a babysitter for my daughter, nothing else."

"Nothing else," she mutters under her breath. Her still-red cheeks round as she puffs in exasperation.

"Our time is up. Thank you for coming," I say.

The woman nods, stands up from the table, and heads to the hallway. I follow her to the front door and watch her open it wide. She halts in her tracks and looks over her shoulder, her eyes wandering over my face.

"Good luck finding a nanny, Mr. Hale," she mumbles snidely and closes the door behind her.

Bad news, Hunter—she was the last one the agency suggested.

Damn it.

Cursing, I go into the living room and check the time on my phone. Four p.m. I wonder what Story and Hayden are doing. The only thing I was able to get out of my brother was reassurance. *Stop being an overprotective jerk. Story and I are going to have a lot of fun today.* As if I could stop being so careful around her. It's not possible, especially not when my brother is involved.

He's a walking disaster...or at least he was. Our age difference is big, but the main problem is we grew up on opposite sides of the world. We've barely seen each other since I was eighteen, when Mom and Hayden moved to the US permanently, leaving me alone in Spain. All those short-lived visits were never enough, and the bond I could've had with Hayden didn't have a chance to form. We're like strangers who share a bloodline. Unfortunately.

I plop down onto the couch and close my eyes. This shit is exhausting for real, and it's far from how I imagined it in my head. For someone who's used to routine and stability, my new reality is total chaos. I'm glad to be home, to spend time with my family, and for Story to get to know her grandparents. But, at the same time, these changes are driving me up the wall. My desire to find balance is full of desperation, and I'm reminded of Amelia's words once again.

Really, Hunter? Going back to the US will end your career—or more like the remnants of your former glory. Is that the life you want for yourself? For your daughter?

She pissed me off that day, and I made a promise to myself. I'll give Story the life she deserves, and I'll be at the top of my game in no time.

Love and relationships are off the table for me. Falling in love again sounds as unrealistic as Sir Alex Ferguson agreeing to come back and coach Manchester United. Marriage sucks, and I have no desire to go down that road ever again. Story and my career are the only things I care about, and I intend to do anything in my power to prove Amelia wrong.

A new message pops up on my screen, and I snatch my phone from the table. I quickly unlock it, and my lips stretch into the biggest smile. I might regret getting married to Amelia, but I'll always be grateful to her for our daughter. Story is my whole world. She filled the void in my chest and gave me purpose, an undeniable strength to help me move forward. For her, I'll move mountains, and I will never second-guess my decisions. If it's good for my little girl, then I'm all in. Another reason I moved to the US. I knew it'd be better for her here.

I swipe through the pictures, feeling happiness overwhelm me. Hayden definitely made sure Story had an amazing day. In one of the pictures, she's sitting on a bench with an enormous ice cream in her hands, smiling at the camera. In another one, she's jumping in the air with my brother. They're both laughing, and their eyes are full of mischief.

The third photo confuses me a bit, and I zoom in to look more closely. Some blonde is holding Story's hand. They both have their backs to the camera. I frown, trying to find an explanation. Then it hits me—she must be Hayden's best friend. I haven't seen her in years, but I recall a girl with blonde hair. Nothing else comes to mind because I barely know her, let alone remember her name.

ME:

When are you going to bring her back?

HAYDEN:

7pm?

ME:

Story needs to eat.

HAYDEN:

Don't worry about it, big bro. I'll take care of everything.

Tossing my phone onto the table, I stand up from the couch and stroll to my bedroom, passing Story's room and a guest room on my way. I have three hours to myself, and I know what to do. I've been way too tense the past few days, and the need to relieve my stress is stronger than ever. A hot shower is a must, and then I can start my search from scratch. My first practice with Los Angeles City FC is on Monday, so I have about four days to find the perfect nanny for Story. Hopefully this time, luck will be on my side. I need it.

"DAD!" Story's yell pierces the air, and I jump to my feet, leap over the table, and run to the hallway. I stop in my tracks the second my eyes land on Hayden. He stares at me with his eyebrow arched in question, not understanding my bewildered look. "Daddy, you're not going to believe what I did today."

I shift my gaze to Story and crack a smile, leaning against the doorframe. "Tell me."

"I was a lost girl." She grins at me and steps closer, holding my gaze. "Piper and I snuck away from Hayden and went to watch the fennecs. They are her favorite animal."

Her words ignite my anxiety, and it takes a toll on me not to snap. Being a lost girl and sneaking away with someone she just met doesn't sit right with me.

"Weren't you afraid to leave your uncle?"

"No. I was sure he was going to find us."

"But what if he didn't?" I ask Story, but Hayden decides to step in.

"And that's why I was sure she shouldn't tell you anything," he mutters, the disappointment clear in his voice. "I trust Piper like I trust myself. She would've never done anything to hurt Story, would've never let anything bad happen to her. She's wonderful, and she made the day a thousand times better."

"I didn't—"

"I know you, Hunter." Hayden scratches his platinum blond buzz with his hand. He's annoyed and disappointed, and I feel torn. Yes, questioning his decisions and his friend's intentions isn't nice. But at the same time, he has no idea what it means to be a dad.

"Sorry, it won't happen again," he says.

I open my mouth to tell him that he's taking this the wrong way, but Story's words make me freeze. "I want to see Piper again. She's the best."

"When did I say you can't see her?" I crouch in front of her, taking her hands in mine. "You know how much I love you, and hearing about you getting lost scares me to death."

Story's eyes roam over my face, the corners of her mouth twitching. She tries hard to suppress her smile, but fails. "We didn't get lost. Piper sent a message to Uncle Hayden when we left. She gave him a clue."

"Like a scavenger hunt?" I glance between Hayden and Story, and they nod. "Nice. She must really know what she's doing."

"Piper rocks. I've never met anyone who's so good with kids. It's like she understands them," Hayden murmurs, grinning at me. "I felt like a third wheel."

Chuckling, I stand. "Sorry if I upset you. It wasn't my intention."

"Nah, it's all good." He steps closer and covers Story's ears with his palms. "I'm kinda used to my brother being a jerk."

"Fair." I lower my gaze to Story's face. She reminds me of her mom so damn much, and sometimes that's not a good thing at all. "Go to your room, change your clothes, and wash your hands. I'll be waiting for you in the kitchen."

"Okay." Story runs to her room without looking back.

I focus my attention on Hayden. "Want some coffee?"

"Definitely."

In the kitchen, I quickly make the coffee while Hayden tells me more about his day with Story and Piper. The longer I listen to him, the harder it is not to smile. Thanks to him, my daughter had an incredible day, and I should be grateful to Piper. I'll make sure to thank her later.

"What about you? Did you find a nanny?" Hayden asks, taking a sip of his drink.

My eyes zero in on his tattoos. They cover his fingers and knuckles and go up higher, hiding under his tee. I have my fair share of tatts too, and they all are special. I could talk for hours about the things I've inked on my body, but I know nothing about my brother's. Another thing I need to fix.

"Unfortunately, no." I shake my head and lean back on the stool. "I need to find a new agency, because the last one was a total fiasco."

"What are you looking for? I mean, I have no clue what you need from a nanny."

"At this point, I just need someone who'll love Story and be happy to spend time with her. Someone your niece will like." I heave a sigh, looking around the kitchen. "Heck, I don't even need someone with a degree. Just someone kind and attentive to my kid's needs."

Hayden watches me as if he's in a daze. Slowly, he inches forward, setting his elbows on the table. "I know the perfect person for the job."

"What? Who?"

"My best friend. Piper's exactly what you're looking for."

4

let the right one in

HUNTER

I stare at Hayden in stupefaction. I don't remember much about Piper, but I'm more than certain she's a college student. Does he expect her to work for me and study at the same time? It doesn't make any sense.

"I don't think that's going to work," I finally say, and he frowns, a look of confusion crossing his features.

"Why not?"

"Well, I need someone who'll be able to live here, and if I'm not mistaken, Piper is still in college."

"She's not. Pip is taking a year off, and she needs a job. She wants to earn money to pay for college next year."

"Look, Hayden, I get it." I take my mug between my palms and stare him in the eyes. "She's your best friend, and you want to help her, but—"

"What the hell?" He leans away, looking at me as if it's the first time we're seeing each other. "Do you think my friendship with Piper is the only reason I'm suggesting you hire her?"

"Isn't it?"

"Fame sucks, I get it, but not everyone's after your money." Hayden pokes his tongue into his cheek. "I'm your family. I'm Story's uncle, and I'm invested in her well-being too. That's why I think Piper is the best shot you have. Especially after today."

I lower my gaze to the table, and my mind goes into overdrive. I have a thousand different thoughts and feelings, and the tiniest ray of hope flutters in my chest. I'm always more than practical, yet as an athlete I also believe in luck. Sometimes winning is not just about teamwork. Sometimes it's a confluence of circumstances—pure luck. What if it's like that with Story's babysitter?

"Why did she decide to sit this year out?" I ask.

"Pip doesn't like to talk about it, so let me put it this way: her little sister's health declined. They visited a ton of doctors, did tons of tests, and finally found the reason. Riley's good now, but someone needs to pay the bills."

"She took money from her college fund? What about their parents?"

"Riley's dad gave them what he had, but it didn't cover everything. Their mom was looking for a job at the time and couldn't help at all. Piper's college money was the only way they could pay for it."

I set my mug on the table and narrow my eyes. "I'm sorry, but... you have money. Why couldn't—"

"I tried." He shakes his head, holding my gaze. "Piper Evans is the most stubborn person I've ever met. According to her, the fact that I *can* lend her money doesn't mean I should. I can't even tell you how many times we fought because I wanted to help and she refused to take my money. That's how she is."

"Admirable," I say, and Hayden bursts out laughing.

"Not the word I would've used." He finally stops his cackling. "Anyway, she needs a job, and you need a nanny. It's a win-win if you ask me. Plus, she's not a stranger; she's my best friend. Our parents know and love her. You can talk to them if you don't trust my judgment."

"I trust you," I reassure him. "Though...just because she and Story got along doesn't mean she'll be a great nanny."

He sighs and rolls his eyes. "Pip is kind and incredibly caring. She loves kids. She was studying to become an elementary school teacher because she likes spending time with children. It's not a burden for her. She enjoys it."

Gawking at Hayden in silence, I weigh my options. Practice starts next week. I could go to another agency and try to find a babysitter before then, or I could hire my brother's best friend and have it taken care of today.

Dammit, I'd be an idiot to say no.

"Okay, you're right. She does sound perfect."

Hayden grins, winking at me. "I told you."

"When do you think she can start?" The second the question leaves my mouth, his face drops. I cock an eyebrow at him just as Story enters the kitchen. "What?"

"Didn't I tell you she's stubborn?" he mutters. *Unbelievable.* My daughter climbs up onto the chair beside me, puts her elbows on the table, and lowers her chin into her palms. "I'll need to figure out how to convince her."

"So there's a chance she won't agree?"

"A tiny, itsy-bitsy chance." Hayden shrugs awkwardly and then shifts his gaze to Story. "I might need your help, kid. Will you go with me to see Piper tomorrow?"

Story instantly sits up straight. Her eyes are round, and her mouth is agape. She looks excited, and my lips involuntarily stretch into a smile. "Can I? Dad?"

"Definitely." I ruffle her hair, making her giggle. "Seems like you're going to have lots of fun with your uncle again."

SITTING on the side of the pool with my legs in the water, I watch Story swim. It's one of her favorite things to do, and the happy look on her face is evidence of how much she enjoys it. She catches my gaze and swims to me. I help her climb out of the pool, and she nestles beside me, looking at me with a playful smile.

"What's wrong, Daddy?" she asks.

"I think I'm a bit worried." I drape a hand over Story's shoulders and haul her to my side. My tee is instantly soaking wet, but I don't care. These simple moments are what I love the most, and I'd do anything to prolong them. "I'm going to start practicing on Monday, while you'll be left with someone you barely know."

"It won't be the first time!" Her laughter is melodic, but shivers run down my spine. I failed this kid so many times, always reassuring myself that at least she had her mom. While in reality Amelia was on the road more often than I was over the last few years. Her career took off two years ago, and she's in her prime now, taking project after project.

"This time it'll be different. Piper is nice."

"You really like her, don't you?" I squint at her, and she nods, cuddling closer to me. "Well, I look forward to meeting her today, even if I was skeptical about her agreeing to work for us. I didn't think your uncle would be able to convince her to accept my offer."

"That's why he took me with him. Piper couldn't say no when I told her I'd love for her to be my nanny." Story grins, batting her eyelashes at me. "Uncle Hayden said I was his secret weapon."

"You definitely were." I laugh wholeheartedly, leaning down to plant a kiss on the top of her head. She smells like strawberries and coconut, and I can't help but smile wider. "I haven't seen Piper in six years, and even then I never talked to her. So I hope we get along."

"You will." Story pats my knee, wiggles a little, and jumps back into the water. "She's great."

I stand up and walk to the table, where I left my phone. It's almost two p.m. already. "Sweetie, you need to get out of the pool. Your uncle will be here in five minutes."

Story nods curtly and climbs out of the pool. She takes a towel and wraps it around herself, puts on her flip-flops, and goes into the house. I wasn't often there for my child, but I was still able to form a bond with her. She trusts me, respects me, and always listens to me. I treat her the same way, explaining my decisions to her when I say no or forbid her from doing something. I earned her love, and it's the most precious feeling in the world.

I follow Story inside and head to my bedroom. I pull off my tee and halt in my tracks, seeing the front door open and Hayden step inside. First, he's early. Second, maybe I shouldn't have given him a key. I don't like when people barge into my house, even if they're family. It feels like an intrusion. I want to be the one to decide who enters. Let the right one in, not the other way around.

"Hey, Hunter." Hayden waves, and I nod in greeting. "This girl is as punctual as the spring tide. You can never be late with her."

He moves aside, and Piper walks into my house. I don't know what I expected, but it wasn't this. She's lean, with full breasts and round hips. Feminine and petite with a narrow curve to her waist. Piper is not how I remember her, and, based on her shocked expression, I don't think I look the way she remembers me either.

"Fuck..." she whispers.

Well, fuck, indeed. How on Earth did I agree to hire someone who looks like that? This is going to be a disaster.

I clear my throat and force a smile. "It's very...um, nice to see you again, Piper. Please, come inside. I need a few minutes to change."

"Sure," Hayden chimes in. He grabs Piper's hand and drags her to the living room. She keeps her eyes zeroed in on the tile, not allowing herself to look at me.

Could this be less awkward, please?

I hope Story is still changing. That will buy me some time to get used to Piper. She's completely different from how I remember her. Where did her glasses go? What the hell happened to her always pale face? Dammit. Looks like my best friend, Angelo Russo, was right—not having sex for months has made me way too agitated. I'm acting so out of character right now.

Quickly, I put on a white T-shirt and black sweatpants and go back to the living room, Hayden's voice gets louder. He's going on and on about my house, my future with the team, and Story's classes. He's overloading this girl with information I was planning to share myself. And I don't think I like it. I shouldn't have agreed to him joining us today.

I linger in the doorway. My eyes land on Piper. She sits on the couch with her legs crossed; her blonde hair is in a high ponytail, bouncing up and down as she swings her leg back and forth. I let my eyes wander over her form, taking in her tight pink tee and bleached blue jeans. Piper looks simple and effortless, and I like it. She doesn't need fancy clothes to bring out her beauty.

She meets my gaze, and her rosy lips part. A sparkle flashes behind her chocolate brown eyes, and her cheeks turn pink. Her fingers fly to a little pendant on her necklace, toying with it. The best testament of her nervousness. Apparently, it can get even more awkward than it was.

5
under control

"So, um, I want to thank you for going with Hayden and Story to Griffith Park. She couldn't stop talking about it when she was getting ready for bed that night. I appreciate it." I smile at Piper, looking her in the eyes as we sit on the couch. Her face lights up, and she nods.

"I'm glad she enjoyed herself. We had a great time together, even if at first I wasn't so sure about the place Hade had chosen," she says, leaning back against the couch. Her leg finally stops swinging.

"I still don't understand what's wrong with Griffith Park," he mutters, plopping down beside her and draping an arm over her shoulder. "You're just being obnoxious, Pip."

"I love Griffith Park," I exclaim slowly. "If I hadn't been so busy these last two weeks, settling into this house, getting Story registered for school, and negotiating my contract, I would've taken her there myself."

"Looks like the Hale brothers have me outnumbered." Piper nudges Hayden with her elbow, and he laughs. I smile, watching them. The memories emerge in my mind. It's exactly how I remember them—always together, making fun of and then defending each other, shouting themselves hoarse. Their friendship reminds me of my own lack of friends.

I *do* have friends, but none of them are from my childhood. Those times were pretty darn lonely.

"Looks like it, Pip." He squeezes her shoulder, and I lift an eyebrow. I know they're just friends, always have been. *Do they act like that around other people?* If I were interested in this girl, I would want her best friend to stay away from her. Or I wouldn't have approached her at all. Who wants to compete with another man?

"When would you expect me to move in?" Piper's voice draws my attention back to her. I blink, shooing away all my other thoughts. I like quickly how she changed the subject. She means business, and it's something I respect.

"Tomorrow evening," I answer, and she instantly bites the inside of her cheek. "If it's okay with you, of course."

She sighs, glancing at Hayden and then focusing on me. "You start practice on Monday, so it makes sense you want me here tomorrow. Just...I have a sister. Riley. She was invited to a birthday party, and I promised to take her and bring her home."

"When does the party end?"

"Around eight. It'll take about an hour to get her home and then drive here. Is it okay if I get here around nine?"

"Sounds great," I assure her, and her lips stretch into a genuine smile. "Hayden told me a little about Riley, so if you want to, you can bring here from time to time. I'm sure Story will love her."

Her eyes dart between Hayden and me. She looks so damn cute, I can't help but grin.

"You have no idea what that means to me. Honestly. Thank you so much, Hunter. Oh...I'm...um..." Her cheeks flush red, and she tucks a strand of hair behind her ear. "What should I call you? Is Hunter okay? Or maybe Mr. Hale?"

And I suddenly feel old. Her question isn't about our thirteen-year age gap, but about me being her employer. Yet it still gives me an ick. "Hunter is fine."

"Okay."

"I would've been surprised if you said Mr. Hale," Hayden says, and I look at him. "Your fans call you Hale, and I think that's more suitable."

"Good thing I don't have fans here." I shrug and catch Piper's gaze on me. The doubt in her eyes is evident, and I snort loudly, just as Story enters the living room. "Since I've been in LA, only one person has recognized me. But it was vague. Like, 'Oh, look, the soccer guy.' I've never been happier, walking down the street, going to the store without being noticed."

"You're the weirdest celebrity I know," he adds and moves away from Piper. He leans forward and grabs Story, pulling her onto his lap. She giggles and winds her arms around his shoulders, pressing her head into the crook of his neck. "You were on the Olympic—"

"That doesn't mean anything. Of the most popular sports in the US, soccer takes fifth place, according to some research. I'm not Tom Brady, and I'm not LeBron either. I'm fine with it."

"I love it here," Story says quietly. She meets my gaze and smiles hesitantly. "You can just be my dad when we go out."

My skin warms. Moments like this are exactly why I moved back home. I can finally be Story's dad and play my favorite sport without being afraid that I'm failing as a father or failing my team. I can have both with no sacrifices and more anonymity. Exactly what I longed for.

"Your dad is not just your dad," Piper murmurs, inching closer to Story and tapping her nose with the pad of her finger. "He's your superhero. No matter where you are."

Story's eyes are shining bright as she grins at Piper. "And you're going to be my best friend," she exclaims, leaning away to get a better look at her uncle. "Hear that, Uncle Hayden? Piper will be my best friend forever in no time."

"Looks like you have some competition, Hade." Piper laughs loudly, pressing her palm to her belly. My gaze falls to her chest, and I feel fucking weird. My eyes hone in on the outline of her lacy bra under her tee. Licking my lips, I swallow my nerves. "Er—"

I tear my gaze away from Piper's chest and focus my attention on her face. *Play it cool, Hunter.* There's no way I'm admitting to ogling my daughter's nanny's tits. Very nice, round tits...oh, fucking awesome.

"I already asked my lawyer to prepare a contract for you," I drawl.

"Lawyer?" She blinks, her lips parting, and I suddenly realize she caught me staring at her. "That's great. When can I sign it?"

"I have practice and a few team meetings on Monday, then I'll meet with Mr. Smith. So as soon as I get back home, you'll be able to sign it." This time, I keep my gaze glued to her face. She nods, and a smile blooms on her lips. "Is there anything you want to know about the contract? I don't really know what Hayden told you."

"I told her everything about Story's schedule, about—"

"Hayden." My voice is dry and full of warning. Why can't he just let her speak for herself? It's frustrating. "I'm hiring Piper. Not you."

Piper laughs heartily and puts her head on my brother's shoulder. "I never thought there would be someone capable of putting you in your place."

"My big brother does it with ease," Hayden deadpans and slowly stands up from the couch, still holding Story in his arms. "Let's go to your room, kid. I remember you wanted to show me your toys."

"And I want you to play Monopoly with me. Will you?" she asks.

"Why not? Let's go play while *the adults* talk," he says snidely.

Once Hayden and Story leave the room, I meet Piper's gaze.

"He doesn't handle it well when people criticize his behavior," she tells me.

"Oh, I know. He's my brother, after all. I'd hoped he outgrew that habit, for his own good." I smack my lips together. "He's not a teenager anymore, but he still acts like one."

"You're wrong."

I frown. "Why?"

"Hade is not how you remember him, and it'd be amazing if you both used this time to get to know each other again. Start from scratch. You'll be surprised."

"Maybe, but I know my brother." That's not really true, but I'm too stubborn to admit it. "Since the moment I returned, he's yet to prove me wrong."

"You're a little arrogant, don't you think?" she challenges me, and my frown grows deeper. "You act like he's constantly making mistakes and bad decisions, while you're the perfect big brother, a real example to follow."

"That's not what I said."

"That's how it sounded."

Fuck. She's not afraid to talk back, is she? I like it, but at the same time I hate being lectured. Just like Hayden.

Now I'm the one to say, "You're wrong."

Piper sighs, moving her hands up and down her thighs. "I think it's better if we stop there. Hayden is family, and I'll never let anyone talk badly about him. Not even his brother."

Point taken. She'll go all mama bear for the people she loves. "Okay. Did Hayden talk to you about your salary? Days off?"

"Salary, no. And he mentioned I'd be able to take days off when you're not at practice or other soccer related activities."

"Yup, I'll have at least two days off a week, so you'll be able to do anything you want. As for your salary, it's five thousand a month."

Her rosy lips part, and her eyes widen. "What?"

"Is that not enough? You'll live here rent free, plus you won't need to buy food or anything, so I thought it would be okay...but if not—"

"It's more than enough. I didn't expect that," she mutters, grasping her necklace with the little butterfly pendant and toying with the chain. "Thank you so much for this chance, Hunter. I appreciate it. You won't regret hiring me."

"I'm sure I won't," I answer, and we stare at each other for an awfully long time.

I know she's exactly what I was looking for in a nanny. She likes my daughter, and Story is drawn to her. The problem is me. Keeping my emotions under control around someone like her will be incredibly hard, because I haven't gotten laid in months.

Damn, I need to talk to Angelo. I need perspective.

"HEY, MAN. HOW ARE YOU?"

"Hey, Hale. Took you long enough to call." Angelo laughs loudly. "I started to wonder if you got lost on your way to LA, maybe with some sexy chick you met on your flight."

"Very funny," I say, stopping near the floor-to-ceiling window in my living room. I stare at the water in the pool, glimmering under the moonlight. Water always has a calming effect on me. Watching it, being in it—anywhere around it, literally. It helps me sort out my thoughts, relax my muscles, and it brings solace to my worries if something is on my mind for too long. "The only chick I have is Story."

"Haven't you hired a nanny for her yet? Your practices start next week," Angelo states, and I roll my eyes. This guy remembers everything, even the little shit I tend to forget. He's kind and funny, and he's one of the best goalkeepers I've ever had the pleasure of working with. For seven years, he's been my best friend, and even if we haven't played for the same team in two years, we still stayed in touch, and our friendship only got stronger. I'd do anything for him, and he'd do the same for me.

"I finally did. I met with a ton of candidates, but I hired Hayden's best friend."

"Hade's best friend?"

"Um, yeah, his best friend is a girl."

"I know, I remember him talking about her." Of course he does. "Isn't she, like, twenty and in college, just like your brother?"

"Piper is twenty, and she's not in college. She's taking a year off."

"Wow, you've got yourself a hot young nanny. I didn't expect that. Good job, man."

"Russo, you're getting on my nerves," I grit through my teeth, heading out to the terrace. Story fell asleep not long ago, and I don't want to wake her up. "I hired a nanny for my daughter, not me."

"Isn't she going to live with you? In your house?" he taunts me.

"I'm not going to fuck her, if that's what you're implying."

Angelo heaves a sigh and lowers his voice. "Chill, Hale. I'm only joking, and you know it." I do. That's how he is, and I expected him to act like that. But his words, combined with the thoughts I had while Piper was here, agitate me to no end. "All I'm saying is, if you're still keeping your promise to swear off women, it might be hard to have someone beautiful around all the time."

"I'm aware."

"You don't owe Amelia anything, Hunter. Rumor has it she's dating her costar right now. Why are you depriving yourself of something you love for someone who was a total bitch to you?"

"I want to prove her wrong."

"It's been seven months, right? I think you're already winning. Stop this."

"You don't get it, Angelo. It's important to me. Amelia doesn't even know about my promise to myself," I exclaim, sitting down on a lounge chair near the pool. "But I'll need to figure out what to do about my needs for real. Piper is far from my type, and she's young, but also very beautiful. She triggers thoughts I haven't had for a while."

"Buddy, a hand job does wonders. Did you forget that already?" He snickers, and I roll my eyes. He can't stay serious for the life of him. "But in all honesty, Hale, your ex can go to hell. Get on Tinder and find a girl who doesn't need anything more than a hookup. It's easy."

"Maybe."

"You're not going to do that," Angelo says, and I chuckle loudly, "so I wish you luck. You'll need it...to keep your dick in your pants."

"Fuck off, Russo," I snap while he dies of laughter. "My dick will be staying in my pants just fine. I have everything under control."

At least, I hope I do.

6
not my prince charming

PIPER

"So, are you nervous?" Riley asks as I drive away from our house. I'm taking her to the birthday party, then I plan to go home and finish packing.

"Why would I be?" I squint at her as we slow at a traffic light.

"I don't know...I just think I'd be about to pass out if I were you. You're moving in with a dude you barely know."

I press my lips together, but I can't keep from bursting out laughing. "Ry, thanks to Mom, I've lived with lots of guys I barely know. It's going to be alright. Hunter is Hayden's brother. That's already a huge bonus. I can always talk to Hade if something bothers me."

"I hate that it's normal for you, that it doesn't bother you. It's wrong." Riley's cheeks flame up red as she crosses her arms over her chest. "Mom is Mom, and I can't be angry with her forever, but what she did—"

"Is in the past." I reach over and put my hand on her knee. "Like you said, Mom is Mom, and she'll never change. I've made my peace with it, and her antics don't get to me so much now."

Riley stares at me silently, and then she slowly nods. "Okay. Sorry, Piper. I'm just mad."

"Mad? Why?" I ask as we near her best friend Madison's house.

"What happened? Are you upset about staying with Mom and Wade after I move out?"

"No." I knew that wasn't it, but I needed to make sure. The girl practically threw a party when I told her about Hunter's offer. She was incredibly excited and supportive, reassuring me over and over that she'd be okay.

"Then is it about Lola and Josh?"

She groans dramatically and presses her palms to her face. "I hate you, Pip."

"Ry, if something's wrong, I want to help."

"Everything's okay, just...they are both going to be at Maddie's birthday, and I'm afraid it'll be awkward."

"Because he chose you?"

"Yeah. Lola played it cool, but I know her. She's upset," she mumbles, fiddling with the hem of her dress. "I'm not sure I should—"

"Stop this," I command, parking the car in Maddie's driveway. "Lola never told you she liked Josh, right? But once she knew he liked you, she suddenly decided to stake her claim on him. It's manipulative. A real bitchy move, sis. The sooner you get it, the better. Lola doesn't deserve your friendship or your worries."

"But what if she wasn't lying?" Riley asks as we climb out of the car. She gets her gift from the backseat of my Toyota Corolla and turns to me.

I glance up at the sky and then focus on my sister. "First, please answer my questions. Do you like Josh?"

"I do."

"Did you know anything about Lola liking him before he told you he liked you?" She shakes her head no, and I barely stop myself from smiling triumphantly. "Then you don't owe her anything. Just enjoy your best friend's party with the guy you like. Okay?"

"Okay." She gives me the cutest little smile.

I wrap my arms around her shoulders and pull her to my chest. "Have fun, beautiful. I'll be here to pick you up around eight."

"Thank you, Piper." Riley squeezes me hard, almost knocking the air out of my lungs. "See you later."

"See you." I wait for her to step inside and only then climb back into my car. I have too many things I need to accomplish today.

ONCE INSIDE THE HOUSE, I lock eyes with my mom. She halts in her tracks, and a gentle smile lifts her plump lips.

"Hey, Mom."

"Hey, Piper. Did you take Riley to the birthday party?"

"Yeah, I hope she's having fun. I need to pack, and then I'll pick her up and bring her home."

"Thank you, sweetheart," she murmurs, her ice-blue eyes full of curiosity as she studies my face. "I barely see you, even when you're home, and now you're moving out."

"I'm the quiet one," I tell her, referring to how she compares me to Riley. "I prefer to stay in my room."

"I know you do, but I often think it has something to do with me. When I get home from work, if you're here, you're with Riley in the living room or the kitchen. When I'm here, you're in your room."

"Ry hates being alone, so if you're not here, she wants my company." I'm not exactly lying. That's really how she is. Though she prefers my company over Mom's any day of the week.

"Then it's fortunate Wade moved in last week. He'll keep her company if she wants." She grins, while I suppress the urge to roll my eyes. Another man, another attempt to build something, another candidate for stepdad. "He's a great man."

"Maybe," I mutter. To be fair, Wade isn't like any of her other men, in a good way, and she acts differently when he's around. Softer, kinder, and more attentive to her kids. But I'd rather not get my hopes up in case it turns out to be another disaster. "I'm glad you have someone to help with the house while I'm gone. Wade is a nice guy, and he's only been kind and respectful to me."

Mom nods and smiles. "How are you holding up? It's quite a change, if you ask me. Moving in with strangers, working, looking after someone's child."

"Story is adorable, and I enjoy spending time with her. It won't be a problem. I'll get used to everything else. People get used to anything. I'm not worried."

"Have you asked who decided to name her that?"

Mom and her prejudice. It's ridiculous she's so judgmental considering how many times our neighbors have criticized her actions and behavior.

"No clue. It's just a name," I say.

"These famous rich folks always choose the weirdest names for their kids." She tsks. "I don't get it."

"Hunter seems like an ordinary person. If I met him on the street, I'd have never even thought he was a celebrity."

"But I'm sure you would've noticed him. He's incredibly handsome." Mom winks knowingly, and my brows knit together. "I googled him. Needed to know who my daughter is going to be working for."

"He's my boss and Hayden's older brother, Mom. I don't think about him in any other way." I hold her gaze, pursing my lips. I can't deny the fact that Hunter Hale is gorgeous, and feeling his gaze on me yesterday sent a billion tingles through my whole body. But him being my boss and my best friend's brother overrules anything I might feel when he's around.

"We'll see." She smirks and disappears into the living room.

It was really nice talking to you, Mom.

I shake my head and pad to my bedroom. I need to get rolling, or I might be late.

"Hey." I wave in an awkward greeting, earning a surprised look from Hunter. The white tee and black shorts he has on save me from reviving the embarrassment I felt after cussing when I saw him last time. "I'm a bit early."

"That's totally fine," he says, stepping aside to let me in. I drag my suitcase after me, and then stop in the middle of the hallway.

"Do you have more stuff in your car?" he asks.

I look over my shoulder, meeting Hunter's gaze. "No, this is all I brought with me. I don't live very far, so if I forgot something, I can always go back and get it...while Story is at school, for example."

He smiles and closes the door. "Let's go; I'll show you your room, and then we can talk about our plans for tomorrow."

"Great."

Hale gestures for me to follow him. He's tall, maybe six feet, and the top of my head reaches his shoulder.

"Where is Story?" I ask, and Hunter glances at me. He stops near the door and opens it for me.

"She's in her room, talking to her mom on FaceTime." He shoves his hands in his pockets. "She wanted to finish the call before you got here, so she could greet you."

"Oh...I hope she's not upset."

"You're here, so she'll be the happiest girl alive. She was literally buzzing all day, waiting for your arrival."

I grin at Hunter, moving to step inside the room, but a door to my right suddenly opens, and Story bursts through. Her gaze lands on me, and she squeals, runs over to me, and wraps her arms around my waist. "I'm so happy you're here. I've been waiting for you!"

"Really?" I let go of my suitcase and kneel in front of this adorable little girl. "I've been waiting to see you too. How have you been?"

"Amazing," she murmurs, her eyes roaming over my face. "You're so pretty."

"Not as pretty as you." I take her hands in mine, and her smile grows bigger. "Will you help me unpack?"

"Yes," Story breathes, and I look up at her dad. Hunter stares at me, looking...annoyed? Did I do something wrong?

"Hunter, what time does Story usually go to bed?"

"Bed?" he asks, frowning and then instantly shaking his head.

"Usually, on the weekends, she's asleep before ten p.m., but I think we can make an exception for today."

"Thank you."

"Thank you, Daddy." Story lets go of my hand as I stand up.

I take my suitcase, and we both step inside my bedroom. Hunter stays behind to turn on the lights. The place is decorated in beige and white, with a king-size bed, a desk with a chair, a spacious walk-in closet, and another door that leads to the en suite bathroom. It's way bigger and brighter than my room at my Mom's, and I feel like Cinderella after she finally moved out of her evil stepmother's house to share a palace with her prince. The only difference: Hunter Hale isn't my Prince Charming. With the way he keeps frowning, he's starting to remind me of Gru from *Despicable Me*. I wonder what his problem is.

"I'll be waiting for you in the living room. Take your time," he mutters, and he disappears from view. Story and I exchange a glance, and she shrugs.

"It's not about you," she tells me as I close the door. "It's about Mom. They can't stand each other."

7
unpleasantville
HUNTER

WHAT THE HELL IS WRONG WITH ME? EVERYTHING WAS great until I saw her talking with Story. Piper doesn't try to impress me, and she's interested in what my daughter's saying. That's...fuck, it feels better than anything. And yet I looked at her as if she just blocked my penalty kick. *Damn*. I need my routine back as soon as possible. It'll help me sort out my thoughts. It always does.

Growing up, I loved playing football. Practicing my dribbling skills any chance I got, passing long and short, driving my friends nuts with my constant desire to be the best of the best, refusing to settle for anything less. It was my whole life, my personality, and I couldn't imagine my future without it. Right up until I caught my dad talking to one of his friends, a big LA Lakers fan. I was nine years old when the dude decided to mock my love for football. *You should've made Hunter join the basketball team. What's the point of soccer if it's not big here? He'll never be famous.*

Famous, my ass. I couldn't care less about fame, and I was disappointed and angry that my dad said nothing. As if silently agreeing with his friend.

It affected me so much that I barely played for a whole month, slacking at practice and letting my coach roast me for my behavior. I lost my motivation. If my own father didn't think I could achieve something, why should I bother at all? Why work so hard if no one notices it? But I was wrong. There were people who watched me. People who noticed. People who knew I had the potential to make a name for myself. And one of them was my mom.

I still remember the day she came to pick me up from another disastrous practice. In the backseat of her car, I was trying to avoid her questions and her penetrating gaze. But the woman needed answers, and she wasn't buying my bullshit anymore. She wanted to know the reason for my downfall, and I told her everything.

Four months after that talk, my mom and I were on our way to Spain. She gave up her career to help make my dreams a reality. A new country and a new language were a whiplash to the brain, but she was there for me through thick and thin. She's my biggest supporter, and she's also the only person who's always told me the truth about my skills, failures, and strengths. I'll be forever grateful to her for everything she did for me. Heck, the Ballon d'Or that proudly sits on a shelf in my parents' living room is hers too. Her sacrifices, her support and help, her love and faith in me made me who I am today.

"Daddy, you're not going to believe what Piper and I are going to do tomorrow." Story runs into the room, interrupting my thoughts and bringing me back to the present.

"Story, let's not get ahead of ourselves, okay?" Piper follows her into the room with a timid smile on her face. Our eyes meet, and I tilt my head, encouraging her to continue. "I thought of something that might be fun for us to do tomorrow, and I told Story about it. But I warned her we'll only do it if it's okay with you."

"And she's already assumed I'll be okay with it," I say as Story climbs onto my lap. She winds her hands around my neck, looking me in the eyes without blinking. *Oh hell no!* There's no way I'm agreeing to something without knowing the details. "Story, what did we agree on when we moved here?"

"That we'll always talk about things we want to do."

"And do you know about my plans for tomorrow? About my plans for your day?"

She instantly starts to sulk, knitting her brows together and looking up at me from under her eyelashes. Definitely her mother's daughter. "You said you'd be gone for most of the day, and when you're back we're going to dinner with Granny and Grandpa."

"Glad you remember." I kiss the tip of her nose, and her lips stretch into a smile, even if she's still trying to pout. Slowly, I lock eyes with Piper. She's still standing near the couch with her hands hidden in her pockets. "Sit, Piper."

Something flickers behind her irises, and I frown. I have no idea what she thinks of me or this arrangement. She likes Story, and she's genuinely happy to spend time with her. But with me? She's careful and hesitant. She's not trying to befriend me; she keeps her distance and stays professional. So far, I'm the only one who's acted like a perv. I need to fix it. The last thing I need is her thinking I'm lusting after her.

"Please."

She twirls a strand of her hair around her finger and finally does as I say, lowering herself onto the couch beside me.

"Are there any errands we need to run? Anything we need to do while you're away?" she asks.

"Not tomorrow," I tell her. "I want you to spend the week getting to know Story and getting used to the house. Use this time to find out about my daughter's likes and dislikes, about her food preferences. She doesn't have any allergies, but she's a picky eater."

"Piper knows I love strawberries and cocoa with marshmallows," Story exclaims, and I smile.

"Unfortunately, baby, that's not enough to keep you hydrated and well-fed, but it's enough to win you over."

Piper shrugs, smiling at me. "I'm not entirely sure I've won her over yet, but it earned me some points."

"Definitely *some* points," I tease her, wrapping my arms around Story. She presses herself closer to me and leans her head on my chest. "School starts next week, so hopefully we can settle into our routines before that."

"Everything's going to be fine as long as we work as a team." Piper shifts her gaze to Story, and the corners of her eyes soften. "Will you be on my team?"

"*You* will be on *my* team," Story corrects her, and we both burst out laughing. It's impossible to stay serious when she says things like that. "Dad, you and I are going to make the best team in the world."

"Just one thing, baby. I'm afraid your uncle will be upset if you don't include him," I say, making Story giggle.

"Uncle Hayden doesn't need to know. It's a secret team." Piper winks at me, and I shake my head. That's what I get for agreeing to hire my brother's best friend. She's playful and full of mischief—of course she gets along with Story.

"Definitely," I confirm, and Story yawns. "It's time to go to bed, sweetie."

"But Dad—"

"No buts. It's past your bedtime."

"Sorry about that," Piper mutters under her breath, and I glance at her. "I should've gotten here sooner."

"Didn't I say it was okay?" I ask her, and she smiles at me weakly. "I'll put Story to bed, and I would be grateful if we could talk for a bit after that."

"Sure, I'll wait for you here." She nods curtly and focuses her gaze on my daughter. "Good night, Story. See you tomorrow."

"Good night, Piper," Story murmurs.

STORY IS IN HER BED, tucked under her Princess Elsa blanket. The lights are off, and I'm sitting on the floor with my phone. I have a few emails from my agent and the team representative, and I know tomorrow is going to be one hell of a day. Disappointment seeps into my veins, spoiling my mood and making me frown. They want to make a big deal out of me signing my contract, and I can't say I'm happy about it. I knew that was going to happen, but I'd just hoped to enjoy my freedom more.

"Dad?"

I blink, peering at Story.

"Mom was asking me about my new nanny."

"What did you tell her?"

"I said you hired Piper because I liked her. I told her you let me choose." She lowers her voice and stiffens. "Mom wasn't happy about it. She said you shouldn't have trusted the judgment of a seven-year-old."

"I also trusted Hayden's judgment, not just yours." I put my elbows on her bed to get a better look at her face. "Don't worry about it, honey. You're going to spend a lot of time with Piper, so you should decide if you want her to be your nanny or not. That's only fair."

"Thank you, Daddy." She smiles, her eyelids fluttering. "I love you so, so much."

"I love you too." I plant a kiss on her forehead as she closes her eyes and falls asleep almost instantly.

I wait for another ten minutes and then go to the living room. Piper's sitting on the couch, typing something on her phone with a focused look on her face. I slowly come closer, and when she notices me she puts her phone on the couch.

"Do you always wait for Story to fall asleep?"

"Always," I confirm, sitting beside her. "No matter what. If I'm in town, I put her to sleep."

"Was it hard for her to fall asleep when you weren't around?" she asks. "My sister is five years younger than me, and I was the one who got her to bed since she was two. Anytime my mom tried, Riley just refused to sleep."

I can't help but smile, even if it feels forced. She sounds totally fine with it, while in reality she took her mom's place when she was a child herself. It's not right.

"Story didn't have trouble falling asleep with her mom, or with her babysitters. She just preferred me."

"No surprise she loves you so much."

"Yeah, but she loves both of her parents. Not just me."

"Oh, I figured that out when I first met her. She's proud to be her mama's girl." Piper drops her gaze to her lap, a blush creeping onto her cheeks. "Story told me today you don't get along with your ex-wife."

My smile fades, and I grit my teeth. I hate when people pry. I hate nosy motherfuckers with my entire soul, and her words piss me off. Even if she probably doesn't mean anything by it. She's just letting me know what Story thinks about my relationship with her mom. Still, I don't appreciate it.

"What happens between me and Amelia is none of your business, Piper."

"I know," she blurts, looking up and catching my gaze. "Story was sad, and that's why I wanted to bring it up."

"It's not something you have to worry about. I didn't hire you to be my therapist. You're just a nanny." *And now I sound like an asshole.*

"I'm just a nanny," she echoes, setting her jaw hard. "It's late, so if you don't have anything else to discuss regarding my job, I'd prefer to go to my room."

"I hope I made myself clear, and—"

"I'm just *a nanny*, Mr. Hale. I'm aware." She grabs her phone from the couch and stands up. "Is there anything else?"

Is she going to be this difficult any time we don't see eye to eye?

"Did you get the notes about Story's schedule and her preferences? I sent them to the email address you gave me."

"I did. I printed them out to make sure I remember everything." Piper takes a step back, hiding her hands behind her. "Can I go now?"

"Sure."

She storms into the hallway, holding her head high and her shoulders squared. She's pissed, and I sigh, closing my eyes.

I thought it might be awkward after she caught me staring at her breasts. It might be uncomfortable. But I never thought it would be so unpleasant. This little out-of-nowhere argument messed up everything, turned the atmosphere between Piper and me into a real Unpleasantville. Exactly what I fucking needed.

8
a wonderful lie

PIPER

I PARK THE CAR NEAR HALE'S HOUSE AND SIT FOR A FEW minutes without moving. Everything is going well. Story and I are getting along amazingly. In just two weeks, I've set up a routine for myself, enjoying every second with her. Until her dad gets home, that is.

Hunter Hale...fuck, he frustrates me to no end. He's an incredible father, I can give him that. A very talented soccer player, a legend who made a name for himself in Europe, which isn't easy coming from our side of the world. But as a human being? He sucks. The way he snaps without any hesitation or remorse, the way he only sees the negative and expects the worst. It's horrible. I feel like I'm walking on eggshells around him, and it's not what I expected. I couldn't have imagined working for him would be this unpleasant.

My phone dings, and I take it out of my purse. It's another message from Hayden, and I have no desire to deal with him. I shove my phone back in my purse and climb out of the Range Rover Evoque, the car Hunter insisted I use. Story's at school, so I'll have a few hours to myself after I finish cooking. Tomorrow is my day off, but I want her to have the food she likes. Just like her father, actually. Hunter always compliments my cooking, but it gives me an icky feeling instead of making me feel flattered. I'd rather he not talk to me at all, pretend I don't exist. It would be a thousand times better.

The first thing I register inside the house is the scent of cinnamon and freshly brewed coffee. Knitting my brows together, I lock the front door and go through the living room to the kitchen. I stop in my tracks, meeting Hayden's gaze.

"Want some?" He smirks at me, taking a bite of his cinnamon roll.

I blink away my confusion, huffing through my nostrils. His insistence pisses me off, just like Hunter's asshole behavior. They're cut from the same cloth.

"What are you doing here?" I ask, propping my hip against the kitchen counter.

"Waiting for you." He shrugs, taking a sip of his coffee. "You haven't answered my texts."

"Because I already told you my answer."

"It's the wrong one, Pip."

I roll my eyes and go to wash my hands. I don't have time for his attempts to guilt-trip me into going to the party tonight. Tomorrow is my day off, and I want to enjoy it peacefully in Riley's company. Sleeping and being hungover isn't what I have in mind.

"Pip, summer break is almost over, and I want to let loose a little."

"Go ahead. You don't need me to have fun." I open the fridge. I've already marinated the chicken and cut the potatoes, and the oven is preheated, so I just put the pan in and set the timer. It should be delicious, and I have no doubt Story is going to love it. So far, the only time she scrunched her nose at one of my meals was when I made steamed salmon because her dad asked me to. But she ate it anyway, confessing to me later in a conspiratorial whisper that she'd never liked it.

"Pip, I need my best friend there to enjoy the party."

"That's something you tell your girlfriends. You'll be perfectly fine without me," I mumble and turn around, almost bumping into Hayden, who's hovering over me with an irritated look on his face.

"Why do you need me, Hade?"

"I want you to have fun. You spent most of the summer at home, nervous about not finding a job. You've got a job now. You have nothing to worry about. It's time for you to at least enjoy the end of summer break."

He has a point. I barely went out this summer, fussing over things I couldn't control and being a mood-killer. Is that how I want this summer to end?

"We're going to Bo's beach house." Hayden wiggles his eyebrows, winking at me with a ridiculous grin. "It'll just be our friends—no outsiders, no groupies."

It sounds good. Like, really good. "When?"

"I'll come pick you up around eight." Hade smiles, visibly happy with himself, while I frown. I was planning to spend the night here and go home in the morning. Do I need to talk to Hunter about it? Give him a heads-up? "I can talk to Hunter, if that's what you're worried about."

"It has nothing to do with him," I snap, and Hayden's eyes widen.

"How are things between you two?"

"He's my boss," I comment dryly, skirting him and plopping onto a stool.

"I'm aware." Hayden sits beside me. "Do you want me to talk to him?"

I punch him in his shoulder. "Don't you dare get involved."

"What the hell happened? You've been in this house for...what? Two weeks, and you already can't stand him?"

"It's not like that."

"Then what is it? Because I was sure everything was going fine."

"Being Story's nanny is a blessing. I love spending time with her, helping her with her homework, cooking for her, and playing with her. It's all good." I fold my arms across my chest. "Her dad is complicated."

"How so?"

I open my mouth to say something, but then I think otherwise and shut it. "Hayden, I love you, and I appreciate everything you've done for me, but he's my boss. And I'm not going to speak ill about him, especially in his house. Besides, he hasn't done anything bad.

We're just too different, and sometimes we don't understand each other."

Hade sighs and slings an arm over my shoulder. "If his behavior starts to *really* bother you, please tell me. I know what an asshole he can be."

"Thank you." I cuddle into him, closing my eyes. "Can you come earlier? I'm sure Story would be happy to see you."

"Totally." Hade kisses my temple, then leans away and looks around the kitchen. "Maybe I should just stay? What you're cooking smells delicious."

"It's for Story, not you."

"I don't believe the whole thing is just for my niece. Do you cook for Hunter too?"

"I cook for all of us. I eat here too." I get up from the stool. "And if you want to stay, call your brother, or at least text him. He won't be happy to know you barged in again without letting him know."

"I'll shoot him a text." He takes his phone out of his pocket and glances up at me. "What are you going to do?"

"I had plans to take a shower and read."

"Reading is boring," Hade whines, sulking. "Will you watch something with me?"

My plans to continue my book are dumped into nothingness. The dude's like a dog with a bone. He won't stop until he gets his way. "Okay, fine. Wait for me here. It won't take long."

"Take your time, beautiful. No rush."

"I still have a dish in the oven, Hade." I give him a pointed look as I edge to the door. "I'll be quick."

The last thing I need is to set the whole place on fire. Though with how cold the atmosphere between me and Hunter is, maybe that's exactly what we need. A little spice to heat things up...but I'm just the nanny. He's entitled to act however he wants. His trust issues aren't my problem. I'm better than that.

I CLOSE my bedroom door and pad to the living room. Story and Hayden are laughing, and even singing. From the moment I brought Story home and helped her with homework, the house has turned upside down. Hayden's presence created a warm and funny atmosphere. Oddly enough, Hunter's return didn't ruin it. The guy was in a good mood, and I thought it was because of me, because I'm off today and won't be getting in his way. I won't be shocked if my guess is right.

I stop in the doorway, watching Hade and Story play Monopoly. Smiling, I step inside and head to the table.

Story looks at me, and her mouth drops open. "You're so beautiful."

"Thank you, honey." I plop down onto the couch beside her. Her gaze roams my face, and she has a fascinated glimmer in her eyes. Abruptly, she switches her attention to Hade and purses her lips.

"Uncle Hayden, I have no idea why you don't want to date Piper. She's stunning."

Hade blinks, then blinks again, and then he just bursts out laughing. "Kid, Pip is gorgeous, no doubt about that, but she's my friend. I don't want to ruin that."

"But why?"

I bite my bottom lip, trying to cover up my smile. Hayden is perplexed; he doesn't know what to say. I keep quiet, enjoying watching him squirm. Until I hear Hunter's voice behind my back.

"You're asking the wrong question, baby."

I turn my head and peer at Hunter's face. He holds my gaze for a second, then focuses on Story.

"Why is my question wrong?"

"You're asking why Hayden doesn't want to date Piper. But it should be up to Piper to decide if she wants to date your uncle."

"I'm perfect boyfriend material," Hade yelps, and this time I can't help myself. My loud giggles fill the room as I cover my face with my palms. My best friend is the most delusional person ever.

Hunter chuckles. "I think Piper's reaction speaks for itself."

When I finally stop laughing and take my hands away from my

face, I see Hunter sitting across from me. His dark green eyes find mine, and a very strange feeling forms in my chest. It's warm and pleasant, and I don't want to look away. He has chiseled cheekbones and serious stubble forming on his jaw. His full lips quirk into a broad smile, barely visible lines bracketing his mouth. Why can't he be like this all the time? Things would be a thousand times better.

"Pip has no idea what she's missing," Hade mumbles, snatching his phone from the table. He glances up at me and subtly nods at the door. "We need to go if we don't want to be late."

"Okay." I follow him out of the room, feeling someone's gaze on my back. It could be Story's, but I'm sure it's Hunter's. I know what it feels like when he's watching me.

We stop by the front door when I hear footsteps, and Story appears in the doorframe. She grins at me, walking closer. "I'll miss you."

"I'll miss you too." I kneel to get a better look at her face. "Have fun, sweetie. I'll see you on Sunday morning."

She inches forward and plants a smooch on my cheek. "See you."

I stand up and smooth my hands over my dress. It's a white summer dress with lacy details on the chest and a skirt that ends just above my knees. It's incredibly simple, but it fits my body perfectly. Riley calls me a sexy bombshell any time I wear it. Once in a while, I want to look hot instead of cozy.

"I have practice at eleven." Hunter's voice reaches my ears, setting my whole body on alert. He lingers by the door, his eyes glued to my face. "It'd be great if you could be here at nine."

"Of course. You don't have to worry about it."

"Great." He nods, hiding his hands in his pockets. "Have fun."

"Oh, I'll make sure she has *a lot* of fun today." Hayden grabs my hand and pulls me out the door. "Bye, Hunter. Bye, Story."

"Bye," I mutter, waving to Story. She waves back and runs down the hallway to her room. I shift to look at her dad and instantly regret it. The intensity of his gaze burns holes in my body, awakening butterflies in my stomach. His eyes travel down the length of me, his pupils dilating and darkening. The heat in my lower abdomen makes me let go of Hayden's hand. *No, no, no.* I don't want him to act like that with me. I don't want him to look at me like that. It's better if he continues to be an ass...because I can't be attracted to my boss. No fucking way.

"Pip?"

I tear my gaze away from Hunter and focus on Hayden. He's standing near his car, his forehead wrinkled. "Is everything okay?"

"Yeah, sure." I shrug, hurrying to his vehicle. "Can you please tell me who else is going to be at Bo's?"

Hayden starts the engine of his car once we are both inside. He cocks an eyebrow at me with a grin on his face. "If you're looking for a hookup, I'd suggest Bo. The guy is still not over you."

"My hookups are none of your business," I hiss, and he cackles, patting my knee.

"Nonexistent hookups, you mean?"

I flip him the bird and shut my mouth.

"Pip, I'm just joking."

"And I'm not talking to you." I stick my tongue out at him and look out the window.

The idea of hooking up with someone sounds appealing. I have no problem giving myself an orgasm, but sometimes I just want someone else to take care of my needs. It's been a while. Maybe I should go wild? Maybe even with Bo? At this point, anyone is better than having fantasies about my best friend's brother.

I didn't like the way I felt when he was watching me. I didn't like my arousal skyrocketing from just feeling his gaze on my body. Most of the time he annoys me, with his snobbish behavior and closed off personality, and I should focus on that. I don't like him. End of story.

What a wonderful lie.

9
remains of pip
PIPER

"So, Piper, how's life?" Bo asks, taking a swig of his beer. I shrug and take a sip of my drink as well. I came outside to enjoy the quiet of his beach house, to listen to a sound I'll always love: waves. "Is it so bad you don't want to talk about it? Or is it so good you don't think we ordinary people deserve to hear about it?"

"Oh, screw you, Bo," I mutter, hitting him on his forearm. "I just...I don't know what to tell you. Everything's fine."

His dark brown eyes are focused on me, and a faint smile crosses his lips. "Why were you so afraid to tell me you were going to work for Hade's brother?"

"Afraid to tell you?"

"Remember, we talked at the beach, and you said you didn't want to jinx—"

"Oh, that wasn't the job I was talking about. I meant a job working for Mr. Russell. At the coffee—"

"No fucking way," Bo yelps, startling me. "Didn't Hade tell you what happened with that dude? He was harassing a girl from our college who worked for him."

"No, I didn't know. Hayden didn't mention it until I said I was going to work for him," I say pointedly, taking another sip of my drink.

"Did you meet him?" Bo bends to get a better look at my face.

"Just during my interview. He seemed fine." I look away, fixing my gaze on the waves as they reach the shore. Back and forth, back and forth. The motion is so simple, and yet it has the power to calm my nerves and make me feel at home.

"You should've left right away." Bo grabs my hand and makes me look at him. "Something is wrong with that dude."

I pull my hand out of his grip, and my brows pinch together in annoyance. "Well, eventually Hayden showed up with Story and suggested I work for his brother. I haven't seen Mr. Russell since."

Standing up from the porch, I shake the sand off my dress. I hate when people treat me like I'm some damsel in distress. I'm fully capable of standing up for myself, and I appreciate when people treat me accordingly. Even Hunter being an asshole doesn't affect me much since I can always return the favor. I know my worth.

"Piper, I-I didn't mean—"

"Please stop." I stomp back inside the house, thankful for the blaring music that fills the whole space. No one is paying any attention to me as I head down the hallway. I need a minute to myself before I go back to my friends.

I walk into the bathroom and close the door, leaning my back against it. Why am I so snappy? Especially with Bo? I know he likes me, and he's always ready to support me in any way he can. His overprotectiveness isn't new, and usually it doesn't bother me. Usually, but not now. Why?

Pushing myself off the door, I breeze to the sink. I brace both palms on the vanity and stare at myself in the mirror. My dilated pupils are the best evidence of my not-so-sober state. That was the plan, right? To let loose a little? To relax with my friends? Yes, but the reality is very different. I don't want to be here.

At first, everything was fine. I was happy to see my friends, hang out with Hayden, and forget about my responsibilities. My mood was light and playful until Sean said something about college. Hearing my friends talk about their classes, about professors and classmates, sounded foreign to my ears. I instantly felt out of place, like an outcast. They didn't even notice when I snuck away because I was tired of listening to their plans for next semester. I was outside for twenty minutes before Bo found me sitting on the porch.

My days off are all over the place, so there's a chance I won't see my friends once school starts. I feel sad about it, about the situation I got myself into. If only I wasn't so stubborn, I wouldn't be alone in the bathroom, whining to myself about how miserable I am. I'd be in the living room with everyone else, drinking, dancing, and laughing. Thinking about the parties I'm going to attend, all the boys I'm going to go out with, and my grades. I could've had all that, but instead I'm alone, and I just want to be at home. Or with Story...

A smile forms on my lips the second I think about Story. She's my personal ray of sunshine these days, making me love every minute of our time together. Everything in her is genuine and pure, so I'm drawn to her. She's like my sister, and I can't wait to introduce her to Riley. Hopefully her father won't change his mind. He does that all the time.

I turn on the faucet and splash some water on my face. Irritation swirls inside my chest. One fleeting thought about Hunter Hale, and I'm ready to scratch his eyes out. At least that would save me from feeling his gaze on my body.

God, I'm hopeless.

Leaning against the countertop, I fold my arms over my chest. Hunter is the most complicated man I've ever met, and, considering who my mom is, that's really saying something. Her collection of men usually consists of guys who proudly fly their red flags in her face, and she continues to ignore them until it's too late. My boss isn't *that* horrible, but his behavior is shaped by his experiences. He expects only bad things from others, doesn't give them a chance to explain themselves. Good thing I can sass him back and shut him down with ease.

The bad thing? It turns me on.

I freeze. My breath hitches in my throat. Did I just acknowledge the fact that arguing with Hunter makes me not only angry, but also horny? I lick my lips, shifting a little and spreading my legs apart. I haven't had sex in four months. The last time I touched myself was more than a month ago, and right now it's the only thing I want to do.

Slowly, I press my palm to my chest and glide it over my breasts, feeling the hard points of my nipples. I slide my palm down until it reaches the hem of my dress. My vision is blurry, and my heartbeat pummels my chest, going up into my ears and echoing in my head.

Moving my hand lower, under the hem of my dress, I slip two fingers beneath my panties. Oh God, I'm so wet already...for someone who isn't even here. For someone who's been playing hot and cold with me for two weeks, making me irritated when he picks fights with me and lets me off the hook after I talk back. For someone I work for. For someone who's my best friend's brother. I'm dripping just thinking about Hunter Hale.

I press my fingers to my aching clit and slowly start to rub it between my fingers. The friction does wonders to my body, sending my mind into overdrive. Massaging my spot, I sigh loudly as my head lols back, and pleasure ripples through my veins as my orgasm builds in my lower abdomen. Hunter's image pops into my head, and it feels like he's watching me. His dark green eyes are fixated on me. Both of his hands are hidden in his pockets, and his posture is tense. He's shirtless, wearing only shorts. A sexy-as-fuck motherfucker.

My movements become more frantic and more hurried. I rotate my hips, meeting my fingers as I slowly push them inside me. Oh my fucking God. I need to come, viciously. It's the only thing on my mind, and I'm drowning. One more second, one more, and I'm going to explode. I moan, and it echoes through the bathroom, bouncing off the tile and coming back to me. Floating on cloud nine, I feel my insides squeeze and contract around my fingers. My legs are shaking, and it takes a good five minutes to get myself back on track.

After washing my hands, I quickly dry them with a towel and step out of the bathroom—instantly regretting it. Bo is there, and the smug smile on his face says it all. He heard everything.

"How did you like my bathroom?"

"It's beautiful." Beautiful? *Piper, you're a dumbass.*

56

"The acoustics in there...damn." He licks his lips, steps closer, and wraps his arms around my waist. "Never in my life have I wanted to break down a door as much as I did tonight. Why didn't you ask me to join?"

"Bo, we've been there, and you know the promise I made."

"Hayden doesn't need to know." He tips his head, his eyes zeroing in on my mouth. I'm still riding the waves of my orgasm, barely thinking straight. I put my hand on the back of his neck and pull him into me for a kiss.

It's hard and fast, but something is missing. Feelings are missing. There's no passion, no eagerness. I don't feel anything, and it scares me. I gave myself an orgasm thinking about one man. And now, when a very real guy is kissing me, I feel numb.

I gasp for air, and Bo's mouth moves down my cheek and to my throat. He licks my skin and suddenly sucks hard, leaving a hickey on my neck. It snaps me out of my daze, and I stumble back.

Bo opens his eyes. "Piper?"

"I hate hickeys, Bo." I press my palm to my neck. "You know that."

"Shit, Piper, I'm sorry." He runs his fingers through his hair, flashing me a smile. "I'm just so into you, it was hard to stop myself."

I hate myself. Period. "Um, thanks...I just...I don't think I can do this."

"What? Why?" He takes a step forward, and I instantly take a step back. I want him to keep his distance. What remains of Pip needs a bit more recovery time than just a quiet moment.

"It's for the best," I mutter, ambling to the living room.

When I spot Hade, I go straight to him. He's sitting on the couch, talking to Decker and Nelly, when I plop down beside him. He drapes an arm over my shoulder, pressing me to his side. I cuddle closer; my cheeks and neck feel hot. I just had an orgasm thinking about his brother. And a few minutes later, I let his friend kiss me. I'm pathetic.

10
plan b, c, and even z

HUNTER

My parents' front door opens, and I see my mom's smiling face. "Hey," I say, stepping aside to let Story come in. We spent the whole morning in Griffith Park, enjoying each other's company and watching animals. She told me so many things she memorized during her last visit with her uncle, leaving me perplexed. How the hell did she remember that fennecs don't drink much water, that they prefer a wide variety of food, from grasshoppers to birds to leaves, instead? When she noticed my shocked state, she said, "Piper told me that," and it immediately explained everything. Her nanny is her new favorite person.

"Hey, Mom." I push the door closed and follow Story inside. My mother is already holding my daughter's hand, and they both smile at me. "Sorry it took us so long."

"Dad loved the zoo, he didn't want to leave," Story explains, batting her eyelashes at me. Sure, it was me who didn't want to leave. I shake my head, lean forward, and kiss my mom's cheek.

"Your dad has always loved animals, so I'm not surprised." Mom plays along, tugging on Story's hand and heading to the living room. "Did you like the zoo?"

"Yes! Last time I went with Uncle Hayden and Piper, so today I was the one who told Daddy about the animals we saw. And let me tell you, he didn't know a lot."

"Ask your dad to name all the captains Real Madrid has ever had instead. He only remembers things that are important to him." Mom ruffles Story's hair, making her giggle. "Are you hungry?"

"I could eat a lion," Story murmurs. "I want your favorite chocolate cake."

Mom blinks, bursting into laughter a second later. "You're lucky I have some in the fridge."

Story squeaks in delight and rushes to the kitchen. She has a real sweet tooth, and it drives her mom up the wall. In Amelia's perfect world, her daughter wouldn't enjoy sweets, would always choose fruit instead. Unfortunately for my ex-wife, Story takes after me with her love for candies and cakes.

"Hunter?" Mom says, and I glance at her. "Can you please go to Hayden's room and wake him up? I don't care how many hours of sleep he got. It's time for him to wake up."

"When did he get home?" I ask, chuckling.

"Your dad said Hayden and Piper got home around five a.m. They woke up Bernie and made so much noise, I'm surprised they didn't wake me up."

"Is Piper here?"

"Yes, she's sleeping in the guest room, but you shouldn't wake her up. Let her sleep, but get your brother's ass to the kitchen. Okay?"

"Sure." I nod, stalking to the second floor. I don't know what they did last night, but I'm sure they were both wasted. Dammit, I don't want Story to see Piper looking like—

That thought flies out the window as the door to the guest room opens and Piper sneaks outside. She's still in her dress from last night, but her face is makeup free, and her hair is collected into a high ponytail. She looks cute and well-rested—not how I expected her to look.

Her eyes land on me, and we stare at each other in silence.

"Hey," I say, and she nods curtly. "Leaving already?"

"Y-yeah." She toys with the chain on her bag, avoiding looking at me. "Riley sent me about twenty messages, so I need to get home."

"I hope she's okay."

"She's fine, but thank you. See you tomorrow, Hunter." She takes a few tiny steps in my direction, and that's when I see it. Piper has a huge hickey on her neck, and all at once I feel lost.

"You have a hickey," I grunt, louder and harsher than I intended. She halts in her tracks, gawking at me with eyes like saucers. Without any particular reason, I step closer and trace the mark with my finger, inhaling her scent and feeling my dick harden. *Jesus fuck.* "Here."

Piper loudly sucks in a breath, holding my gaze and covering the spot with her palm. Her fingers brush mine, and I start to wonder if everything is okay with me. Because the idea of lifting her, pinning her to the wall, and fingerfucking her till she comes is the only thing I can think about right now. Desperately. And it's so wrong.

She steps back, lowering her eyes to the floor. "I'll cover it up. Story won't see it."

Story? The problem is me, not her. I'm the one who's dying to know who she was with last night. Does she have a boyfriend? Does she...*oh shit.* I need a fucking plan. Plan B, C, and even Z. Or she's going to be the death of me.

"See you tomorrow, Piper," I grit through my teeth, rounding her and heading toward my brother's bedroom. I have a boner from touching her skin. What a disaster.

"YOUR SON WILL BE DOWN in ten minutes," I announce as I step into the kitchen.

Mom and Story are sitting at the table, each with a steaming mug and a plate of cake in front of them. Story glances at me and takes a bite of cake. She closes her eyes, a blissful expression on her face. Just looking at her makes me want to try the cake too. I'll never say no to something sweet.

"My son?" Mom asks as I sit beside Story. "I don't remember

disowning you, Hunter. You probably meant to say 'my brother', right?"

I roll my eyes. "My brother will be down in ten minutes. Better?"

"Absolutely." She smiles at me, taking a sip of her coffee. "Did you see Piper? She swung by to say hi before she left, just after you went upstairs."

"I did. She told me she was going home." I shift in my seat, my level of discomfort at its peak. Thank God I chose black sweatpants this morning. It would've been way harder to hide my erection in my jeans.

"Piper said her sister has a date, and she needs to help her get ready," Story murmurs, sneaking a glance at me. "It's so exciting!"

"It's exciting when you're fifteen like Riley is." My mom tsks. "I swear, kids these days. You're going to give me a heart attack!"

"I had my first kiss when I was four, because love is not about age. It's about feelings," Story says. *And I'm fucking dead.* My mom's going to kill me. I meet her gaze, and her eyebrows are at her hairline. *Please, Story, don't say a word, don't say—* "But you shouldn't be worried. I'm not going to date anyone until I'm at least eleven. Piper said I should enjoy my childhood, and boys can wait."

Mom clears her throat, coughing loudly. "You should listen to Piper. She's a sweetheart, and she's totally right." She narrows her green eyes on Story. "Who told you love is about feelings, sweetie?"

"Mom." Story shrugs, taking another bite of cake. She looks nonchalant and carefree, while I'm seriously debating whether I should run. When my mom's angry, it's better to stay away from her. Like, on the other side of the world away. "Love is one of the most beautiful and powerful things in the world. If Dad didn't love Mom, I wouldn't be here at all."

My gaze flicks to my mother, and she purses her lips. She takes a deep breath and sets her mug on the table. "Did your mom talk to you about all that?" she asks.

"Yes. No. Not really." Story blushes, and her brows knit together. "She used to take me with her to meet her friends, and I heard them talking."

"Jesus," Mom blurts, and a deep wrinkle appears on her forehead.

"Is something wrong? Did I do something?" Story turns to me, her gaze pleading. "Daddy?"

I press my palm to her cheek and dip my head to look her in the eyes. "Everything's fine, baby. Your granny is just surprised you know so much about grown-up stuff."

"Story," my mom says softly, and my daughter looks at her. "I'm sorry, sweetie. You didn't do anything wrong. Your granny is just old-fashioned. I'll do better next time. I promise."

Story sighs, jumps off the chair, and ambles over to my mom. She hops up onto her lap, winding her hands around her neck. "You're amazing, Granny. You don't need to change for me. Or anyone. Piper says if someone makes you feel like you don't belong, it's not about you. It's about them. I think she's right."

Does Piper mean me? Do I make her feel like she doesn't belong? Is that how she feels when I get home from practice?

"Aw, I'm so happy your dad hired Piper for you." Mom wraps her arms around Story, cuddling her to her chest. "She's an incredible girl, a real blessing. First for Hayden. Now for you."

"My best friend is a sunshiny girl," Hayden says from behind me. "You gotta love her. No one stands a chance against her charms."

"Not sure she's trying to charm anyone," Mom chuckles, fixing her gaze on Hayden. "She's just always nice, and people love her for that."

"Not Hunter."

What? I watch Hayden edge closer to the table. He slumps down into a chair and only then meets my gaze.

"Care to explain yourself?" I demand.

"Chill, bro." He waves his hand, yawning loudly. "Piper loves being Story's nanny, so she'll put up with your antics."

"My antics?" *What did she tell him?*

"Damn, my head is killing me." Hayden runs a hand over his face, ignoring me. *What the fuck did she tell him?*

"What do you mean my antics?" I ask through clenched teeth, and the kitchen drowns in silence.

"You're so annoying," he mutters under his breath. Then he looks up to meet my gaze. "Pip never complains, so to answer your question —she didn't tell me anything. But I know her, and I know when something is bothering her."

"Don't you think it's a bit presumptuous to put the blame on your brother just because you're suspicious?" Mom chimes in, giving Hayden a pointed look. Then she shifts her gaze to Story, and then to me. She doesn't want us to argue in front of my daughter. "And besides, Piper is an adult. She makes her own decisions. If she hasn't quit and she isn't talking to you about Hunter, then you can't assume it's about her job."

"Then what could it be? She needed a job; she got one. Everything she was worried about has been resolved."

"She misses going to college." Story's voice draws our attention to her. "She didn't want to go to the party with you, Uncle Hayden. Piper was worried everyone would be talking about college, and she'd feel left out."

"Fu—" Hayden stops himself before cursing. "*Funny* she never told me that. Not funny—she was totally right. We did talk about college a lot. She even disappeared for a while, probably because she got tired of our ramblings. I'm the worst best friend in the world." He pouts and then sneaks a glance at me. "Sorry, Hunter. I guess I was wrong."

"That's okay." I nod and stand up, intending to go to the bathroom. My brain is ready to explode from all these revelations about Piper. Things aren't easy for her, and me acting like an ass doesn't help.

"Are you going to stay for dinner?" I'm almost at the door when my mom calls out to me.

"Yeah, I'd love to."

"Great. I'll start cooking then." Mom lets go of Story, and she goes to her uncle. She takes his face in her hands and stares at him long and hard. Then she scrunches her nose and steps back.

"You look exhausted, Uncle Hayden. Have you thought maybe you should stop drinking?"

I snort and rush out the door, dying from laughter. Yes, she knows things she shouldn't. Yes, she says things no one expects, and sometimes it's too much. But not today. Her reaction to Hayden is priceless. Tips and tricks from a seven-year-old—nothing is better than that.

STANDING IN THE KITCHEN, I look out the window, holding a mug of coffee. Story and I spent time with our family last night and got home around nine. She was in an incredibly good mood, chatting nonstop about her school and the friends she's made there. Story genuinely loves her grandparents, but her uncle is her absolute favorite. Their energy is somehow matching, and he enjoys playing with her, agreeing to do whatever she asks.

Hayden isn't how I remember him. I never thought I'd say it, but he's mature and responsible. He has the right principles and loves his family.

Piper was right when she said he'd changed. I shouldn't have dismissed her. She knows him better than I do.

I glance at my watch. 8:45 a.m. She should be here soon. I just hope it's not awkward. I intend to do anything I can to make sure it's not. I've been giving her whiplash with my attitude, and I don't blame her for being careful around me. It's like dealing with two kids instead of one, and I'm not sure who's more of a handful. Probably me, because Story knows how to control her emotions.

A door closes, and my body goes rigid. I don't have any doubt that it's Piper. She's on time, as always. Punctual as the spring tide, my brother said, and he's not wrong. A huge difference from Amelia, who was always late.

"Oh." Piper freezes once she sees me. "Hey."

"Hey. Sorry if I scared you," I say, and she crooks a smile as she heads to the fridge. She has a plastic box in her hands, and when I look more closely I can't hide my surprise. "Cheesecake?"

"Strawberry cheesecake, to be exact." She puts the box in the fridge and turns to me. Her hair is collected into a messy bun, a few wild locks framing her beautiful face. In jean shorts and a pastel pink tee, she looks incredible. "I know Story loves it, so I wanted to treat her."

"Where did you get it?"

"I made it." Piper shrugs, leaning against the kitchen counter. Her plump lips ease into a big, radiant smile. "I didn't have much to do last night, so I thought why not make something for Story and Riley. They both have such a sweet tooth, it's honestly adorable."

I chuckle, taking a sip of my coffee. "Story's love for sweets comes from me. Amelia hated me for all the cakes and cookies I kept in our cupboards."

"I've never seen you eat anything sweet." Piper's brows pinch together, and I feel a rush of energy slowly spread through my whole body. She's not only attentive to Story, but to me as well. And it turns me on. "Do you want a taste? I'm not sure Story will leave any for you."

Do I want a taste, Piper? I do. Just not of the cheesecake. "No, I'm good." And hard, but that piece of information shouldn't leave my mouth. Ever.

"You don't think it's delicious?" she asks, her chocolate brown eyes trained on me.

"I have no doubt it's delicious." My voice drops an octave lower, and I angle my body closer to her on instinct. I catch the scent of her perfume, and I want to bury my face in her neck. Lavender mixed with vanilla hits my nose, and I tighten my grip on my mug. "I just... ate."

Her lips part as she holds my gaze. All I'd need to do is curl my hand around her waist, and she'd be up against my chest in no time. The problem? It'd be highly inappropriate, and she'd quit faster than I could say "goal." I can't afford to look for another nanny.

"Your loss then." She takes a step back, tossing her hair aside, and my eyes land on her neck. There's no sign of her hickey, and for a second I want to smile, but my relief is short-lived. Who was she with?

Does she have a boyfriend? Do I need to worry about catching her with someone in my house? In my car? Because the girl has needs, just like all of us, and I can't blame her for wanting to be satisfied. I just need a heads-up...I guess.

"I'll be home around five, so if you want to go out..." I trail off, noticing her frown. "You know, if you want to see your boyfriend—"

"My boyfriend?"

"Well, your hickey..."

Her face instantly darkens, and I regret not biting my tongue. "Can't I just hook up? Do I really need to have a boyfriend to get a hickey?" She puts her hands on her hips and purses her lips. "What if it was a girl?"

"You swing both ways?" I ask, only realizing how I sound when the last word leaves my lips.

"Do you have something against that?"

How on Earth did we move from talking about cheesecake to discussing her sexual orientation? I exhale a long and exasperated breath and set my mug on the kitchen counter.

"You can sleep with whoever you please. It's none of my business, and I'm sorry I brought it up at all." I take a step back, my eyes roaming over her face. She looks just as perplexed as I feel when she meets my gaze. "What I mean is, if you want to go out, to visit your sister or anyone else, you can always do that once I get home. You're young, and I don't want you to feel obligated to spend all your time in this house."

Skirting her, I head to my bedroom. I have about twenty minutes to get ready for practice, and I prefer to spend that time in my room. It'll be much safer, and it will help me keep my mouth shut.

They say you should know your enemy. Well, I know mine. It's me. I'm my biggest enemy for sure. Instead of making things right, I only make them worse. I have a fucking talent for it.

11
bringing out the bad

PIPER

Boring. Boring. Boring. I scroll through my feed faster than a cheetah runs after its prey. I ignore cute dogs, food recipes, dances, and—God forbid—books. My to-read list is so long, I'll need another life to be able to finish everything. So I've been staying away from all new book recommendations, even if they're tempting.

I sigh, lock my phone, and toss it on my bed. Two hours. I just need to wait for two more hours before I pick up Story from school. It's nothing unusual, except for the fact that her dad is home. Hunter barely talks to me if it's not about his daughter. Yes, it's something I wished for a month ago. Yes, it's less awkward this way, but he makes me feel like I'm annoying and unwelcome, and that's not how I want to feel when I spend almost twenty-four seven with someone.

When was the last decent conversation we had that wasn't about Story? Exactly a month ago, when I found him in the kitchen as I put some cheesecake in the fridge. That's when he decided to bring up my hickey again. He insinuated I have a boyfriend and told me I can go out. Because I'm young. *Well, Mr. Hale, if you'd bother to talk to me, you would know how much I love spending time at home.* Instead, he made assumptions and dragged his pompous ass out of the room. Asshole.

I plop myself down on my back and stare at the ceiling. I love Story. I love my job; it's a blessing. Two more months, and I'll have enough money to pay for my next year of college. I was also able to buy some nice stuff for Riley; she was thrilled. It's all good, but... Hunter makes it hard to fully enjoy it. His presence and his emotionless stare play on my nerves even more than the sound of nails across a chalkboard. He's just weird.

Patting my hand over my covers, I grab my phone again and unlock it. It's only been three minutes? I'm screwed. I sit up and look around the room. Why should I feel like a hostage in his house? Why do I need to stay locked in here just because he stayed home for some reason? It's on him if my presence irritates him. He's free to go to his room and do whatever he pleases. I don't care.

I scramble off the bed, beeline to my walk-in closet, and quickly take out my swimsuit. We all have our own routines, and swimming has been mine since I started living in this house. I often do laps when I don't have anything better to do, when everything is ready for Story to come home and I still have time to kill. Why can't I enjoy that now? It's ridiculous. He said so himself—I'm free to do whatever I want. And right now? I want to swim.

Once I'm in my one-piece swimsuit, I look at myself in the mirror. It's all good, but for some reason I don't like it. I want something else...something more revealing. *What. The. Fuck? Piper Meadow Evans, are you looking for trouble? Because it feels like it.*

Suppressing all my dirty thoughts, I change into my pink bikini, pull my dress on, grab a towel, and stomp toward the backyard. The house is silent, and I wonder if I missed him leaving for practice or somewhere else. I'm sure he wouldn't have given me heads-up. So what if he left? Even better.

The second I get to the backyard, I want to be back in my room. Hunter fucking Hale is here, and he just got out of the pool. Water is dripping down his form, and he runs his fingers through his dark brown hair, holding his face up to the sun. My lower abdomen instantly warms, and my clit pulsates. Those pecs, ripped muscles, and rock-hard abs make my mouth water. But who cares?

The right side of his chest is covered with tattoos. They go down his right arm and all the way to his wrist. The mix of thick black lines, geometric symbols, and abstract patterns interlocked into one composition makes me want to look closer.

I drag my eyes down his body, and they become fixed on his crotch —he's fucking huge!

Hunter lowers his gaze, and our eyes meet. Good thing I could finally focus on his face, because the last thing I want is him seeing me eye his dick. Because I was. Just a heartbeat ago. *I'm such a desperate little shit.* Memories of the orgasm I gave myself come rushing back, and I'm having a hard time concentrating on what's happening now.

I bite my inner cheek, squirming in pain, but at least I'm back to reality. *Okay, I can do this.* I came to swim, and that's exactly what I'm going to do. Swim. And maybe eye-fuck Hunter, because that's the only thing that flashes in my mind. It's like I'm fixated on the idea. Or I'm just feeling unsatisfied and extra horny, and that's the reason I'm considering jumping his bones. *Oh my God.* I should've agreed to go to the party with Hayden last weekend. I could've hooked up with someone and solved my problem. Yet I stayed home, watching movies with Story and Riley, who came over for a sleepover. Yay to Hunter for letting Riley stay, nay to me for ignoring my urges. I'm hopeless.

Giving him a tense smile, I saunter closer to the pool. Hunter's gaze moves down my body, and my nipples pebble immediately. The way I react to him is absolutely brainless, no matter what we're doing, especially if we're arguing. When that happens—and it happens way too often for my liking—I get close to an orgasm just by putting the asshole in his place. The weird sensations in my lower abdomen quickly speed up and spread through my body, forcing me to almost come. I've never experienced anything like it around any other guy, and I can't blame it on lack of experience. Just...there is something really exquisite about him, unique and overly erotic, something that awakens so many different emotions within me, so most of the time I feel lost. And today isn't an exception.

I hesitate, stopping by the pool, and my fingers fly to the hem of my dress. I need to take it off if I want to swim. Easy-peasy, right? Well, yes, but not when my hot boss, aka my best friend's brother, stands near me wearing only his briefs. *Ugh, wrong thought, Piper.*

"The water is nice." I turn my head toward the sound of his voice and meet his gaze.

"I know. I swim almost every day."

"Really?" He half-turns to me. "I've never seen you by the pool."

"That's because I prefer to swim in the mornings when I'm not bothering anyone."

"You can swim whenever you want; you're not bothering me." I nod, and he peers at me. "So, are you an early bird?"

I wrinkle my brows and tilt my head. "What?"

"Are you a morning person, Piper?" This time I realize what he means.

"Definitely. There are so many things you can finish faster if you start working earlier."

Hunter laughs, and the sound scatters all over my skin. It's deep and a bit husky—and also incredibly sexy. *Yeah, Piper, such a great idea to think about him like that. It's not enough you're dreaming about him at night, waking up with clenched thighs because your pussy is dripping.* It's becoming a huge problem, and I'm not sure how to change it...aside from quitting.

"Any plans for today?" I ask, finally deciding to take off my dress. My hair spills over my bare shoulders the second I'm in only my bikini. I collect my hair into a messy bun as I wait for Hunter's answer. I put my dress and towel on the sunbed, and my breath gets stuck in my throat when I meet his gaze. The way he looks at me sends shivers down my spine.

"Not really. I have a press conference tomorrow since my first game is on Wednesday. Everyone wants to know what Hunter Hale is thinking. Surprisingly." He plops down onto the second sunbed. His eyes never leave my face.

"Story's very excited to go to your first game. She wants to see her dad play," I say, lowering myself on the edge of the pool and putting my legs in the water. When I look over my shoulder, I lock eyes with

Hunter, who sits with his elbows on his knees. "What about you? Are you excited to be back in the game?"

"Of course. I missed being on the pitch. It was my whole life for a very long time, so this break took a toll on me."

"But the season ends in October and doesn't restart until February. What are you going to do during the break?" And, most importantly, what am I going to do during his break?

"Well, there will be playoffs in November. And after that, I'll still be practicing, to stay in shape. I've also planned something...for my future, and I just hope everything will work out." His lips suddenly curl into a grin, and he arches an eyebrow at me. "I'll still need a nanny for Story. I'll still need you."

Oh no, Mr. Hale. No, no, no. Take it back. These butterflies in my stomach drive me up the wall, but at the same time...I can't help but smile. "Good. Because I love Story, and I love being your—*her* nanny."

"Did you almost say 'your nanny'?" He laughs, putting a hand on his belly.

"You could've pretended you didn't notice," I huff and slide into the water, boring my gaze into his yet again.

"And let a golden opportunity to tease you go to waste? Nah." Asshole. But the way he smiles at me makes my heart melt. Hunter is a very handsome man, charming and hot. And he can be absofucking-lutely awesome...when he doesn't act like a jackass.

"I see you enjoying making me squirm."

"What's not to enjoy?" he murmurs, licking his lips, and I trace the movement of his tongue with my heated gaze. I'm hot and bothered all over again, and I'm in the fucking water, where it's supposed to be cool. "Hayden was right. He said you're cute when you're feeling shy."

"I thought you liked me angry," I blurt without thinking, and I instantly want to disappear. His gaze darkens, and he takes a long, shaky breath. "I just...we argue a lot, and—"

"I wouldn't say we argue." Hunter stands up. "We just don't see eye to eye sometimes."

"Yeah..." I trail off, keeping myself above water even if I want to disappear from view.

"Enjoy your swim," he says.

My eyes zero in on his butt as he pads into the house. Is there any part of him that isn't perfect? It sure doesn't look like it. What's more...he's bringing out the bad in me, and I'm acting like a brat who thinks that flirting and arguing with their boss is okay.

It's official: I'm the worst.

I do five laps and realize my head isn't in it. That was the first decent conversation I've had with Hunter in weeks, and then I ruined it with my flirting. The man was just teasing me, but I took it as encouragement. Even if there is some attraction, it's just because he's single and I'm constantly around. I don't need to be a genius to figure that out.

I climb out of the water, grab my towel, and quickly dry my body. With my dress and my wet towel in my hands, I head into the house. Unfortunately, swimming didn't bring me any solace today. Good thing Hayden is coming over tonight. With him around, things are easier.

I pass Hunter's room and hear the faint sound of water running. Is he taking a shower? My cheeks feel warm, and I shut my eyes. This is becoming ridiculous, I swear. I need to let out this frustration. The Sabotage show on Saturday can't come soon enough, because I need to get out and unwind. Staying professional is a must for me, and I intend to do everything in my power to keep my panties on and my thoughts in check. The last thing I want is to think of him again when I masturbate.

I close my bedroom door, go to my bathroom, and open the drawer to take out my hairdryer. My hand hovers over it, ready to seize it and work a little magic, but instead I feel paralyzed. *Is this really happening?*

I move closer and press my ear to the wall. Listening carefully, I try to muffle my inner voice and all the thoughts it continues to produce, and soon all I hear is the sound of water from Hunter's en suite. I'm almost ready to move away when I hear it again. A low grumble, a louder groan, and then my name. Again and again and again.

My jaw drops as I press my back to the wall. My eyes are wide and unblinking, and my heart gallops. Hunter Hale is in the shower just behind this wall, jerking off...while calling my name. Does it mean he likes me? Or is he just lonely and sexually deprived? Or both? I don't know what to think, but I know what I'm going to do.

Slipping my hand under my panties, I touch my clit. I close my eyes at once, as soon as this feeling settles in. It feels too good. Too arousing. Too sensational. Picking up the pace, I fingerfuck myself, listening to Hunter getting off behind the wall.

What if it's not just him bringing out the bad in me? What if I'm doing the same to him?

12
haunted

HUNTER

STANDING UNDER THE STEAMING WATER, I STARE AT THE wall, not seeing anything. My hand is wrapped around my dick, and I feel numb. I've been doing so well, keeping my distance, staying nothing but professional. We argued a few times, but it was short-lived and didn't affect my resolve in any way. Piper is Story's nanny, and she's off-limits. Easy, like kicking the ball into an empty net. Not easy when she waltzes out of the house wearing nothing but a short summer dress over her bikini. Her clothes and her sass sent me over the edge, like a flick of the switch, making me horny.

I thought you liked me angry.

Damn right, girl, I fucking like you angry. What I like even more is thinking about all the ways I could make you drop the attitude. On your knees, on top of me, or on my bed on all fours.

I'm getting dangerously close to not caring about any of my rules. What's stopping me is the realization that it would ruin everything, and I can't stand even the thought of her leaving. Story already loves Piper, and separating them would lead to my daughter hating me. I have no doubt about that.

The most frustrating part? I have my first game in two days, and I can't shake off my irritation. Having Piper around is torture. I'm not sure what I was thinking when I hired her. Of course, it was for Story, but I should've put more thought into the decision.

"Fuck," I groan, dropping my hands to my sides and leaning against the glass wall of my shower. I'm emotionally spent, and that wasn't what I wanted when I went outside to swim. I wanted a refresher but got a boner. Excellent.

I stay in the shower, washing my body and trying to figure out my plan of attack. I need one before I completely lose my cool and do something stupid. Hunter Hale has a reputation as one of the most level-headed people in the game. The only spontaneous decision I ever made was asking Amelia on a date. I would prefer for it to stay like that. I don't want to be known as the guy who had an affair with his daughter's nanny.

What affair though? I pull on my tee, clenching my jaw hard. Okay, it's not an affair, but it's still wrong. I'm her boss, and I'm not looking for a relationship. Fucking Piper sounds tempting, but it's not worth destroying what she has with Story.

Once I'm fully dressed, my phone starts buzzing. I glance at the screen and smile. My best friend has the best timing ever. "Hey, Angelo. What's up?"

"Hey, Hale," he mumbles, yawning loudly. "Cissy is trying to turn the whole place upside down."

"Why?"

"Because my daughter is evil reincarnate," he whines, making me chuckle. "She wants to play, and when I say it's time for a nap, she starts crying and saying she wants her mommy back."

"When does Luna get back from her parents' house?"

"Tomorrow. I swear, man, this is the last time I'm going to agree to this. Either she takes both kids with her to visit or waits until I'm off."

"Well, she deals with two of them when you're on the road. You can't look after one?"

"Fuck off. I called you for support, not a lecture!" My friend scoffs as I walk out of my bedroom. "Not everyone is as good with kids as you are, Hale."

"I'm only good with my own kid." I laugh heartily, feeling the tension leave my body little by little.

"Nah, you're shitting me. If you were only good with Story, you wouldn't want to coach kids," Angelo counters. He's one of the few people who knows about my plans to open my own football school next year. Dream big and make it happen. Always.

"You're not wrong," I tell him, heading to the couch, where I plop down and prop my feet up on the coffee table. "We'll see if I can actually pull it off."

"I'm sure you will; I believe in you, Hale. And mark my words: I'll be the first to fly to LA when you open. I promise."

"Thanks for believing in me, man."

"How's the sex life? Did you find yourself a hookup?" he asks nonchalantly.

"Russo, this is—"

"Or wait, is it the nanny?"

"Shut the fuck up," I hiss, balling my fist so hard my knuckles turn white. I just fucking got off thinking about Piper, so his question hits too close to home.

"So defensive again." Angelo sighs, then clears his throat. "You have your first game on Wednesday, and I hope you win...but you gotta do something about your needs too. We both know how grouchy you can be when you're—"

"God, Angelo, I want to hang up on you." Growling, I close my eyes. "I'm open to conversation, but right now, that's not what I want to talk about."

"Sorry, Hale. I'll try to tone it down. For now."

"What a fucking shocker," I mutter, and he laughs.

I talk to Angelo for another twenty minutes before he has to finish the call because his daughter broke a vase. Thanks to Angelo, my irritation has dissolved into nothingness, and I'm grateful to him for that.

"Hunter?" I turn my head toward the sound of my name and find Piper standing in the doorway. Her hair is in a high ponytail, and she has lip gloss on her rosy lips. She's wearing a light pink crop top and a black leather jacket over it. My eyes zero in on her bare midriff, devouring every inch of her golden skin, her flat stomach, and moving down her legs in jeans. Perfection. "Hunter?"

I blink and return my gaze to her face. A faint smile plays on her lips, and a fire dances behind her irises, adding a honeyed shade to her chocolate brown eyes.

"Yeah, sorry, I have a lot on my mind today. I kinda hate press conferences, and it plays with my mood."

"Uh-huh," Piper murmurs. "I'm leaving to pick up Story in ten minutes. Should I stop by the grocery store on our way home? Your brother will be here for dinner."

"I have a feeling Hayden is going to move in soon. He's here almost every day. All because of your food."

"It's not my fault I'm a good cook." She shrugs, grinning. "And you can always say no to him. It's not like you're obligated to have him over whenever he pleases."

"Story loves him, and he's family. I'm trying to get to know him better...like you suggested."

Her smile grows wider as she tucks a strand of hair behind her ear. "Glad to know you're actually listening to me."

"I always do." I stand up and notice as her breath hitches in her throat. This reaction speaks louder than any of her words, and I'm suddenly aware of my surroundings, and more importantly my actions. I need to break this fucking spell she's put on me. I need to let her know that nothing will happen between us, ever. "I'm a bit old-fashioned, and I still don't know a lot of places here, so maybe you can help me. Where do people usually go if they want to have fun? Like, to meet someone?"

The change in her emotions is swift, like a snap of a finger. Piper isn't smiling anymore, and her eyes are narrowed.

"Use Tinder. It's always good if you just want to have fun and meet someone new." She takes a step back, hiding her hands in her jacket pockets. "Hade knows everything about it. You can ask him."

"I will. Thank you, Piper." Awkward? Yes. Inappropriate? Yes. But it served its purpose. She's furious, but she knows I'm setting boundaries. It's for the best. I stop right in front of her. "And it's okay. You don't need to buy anything at the store. I'll order takeout."

She watches me from under furrowed brows, then lifts her chin and nods. "Okay. I gotta go."

The aroma of her perfume hits my nostrils. I inhale deeply, and regret floods my mind. What I feel around her is different from every other woman I've ever been with. She's not even my type. And still, the attraction is there, and it's hard to ignore. I just need to know... what if I'm only feeling this way because I haven't had sex in months?

My sex drive has always been incredibly high. Sometimes it even overwhelmed Amelia. I've tried so many things in bed, and now I'm celibate because my ex-wife shamed me for my sex life. Because she insinuated I wouldn't be able to keep my dick in my pants and would find a new mommy for Story just to keep myself satisfied. That's why I'm dead set on keeping my promise to myself. Story is my everything, and I'll do anything for her. Only for her.

The sound of the door closing breaks me out of my daze. I blink, realizing Piper left. Heaving a sigh, I drag myself back to the couch. I should use this time to figure out what I want to order for dinner. Maybe takeout will help drive Hayden away from this house, at least for a while.

"ARE YOU KIDDING ME?" Hayden yelps, almost spilling his beer. "Of course I'm going to your first game. How could I not? How could you even think I was going to skip it?"

"Dunno. I didn't think you were interested in football." I shrug, taking a sip of my whiskey. Hayden and I are alone, as Story went to bed an hour ago, asking Piper to stay with her till she fell asleep. She wanted me to spend more time with her uncle. Did I expect Hayden to leave as soon as dinner was over? Probably not. But I definitely didn't think he would stay past eleven, yet here we are. Bonding, as Piper called it.

"I'm interested in my brother, asshole." He purses his lips and eyes me for a minute, then breaks into a smile. "Piper said you wanted to talk to me about something...relationship related."

She did not. Fuck, that girl will be the death of me. "I'm not interested in anything relationship related."

"A hookup then?" He takes a sip of his drink, barely holding back his laughter.

I roll my eyes as I set my empty glass on the table. "I already have Tinder. I'm good."

"Do you need me to teach you how to use it?" The geeky smile on his face makes me want to punch him. He's infuriating.

"Fuck off, kid. I'm not that old."

"Says the man who just called his brother 'kid.'" Piper's voice fills the room, and Hayden and I both look at her. She lingers by the door, leaning against the doorway. She's in black leggings and a white tee, and her hair is in two braids.

"He's thirteen years younger; he'll always be a kid to me."

"Hunter, you're ruining my image, for real," Hayden scoffs. He exchanges a glance with Piper. "I have a better idea for you, actually. I mean, for your problem."

"Which is?" I grab the bottle from the table and pour myself another drink. This is becoming highly entertaining, and I didn't expect it.

"Sabotage has a show this Saturday. Why don't you come? Listen to me play, have a great time, and meet someone new." He gestures at Piper, and for a second her gaze flicks to me. "Pip can keep you company if you're afraid to go solo."

"You're forgetting about Story," Piper retorts, coming closer and lowering herself onto the seat next to Hayden.

"I'm not. Mom and Dad will be happy to have their grand-daughter for a sleepover. I can call them—"

"It's late," I say, and he stares back at me with a deep frown. "Besides, I'm not sure that's a good idea."

"You've never heard me play in person," Hayden mutters, and

guilt drips over my body and finds its way to my heart. He's not wrong, and it makes me a shitty brother. "Forget it."

"I'll come. I promise," I blurt, and he grins, draping an arm over Piper's shoulder. "Hopefully Piper isn't against spending time with me outside of this house."

"Don't worry. I can even introduce you to some of my friends," she mumbles. Then she covers her mouth with her hand, stifling a yawn. "Sorry, I'm going to bed."

"What time is it?" Hayden fishes his phone from his pocket and instantly curses when he sees the screen. "Dammit, I need to get going too."

Forty minutes later, I'm alone in my bedroom, getting ready to climb into bed. I pull back the covers and pause, deciding to go get a glass of water in case I wake up feeling thirsty.

When I step into the kitchen, I hear a squeal. My eyes widen as my gaze snaps to Piper. She's standing in front of the cupboard with her mouth open, staring at me in total bewilderment. I swear I'm feeling haunted in my own house.

13
because the night
PIPER

Hunter clears his throat. "Didn't think you were still up."

"I could say the same," I mumble, grabbing a chocolate bar from the cupboard. "I was sure I was the only one who was still awake."

He rests his elbows on the kitchen counter. "I was going to bed when I realized I needed a glass of water."

"Yeah, I came to get some too."

"And food." He points to the chocolate bar in my hand, and I chuckle. I took the first thing my eyes landed on because he startled me.

"Yeah, and food."

We continue to stare at each other in silence. My cheeks warm; I'm suddenly aware of what I'm wearing. A light blue satin nightdress barely hides my butt, and its deep-cut neckline highlights my boobs better than any push-up bra I own. It's sexy, and it's not something I should be wearing in front of my boss...especially a boss who's been sending me mixed signals all day.

"I'll go." I take a step toward him, and he steps to the side, as if avoiding me. I take another step, and he ambles further to his right. Another step and he moves behind the counter, facing me from the opposite side of the kitchen. "What are you doing?" I ask.

"Nothing. I'm going to pour myself some water and go to bed."

Shifting my gaze to the empty glass I left on the counter, I shrug. It'd be great to have some water in my room too. I go back to get my glass, and in my peripheral vision, Hunter edges away again. Is he kidding me?

I grab the empty glass, quickly pour myself some water, and turn to look at him. "What's your problem with me?"

"What do you mean?"

"Any time I'm close to you, you move away. Is something wrong? Do I stink?"

"What? No. You smell very nice. I like it," he says. "I'm just...it's better if I keep my distance."

Shaking my head, I turn around abruptly, slamming my knee on the edge of a cabinet. I squeal in pain, dropping my glass and the chocolate bar on the floor. Water and shards of glass are everywhere, so I stay rooted to the spot, pressing my palm to my knee and keeping my eyes closed.

"Okay, let's get you out of here." His deep, muffled voice sounds like honey: sweet and pleasant to my ears. I snap my eyes open and see Hunter in front of me. He wraps his arms around my waist and lifts me with ease. The next thing I know, I'm sitting on the kitchen counter with Hunter standing between my legs. "Can I have a look?"

"It's nothing. It'll just leave a bruise."

"Can I have a look, please?" he insists, and I remove my hand from my knee. "That's better."

His long fingers skim along my skin, pressing slightly on my knee, and I suck in a breath. His touch is so light, but at the same time it's sizzling hot. My hard nipples poke through my nightdress, and my chest rises and falls fast. The things his presence does to me are infuriating.

"What's the diagnosis, Dr. Hale?"

Hunter snorts, and his hot breath gusts over my skin. "You have a little cut. Nothing serious."

"Yeah, except your kitchen is a complete mess." Our eyes lock. "I'm sorry for that."

"It's okay. Don't worry about it. I'll take care of everything." He smiles. "Including you. *Sit.*"

I have no desire to move, sir.

Hunter cleans up the floor, sweeping away shards of glass. Then he wipes it with a paper towel. All his movements are effortless; he doesn't dwell on any one task. If it needs his attention, he's up to it, no matter what. And right now, I need his attention. A lot.

Once he's done cleaning, he opens a few drawers and then comes back to me. "Can I?"

"It's just a cut," I tell him, trying to feign indifference, while in reality I'm close to begging him to touch me.

"Then I'll just clean it and apply a little ointment. What do you think?"

"Okay."

Hunter thoroughly cleans my wound with a drop of peroxide. It stings a little, and I squirm, hissing through clenched teeth. He blows on it to make it less painful, and I start smiling, butterflies somersaulting in my stomach. It feels too good to have his hands on me.

"You know what you're doing when it comes to cuts and bruises."

"I play professional sports, Piper. Wounds, bruises, and even fractures are part of the job; it's my everyday life. I *have* to know what to do in case something happens. Even if the team doctors and physical therapists are there to keep an eye on me." He takes out a tube of Neosporin and gently applies it to my wound. "But I'm also a father. Taking care of my kid when she needs me is the least I can do."

"Story is lucky to have a dad like you."

"I'm trying my best. I just hope she's happy."

"She is. Very." And so am I. "Thank you, Hunter."

I cover his hand on my knee with my own, and a blinding rush of energy surges through my whole body. A gasp escapes my parted lips, and I move forward an inch. And just like that, I discover the reason he's been avoiding me. His erection pressing against my pussy makes my eyes go wide. Has he been hard since the moment he walked into the kitchen and saw me?

Hunter digs his fingers into my thighs, setting his jaw hard. "That's not what you think," he mutters, not moving.

"I don't know what I think...but it feels like a boner," I murmur. I see his Adam's apple bob up and down. He exhales loudly and then leans forward, boring his gaze into mine. The shy and reserved side of me disappears, and he's left to deal with the more adventurous and daring Piper. I glide my hand over his, higher and higher until I reach his chest. "And your heart is beating insanely fast."

Hunter smirks and pulls me closer, pressing his hard-on against my wet core. "Do you understand this is highly inappropriate?"

"Do I look like I care about that?"

A low growl reaches my ears when he palms my ass, and I think I could come just because he's so close to me. Hunter inches forward, his hot breath all over my face. My level of anticipation soars through the roof, and I feel my body trembling.

Suddenly, he moves away, a stony expression on his face as he holds my gaze. "I haven't had sex in months, and that's why I reacted like that. You're not my type, Piper. Google my ex-girlfriends or my ex-wife, and you'll understand everything. If I feel a desperate need for sex, I'll use Tinder. I'm not going to fuck Story's nanny."

I drag my eyes up and down his form and jump to my feet. Hunter stands still, arms dangling at his sides.

"Unbelievable." I hiss, pushing past him. Glancing over my shoulder, I catch his gaze focused on me. "From now on, don't even think about talking to me about anything that isn't related to Story. I'm just a nanny, Hale."

Rushing out of the kitchen, I stride to my bedroom. I have no idea what I was thinking, acting like that with him, or what I expected from him, but it definitely was not that. Why did I let that happen? Because the night belongs to lovers, but not to heartless jerks like Hunter Hale. I'm done with him.

I TAKE Story to school after her dad has already left the house. I try my best to hide my irritation, but unfortunately I'm not successful. She notices that I'm moody.

"Is everything okay? Did I do something to upset you?" Story pleads, her big green eyes glued to my face.

"Honey," I mutter under my breath, brushing my fingers over her skin. "I just didn't sleep well, and it affected my mood. Everything's fine; don't worry."

"Really?"

"Yeah, I promise." I cup her cheek with my palm, and she leans into my touch, smiling brightly. "How about we get some ice cream after school?"

"Sounds perfect." Story wraps her arms around my waist and hugs me tightly. "Can I tell you something?"

I bend down to her and smile. "What?"

"I can't wait to go to the game tomorrow. I know how much football means to my dad, and I want him to do well. Just...can we stop by the stadium on our way home? I want to see it today." Dammit, I totally forgot about the game. Maybe I can bail? Hayden and his parents will be at the stadium tomorrow, and they can easily watch Story. She won't—

"I'm so excited you'll be there with me to see my daddy play. You can cheer for him with me. It'll be awesome!"

"I'm sure it will." My smile is so fake that my cheeks hurt. "And of course we can stop by the stadium. Whatever you want."

"You're the best, Piper," Story chirps, tightening her arms around my waist. "I love you."

"I love you too," I murmur, hugging her back. It's a simple truth. The only reason I don't quit. She's way more important than her insufferable father. He can go straight to hell. I wouldn't shed a single tear.

14
pictures of her

HUNTER

"MR. HALE, ONE LAST QUESTION, I PROMISE." A BEAUTIFUL woman grins at me, and I force a smile in return. I don't even remember what magazine she represents. The coach, a few guys from the team, and I have been answering questions for an hour already, and I'm on the verge of storming out of the goddamn room. I'm just a football player...I don't like being a talking head. "How do you like LA?"

I blink, reclining in my seat. "I like it here. It's my hometown, my family is here. And I've got an awesome team, one of the best I've ever played for."

"That's nice to hear. Wishing you all the best for your next game." Her gaze slowly coasts over my face, and she licks her lips. I've seen this look way too many times. I can read the signs, recognize her body language. Fucking a reporter is on the same level as fucking my daughter's nanny. It's never going to happen.

"Thank you, Ms. Dunn," Coach says. "It was great talking to you all, but we have a game to win tomorrow. I need my guys on the field."

Chatter fills the room, chairs scrape against the floor, and a few exasperated breaths come from me and the team's goalkeeper, Marek Vavro. We exchange a glance and chuckle as we stand up from our seats.

"I wonder if there will be a day when I actually like talking to them," Vavro says.

"I've been doing it for fourteen years, and I still hate it," I say as we stroll out the door.

"You're not helping, you know that?"

"Really?" I laugh, and he nudges me with his elbow. "I truly thought I was."

"Not in the slightest." Vavro looks me up and down, his mouth twisting into a smirk. "Ms. Dunn was drooling over you. Just saying."

"I'm not interested. Just saying."

"Dunno, she has some moves, for sure. Always so prim and proper, staying one hundred percent professional," he says, wiggling his eyebrows. "Not today though. I think she has the hots for you."

"You've got it all wrong, buddy." I shake my head and open the door to the locker room. I don't have time for this shit; I need to focus on tomorrow's game. It's gotta be perfect.

"I know the pattern, Hale. Girls like Autumn Dunn remind me of sharks. They see their prey, they chase it, and then they fucking swallow it whole. You won't even notice it until she jumps your bones, trust me."

"Well, I know the pattern too. And I know what I want. It's not her."

Vavro looks at me pensively and then starts to grin. "Fair. I love how levelheaded you are. A huge difference from some of the divas we've had on the team. I like you, Hale."

"I like you too." The door closes behind us with a bang, and we go our separate ways to our lockers.

Vavro might be right about the reporter, but my head is already too busy dealing with another woman in my life. One I can't really escape just by walking out of the room.

What are things going to be like now? The question found its way into my head last night, and I wasn't able to get rid of it, but I tried. I'm her boss. I'm the father of the child she's looking after. I'm her best friend's brother. The last one is just a nuisance—I wouldn't take it into consideration if I decided to pursue her. But I won't. I'd need to deal with the aftermath of banging my kid's nanny. The same nanny who lives in my house, who I'd have to see every day. It'd push her to quit, and I don't want that for my daughter. A mindless fuck isn't worth ruining Story's happiness.

"YOUR STADIUM IS SO BIG. It's so big and so beautiful," Story says the second I step into the house. She runs to meet me. I set my sports bag on the floor and catch her in my arms, giving her a big hug. "I can't wait to go back tomorrow."

"And I can't wait for you to see me play." I kiss her cheek, making her giggle. "But I'm a bit confused. When did you see it?"

"Piper took me there after school," she explains, winding her hands around my neck and pressing her cheek to mine. "She also bought me an ice cream. With strawberries."

"Of course she did. You have Piper wrapped around your little finger."

"No." Story suddenly pouts, pinching her brows together. She leans to my ear and lowers her voice. "Piper is upset about something. She says it's nothing, that she just slept badly, but I don't think it's the truth. Maybe we can cheer her up?"

Cheer her up? I have no idea how she's going to act around me now, but I guess I can expect her to keep her promise for a little while and not talk to me about anything that doesn't concern Story. And that sucks.

"Daddy?" Two warm palms cup my face, and I meet Story's gaze. "Can we cheer Piper up? Please?"

"Of course. Do you have something in mind?" Because I'm pretty sure no one is going to like my suggestions.

"You're the best," she whispers, and then kisses my cheek. If she knew I was the reason for Piper's moodiness, she wouldn't be so kind. She would probably stop talking to me too, just to teach me a lesson. I should learn to keep my hands to myself.

FINGERS CROSSED this won't be awkward. The last thing I want is for Story to suspect anything, to feel the tension between Piper and me.

"Oh my God, Story, you shouldn't have done that." The closer I get to the living room, the more clearly I hear them. Another tentative step, and my eyes land on Piper, sitting on the couch with Story on her lap. My daughter is playing with Piper's hair, twirling her locks around her fingers. There is so much adoration in her eyes that it throws me off. Was I really ready to risk that just to wet my dick?

"I wanted to make you smile. Daddy helped me with it." Story glances at me with a cute smile and then returns her attention to Piper. "I love it when you're smiling, and I'm sure my dad feels the same way."

Piper's gaze swims to me for a brief moment, feigning total indifference. She nods and instantly looks away. I'll be getting the silent treatment then. What a life.

"What are we going to watch?" I ask, plopping down on the couch.

"Can we watch *Frozen II*? Please?" Story clasps her hands together, rounding her eyes. "Please, Daddy?"

"How many times have we watched it already?" I smirk, pulling a pizza box closer to me and opening it.

"Five." She grins, making Piper snort. "But I love Elsa so much."

"Whatever you want, baby," I tell her, and then I look at Piper, who already has the remote in her hand. "Can you please turn it on?"

She meets my gaze and again just fucking nods. I should be happy she's keeping her distance, but I don't want it to be like this. I don't want it to be so ice-cold between us. I don't want her to ignore me.

Later, I have two crying women in the room. Story sits between Piper and me, leaning on my shoulder and sobbing. Her nanny is more discreet, wiping away the tears on her face with her fingers. I sling a hand over Story's shoulder and pull her closer.

"You know they're fine, right?"

"I-I do...but it's still *saaaaaaaaaaaaad.*" She sobs louder, hiding her face in my tee. I smile and shake my head, bringing my gaze to Piper. She feels it and sneaks a glance in my direction.

"Is this your first time watching this? Piper?" Tears are brimming on her eyelashes, but by the way her pupils widen, I know she hates that I'm forcing a conversation on her. Not that I care. I *want* her to talk to me.

"No." She focuses on the screen again.

"Then what's your excuse for crying?"

The next time our eyes lock, she glares at me. Her rosy lips form an adorable pout, and she clicks her tongue in exasperation.

"I'm very sorry for being so...emotional." This is her jab at me. She probably thinks I have a stone where my heart should be. "I'll try to do a better job of hiding how I feel."

"I didn't say that."

"Oh, you most certainly did." Her lips quiver, and suddenly she breaks into a smile. "You were very convincing...in the shower."

I narrow my eyes, staring at her in confusion. I expected her to mention last night, in the kitchen. Not this. What does she mean?

"You should think about soundproofing. It might come in *handy* when you're in the shower."

Did she hear me? Does she know I was jerking off? Calling her name? She needs a fucking spanking to teach her a lesson. *What happens behind my bedroom walls stays behind my bedroom walls, Piper.*

"You're talking in riddles," Story mutters, moving away from me and crossing her arms over her chest. "Can you stop? I don't understand."

"Sure, sweetie." Piper flashes me a smile, enjoying my shocked state. "My lips are sealed."

Her lips are sealed? They will be when she's gagging on my cock, begging me to give her more...*Jesus fucking Christ.* I need a shitload of ice to cool down. The last thing I need is Story noticing my hard-on.

I stand up and head to the kitchen without another word. I lean against the counter and stare in front of me. Piper's image from last night pops into my head, and my veins instantly heat up. She felt incredible in my arms; her skin was so soft and silky, and those sensual hips and her scent totally blinded me. I wanted nothing more than to taste her, make her choke on my cock and then bury it in her juices. I wanted it so badly, but...I couldn't.

Back in the living room I look at Story and Piper on the couch. My daughter has her eyes glued to the TV, holding a pizza slice in her hand. Piper is watching me, and the satisfied grin on her lips says it all. She loves making me irritated and so fucking horny. I'm tempted to go back to my room and take care of myself. I just want to let go, like the fucking Queen of Arendelle sang. Just move on and push everything aside.

But the pictures of her in my mind make it absolutely impossible.

15
the nanny's tale

PIPER

"WHY IS DADDY NOT PLAYING?" STORY ASKS FOR THE thousandth time. "It's the second half of the game already."

Hayden and I exchange a look. There are only twenty-five minutes left, and I can sense Story's disappointment. She was so excited to see her father play, but she's spent most of today's match impatiently waiting for him to step onto the field.

"Honey, do you see him?" I point at Hunter, who's warming up on the sideline. "I'm sure he'll be in the game soon."

"But he's a great player. Why can't he play the whole game?" she whines, folding her arms across her chest.

"Sweetie," Colin, her grandpa, leans forward, diverting her attention to him. "You have to trust Coach's decisions. If he thinks your dad will be more useful in the last part of the game, then it's the truth."

"You're not helping." Willow slaps her husband's knee, frowning. "Story, it's the first official game for your dad in a while. The season is almost over, and the team is very strong already. They all deserve to be on the field just as much as your dad does. I'm sure he'll do his best and prove himself to be a very useful asset to the team. And who knows? Maybe next time he'll be on the field from the start."

I love Mrs. Hale. She's the absolute best when it comes to her kids.

She easily deals with their tantrums and antics and always explains everything thoroughly. Story holds her grandma's gaze, then slowly nods and brings her eyes back to the field.

When I see the referee hold up two numbers, I narrow my eyes on Hale's figure. He's on the halfway line at the edge of the field, ready to substitute for one of his teammates. The black of his kit looks incredibly fine against his tanned skin and dark brown hair. The number thirteen on his back draws my attention, and I can't help but smile. Story's birthday is on December thirteenth, and I'm sure that's why he has that number. Even if he's a jerk, he's an amazing father who loves his child to the moon and back.

Once it's announced that Hunter Hale is joining the match, there's an excited chattering all over the stadium. People are curious to see him play, and even if I hate to admit it, I'm curious too. LACFC is winning two to one, but with how they've played in the past twenty minutes, I think they'll score one more time. Will Miami go home without a win, or will they be able to steal the spotlight and turn the game around? Something's telling me Hunter will do anything to finish the game on his team's terms. He's a real pro when it comes to soccer. Being a nice person is the thing he really sucks at.

For the next ten minutes, my eyes are glued to Hale. I've watched plenty of games with Hayden during our years of friendship, but this is the first time I've seen a game in person. And it's so exciting! It's fast-paced, passionate, and very raw. As we get closer to the end of the game, things get dirtier. Miami is trying hard to steal the ball and score, but so far LACFC's defenders are doing their job to a tee. I'm on the edge of my seat, and my heart beats wildly. It's unreal how captivating this game is.

"I think he's going to score," Hayden mumbles, and I shoot him a curious glance. His eyes are fixed on the field, and it's clear he's talking about his brother.

Bringing my attention back to the game, I easily find Hunter. He's running fast toward the Miami net alongside another player from his team—a short pass, and now he has the ball. I watch as Hale slows down in the space outside of the box and then steers a fine finish past the Miami goalkeeper. Three against one, and Hunter Hale scored his first goal for LACFC. To say the stadium erupts would be an understatement, but it's nothing compared to the cheers of Hunter's brother and daughter.

Hade hauls Story from her seat and presses her to his chest, jumping in the air. Yelling at the top of his lungs, he announces to everyone around that that's his brother. I sneak a glance at Willow, and she chuckles, meeting my gaze, also amused by her son's behavior.

For the rest of the game, I'm riding a wave of euphoria, just like anyone who came to support LACFC. The final score is three to one, and I'm grinning so much my cheeks hurt. Coming to the game, I didn't expect to like it as much as I did. It made my day a thousand times better.

Instead of going with the Hale family to congratulate Hunter on the win, I make an excuse and go to the parking lot. During one of our arguments, he told me to know my place, and that's exactly what I'm doing. I'm steering clear of any innuendos, any of the inappropriate thoughts I've had for days. He's Story's dad, my boss, and he's off-limits. The nanny's tale ends here.

Sitting in Hade's car, I take my phone out of my purse and launch the web browser. Might as well use this time and find more reasons to keep my distance. I type "Hunter Hale wife" and start chewing my bottom lip while waiting for the results to load. The first thought I have once Story's mom's face pops up on my screen is simple: Hunter is right. I'm not his type, if this is the woman he spent eight years with. Amelia Hale is a brunette with pearly white skin, sprinkles of freckles on her nose, puffy lips, and light-blue eyes. She's gorgeous, and her flawless body only adds more appeal to her looks. Story takes after her mom almost completely, except for her deep green eyes, which she got from her dad.

I google some more, and bitterness fills my mind and my mouth. Hunter has never even been seen with a blonde. At least he was honest. My closeness is the only reason he reacts to me. I'm sure he would react the same way to any other woman who worked for him. He did the right thing telling me off.

The car door suddenly opens, and Story climbs inside, settling into her booster seat. I hide my phone in my purse as Hayden slides into the car. He starts the engine and squints at me.

"You should've come with us. It was fun," he says.

"We met other players from the team," Story exclaims in a cheerful voice. "They were all incredibly nice and friendly. Their goal-keeper even did a happy dance with me."

"I'm not family." I shrug, averting my gaze and looking out the window. "It wasn't my place to be there with you."

"Bull—um, you're wrong." Hayden reaches over and grasps my hand in his, entwining our fingers. "You're my family. You do belong."

"Thank you, Hade. I appreciate it."

"And I'd appreciate it if you kept my brother company at my show."

My eyebrows hit my hairline. This sudden change in topic throws me off.

"Why?"

"Because Daddy thinks he'll be out of place, but with you...it'll be different." *Very different, dammit.* I sigh, holding back every word that burns down my throat.

"I told him I'd be waiting for him to return the favor and come to my show. Hunter being Hunter, he promised. He said he was excited and he couldn't wait for Saturday. But then, bam! He says it'd be better if he skips it. He doesn't want to bother you."

Very nice of you, Hale, to make it all about me. Asshole.

"He won't bother me," I murmur, faking a smile. I don't like the idea of being with him alone at the show, but at the same time, why not? I could always meet someone new and go back to their place for a hookup. It'd be for the best. "No problem at all. Don't worry."

Finding someone who can take care of my needs is exactly what I'm going to do. I don't need Hunter Hale for that.

16
down the rabbit hole

HUNTER

I STOP THE CAR NEAR MY PARENTS' HOUSE, QUICKLY JUMP out, and open the door for Story. She smiles at me when I take her hand and help her climb out of the backseat. She's been in a particularly good mood, chatting the entire ride about all the things she wants to do with her grandparents. I'm grateful for the distraction, because otherwise I would've been thinking about Hayden's show the whole time. My brain refuses to believe it'll be anything but a disaster.

"Are you excited about tonight?" Story's voice interrupts my thoughts, and I focus my attention on her as I lock the car.

"Intrigued."

"Why?"

"Well, I've never seen Hayden play in person. I have no idea what it will be like."

"It'll be awesome," she murmurs, clasping my hand in hers as we stroll to my parents' house. "I'm sad I can't go with you."

"You're too little to be at a club. Loud music, a crowd, alcohol. It's not the best place for a seven-year-old."

"Will you be drinking?" Story tugs on my hand, and I squint at her. When I ruffle her hair with my other hand, she giggles. "Daddy?"

"No. I'm the driver, remember?"

Story halts in her tracks. Her eyes widen, and her mouth falls open. "Will you give Piper a ride home?"

My right eye twitches when I force a smile. "As far as I know, your nanny will be with her friends. I highly doubt she'll want to come to our house after the show."

"Yeah, you're probably right." She shrugs and keeps walking. "You and Piper don't get along."

"Wh—" I swallow a sudden lump in my throat as she stops near the front door. "What do you mean?"

"You act like two strangers when you think I'm not around."

"Story, Piper and I aren't friends. And we've never been friends." In two strides, I'm at the door and pressing the doorbell. "I'm her boss."

She silently holds my gaze, shifting a little and grasping her backpack strap. "I know, but it wasn't like that before. You two are starting to remind me of you and Mom, right before...right before you moved out."

Thank goodness my mother finally opens the door, saving me from having to respond. Things between Piper and me aren't as bad as Story thinks. They're just...nonexistent.

"Hey hey, my little sunshine," my mother greets Story. My daughter rushes to her and wraps her arms around her waist. "Did you miss me *that* much?"

"I did." Her voice is muffled, as she keeps her face pressed to my mom's belly. "You're the best granny in the world."

"Sweetie, you make me wanna cry. And I hate crying!"

Story leans away, looking up at my mom's face. "Why do you want to cry?"

"Because you're too sweet." She cups Story's face with her palm. "And because I'm over the moon that your dad decided to come home."

"The best decision I've ever made." I meet my mom's gaze and smile. "Hey, Mom."

"Hey, Hunter. Can you stay for a few minutes?"

"Only a few minutes?" I step inside as Mom and Story move back to give me space. "I can stay for an hour or two."

Mom's expression darkens, and she narrows her eyes. "An hour tops, Hunter. Your brother's show starts in an hour and a half. You'll need time to get to the club."

I can't really bail, can I? I sigh and nod, accepting the inevitable. No way she'll let me skip Hayden's show. Besides, I made a promise, and I'm not a quitter. Who cares if I'll be forced to spend time with a girl who hates my guts and only talks to me if Story is present? I'm the one to blame for that.

Fifteen minutes later, Mom and Story go upstairs to set up for their sleepover. I take a sip of coffee, feeling my father's gaze on me. I arch an eyebrow, lifting my chin in question. "What?" I ask.

"Nothing." *Nothing? Then why are you looking at me like that?* "When do you think Amelia will visit?"

"In December. She'll be here for Story's birthday."

Dad smirks and shakes his head. "What a mother. When was the last time she saw her daughter?"

"In August." I know where this conversation is going, and I can't say I like it. He doesn't have any right to comment on Amelia's parenting skills.

"Why do you look so calm? Story loves her mom, and she misses her. Why can't you insist on her visiting more often?"

"Would you have visited more often if you knew Hayden and I were missing you?"

"Hunter," Dad mutters, shifting uncomfortably in his chair. "It's different."

"How? She has a job that requires constant traveling. You had a job that required you to stay here while Mom and I were living in Europe. What's the difference, Dad?"

He averts his gaze, staring off into the distance. I wait for his answer, feeling indifferent. I'm not the little boy who craved his dad's presence anymore. I don't hold grudges, even if I can't quite forgive him for his mistakes. But if he's going to criticize Amelia, he better look back on his own life and realize how it was for me, and then for my brother also.

"You're right. There's no difference," he finally says, meeting my gaze. "I didn't even think about comparing it, and that was wrong of me."

"Glad you see it that way now." I take another sip of my coffee and heave a sigh. "Story misses Amelia, but they FaceTime a few times a week. And she also has Piper. She won Story over in such a short time, I'm baffled."

Dad smiles, and his shoulders instantly relax. "Piper is a real gem. You're lucky she agreed to work for you."

"Yeah, I am."

"You know, your mom and I often wondered if Piper and Hayden would ever become more than just friends," Dad confides, and my heart pounds. "But those two are living proof that friendship between a man and a woman is possible. They act like siblings more than friends."

"I've asked myself the same question."

Dad slowly sets his mug on the table, peering at me. "How do *you* like Piper? She's a beautiful—"

"No, no, no." I shake my head, immediately shutting him up. "Piper is Story's nanny. End of story."

My father blinks at me from under furrowed eyebrows. I'm too defensive; I'm giving myself away. The buzzing of my phone startles me, and I grab it from the kitchen counter.

"Hey, man," Hayden mumbles, out of breath. "Any chance you're on your way to the club?"

"I'm still at Mom and Dad's, but if you need something..." I let the words linger in the air, hoping for the best. Dad continues eyeing me, and I feel uncomfortable. The last thing I want is my parents thinking there's something going on between me and Piper.

"You'd be my savior if you could stop by Piper's house. I forgot my lucky pick at her place, and I can't fucking play without it." Lucky pick? But who am I to judge. My lucky charm is a little stone I found years ago in Madrid. I always have it with me.

"No problem. Can you send me her address?"

"Sure, one minute." A shuffling sound makes me take the phone away from my ear. "Piper's home. I told her I'd come pick her up, but things got crazy, and...Hunter, you're doing me a huge favor. Thank you."

Do I really think this call is a blessing? A forty-minute ride to the club with someone who can't stand me. *Splendid.* "No worries. You can count on me."

"Thanks again, Hunter."

I end the call, meet my father's gaze, and say, "I need to get going. Hayden needs my help."

"I heard," he says slowly, his lips stretching into a huge grin. "Piper's house is ten minutes from here."

"Great." I stand up and rinse out my mug. "I'll go tell Mom and Story I'm leaving."

"Sure. See you tomorrow, Son."

"See you tomorrow."

I PARK near a small one-story house with an earthy red facade and a neatly manicured lawn. I take out my phone and call Piper, waiting for her to answer. To no avail. I close my eyes and groan. Why do I get the feeling she has no idea I'm coming to pick her up? *Dammit, Hayden.*

Knocking on the front door, I feel like a fucking teenager picking up his homecoming date. Ridiculousness at its finest.

The door opens, and my eyes land on Riley. She stares at me slack-jawed, in total bewilderment.

"Mr. Hale?"

"Hey, Riley." I smile. "And please, call me Hunter."

"Sure, Hunter." Her cheeks flush, turning red and reminding me of her sister. They don't look that much alike except for their blond hair, but right now the resemblance is striking. "Is everything okay with Story? Do you need Piper's help?"

My smile grows wider as I hide my hands in my pocket. "Story's fine; she's with her grandparents. Thank you so much for asking."

"Your daughter is precious. It's impossible not to love her." Riley flashes me a lopsided grin. "Our dance teacher, Ms. Martinez, adores her. She always has something nice to say about Story and her talents. She'll be a great dancer someday."

"I hope so, because she's very passionate about it." I fall quiet. The sound of footsteps reaches my ears, and in the next moment Piper shows up in the hallway. Our eyes meet, and she scowls.

"Hey, Piper."

"Hey, Hunter." She stops by Riley's side. "What are you doing here?"

"Lucky pick," I say, and her face drops. "Hayden asked me to come pick you up so you can bring it."

"Gah, he's impossible. I was going to call an Uber."

"Hade thought you would look better in a Lexus…" Riley laughs, looking at me for help.

"Lexus RX."

"Yeah, Hade thought you'd look better in a Lexus RX, sis. I can't really blame him."

"I hate you, kid," she mutters, threading her fingers through her hair. Then she brings her gaze back to me. "I need twenty minutes."

"I'll wait in the car, don't worry." Without saying anything, Piper disappears into the house, and I shift my gaze to Riley. "Bye."

"Bye, Hunter."

The door closes, and I edge back to my car, taking my phone out of my pocket. Might as well use this time to read some news.

I immediately regret my decision. Photos of Amelia and her new boyfriend pop up on every account I follow. I curse and toss my phone onto the passenger seat, then fold my arms over my chest. I'm not jealous. Just mad at myself. More and more I think that Angelo was right. Maybe I'm making a mistake in neglecting my needs.

I spend the next ten minutes scrolling through Tinder, swiping left over and over again. No one seems to pique my interest—until I stumble upon a familiar face. I'm so surprised to see Autumn Dunn that I swipe right on impulse and then just stare at the screen in horror. What have I just done? *No, fuck no.* I bang my head on the steering wheel. Another complication I don't need.

"Um, is everything okay?"

I sit up, turn my head toward Piper's voice, and feel as if I'm falling down a rabbit hole. Can I fucking skip to the good part of this night? To when I'm alone, not swiping right on the reporter who was making bedroom eyes at me, with no nanny looking sexy as hell in a little black dress?

"Hunter?"

"Is there any way to swipe left retroactively? Like, if you swiped right but didn't want to?" I plead, and she blinks. "I mean, on Tinder...do you know if I can take back my swipe?"

Piper holds my gaze, and I see her expression waver. Irritation and anger are the two most recognizable emotions on her face. She exhales loudly and climbs into my car, buckles the seatbelt, and only then turns to face me. "Give me your phone."

I hand it to her and watch as she taps the screen, once, twice, and then shows it to me. "This one?" I see Autumn's face and nod. Piper takes my phone back, taps a few more times, and shoves it back into my hand. "Done."

"Thank you, Piper. Honestly—"

"Can we go? I don't want to be late. Hade needs his pick."

"Yeah, of course." I start the engine and drive away from her house. The silence in my car becomes suffocating, and I hate it. "I'm very sorry for being rude to you the other night. I should've handled it differently."

Piper continues staring out the window, toying with her butterfly pendant, and for a moment I think she's going to ignore me for the whole ride. But I'm wrong. Eventually she says, "Thanks."

"I should've apologized right away, but...I kinda freaked out."

"Uh-huh." She trains her deep brown eyes on my face. Her bright makeup highlights her cheekbones and eyes, and her lips are painted red, making it impossible not to admire her. A heavy curtain of hair veils her shoulders, with two little braids framing her face. "Why did you cancel your swipe? That woman looks exactly like your type."

And that's how I know she followed my advice and googled my exes. It only gave her more reasons to believe me. Reasons to turn against me completely.

"She's a sports reporter. I met her during my press conference, and I swiped right on instinct, because I recognized her. I was surprised to see her on the app."

"Of course...because it'd be highly unprofessional to date her, right? And you're keen on keeping things professional."

"Yes." I set my jaw hard and keep my eyes on the road. "Piper, I've been single for a while, and also—"

"Can you please stop?" She raises her voice. "I'm Story's nanny. You're my boss. We're not friends, and we don't have to talk about anything that isn't related to my job. So please, spare me the stories about your single life. I'm not interested."

"But it's your day off. And we're going to my brother's show together."

She focuses her gaze on me. "Then we can talk about Hayden and Sabotage, about the club we're going to, about the people around us... and nothing else."

I watch her for a second and then nod. "Good. Should I turn on the music?"

"Do whatever you want." She takes a deep breath, putting her hands on her bare legs. Her little black dress ends just above her knees, and I force myself to look away. The view is perfect, but I have no right to enjoy it. "I just want to get to the club already."

You and me both, Piper. You and me both.

17
disturbing behavior

PIPER

"Hade!" I call out, and he finally notices me. The club is already packed, and it wasn't easy to make my way up to the stage. Especially since Hunter decided to shadow me the whole time. "Don't you need this?"

"I love you." He snatches his pick from my fingers, leans in, and kisses my cheek. "So happy you made it on time. Good thing I called Hunter—"

"About that." I grab his ear and pull him closer. "Next time you make a decision for me, I'll block you."

"Ouch, Pip!" Hayden yelps, moving away from me and rubbing his ear. "What's the matter with you?"

"She wasn't happy you forced her to spend time with me." Hunter's voice reminds me of his presence, and I shiver uncomfortably. "You should've given her a heads-up I was coming to pick her up."

"You fucking live together six days a week. Couldn't you survive one car ride?" Hade huffs, taking a step back and glaring at me. "See you after the show."

I roll my eyes and find the booth Hayden booked for us. Once I've sat down, I meet Hunter's gaze. He stops near the table, looking down at me with his hands hidden in his pockets.

"Do you want something to drink?" he asks.

"Cuba libre," I tell him. Hunter nods and wanders to the bar. My eyes zero in on his ass, but this time, instead of ogling him as usual, I decide to examine the club.

It's better this way.

Looking around, I catch someone's gaze on me. It's Nick Davis, our college's quarterback. He's a senior this year, and we've talked a couple times, but it's never been anything more than small talk. I smile at him, and he smiles back, instantly heading in my direction.

"Hey." He stops by the table, puts his hands on the surface, and bends down to me. "You're Piper, right?"

"Hey, Nick. And yes, I'm Piper. Glad you remember me."

"Someone as beautiful as you are is hard to forget." Cheesy, but I'll take it. "I haven't seen you in a while. Where have you been?"

"I'm taking a year off, so..." I shrug. "What about you? Are you going to win the championship this year?"

"It'd be a dream come true to win the championship in my final year." He grins, and I see a dimple on his cheek. "Are you here alone?"

"I'm here with Hade's brother. He asked me to keep him company."

"And are you going to babysit Hade's brother all night?"

"Just during the show," I murmur, and he licks his lips.

"I'll find you after then. I'd love to get to know you better, Piper."

"I'll be looking forward to it."

"Your drink." Hunter's dry voice breaks the spell, and I jerk in my seat when he sets a glass in front of me. He slides into the booth and peers at Nick. "Can I help you?"

"Um, I was just...I was talking to Piper." Nick gapes at Hunter in total bewilderment. Then he squeals like a girl. "Oh shit. Are you Hunter Hale?"

Didn't I tell him I was here with Hayden's brother?

"Yeah, that's me. Who are you?"

"Oh, I'm Nick. I play football too—American football though. I go to school with Hade and Piper." He extends his hand to Hunter, smiling. "It's so nice to meet you."

"You too." Hunter puts his glass on the table and shakes Nick's hand. "How long have you and Piper known each other?"

"We don't really know each other. Yet." Nick steps back and winks at me. "I'll find you after the show, Piper. Bye, Hunter."

"Bye." His jaw twitches.

In your face, Mr. Hale.

I pick up my drink and take a sip, enjoying the taste of Coke and rum on my tongue. It's delicious, and I close my eyes, feeling Hunter's gaze on me. I know he's watching, and goosebumps scatter over my skin. It feels amazing.

"Do you like your cocktail?" I snap my eyes open and look at Hunter. He's no longer sitting across from me. He's moved closer. Much closer. His knee is an inch away from mine.

"Yes, it's good. Thanks." I take another sip, not showing him how his closeness affects me. "What's your poison?"

"Just Sprite."

"No whiskey?" I know it's his favorite; I've seen him drink it several times.

"I never drink when I drive."

"Okay." I hear a familiar sound from the stage. It's Bo's drums, and it means one thing: the show is starting. "I hope you're ready to hear your brother play. He's really talented."

"I know he is," Hunter answers, eyeing the stage with curiosity. "His baritone is different, and I like it. It reminds me of Dan Reynolds's voice, from Imagine Dragons, but it's still unique. In a year or two, he'll be playing much bigger stages than this, all around the world. I believe in him."

I bite the inside of my cheek in annoyance. He's not allowed to be this nice. He's not allowed to act as if he knows anything about my best friend. He's an asshole.

For the next forty minutes, I sing along with Hade, yell with the crowd, and clap like crazy. My hands hurt, and Hunter starts making fun of me. He says he never expected me to be a groupie. I can't say he's much better—he looks mesmerized, and I swear I saw him dance a few times. The atmosphere of the club and the sounds of my favorite music have made me forget how things have been the last two months. It made everything better.

After my second cocktail, I decide to go to the bathroom, and on my way back I stumble into Nick with his friends. He catches my hand, pulls me into his side, and gazes at me with a gentle smile playing on his lips.

"Never thought the girl of my dreams would literally fall into my arms." Another cheesy line makes me cringe. Maybe I don't want to see him after the show. I'll be perfectly fine with my friends.

"I'm very clumsy." I put my hand on his chest in case I need to push him away.

"Or a little drunk," he purrs. "Have you been drinking?"

"Not really. Why?"

"Just want to know what I should order you later. Cosmopolitan? Margarita?"

"Nothing. You shouldn't bother." Nick bends down and takes my chin between his fingers. "Nick?"

"I like you, Piper, and this feels like a great opportunity to get to know each other. To spend some time together. To drink. Dance. Laugh. Anything. Whatever you want, I'm in."

"Good to know." I step back, and his hand drops from my face. "But I'll need to find Hade and the guys from the band after the show."

"I'll find you, Piper. Don't worry. I have my eye on you," he assures me.

"See you." *I hope not.*

The second my eyes land on Hunter, I know he saw everything. He's standing near our booth with his arms crossed. His jaw is hard, and a deep frown has replaced his smile.

Rounding him, I slide into my seat, not paying him any attention. He follows me and sits down as well. I focus on the stage, refusing to acknowledge him. I'm here for my friends, to enjoy a night out and my favorite songs. Hunter Hale's lectures aren't something I'm interested in.

"That guy seems handsy." His deep voice indicates how close he's moved yet again.

He is, but I'm not going to admit that. "He likes me."

"He also likes touching you without your consent."

I curse under my breath and turn to face him. "Why do you care?"

"You're my employee. I want you to be safe." *Fuck you sideways, Mr. Hale.* Playing the employee card again?

"And I want you to find someone to take care of your needs so you won't be interfering with things that don't concern you," I bite out, pinching my brows together. "Get back on fucking Tinder, Hunter, and leave me alone."

Sabotage is playing my favorite song, "Survivor," but I don't care. I'm angry and disappointed, and this version of me never makes the right decisions.

"Fuck Tinder," Hunter mutters. He inches even closer and cups my face with his palms, forcing me to look at him. My eyes widen when he cuts the distance between us and presses his lips to mine. Just like that, Hunter fucking Hale is kissing me...but why am I kissing him back?

18
carnal knowledge

HUNTER

Piper's lips are soft and taste like peaches. I suck on her bottom lip, nibbling and urging her to open her mouth for me. Her hands land on my knees as she tries to find balance, and my skin ignites as my blood runs hot through my veins. I feel drunk; my head starts to spin when her tongue brushes mine.

This kiss is nowhere near gentle. It's raw and full of longing, and it's sweeter than my favorite chocolate bar. My fingers weave through her hair, and I groan when her tongue slowly twirls around mine. My dick strains against my jeans, and my desire to see it deep inside her pussy pushes me way past my limits. I glide my lips over her cheek and inch toward her ear.

"Get comfortable. Lean your back against the booth. Now," I command.

Once those words leave my mouth, I scoot away from her and stand up. I'm risking ruining the mood, but I don't want anyone to see what I'm going to do to her. No one is watching us right now, and the booth we're in is pretty dark and secluded, but that doesn't mean no one could notice. And that's the last thing I want. Her fucking pussy is mine.

I plop down in the booth and slide over to her, driving her to scoot over a little more. Leaning my side against the booth, I catch

Piper's heated gaze. Her parted lips and disheveled hair make her look even more beautiful. She's perfect, and I can't wait to get her alone, as far away from this place and all these people as possible. But not yet. I kiss her bare shoulder, and she shudders. I smirk and ease closer to her ear.

"Spread your legs for me, Piper."

She holds my gaze. I know she wants it, and I can only hope she'll go for it. She exhales loudly and sets her legs wide. "Like this?"

"Good girl," I tell her, and her whole body trembles.

I put my hand on her thigh and move it higher until it reaches her panties. It only takes one second to notice how wet she is, and it sends me spiraling. So fucking wet for me. I massage her clit through her silky panties. Once, twice, I move my fingers in circles, and a quiet moan reaches my ears. Perfection.

I grab her leg and hook it over my knee, spreading her wide open for me. My hand drifts back under the hem of her dress, and then I push her panties aside. Piper digs her fingernails into the seat as I press my finger to her clit. I rub her sweet spot between my fingers, lowering my mouth to her shoulder and caressing her skin with my lips and my tongue. Her perfume mixes with the smell of her arousal, driving me wild, and I'm not sure how long it'll be before my own release. A fucking minute?

"Does that feel good?" I ask, sucking her earlobe into my mouth.

"Yes." Her voice cracks, and she starts to rotate her hips, meeting my fingers. "I'm so close...make me come, Hunter..."

As if she needs to ask me twice. I run my hand down her folds, plunging two fingers inside her and pressing my thumb to her clit. Fucking her pussy with my fingers, I continue to stimulate her clit, barreling her closer and closer to her orgasm. It hits her suddenly and strongly, and she pinches her brows and bites her bottom lip to stifle any sounds. Her walls squeeze around my fingers, and a satisfied grin forms on my lips. I just made her come...in a club full of people...with my brother singing on the stage. Is this wrong? Most definitely. Do I regret it? Not even a little bit.

I take my fingers out of her and fix her panties. Piper watches me, her hooded eyes glued to my face. Slowly, I put my fingers in my mouth and suck them clean. Her gaze darkens as she sits up straight, her chest rising and falling rapidly. I can't help but smile, and a lopsided grin dances across her lips in return. I drop my head and steal a quick kiss.

"I can't stay away from you...even if I try," I confess, holding her gaze.

"I never said you should," Piper murmurs. Then she freezes with her lips parted slightly. "It's the last song. They're almost done."

"So you're *that* kind of fan," I state, resting back against the booth.

"I'm a loyal friend, Hunter, and I'm very supportive of my people."

"So you not joining my family after the game was exactly what I thought it was. You don't support me."

"I was actually cheering for you, just like everyone else. I wanted to see you score, and you did. I wanted to see you win, and you did. I just didn't want to be there because of your words. You said I was just the nanny, that I should know my place." She licks her lips, glancing at the stage. "I did as you told me."

"Do you always do as you're told?"

"You've yet to find out." Piper puts her hand on my knee and brings her lips to mine. "I can be very different."

"Oh, I noticed that," I say, grabbing her hand and laying it on my hard dick. "I can be very different as well."

Her cheeks tinge red, and my gaze zeroes in on the pulsating vein in her neck. The way she reacts to me stirs so many different emotions within me, making me thick with longing. It's crazy, and I'm not sure what I can do to get rid of it. Except fuck her senseless, but even that won't be enough.

"Will you stay?" she asks, and I jerk my head no. I came to hear my brother's band play. I never planned to stay longer or hang out with Hayden and his buddies. Piper moves away from me and looks around the place. "I expected that answer. You're so predictable."

"I'm too old for this shit, Piper."

She rolls her eyes and fixes her dress, heaving a sigh. "At least come with me backstage? Hade will be happy to see you."

"Fine."

Piper and I find our way backstage. She strolls in front of me, and I'm having a hard time keeping my hands to myself. I want her back pressed to my chest, my palms cupping her breasts and my hard dick poking her in the ass. But I restrain myself. She's going to stay, and I'm going home. That's it.

Opening the door of the dressing room, I let Piper go first and follow her in. She takes a few steps and throws herself at Hayden, wrapping her arms around his shoulders.

"You were incredible."

"Praise from my biggest fan." Hayden hugs her back, laughing heartily. "Love you, Pip."

"Love you too, Hade," she murmurs, stepping back and sneaking a glance at me. It's her way of letting me know I should say something too. God, does she think I'm *that* hopeless?

"I thought my brother was talented," I exclaim, "and I wasn't wrong. You're a star, Hayden. Your music will take you places. I'm a hundred percent sure of it."

He watches me in silence, and then starts dancing like the fucking child he is. "Did you all hear that? My famous brother thinks I'm cool. Any chance I can make you repeat all that for our social media?"

"Fuck no," I mutter, and they all start laughing.

I stay for a few more minutes, chatting with Hayden and the guys from his band, Jimmy and Bo. They're levelheaded and respectful—not what I expected, but I only recently started to get to know my brother. It's refreshing how different he is from the guy I knew in my youth.

"Are you sure you wanna go home? Story is with our parents." Hayden hides his hands in his pockets once I announce I need to get going. "We'll have fun."

"Listen, your show was great, and I'd love to hang out with you some more, but not at a club. I feel out of place here, and I don't want to ruin it for you. Enjoy your time with your friends and your fans."

"You're impossible," he utters, draping a hand over my shoulder to give me a quick hug. "Thank you for coming, Hunter. It means way more than you think."

"For me too."

"Bye, Hunter." Piper appears out of nowhere, like a fucking genie from a bottle. "See you tomorrow."

"See you tomorrow, Piper." I echo her, shifting uncomfortably, because just the sight of her brings my dick back to life. My gaze falls on Bo, the drummer, as he stands close to her. "Bye, Bo. It was nice to meet you."

"You too." We shake hands, and he wanders away, joining Jimmy on the couch. Since there's nothing left for me to do, I place my hand on the doorknob. I'm very close to opening it when I feel her presence behind me.

"Are you sure you don't want to stay?"

Looking over my shoulder, I meet her gaze and shake my head no. "Are you sure you want to stay?"

"Hayden will be upset if I go." Who cares? He's not her boyfriend.

"See you tomorrow then." I push the door open.

"Do you remember the hickey on my neck?" Her words halt me in my tracks; my back tenses. I keep my eyes focused on the wall ahead of me. "Bo did it."

My head whips back before I have time to think. Her gaze is full of fire as she stares at me with a smile ghosting at the corners of her mouth. She let me know what Hayden's bandmate thinks of her. What he did to her. Fucking carnal knowledge, that's what it is. My jealousy blinds me again, but this time I refuse to give in.

Two can play that game, Piper.

"Good night, Piper." With that, I stalk down the hallway and head straight to the exit. I'm not some boy who will run after her and do whatever she wants. That's not how this is going to work.

19
do not go gentle
PIPER

"Pip, what do you want to drink?" Hade asks.

"Nothing," I answer curtly, looking away and focusing my gaze on the crowd. I shouldn't have stayed. At the same time, I shouldn't have gone with him either. I have no desire to look desperate to fuck him, even if I am.

"Okay, that's it," Hayden mutters and plops down onto the couch beside me. "What's the matter with you?"

"Everything is fine."

"It's not." He slings an arm over my shoulders and pulls me to his side. "Did Hunter do something?"

Does fingerfucking me count as something? *Bad idea, Piper.*

"No, he was surprisingly nice."

"Then what?"

"I wanted to unwind, to have fun. But I don't think I'm in the right mood."

"Why don't you have some fun with Bo?" he asks.

"Hade, stop it. Bo is a friend, and I don't want to ruin it."

"He wants to date you." *And I want to date your brother. Our wishes don't always become reality.* "Why don't you want to date him?"

I hold his gaze, etching my eyebrows together. Sometimes he's so

114

ignorant that it irks me to be his friend. "Because I don't like him. He's my friend, nothing more than that."

Hade watches me in silence, then nods. "Okay. I understand."

"Really?" I quirk an eyebrow. "Because I've been saying it over and over and over, and you never seem to understand."

"I was just a shipper. I wanted my best friend to date a really decent guy. One who likes her and respects her. One who will never cheat on her or lay a hand on her."

"Well, sorry for ruining your dream, but Bo and I are never going to happen." An idea pops into my head, and after a short debate, I decide to go for it. "Are you like this with Hunter too? Did you ever say anything to him about the women he was with?"

The look on Hade's face is ridiculous. His deep green eyes go wide, and his eyebrows fly up to his hairline. "Are you insane? Hunter would stop talking to me if I meddled in his personal life."

"So you never told him you didn't like Amelia?"

"I never said anything about her when they were together, but I wasn't silent when he filed for divorce. When he called me after meeting with his lawyer, I said it was the best decision of his life."

"Did he agree with you?"

"He did." Hade looks away. "Hunter has a type, Pip. He has a thing for money-hungry harpies, and unfortunately, even if he knows that, he still makes the same mistake again and again."

"I thought his type was brunettes," I blurt, and Hayden snaps his gaze toward me. He frowns, eyeing me suspiciously, while I keep a straight face, even if it's hard. I'm not his type in looks, and apparently in personality too.

"Brunettes," he confirms, moving away. For whatever reason, I feel the atmosphere between us drop to zero degrees. "Not blondes with sunshiny personalities."

"Why do you say that?"

"Because I don't want you to have any fantasies about Hunter."

"Am I not good enough for your superstar brother? Is that what you're saying?"

"No." Hade shrugs, standing up from the couch. "*He* isn't good enough for *you*, Piper. So whatever you feel for him, it needs to go away."

A loud snicker escapes my lips, and I instantly cover my mouth with my palm. Hayden frowns even more, bending down to get a better look at me.

"We barely talk to each other when Story isn't around. Do you think I'd be attracted to someone who told me I should know my place when I brought up what bothers his daughter?"

Bad move, Piper. Such a shitty way to divert attention, oh my fucking God.

"Hunter told you that?"

"He apologized," I add, feeling my heart gallop so hard and so fast, I'm on the verge of passing out. "He knows he was wrong...so yeah, he apologized."

"Is that why you were unhappy that I asked him to give you a ride?"

"No, not really. I was unhappy because you didn't leave me any choice, like always," I mutter quietly, and Hade lowers his head even more. "You should stop doing that."

Hayden clenches his jaw and takes a step back. He looks pissed and puzzled at the same time.

"It's like you suddenly decided to get back at me and my family for some fucked-up reason," he remarks sharply.

"Just like you assumed I was crushing on Hunter because I mentioned his taste in women."

"How do you even know what his type is, Pip? Why do you care?" Hayden counters, drawing the attention of his bandmates while I'm trying my hardest to keep calm.

"I've spent the past two months around him. I never really knew Hunter before this year, so forgive me for trying to get to know him. I was just curious who I'm working for, Hade."

"You could've asked me, and yet this is the first time we're talking about Hunter. So forgive *me* for finding it weird." Hayden sneers, his nostrils flaring. "Especially bringing up his taste in women. Double weird."

I blink, anger filling my every pore. "Drop your fucking assumptions, Hade. I don't like Hunter." *You're such a fucking liar, Piper.* "Besides, *he* isn't even *my* type."

Hayden glares at me for a moment, and then his shoulders slump. He sighs, rubbing his face with his palms. "Sorry, Pip. You caught me off guard with your questions, and I'm just...I don't want you to get hurt. And that means you shouldn't be attracted to Hunter in any way."

"Duly noted." I stand up from the couch. "I'm going home. I wasn't in the mood for this before, and now it's even worse. See you, Hade."

"I'll come visit tomorrow, on my way to campus."

"Do whatever you want." With that, I nod to the boys and stride to the exit, forcing my way through the crowd. I hate how this day turned out, and I'm so ready for it to be over.

ON MY WAY HOME, I take my phone from my purse and check the time. It's two a.m., and I feel disappointed. This is not how I imagined my night would go. It's not how I planned it would go. Why the hell did Hayden feel the need to ruin it for me? Why does he think his brother is bad news? It's the first time he's talked this way about Hunter, and I have no idea why. It's bugging me so much, I don't even notice the car is in my neighborhood until it's stopped in front of my mom's house.

"Thanks," I mutter. I climb out of my Uber and linger by the car door without closing it. My fingers fly to my butterfly pendant, slowly tracing the lines as I make a decision. I know it's a bad idea. No, scratch that—it's a horrendous idea, but I still want to do it. Desperately. "You know, I changed my mind. Can you take me to another place?"

The driver, a guy in his forties, looks at me nonchalantly and then nods. "Just add another address."

"Great." I slide back into the car, add Hunter's address, and relax against the seat.

I'm just as excited as I am scared to make a mistake. There was a reason I didn't go home with him in the first place, and now I'm completely dismissing it...because I want him to make me forget. I want him to make my night better, even if I'm not sure he'll want me there.

I close my eyes and think back to our moment in the club. To his hands on my thighs, his fingers in my pussy, his lips on my bare skin. It feels divine even as a memory. Forbidden and wrong in so many ways, considering I'm his employee and his brother's best friend, and yet... I've never been kissed like that before. I've never wanted anyone more than I want Hunter Hale. His whole existence is living proof that people don't always know what they need until they have it.

Every step toward Hunter's house is accompanied by a wild beat of my heart. I'm so nervous my chest hurts. I try my hardest to keep my emotions at bay but fail miserably. What happens if he kicks me out? Will I be able to keep working for him and Story? Should I even risk it? I love Story, and even thinking about making her upset pushes me to the edge. Why am I here?

I take out the keys from my purse and toy with them. My mind is full of doubts and worries. I'm scared to take this step, but I still can't resist it. My willpower is nowhere to be seen as I put the key in the lock and turn. I want what I want, and I'm not sorry about it. At least, not tonight. I can always regret my actions tomorrow.

I step inside and close the door behind me. Is he asleep already? Is he even home? What if he never—

"Piper?" His silhouette is barely visible in the darkness of the hall-way, and I move forward to have a better look. Just because I want to be close. "What are you doing here?"

"I shouldn't have stayed," I whisper, taking a few tentative steps forward.

"Did something happen? Was that jock bothering you?"

"No." I stop in front of him. My eyes are glued to his face. "Hade and I got into an argument."

"Why?"

"Because of you. He told me I shouldn't be attracted to you."

"You shouldn't. I'm bad news when it comes to women. Hayden knows it." He tilts his head, watching me intently. "What did you tell him?"

"I told him he was wrong." I take another step forward, and my breath hitches in my throat. He's in only his briefs, and the view sends my emotions into turmoil. "He said he was sorry."

"You made him believe you."

"I did." I unzip my leather jacket, letting it fall to the floor and dropping my purse there as well. "I didn't plan to be here."

"Then why are you here?" Hunter demands. "Piper?"

"Because I'm a bad friend," I confess. I kneel in front of him, my eyes falling to his crotch. "Because I want his brother."

"What exactly do you want, Piper?" He inches closer and takes my chin between his fingers, making me look him in the eyes. "Use your words."

I lick my lips and notice his heated gaze. I put my hands on my knees, and my panties become a puddle. I'm way too far into this to back out now.

"I want you to fuck my mouth," I say, and his lips stretch into a smile. "And don't you dare be gentle. Do not go easy on me, Hunter. I don't want that."

"Whatever you wish, Piper." He pushes down his briefs, and I finally see his cock. Well damn. I'm in for a fucking treat.

20
enough

HUNTER

My cock is hard, and her eyes focus on it. A smirk tugs on my lips as she lifts her hand and glides her palm over my length. I watch her every move, locking my hands behind my back.

"I figured you were big, but this..." She wraps her palm around my dick, giving it a light pump. "This is way more than I expected."

"You better get used to it," I say hoarsely. Our eyes meet as she continues to jerk me off. "Later, I'm going to stretch your pussy with it."

"I'll take you up on that, Hunter," she coos. I grit my teeth when she grabs my balls with her other hand, tugging a bit and then fondling them with her fingers. "You better keep your promise—"

"Stop fucking talking." I put my hand on the top of her head. "I want your rosy lips on my cock."

Piper slowly opens her mouth, and I drive my whole length inside. She circles her lips around my dick as I fuck her mouth. Her tongue swirls around it, adding friction. We make eye contact, and neither of us looks away. Everything else disappears, all boundaries and rules. We're no longer who we are. I'm not her boss, and she's not my daughter's nanny. We're a man and a woman who want each other and are driven mad by need. It's pure and wild at the same time, because there's no pretense or boredom. Her usually sunshiny personality has turned into a wildfire, one I can't wait to tame.

"You're so good," I murmur, closing my eyes and feeling my release approach. It's been a long time since any woman did this to me, and she's exceptionally good at what she's doing.

Pumping into her mouth, I go faster and deeper. Piper gags, and I see tears form in her eyes. I slow down and instantly feel her lips tighten around my sensitive skin. She shakes her head, and I barely keep myself from laughing out loud. She's a fucking brat, no less.

Her hand is on my balls, and when she massages them with her fingers I stop controlling myself. My hand on her head keeps her where I need her, and with a loud groan I come, filling her mouth with my cum. *Jesus fucking Christ, she's perfect.*

I step back and stare down at her. She holds my gaze and opens her mouth so I can see my cum on her tongue. My dick is hard again in no time, and my balls tighten. This is unusual, even for me. I always need at least a quick break, but apparently not with her, and not right now. She swallows everything, and I extend my hand and help her to her feet. I pull her close, her body colliding with my own. Her scent intoxicates me. She's the only thing I want to taste.

I cup her breasts roughly. The second I move my hands lower, she moans, pressing herself closer to me. Her hands find my shoulders as I slide mine to her ass. She feels heavenly, and I can't resist any longer. Not that I really want to.

I dip my head and kiss her lips. One of my hands is circled around her waist, and the other is hidden in her hair. My fingers play with her locks, until I grab a handful of them and tug. Piper whines, and her head tips back, giving me the perfect view of her neck. I dive in, leaving a hot trail of wet kisses on her skin, nibbling and drawing moans out of her. She grips my forearm, digging her fingernails into my flesh when I suck harder.

"Hunter." She whispers my name angrily, but I shut her up by covering her mouth with mine. My tongue plays with hers, demanding more until she pulls away. "I hate hickeys."

"Why?" I ask jokingly and twirl her around, pressing her back to my chest with my dick poking her ass. Just like I imagined in the club.

"Because it reminds me of how dogs mark their territory."

I snort and push her toward my bedroom. "Just because you were with someone who wanted to make it known you were his doesn't mean every man is the same." The door closes, and we stop in the middle of my room. "Turn around, Piper."

I see her shiver, and then she whirls around. "I have a question."

"First, take your heels off," I state, wrapping my hand around my dick and pumping slowly.

Piper kicks her heels aside. "What happens if I give you a hickey?"

"As long as it's somewhere others can't see, it's all good." I shrug, moving faster. "Take your dress off."

Her dress lands on the floor, and my eyes land on the most perfect tits in the world. Her next question draws my attention to her face. "Are you clean?"

"Yes," I confirm, and her fingers curl around her bra strap. "Now take off your bra and panties. You've been hiding your breasts from me for way too long."

When she's finally naked, my eyes devour every inch of her body. Her tits are round and full, with rosy buds for nipples. My mouth waters as her fingers brush her chest, pushing her hair off her shoulders.

"Better?"

I invade her personal space, winding my hands around her waist. "So much better."

I lift her, then lower her onto my bed and climb beside her until my head is on the pillow. "Come here and give me your pussy."

"What exactly are we doing?" Piper asks, straddling my legs.

"You're going to bring your ass over here"—I point to my mouth —"and sit on my face, so I can eat."

"Um..." She glances at my dick, and I can't help but laugh.

"I haven't slept with anyone for nine months now, and I wasn't planning to tonight. I don't have condoms in the house."

"Hunter!" Piper gently slaps my chest, knitting her brows together. "You promised to fuck me later."

"Did I say tonight?" I palm her ass and pull her toward me.

"No, but—"

"Tomorrow," I say, giving her ass a light slap. "I'll fuck you tomorrow."

"You better keep your promise, Mr. Hale. I hate being disappointed." Piper moves closer; her pussy hovers over my mouth. She looks down when I put my hands on her hips to hold her in place.

"I never disappoint, Piper."

I suck her clit into my mouth and release it almost immediately. I lick, nibble, and play with her nub with my tongue. Her moans are the only sounds I hear as she starts to ride my mouth, her juices covering my lips. She's so delicious, I can see myself doing this to her every fucking day.

Piper grabs the headboard, and her movements become rougher. She rides my mouth, rotating her hips deeper. Our eyes meet just in time for her body to spasm. She moans my name, coming all over my lips and tongue.

I don't let her move away until I lick her dry, but even then my hands are all over her. I pull her to me, and Piper rests her head on my chest. We stare at each other, not bothered by the silence. Inching closer, I kiss her lips. Slow and gentle.

"You're not going to your room," I whisper, resting my chin on the top of her head.

"I wasn't planning to."

"Good." I close my eyes, pulling a blanket over us with my free hand. "Good night."

"You're not going to tell me this was all a mistake?" she asks.

"Never." I just hope she'll be okay with what I can offer her. Hopefully it will be enough.

21
fuck me if you can

PIPER

I'M AWAKE, BUT I DON'T WANT TO OPEN MY EYES. His strong arms are wrapped around me, keeping me close to his broad chest. I inhale, and his scent hits my nostrils, making my nipples pebble. Hunter Hale is addictive, and getting just a little taste last night piqued my curiosity to the highest. I want to know all of him. I want to see all of him...I just pray he won't push me away.

There is an edge to him. A mystery. I was in a weird mood yesterday, and now it's rushing back. Hunter's words ring in my ears. *I'm bad news when it comes to women*, and Hayden more or less confirmed that. But what does it mean? How can he say his brother isn't good for me? I need an explanation, but I'm not going to ask Hade. At least, not now.

Banning those thoughts from my mind, I focus on more pleasant things. Slowly, I glide my palm over Hunter's back and feel his muscles tense. His grip around me tightens, and he hides his nose in my hair. Smiling, I press my face to his chest. I don't want to leave this bed.

"Your hair smells like cigarettes." The low tone of his voice reverberates through my body, and tingles roll over my skin. "Lavender and vanilla suit you better."

"I love the smell of cigarettes," I confess, keeping my eyes shut. "The ones that smell like cherry and vanilla are my favorites."

"Is vanilla your favorite flavor?"

"No, it's lavender."

"Should've guessed that," he chuckles, and I hesitantly open my eyes. The room is dim because of his heavy curtains, but the sun is peeking through them already. "How did you sleep?"

"Good, but not enough," I murmur, leaning away and peering up at his face. Hunter's eyes radiate warmth as he looks down at me, and his lips curl into a smile.

"You were the one who woke me up in the middle of the night with my cock in your mouth," he whispers, combing my hair with his fingers. I give him a cheeky grin, and he plants a kiss on my nose. After he let me ride his mouth, we both fell asleep. But not for long, because the second his hard dick pressed up against my butt, I was fully awake and wanted nothing more than to suck him off again. He definitely didn't mind. He came even harder than the first time.

"Do you want to sleep more?"

"No. You?"

"I'm good." Hunter's gaze sweeps over my face, and then he stares at something over my head, looking lost in his thoughts. "Do you want to eat? I can make breakfast for us."

"Yes, please," I tell him and wiggle out of his embrace. Sitting up, I glance at Hunter and catch his gaze on me. His eyes travel over my body so slowly that my heartbeat instantly takes off. "Do you want me to cook?"

Hunter quirks an eyebrow at me and then shakes his head. "I want to treat you to something delicious."

"Sounds incredible." I hop out of bed and then just stand there, doing nothing. I need to go to my room for my clothes, but it gives me a weird feeling. Like I'm breaking the magic of our moment. "I'll go change...in my room."

"Okay, I'll meet you in the kitchen." He sounds so normal, and it starts to gnaw at me.

I take a few steps forward and collect my clothes from the floor. Pressing them to my chest, I zip out of the room without looking back. In the hallway, I quickly pick up my jacket and purse from the floor and head to my room. Closing the door, I don't hesitate for even a moment. I just keep moving and moving and moving. I'm a grown woman, and I'm not ashamed of my weaknesses or my desires. Stepping into his house last night, I knew there would be consequences. Whatever happens after breakfast, I'm ready.

The kitchen is full of sounds and smells, and I can't help but smile. I can safely admit the man knows what he's doing when it comes to cooking. Most of the days, his food is delicious. Except for a few times when he suddenly decided it was time for fish and neither Story nor I wanted to eat it. But he's pretty good at everything he does.

Hunter's near the oven, stirring something and not paying any attention to his surroundings. He's fully dressed, wearing gray sweatpants and a white tee. I edge to the table and sit down. He hears me and looks over his shoulder, meeting my gaze in an instant.

"Sit. Don't even think about doing anything. Today, I'm in charge of your meals."

"You're bossy."

"You didn't seem to mind it last night." He smiles, and I roll my eyes, making him laugh. "I know you can be in control too. Just not today, okay?"

I hold his gaze and then nod, adding a little disobedience to my words. "Not *now*, you meant to say."

Hunter keeps silent for a moment, and then shakes his head, smiling. "Not now."

I watch him, feeling content. Usually our mornings aren't like this. They are filled with Story's chatter and laughter. And I love it. She's an adorable girl who likes to share her plans and her wishes. She tells us about school and her classmates, about her teacher and her favorite subjects. But that's nothing compared to how she talks about dancing. In those moments, she reminds me of my sister so damn much, I can easily close my eyes and imagine it's Riley talking. Their passion and enthusiasm are remarkably identical, along with their talents. I was the one who took Riley to dance class when she was a little girl, and now I'm the one who brings Story to hers. Full circle.

"A penny for your thoughts?" I jerk in my seat and focus my gaze on Hunter, then lower it to the table. Two plates with bacon and fried eggs, toast with ham and cheese, and two cups of steaming coffee. I didn't even notice when he set all this down.

"I was thinking about Story and Riley. Their love of dance is pretty similar, and I often feel like I'm going back in time when I take your daughter to Ms. Martinez. I did it for Riley for at least five years, till she was ready to go on her own, with her friends. It brings back a lot of memories."

"I get the feeling you grew up way too soon. You were taking care of your sister, doing things that moms usually do. Am I right?" He slides into his seat and peers at me. I sigh, taking a fork from the table and toying with it. "If you don't want to talk about it, I totally understand."

"It's not that I don't want to talk about it. I just don't like to dwell on the past."

"The past is what shapes our personalities. It makes us who we are." He falls silent, chewing his food and keeping his gaze trained on me. "If you ever want to talk, I'm here."

"Duly noted," I mutter and dig into my food. We're getting way too personal for my liking, and it's not something I want to do with him. At least, not for now. I want to know where we stand. "About last night. Can we talk about it?"

"Sure. But maybe we should finish our breakfast first? It's more comfortable to talk about things when your mouth isn't filled with food."

"You're right. I'm sorry. I shouldn't have—"

"Stop saying you're sorry. You haven't said anything to warrant forgiveness or an apology. You want to know what last night means, and that's totally normal. I want us to talk...just after breakfast."

We finish eating in silence, constantly glancing at each other and smiling. I couldn't have imagined things would ever be like this between us. There's no trace of awkwardness, no shyness. It's as if everything is exactly how it should be, and it makes me nervous.

"CAN I start by stating the obvious?" Hunter asks as we sit on the couch in the living room. "I like you, Piper. A lot. That's not something I expected when I agreed to hire you, nor when I saw you for the first time after all these years, but it's my reality now. I like my daughter's nanny, and I'm not ashamed of it."

"When I agreed to work for you, all that mattered to me was Story, and you were like...a bonus," I say, making him chuckle. "When I saw you in the hallway half naked? I honestly considered saying no."

"Why is that?"

"Apparently I didn't just agree to work for my best friend's brother."

"No?"

"No. I agreed to work for one of the sexiest men I've ever seen, and I regretted not googling you beforehand," I confide.

"I'm glad you didn't. Google remembers everything, even things I'd love to forget."

"Such as?"

"Piper, you're not the only one who doesn't like to dwell on the past."

"You got me," I confirm, eyeing him intensely. "I like you too, by the way. And I'm not ashamed to admit it either."

"Good to know," Hunter murmurs, and my clit aches. This neediness is becoming irritating. He's just a man. Why the hell am I so infatuated with him? "Um, I'm risking sounding awful here, but I want to be honest with you. I think you deserve it."

"Okay?"

"I don't want a relationship. I don't need a girlfriend. And I have no plans to settle down in the future. Marriage isn't for me," he states. I keep a straight face watching him. "Football and Story are the only things I'm interested in, and I plan to dedicate all of my time to them both."

"Where does that leave me?"

"All I can offer you is sex," he says calmly. "No strings attached. If you meet someone, I'll step back and not bother you again."

Well, I'll be working for him till next August. That's what my contract states. I also plan to go back to college and finish my degree, so the next few months are all we have. He can be my friend with benefits...or, considering our circumstances, my boss with benefits. Am I up for it? When the time comes, will I be able to walk away and not be heartbroken? I can only hope I will, because I have no desire to say no to him.

"Should we set some rules?"

Hunter looks at me for a moment, and then his lips break into a coy smile. "Definitely. What's rule number one?"

"No one needs to know. It's a secret."

"Agree. What else?"

"We have our own beds, so we're not allowed to sleep together."

"Ugh, I thought you liked cuddling with me," he whines, and I hit him with my leg—unsuccessfully, because his fingers circle my ankle and he yanks me to him, making me straddle his legs. "Jokes aside, I totally agree with rule number two."

"What if rule number three is about exclusivity?"

"I don't plan on hooking up with anyone else." Hunter dismisses me, cupping my ass with his palms. "I don't need a rule for that."

"Okay, then what should rule number three be?"

"If you meet someone, you tell me, and we stop this." He holds my gaze; his hands are firm on my body.

"And if you meet someone, you tell me, and we stop this. I don't want to be the other woman."

"There won't be anyone. Do we need more rules?"

"I don't think so." I lower my head; my lips are an inch away from his. "I just hope you'll keep your promise about not disappointing me."

Hunter roughly grabs the back of my neck, his hot breath on my face. "I always keep my promises." A second later, our lips collide, and we lose ourselves in this moment.

"Uncle Hayden, it's not fair," Story huffs, crossing her arms over her chest. She's frowning, looking down at the Monopoly board. "I wanted to buy this factory."

"Sorry, kid. Luck isn't on your side." Hade laughs, winking at her and then glancing at me. "It's not on your nanny's side either. Stop being a sore loser, Pip."

I roll my eyes and stand up from the couch, catching Hunter's gaze on me. "I'm going to the kitchen. Do you want anything?"

"Cocoa and toast with Nutella." Story's no longer sulking. Instead, she looks at me with a big, radiant smile on her lips. "Pretty please."

"Okay. What about you guys?" Hunter and Hayden both shake their heads no, and I continue to the kitchen. I want to be anywhere but the living room. Things are weird.

Hunter left to pick up Story around four, after we spent two hours making each other come over and over with our fingers and our tongues. He definitely has a mouth on him, and he knows how to use it and make a woman lose her mind. I was floating on cloud nine after that, happily singing along to my playlist while cooking dinner and waiting for them to come home. Then I saw Hayden step into the house with Hunter and Story.

Hade caught me in the kitchen when Hunter and Story went to change their clothes. He gave me a long lecture, peppered with apologies and reassurances. He promised to do better, to stop being so overprotective and manipulative. To give me space and not bother me about my love life. He said he'd be there for me no matter what, even if that means mending pieces of my broken heart. I was happy he decided to say all that. The problem was, he was watching me like a hawk once Hunter entered the room. He wanted to make sure there was nothing between Hunter and me.

Story is sound asleep in her bed. I slowly close her bedroom door and saunter back to the living room.

"Can I stay here tonight? My first class is at ten, so I'll have plenty of time to get to campus before it starts," Hayden asks, and I freeze in the doorway.

"Sure. There's a guest room upstairs. You can take that." Hunter shrugs. He hasn't noticed me. I clear my throat, and they both look at me. "Story is asleep, and I'm going to turn in too. Do you need anything before I go?"

"No, thank you, Piper. I'll just show Hayden to his room, and then I'll go to bed too."

"See you in the morning, Pip." Hade walks over to me and kisses my cheek. "Night."

"Night," I mumble as he starts to climb the stairs, humming one of Sabotage's songs under his breath. I don't know how I feel. I'm happy they're bonding and spending more time together. But at the same time, it feels like he's staying to keep an eye on me.

"He's here because of you." I bore my gaze into Hunter. "He's been watching you all evening."

"He wants to make sure there's nothing going on between us."

"So far, I think you managed to convince him." Hunter nudges me and takes a few steps toward the stairs. "Night, Piper."

"Night, Hunter," I answer curtly and hurry to my room. "Nice to know you're going to keep your promise."

"Piper," he groans as I put a hand on the doorknob.

"Fuck me if you can, Hunter, or go to bed."

I don't expect him to do as I say, but I can't ignore the opportunity to tease him out of his mind.

22
fade into her

HUNTER

I LEAN AGAINST THE DOORFRAME, WATCHING HAYDEN brush his teeth. My mind isn't here, as my thoughts keep returning to my little chat with Piper. *Fuck me if you can, Hunter, or go to bed.* As if there's anything I want to do more than finally bury my cock deep inside her pussy. Of course I want to fuck her, but sometimes our wishes have nothing to do with reality. Hayden's presence in my house is my reality, and I can't risk him finding out about Piper and me. He won't understand.

"I've been meaning to ask you," Hayden mutters, spitting toothpaste into the sink and rinsing his mouth with tap water. "Is it true you told Piper she should know her place?"

"What?"

"Yesterday she mentioned you told her to know her place when she wanted to talk to you about Story. She also said you apologized but...did you *really* tell her that?"

Is that how she tried to divert his attention last night? How she made sure he believed nothing was going on between us? I somehow understand her logic, but at the same time, couldn't she have warned me? It was obvious he'd try to make things right and lecture me. Exactly what I fucking need when I'm horny and irritated...not.

"I'm a direct person, Hayden. So yes, I told her that, and yes, I apologized."

"She's my best friend."

"So what? She's my employee."

"It's different, Hunter," he grits, crossing his arms over his chest. "Piper doesn't deserve to be treated or talked to like that. Story loves her, and Pip loves her too. You should be grateful, not spiteful."

"I am grateful." I frown. I've said a lot of wrong things to her, and many of them would never have left my mouth if I didn't feel attracted to her. My annoyance with myself got mixed in with my frustration and my growing desire to have her, and it definitely wasn't the healthiest situation to be in. I know how horribly I was behaving toward her, and I'd do anything for her to forget about it and forgive me. I'm not the fucking douche my brother is trying to portray me as. "Things are better now."

"Because you said you're sorry?"

"Because I admitted my faults." I nod, narrowing my eyes on Hayden. "It's between Piper and me, and if I said I was sorry, I meant it."

"Not sure she sees it that way." *Trust me, brother, she does.* There's no lingering misunderstanding between us. We've talked about everything that's happened since the moment she moved in. "You should be more careful with the things you say—"

"Do you like her?" I ask, and his jaw hangs open. Hayden gawks at me with eyes as round as saucers.

"What do you mean?"

"Do you like Piper?"

"She's a *friend*, Hunter," he hisses, dropping his hands to his sides and balling his fists. "Pip is like a sister to me. Always has been, and always will be."

"Then you should think about loosening her leash. You're suffocating her."

Hayden looks stunned for a second, and then he shakes his head. "You're still the same. A fucking jerk who turns things around when he feels threatened."

"If you think you're any different, you're deluding yourself." I smirk and head to the stairs. "You're being defensive because you know you're in the wrong. And you don't like to hear the truth. Night, Hayden."

"Night," he mutters angrily.

I don't look back, but I hear his footsteps and then the door closing. He needs a reality check. The way he tries to control her is ridiculous, and I don't just think that because I got involved with her. She has a good head on her shoulders, and she's much smarter and more resourceful than he gives her credit for. He should know better.

I open the door to my room, step inside, and just stand there, not moving. All that talk about always keeping my promises, and now I'm all alone in my bedroom. Agitated and sexually deprived because of Hayden.

When I saw Piper and Hayden for the first time in all those years, I had this thought about how other guys would need to keep their distance from her because of their closeness and his overprotectiveness. And now that other guy is me. His possessiveness when it comes to Piper is as admirable as it is frustrating. I would've understood if there were a reason for his behavior, but I don't see any. She's not a damsel in distress. If anything, the girl is very aware of how to stand up for herself.

Shaking my head, I stomp to my bed and take off my tee, tossing it onto my covers. My breathing quickens when I notice her panties on my nightstand. *What a sneaky girl.* My lips curl into a smile as I take her panties, fisting them. Is this her way of telling me what she wants? If so, she definitely succeeded.

Screw it.

I shove her panties into the pocket of my sweatpants, grab my tee from the bed, and put it on. I take a few steps toward the door, halt in my tracks, and go back to my bedside table. When I open the first drawer, a new box of condoms is the first thing my eyes fall on. I take a few and saunter to the hallway, quietly closing the door. Story is asleep, and I'm sure Hayden is still up, but I know he won't come downstairs. My words played in my favor, and he'll stay away. His ego is huge, but the last thing he'll want is to butt heads with me. He won't win.

Putting my hand on the doorknob, I slowly push the door open, and amble inside. Piper's bed is empty, but light comes from under her bathroom door. I quickly lock the door and sneak to the bathroom, cracking the door open. Piper is in the shower. I see the outline of her body through clouded glass.

I pull off my tee, and it falls to the ground. Then I add my sweatpants and my boxer briefs to the pile. Stepping closer, I stop by the glass door before I open it. My eyes land on her back, and I let my gaze devour her. Her wet hair spills over her shoulders. Water drips down her shoulder blades to her narrow waist and her amazing ass. Piper is fucking perfection.

"I found your gift," I murmur, and she looks over her shoulder.

"It wasn't a gift." Piper shrugs, locking her gaze with mine. "It was motivation."

I step inside the shower and cup her face with my palms. She puts her hands on my hips and then slowly circles one of her hands around my dick. "It was a gift. I'm not giving it back."

"Whatever you want, Mr. Hale." *Fuck.* Her "Mr. Hale" sounds sexier than any other woman who has ever tried to flirt with me. I pull her closer and tip my head down, kissing her.

She strokes my dick as our tongues dance in a frenzied motion. My head is spinning, and my whole body is in flames from her closeness. Her soft lips are so fucking kissable, I don't want to stop for even a moment. I suck her bottom lip into my mouth and bite hard, hearing her whimper. Her grip on my dick becomes tighter in an instant, and I groan from how good it feels. A hand job was my only source of relief for a while, but it never felt as amazing as it does with her. She makes everything better.

I put my hand on her breast, massaging gently and then tugging on her nipple. Piper leans into me, pressing herself even closer to my chest, as she continues to work her magic on my dick. If I don't stop her, she'll have me coming in no time. And I don't want that. I want to come with her walls squeezing tightly around my shaft. I want to be inside her so bad that it reminds me of an addiction. It's my first time with her, and I'm afraid to even imagine what will happen when I do fuck her. Will I be able to stop?

"Touch me, please." Her whisper rips me from my thoughts, and I glide my lips over her neck and down to her shoulders. I suck, leaving a hickey on her collarbone. "Hunter, please, touch me."

She spreads her legs and I lower my hand to her pussy, my fingers sneaking to her clit. She's so fucking wet, and it has nothing to do with the water. Piper is dripping, and this realization sends me over the edge. I want her now.

I take a step back, and Piper's eyes snap open. Her chest is rising and falling from her erratic breathing. Grabbing her throat, I inch my lips to hers, running my tongue over her bottom lip. "Turn around, bend over, and show me your beautiful cunt."

She holds my gaze, keeping silent, and then she slowly nods. I seize her lips with another long, passionate kiss, and only when I feel her tremble do I step away.

"Do it."

Piper slowly turns around as I open the glass door and reach for my pants. Grabbing a condom, I quickly tear open the wrapper and sheath my cock. I stalk back into the shower stall and close the door, my eyes instantly falling on her fine ass and pussy. Her tits are pressed against the glass as she holds her butt cheeks, spreading herself open for me. Not a single question was asked, and she's waiting for me exactly as I wanted her. She's so in tune with me, I might be a goner.

"I'm going to fuck you senseless, Piper." I run my dick up and down her folds, drawing a long, loud moan out of her. She's not the quietest girl, and even though I'm tempted to make her scream, I won't do that now. My daughter and my brother are still here, and I don't want them to know. For different reasons, but nonetheless. They don't need to know about what I do with Piper. Not now, not ever.

"Fuck me, please," she whispers, and I angle my cock, slowly pushing it all the way inside her pussy. I grip her hips, and a hiss escapes my lips. She's tighter than I expected. "Oh God, I'm so fucking full."

"You're not," I tell her, picking up my pace and fucking her steadily. "I'm going to stretch this pussy until you take me whole. Until I'm fucking balls deep inside you."

"It feels so good," she moans, and I dig my fingernails into her ass. The sounds she makes are the hottest sounds I've ever heard. My mind becomes cloudy as I pound deeper into her. I place my palms on her ass, finding two little spots for my fingers.

Ramming into her deeper and harder, I groan, feeling my balls tighten. I'm so close to my release, but I'm not fucking ready for it to be over. I step back, turn her around, and kiss her lips. I wrap my arms around her waist and lift her off her feet. Her legs instinctively wrap around me as I drive my length inside her all at once. A low growl leaves my lips, because it feels like fucking heaven on Earth.

"Fuck."

Piper winds her hands around my shoulders, her fingers sneaking into my hair. "I'm so close already...please, don't stop..."

"I'm going to make you come so hard, Piper...you won't be able to fucking walk." I hide my face in her neck, her scent swimming around me and filling every bone in my body. I'm on the verge of my release, and I stop holding myself back. "Such a good girl...such a good fucking girl..."

With one strong thrust, I come. I bite down on her neck and continue to move my hips over and over, until she comes too. Her lips seek mine, and our sounds drown in our collided mouths. Her walls squeeze hard around my dick, and I come even more...even if I didn't think that was possible.

Her arms are wrapped around my shoulders, and our lips have minds of their own, refusing to be apart for even a minute. We kiss, pant, and caress each other's skin, prolonging the feeling and enjoying it to the fullest.

I step back, but my hand stays firmly circled around her waist. My gaze is glued to her beautiful face. Her cheeks are flushed, her eyes are glimmering with heat, and those puffy lips look incredible. She's even more beautiful now, probably because I finally saw her. I finally saw all of her, and I don't want to go back to the way it was before. I want to fade into her.

"I honestly thought you were going to make me pass out," she says, dragging her finger down my chest.

"Not tonight," I respond, grabbing her chin between my fingers and tilting her head toward me for a kiss. "I want to make you scream my name...and that's not possible with other people in the house."

"Are you thinking about sending Story to your parents' more often?"

"I definitely am." I kiss the corner of her mouth, and she sighs, closing her eyes. "A little sleepover here and there won't hurt."

"I love the sound of that."

"I know." I take a deep breath and kiss her forehead, then step back immediately. "I need to head back to my room. I have a pretty busy morning."

"Sure. Night, Hunter."

"Night, Piper." I hesitate for a millisecond, and then I mentally slap myself. *Rules, Hunter. They are there for a fucking reason.*

I climb out of the shower, quickly dry my body with a towel, then take off the condom and throw it into the trash can. Putting on my clothes, I glance over my shoulder and see her wash her body under the pouring water. Piper feels my gaze and gives me a little smile. I nod and go to my room. Of course, not all nights will be like this, but I'll be sure to make the most of the ones that are. It's just a silly idea, but I think I finally met someone as insatiable as me.

23
best served cold

HUNTER

"HALE!" I WHIP MY HEAD TOWARD VAVRO'S VOICE. "YOU'RE next."

"Okay." I run in his direction, energy surging through my veins.

Today's practice has been typical. We warmed up by jogging around the pitch and then stretched, to improve our agility and increase our range of motion. What I love about football is that it works the whole body, even if the main focus is on legs. But guys love to make fun of this part of practice. No matter the team or the country, it's always the same.

Racing each other motivates us to run faster, and that's exactly what I was doing before I started to practice my dribbling skills—something I'm really good at, but I don't let my arrogance overrule me. I still have things to learn and skills to improve. Being in top shape is what I love the most.

I should be practicing passing, but the coach, who's standing near Vavro, wants me to practice shooting. After playing football for as many years as I have, my skills should be immaculate, but only continuous practice makes perfect.

"Coach." I stop near Coach Larson, wearing a polite smile. He's been moody all day, so I have no idea what to expect. When I shift my gaze to Vavro, I see the guy grinning. "Marek."

"How do you feel about starting next game?" Coach gets straight to the point. "I want to give this last game of the regular season our best shot, and that means you're on the field from start to finish. Ideally."

"I'm all in." I shrug, and a drop of sweat slides down my temple and onto my cheek. Flexing my muscles, an itching feeling forms in my legs. I fucking need action. I hate standing by and doing nothing when I'm on the pitch.

Coach sweeps his gaze over my face and then starts to nod in approval. "I knew it was the right decision to hire you, Hale. You've been a valuable addition to our team. A new leader. Someone who doesn't want to be, but still is."

"You're giving me way too much credit, Coach." I laugh, and it sounds like a barking dog. Fuck. I don't have time to look for water, but I hear my name again, and Vavro tosses me a bottle. "Thanks, Marek."

"Don't mention it." He jumps a few times and then sets his legs wide, shifting his weight from one leg to the other. I keep watching him, and a smug smirk forms on my lips. *That won't help you against me.* If I want to score, I will. I always do.

Ten shots later, Marek is seething. He runs a hand through his blond hair; his whole face is red with anger. I scored ten out of ten, without giving him a single chance to stop the ball. The Coach laughs, placing a hand on his stomach.

"Are you sure we don't need another goalkeeper for Saturday?"

"Hundred percent," Vavro grits through his teeth. He claps his hands together. "One more time, Hale."

"You want me to make it eleven?" I set my foot on the ball, rolling it back and forth while holding his gaze.

"Ten. Ten will be your record," he snaps. He jumps into the air, hitting the top of the net with his hands. He's pissed, and I'm going to use that in my favor.

I jog away from the net, dribbling the ball and preparing myself for another shot. I'm calm and collected as I take a deep breath through my nostrils. There isn't a trace of the irritation and annoyance I felt days ago. Everything is gone because of her.

The sudden sound of a whistle brings me back to reality. I focus and sprint toward the net, zigzagging until I'm in the best position for the shot. My motion is swift, and it's barely noticeable when I kick the ball. It lands low in the bottom corner of the net. Eleven. And Vavro isn't fucking happy.

"Thank you for destroying my motivation," he growls, taking the ball into his hands and squeezing it hard.

"I think it's exactly the motivation you need. You'll want to play better on Saturday, so no one from Nashville scores," I tell him as he continues to glare at me. "Don't let your anger overwhelm you during the game. You can always focus on that later...if you still feel the need."

Vavro shifts from one leg to the other, puffing his cheeks. Then he suddenly heaves a sigh and nods. "You're right, Hale. I can use this as an example of how I *shouldn't* play if I want us to win."

"Glad my idea worked," Coach mutters, and we shoot him a quick glance. "If we win on Saturday, we'll get the Supporters' Shield. It will give us a great boost before playoffs."

"Winning the Supporters' Shield will suit us perfectly," Marek states, grinning. His broody mood has disappeared, and now he's full of determination.

"Let's not get ahead of ourselves. Calling shots before the game is a bad omen." Coach waves his hand dismissively, then looks at the other players on the pitch. "It's time for an inter-squad scrimmage, guys. Show me what you've got."

"With pleasure," Vavro and I exclaim at the same time. Then we nod at each other and follow Coach over to the rest of the team. It's time for a little game, and I'm here for it.

MY SPORTS BAG hangs over my shoulder as I walk to my car. I can't wait to get home, soak my aching muscles in a hot bath, and have a quiet moment with Story. Well, I also hope to get Piper all to myself so I can convince her to have a little fun once Story goes to bed. It's been three days without any physical contact, and my cock is desperate to feel her tight little pussy wrap around it. It's not like she's avoiding me. A few times, I got to feel her press her round ass to my groin...but that's nothing compared to what I want to do with her.

"Mr. Hale?"

I halt in my tracks when I notice Autumn Dunn strolling toward me. She's wearing a light blue bodycon dress and a black leather jacket, her heels making her look taller than she is. Her long brown hair is collected into a bun, and she has on very bright makeup. She stops in front of me, looks me up and down, and then flashes me a big smile.

"How was practice?"

"Hello, Ms. Dunn," I greet her, furrowing my brows. "Practice was good. Why?"

"Saturday is the last game of the regular season. If LACFC wins, they'll get the Supporters' Shield. Are you excited?" She crosses her legs at her ankles, hands hidden in her jacket pockets.

I blink and scowl in an instant. "Is this an interview?"

"No." She shakes her head, her smile slowly disappearing.

"Then have a nice day." I keep walking.

"Hunter, wait." *We're on a first name basis already? She's annoying.*

"What?"

"I was in the neighborhood, and, well...I knew it was a practice day, and that you'd be here. But I'm not stalking you," she blurts, playing with her earring.

Could have fooled me. "What do you want, Ms. Dunn?"

"Oh God, please don't call me that. I'm Autumn." She extends her hand. I roll my eyes, but I take it, give it the quickest squeeze, and let go.

"Nice to meet you, Autumn. Anything else?"

Autumn sighs and then pinches her brows together. "We were an instant match. Why did you delete your swipe?"

It takes me a minute to figure out she's talking about Tinder. I forgot about that app, this woman, and my mistake the second Piper helped me fix it. I even deleted it on my way home from the club. I knew I wouldn't be using it. But Autumn Dunn wants answers.

"Maybe this will sound like an excuse, but I honestly never planned to swipe right. I was still getting used to the app, and then I saw you, and my surprise got the best of me. I fixed it the second I realized what I did." I take out my phone, quickly tap on the screen, and shove it back in my pocket, bringing my gaze back to the reporter.

"But you don't know what you're missing out on."

A loud snort escapes my mouth uncontrollably. "Highly doubt it."

Her jaw flexes, and the look on her face hardens. She's not one to take rejection lightly, I can tell. Too bad I don't give a—

"How about you go on a date with me? Invite me to dinner?"

"Ms. Dunn, do I need to repeat myself? I'm not interested."

"Aren't you single? I mean, you were using Tinder, so obviously you are...and I don't remember any news stories about you having a girlfriend. Unlike your ex-wife."

"Amelia has a boyfriend, not a girlfriend," I correct her, throwing her off her high horse and making her turn even redder than she already is.

"Smartass," Autumn utters, looking away for a second. When she brings her gaze back to me, she looks malicious. "When I heard you were moving to LA, I was dead set on meeting you. I made sure to be at the press conference. You were exactly how I expected you to be, and more. When I saw you on Tinder, I knew it was a sign. We could be a great couple, Hunter, but only if you give me a chance."

I'm so going to regret this later.

"I can't say I'm single right now. I have someone in my life, and we're getting to know each other. As slowly as possible, considering my daughter."

"I didn't know. How did you—"

"Ms. Dunn, you're a very attractive woman, but that's all there is to it. I'm not interested in being in a relationship or getting to know you." I extend my hand to her, and she reluctantly takes it. "I hope we can keep things professional."

"Definitely." We shake hands, and I step back. The snarky smile on her face makes me cringe. Why is it there? "Though, as a professional, it's my job to find out who you're seeing. It'll be quite a story."

"She's not a public person," I say. I'm still wearing a polite smile, even if I want to strangle her.

"That makes things even more interesting." Autumn Dunn wiggles her eyebrows at me, making me frown even more. "But if you want to keep me from digging...you know what to do. I'd never say no to a date with you."

"Duly noted, Ms. Dunn." I nod and casually saunter toward my car, not giving away the full extent of my anger. This woman has made me furious, and all I want to do right now is make her pay for her blackmail.

As I start my Lexus, I see her car take off. She drives away with a lopsided grin on her face, winking at me as her car passes mine. Revenge is a dish best served cold. If I catch her snooping around, if I find out she's annoying Piper and Story—her career will end faster than she can say her last name.

My past is my teacher. Years ago, when one of my exes threatened to accuse me of sexual assault because I broke up with her while she was hoping to get a ring on her finger, I learned how to protect myself. Having a voice recorder on standby is my salvation.

Agitation rises inside my chest, spreading through my veins and finding its way into my mind. I need my head on straight...and I need my fix. I need Piper in my bed. No excuses.

24
hunter's touch

PIPER

LEANING AGAINST THE DOORFRAME, I WATCH STORY dance. She's incredibly cute in her black long-sleeved leotard and red sparkling tutu. Her hair is in a tight bun, and the look on her face is serious. The way she bites her bottom lip leaves no doubt that she's struggling with this new routine. I smile. Memories of Riley dancing fill my mind in an instant.

There were days when I did my homework in the studio, waiting for her class to be over. I wanted her to thrive, to be successful, and she achieved everything I dreamed of for her. She's the best in her class— prima ballerina, as I often call her. Ms. Martinez always praises her, and now they're planning a recital, a winter-themed showcase, in which my sister will be a principal. The little sneak refuses to tell me anything else, saying it'll be a surprise. Everything she does is magical.

"Hey, sis." A soft voice pulls me out of my thoughts. I turn my head, and my eyes meet Riley's. She's smiling, and my chest swells with happiness. I love being in Hunter's house, love being with Story. But at the same time, I miss Riley so much it hurts. "I knew I'd find you here."

I push away from the doorframe and step out of the dance studio. Wrapping my arms around Riley's shoulders, I hug her as tight as I can, hiding my face in the crook of her neck. She smells like home. Her favorite perfume, Miss Dior, wafts around her, and I can't help but smile.

"I missed you."

"I...can...feel...that," Riley pants, wiggling out of my embrace. I let her go and step back, hiding my hands in my pockets. "If you miss me so much, why don't you invite me to visit again? Or maybe a better question is, when do you plan to come home? Wade is a freaking God in the kitchen; you have no idea what you're missing."

"Hunter has his last game of the regular season on Saturday. Then there will be playoffs, and once they're over he'll be on a break. So I'll have more time to myself in the second half of November, and I'm sure he won't mind if you come over more. We just need to wait a little bit."

"That's nice," Riley gushes. "Any chance I can go to the game with you?"

"Do you want to?"

"I do, but only if it won't be a problem. I don't want to cause any—"

"Stop it," I say, and Riley's eyes go round. "Story will be ecstatic when she hears. You're like an idol to her at this point."

"She's the sweetest, I swear," she murmurs, peeking over my shoulder into the studio. "Tiny problem, sis. It's her father's game, not her recital."

"Hunter never says no to Story."

"And you?" Riley teases me, a lopsided grin playing across her lips.

I roll my eyes and nod. "I don't say no to her either."

"I knew it. You were exactly like that with me."

"I was strict with you when you deserved it. And it's the same with Story. Trust me. No one is trying to spoil her."

Riley shakes her head, adjusting her sports bag. "Story is an incredibly kind girl. Everyone loves her...the girls from my class are jealous of me because I'm her favorite."

I stare at her long and hard, but then I break into a smile. "After me. *I'm* her favorite."

"The audacity," she mumbles dramatically, pressing a palm to her chest. "We are both her favorites."

"Fine. I think I can share her love with you," I state, and Riley pokes her tongue out at me. Quickly taking my phone out of my pocket, I check the time. I still have twenty minutes before Story's class is over. "How about a hot chocolate?"

"Pass." She gives me an apologetic smile. "My class is right after this one, and I hate dancing when my belly's full. How about we just sit on the bench and talk?"

"Sounds amazing," I say.

WHEN I STEP into the house, I know he's home. I close the front door, and my eyes clash with Hunter's. He stands in the doorway, glancing between Story and me. He's smiling, but it looks forced. I frown, trying to figure out his mood. Angry? No. Irritated? Definitely. But why? Did something happen at practice?

"Daddy!" Story notices him and rushes into his outstretched arms. Hunter catches her with ease, lifting her and kissing her on her nose. "How was your practice?"

"It was good," he says calmly. I take a few steps forward, my eyes roaming over his body. I mentally slap myself for my thoughts. I'd love to be in his arms too, but that sounds creepy. He's not my daddy. *Oh my fucking God.* "Hey, Piper."

"Hey." I wave, shifting a little. Hunter's green eyes darken, and he narrows them on me. *Yeah, my aching clit is the best evidence of how much our lack of contact affects me.* There's a very big chance I'll give in and sneak into his room one of these days. Or maybe tonight. I don't think I have it in me to resist him much longer. "How long have you been home?"

"Thirty minutes. How are you two? How was your day?"

"Story had a very eventful day. I'm sure she has things she wants to share with you."

"I can't wait to show you what I made in school. It's so cool," she exclaims, and Hunter focuses his attention on Story. "Can you wait in the living room? I want it to be a surprise."

"Whatever you wish, princess," he chuckles, putting Story down. She squeals and dashes to her room. "Piper?"

I hate the way he says my name. It turns my panties into a wet mess. "Yeah?"

"There's something I need to talk to you about, but only once Story is asleep." And just by his tone of voice, I know it's nothing good. The excitement I felt transforms into unease, and my veins turn into strained cords full of ice.

I pinch my brows together and hide my hands in my pockets. "Sure. I'm going to my room. I need to change before I cook dinner."

"I can order something."

"That's okay." I stroll past him. "Cooking always eases my mind."

As I walk to my room, I feel his gaze on me, and this time I don't know what to think. What could've possibly happened at practice? I was hoping to talk to him about Riley coming over, but now I'm not so sure I should. Hopefully, whatever he has to tell me won't be that bad.

"Hade, if you want me to help you...tell me what you need. Easy." I sigh, pressing my phone to my ear. It's dark and quiet as I sit at the edge of the pool with my legs in the water. While Hunter put Story to bed, I decided to wait for him outside. It's been almost twenty-five minutes, so when Hayden called I was happy to talk to him. Until I realized he was in a mood.

"I don't know what I need. That's the problem," he snaps, frustration rising in his voice. "My inspiration these days is nonexistent. I don't want to write, don't want to play. I don't want anything."

"Is it school? Maybe you're stressed because of your studies?" But

I know perfectly well that's not it. Hade is a messy mess most of the time...with straight A's in all of his classes.

Hayden keeps silent, and I close my eyes, listening to the sound of the water as I slowly swing my legs back and forth in the pool. It's nowhere close to the sound of the ocean, but it's still relaxing. The thoughts in my head are way too frantic.

"Do I really suffocate you?"

At first, I'm not even sure I hear him right. I open my eyes and stare ahead of me, and my brows knit together. "What?"

"Hunter said something when I stayed the night...and I can't stop thinking about it." Hayden's voice cracks, and he takes a long breath. "Do you feel like I'm suffocating you?"

"Hayden..."

"Pip, you told me the same thing at the club. You said I take away your choices. Is that how I make you feel?"

"Sometimes."

"Fuck, Pip...I'm so sorry for making you feel like that. It's not what I want...it's not what I ever wanted..." He trails off, and I hear him pacing, the loud sound of his feet hitting the floor.

"Hade, stop it. Everything's fine."

"No, it's not," he whispers harshly. "But I promise you...I promise you I'll do better. I swear. I don't want you to feel like I'm suffocating you with my care, with my worries...I'll be a better friend. One you really deserve."

"Hade, I love you the way you are. You're my best friend—my best, best friend in the entire world."

"Love you too, Pip. You're the sunshine to my storm, and I'll be damned if I let your light dim," he says.

"Do you feel better?" I ask.

"I do. I needed to get that off my chest, so thank you."

"You're always welcome. See you on Saturday?"

"See you on Saturday. Night, Pip."

"Night, Hade." I end the call and feel someone's presence. Hunter stands behind me with a faint smile playing on his lips. Taking a deep breath, I let my shoulders slump and put my phone on the tiles surrounding the pool.

"How's my brother?" Hunter asks, lowering himself beside me.

"He's fine. I think our talk helped clear his head."

"Good."

I decide to keep the details of my conversation with Hayden to myself. This is between Hade and me, even if Hunter got himself involved by giving his little brother unsolicited advice.

"Story just fell asleep ten minutes ago. Sometimes it's hard to get her to bed when she feels excited."

"Tell me about it," I chuckle and glance at him. "Your upcoming game is all she talked about on our way home."

"She showed me her drawings," he says, and his smile grows bigger. "I have no idea how we're going to win four to one, but I'll do my best. I can't possibly disappoint Story."

"I'm pretty sure you'll never disappoint her."

"Hope so." Hunter sighs, and all his playfulness is gone. As if he turned off all his emotions with this one simple gesture. "Do you remember when you helped me with Tinder?"

"Yes."

"Why didn't you tell me the woman and I were an instant match?"

I look away from him, focusing my attention on the myriad of stars illuminating the sky. "You wanted me to take back your swipe, and I did that. I didn't think the instant match was important because I thought you didn't want anything to do with her. I'm sorry if I took it all wrong."

"You took it all right, Piper," he says softly, taking my chin between his thumb and index finger and forcing me to look at him. "I'm not interested in Autumn Dunn. The problem is her. She doesn't like to be rejected."

"Did she...how do you know that?"

"She was waiting for me after practice. She wanted to know why I removed my swipe. In her head, we were a perfect match, and still are. She told me I should take her on a date."

A green-eyed monster awakes in my chest, the beating of my heart becomes painfully loud and strong. That reporter is exactly his type, at least in looks. She's established, and she's his age. After all, she was his instant match. I swallow my nerves, feeling as if I just gobbled a bunch of rocks.

"What did you tell her?"

"That it was a mistake on my part, and I'm not interested." His long fingers caress my skin, and it feels like a blessing, soothing my ardent nerves. I've been yearning for Hunter's touch since our first time in the shower. "I wanted her to forget about us being together, so I told her I'm seeing someone. And now she wants to know who it is. She's a reporter, after all."

"What does that mean? Will she be snooping around, trying to dig up information?"

"That's what she told me." He shrugs and drops his hand. "She gave me a choice. If I don't want her snooping around, I should take her on a date."

Oh my God. "Isn't that blackmail?"

Hunter blinks, and then a coy smile crosses his lips. "I love how smart you are, Piper. It makes me admire you even more." And now my ovaries are in a twist. How can he say something like that to me? "It's blackmail, you're right. I know what to do in case she keeps her promise and starts stalking me and my family. I recorded my conversation with her, so I have evidence. I just want you to be careful from now on. If you see someone following you or Story, please tell me. Immediately. I need to know when to act."

He recorded their conversation? How did he have time to think of doing that? Maybe it's not the first time someone has tried to pull this trick on him. Has he been blackmailed before?

"Piper?" His voice sends shivers down my spine. "This isn't your battle to fight; it's mine. My mistake led me to this, and now it's for me to fix. I know what to do. I just need you to be careful from now on. Promise me you'll be careful. Please."

"I promise," I say, and he brings his face closer to mine. His hot breath fans over my warm cheeks as he bends his head, and our noses touch. "Can you please...can you please kiss me?"

"With pleasure." Hunter places his hand on the back of my head and smashes his lips on mine. The second my tongue brushes his, I know we won't make it to either of our rooms. He's going to fuck me right here, by the pool in his backyard...and I don't have anything against it.

25

it happened last night

HUNTER

MY MOUTH IS DESPERATE TO FEEL HERS, GREEDILY possessing it with each brush of our lips. I groan into our kiss and grip her neck harder once her tongue slips inside my mouth. This kiss is painfully slow and invigorating. It sets my body on fire, making my skin scorching hot. It's fucking madness, but I don't care. I want what I want, and it's her. Here and now.

Leaning away, I see her panting. Piper's gaze is glimmering in the darkness, looking feverish. She parts her lips, breathing rapidly. Tucking a strand of hair behind her ear, I trace my fingers over her jaw and down her neck. *So fucking beautiful.*

I slowly stand up, holding her gaze. I extend my hand and help Piper to her feet. Without hesitation, I lead her toward a little terrace in a secluded part of the backyard. She doesn't ask a single question, just goes with the flow.

Stopping near a wooden bench, I reach over a nearby chair and take a little flannel blanket from the back of it. I quickly cover the bench, plop down, and meet Piper's gaze. Her impatience is adorable.

"Take your shorts off," I tell her. Then I watch her get rid of them, keeping her panties on. *Such a good girl; she always does what she's told.* I adjust my cock in my shorts, and her eyes zero in on it. "Sit on my lap."

Piper steps closer and lowers herself onto my lap. A quiet whimper leaves her mouth once my hardness pokes against her pussy. She wraps her arms around my neck, holding my gaze. In the darkness, under a sky full of stars, my eyes roam over her face, appreciating her beauty. Moonlight reflects on her tanned skin, making it glow. I notice a little birthmark on her right cheek and another on her left, closer to her mouth. She has full, kissable lips and little dimples that appear any time she grins. Her long black eyelashes are framing her eyes, making her gaze languid. She's an incredibly gorgeous girl.

"Resisting you is harder than I thought," Piper whispers, rotating her hips and gliding her pussy over my dick.

"And why are you resisting me?" I ask, grabbing a handful of her ass, digging my fingers into her skin.

"I don't want you to think I'm needy."

"We could be needy together," I confess, and she smiles as she continues to rub her pussy over my length through our clothes. "There's nothing wrong with wanting to have sex...once a week, once a day, once an hour. Whenever you want me. I'll never say no to you."

"You're setting my expectations really high." She rolls her hips one more time, and a loud hiss escapes my mouth. She's going to make me cum in my shorts. "Ruining me for all other men."

Her words trigger me, make me unreasonable. I grab her hair in my fist and yank. Her head bobs back, exposing her neck to me. I inch forward, showering her skin with wet kisses, devouring every inch of her throat.

"How wet are you for me?" Letting go of her hair, I reach into my pocket and take out a condom.

"I'm soaking wet, Hunter," she murmurs, placing a hand on my groin and pulling my dick out of my shorts. I tear the wrapper, toss it aside, and roll the condom over my cock. Her hand squeezes the base of my shaft, and I growl in warning. "I want you so bad."

"Good." I press my finger to her clit, feeling her wetness through her panties. "I want you to take my dick into your little pussy and ride me till you can't fucking move."

Piper hovers over my lap, then moves her panties aside and takes my cock all the way inside her pussy. She's warm and wet, tightly wrapping around my dick. Her movements are slow and deep. She doesn't rush, enjoying every dip of her hips. The most mesmerizing thing? I look into her eyes, and I don't want to look away.

"You feel so good," I praise her. "So fucking good."

Her pussy is slowly stretching, taking more and more of my cock. I'm so deep it makes me see stars. I cup her ass with my hands, urging her to start moving faster. My release builds within me, making my breath shallow. I pull her face to mine, searing her lips with a kiss. It's rough; I'm ravishing her mouth with mine. She might be my own addiction, the kind of drug I never thought I'd get to try. She's sweet and wild, and the level of trust she demonstrates makes me want her even more.

"I'm gonna come, Hunter. Oh my God..." Piper's moves become frantic as she wraps her arms around my shoulders. She bounces up and down on my cock, rubbing her clit over my lower abdomen, stimulating her approaching orgasm. "Are you close? Hunter, please."

"Yes...make me come, baby," I groan, just as she catches my bottom lip between her teeth, biting it and slowly releasing. A wicked smile illuminates her face. "Such a naughty girl you are...riding my dick so well..."

I slap her ass any time she moans. Her eyes are closed as she fucks me. Harder. Rougher. Deeper. Her need to come intensifies, just like mine. I'm barely holding back my release, but as soon as her body starts to tremble and her walls squeeze around my shaft, I let go too. Fuck, it feels incredible.

We kiss, prolonging the feeling of our orgasms. My hands caress her body as I slowly slide them up and down her sides. Piper is the first to lean away. She cups my face with her hands, her eyes searching mine. Her chest rises and falls as she continues to stare at me.

"What is it, baby? Tell me."

"Do you have more condoms with you? I want you again." I definitely have a little wild thing with a sex drive like mine.

"I have a few," I confirm, and her face lights up with a smile. "I've never been this hard after sex..."

She hops off my lap, takes off my condom, and tosses it aside, while I get a new one from my pocket. My hard dick is the only thing I'm going to take care of tonight. That and Piper.

Straddling me, Piper takes my cock inside her once again. And this time, I simply pull her in for a kiss and lose myself in her. The best fix to my fuckup...enjoying sex with someone I really like.

THIS MORNING, I leave my room after a knock on my door. Story is standing in front of me in the hallway. She's fully dressed and holding her backpack in her hands. I arch an eyebrow in question, and she sighs.

"Piper is asleep again."

"Meaning?" I crouch to her so I can look her in the eyes.

Story giggles, covering her mouth with her hand. "Piper woke me up, told me to get dressed and go to the kitchen for breakfast. The whole time I was eating, she was yawning and rubbing her eyes. I told her to go lie down and catch a few more minutes of sleep. And she did...she's still asleep."

I barely hide my smile. My chest is full of pride. I fucked her good last night, stretching her pussy and making her come over and over. Around four a.m., I took her to her bed, and since she usually wakes Story up at seven, she didn't get much sleep.

"Let's give your nanny a chance to rest, okay?" Story nods. "I'll take you to school, and Piper will pick you up. What do you think?"

"I think you're the best daddy in the world!"

I ruffle her hair and stand up. "Wait for me in the living room. I need five minutes to get dressed."

Story smiles and strolls away, humming some song under her breath. The grin I was trying to suppress blooms on my lips, and this time I don't hide it. She wanted me to make her pass out when I fucked her in the shower...well, I guess I succeeded last night on the terrace.

When I get home, I hear my parents' voices. My ears prick up, and my eyebrows rise to my hairline. I don't remember my mom telling me they were planning to visit.

I linger by the door to the living room. Mom and Dad are sitting on the couch while Story shows them something in one of her books. I clear my throat, and they all bring their gazes to me.

"We've been waiting for you for a while!" Dad exclaims with a smile on his face.

"If I knew you'd be here, I would've made sure to be home earlier." I shrug, adjusting my sports bag. "I hit the gym after practice. I have way too much energy."

"Yeah, it's our fault, we didn't warn you," Mom says softly, looking me up and down. "Story called...she wants to come over for a sleepover."

"And instead of calling me and asking, you decided to just show up?"

"I know, it sounds bad, but Story knows how to masterfully manipulate us. She wanted us here, and well...we're here." My mother gives me a smile. "Tomorrow is Saturday. Your big day. This way you'll have a chance to relax and prepare for the game. We'll bring Story to the stadium."

It's not a bad idea. If anything, the peace and quiet will do me a lot of good, and Story will get to spend time with her grandparents. Win-win.

"Okay, but we need to—"

"We already did." My dad points to a small bag sitting by the couch. "Piper helped us pack. She's in her room. I told her she could have the night off if Story comes to our place."

That, I don't like, but I keep silent. I don't want them to be suspicious. Because, indeed, if Story isn't here, why should Piper stay?

"Great," I say.

THE DOOR to Piper's room is open, so I stop in the doorframe. She's in her bed, hiding under a blanket with a book. I knock softly, and she finally notices me.

"Hey."

"Hey. Come on in." She puts her book on the covers. I come closer and lower myself onto her bed. "You let Story go to your parents'."

"I did. She'll have a great time with them, and they'll bring her to the game tomorrow." I give her a smile, and she smiles back. "Did you tell Riley she can come?"

"I did. She yelled so loud, I wanted to hang up on her."

I shake my head, examining her face. "How do you feel?"

"Now? Good. This morning? Or when I brought Story home? Not so good." Her eyes sparkle with mischief. "When I said I wanted you to make me pass out, I didn't mean it."

"That's your little price for five—"

"Six," Piper corrects me, giving me an eye roll.

"That's the price of six orgasms."

"You make it sound as if I was there alone," she huffs, crossing her arms over her chest.

"You definitely weren't," I murmur, leaning closer and cupping her face. "Have dinner with me."

Piper's eyes widen as she gawks at me. "Dinner with you?"

"Dinner and a movie. Unless you planned to go home?" I hold her gaze, my fingers caressing her cheek.

"Dinner and a movie sounds great."

"Amazing." I give her a quick kiss on her lips and stand up from her bed. "I need to take a shower, and then I'll meet you in the kitchen?"

"You bet," she says, picking up her book again. Smiling to myself, I head out of her room. Tonight is going to be amazing.

26
the thin line between swooning and horny

PIPER

NEVER, I REPEAT NEVER, HAS THERE BEEN A TIME I WASN'T able to walk after sex. There were days I felt a bit sore. Days when my legs were wobbly. I've experienced all that, and it never bothered me. It was something I could deal with. Until Hunter motherfucking Hale. The man knows how to fuck, how to make me pass out from pleasure.

Exiting my bedroom, I head to the kitchen. I'm wearing black leggings and a pastel pink tee, even if I felt tempted to put on something nicer. For him. Like it's a date. Apparently, being fucked so good has the power to make me brainless. I can only imagine the look on Hunter's face if he walked into the kitchen and saw me wearing my white floral dress. Our agreement would've ended right away, and I don't want that. I'm enjoying my time with him way too much.

I hear footsteps, and Hunter joins me in the kitchen. I turn my head to look at him, letting my gaze travel down his form. He's wearing a white T-shirt and his favorite gray sweatpants. His hair is still wet, and I instantly regret not joining him in the shower.

Are you out of your damn mind, Piper? You can barely fucking walk. Don't even think about sex with him!

Great. Now even my inner voice is giving me orders.

I blink and focus my attention on him. "What should we eat?" I ask.

"You love pizza," Hunter says softly, stepping closer and hovering over me. I nod, looking up at him. "I already ordered your favorite, with mushrooms, Parmesan, and oregano. It should be here soon."

"Thank you," I whisper. He saw me eat pizza once, and he heard me talking about my favorite toppings...only fucking once. What's going on? "What did you order for yourself?"

"Pepperoni." He shrugs, edging to the fridge and taking out the apple juice. He only has time to set it on the kitchen counter before the doorbell rings. "Must be our pizza."

Ten minutes later, Hunter and I are sitting on the couch in the living room. Two pizza boxes are on the table, along with a glass of apple juice for Hunter and a glass of white wine for me. It feels so surreal, I want to pinch myself. What if this is all a dream and I'm still sleeping?

"What do you want to watch?" he asks, picking up the remote.

"I don't know. The last few months, I've only been watching Disney with Story."

Hunter chuckles, looking for something on the TV screen. I watch him, admiring every little detail of his face. He has a strong, sharp jawline and a straight nose. His lips are full, and I'll be damned if I say I don't enjoy kissing them. His usual stubble is shorter now, and there are freckles on his tanned skin. Which isn't surprising because of all the time he spends under the sun. He's fucking gorgeous, and his perfect body makes him absolutely unattainable. And yet...he's here with me, eating pizza and serving me wine. I'm pleasantly surprised to see this side of him. Usually, he's only like this with Story.

"Okay, we're going to watch *Lupin*." Hunter catches me staring at him. "Or you can continue watching me. Though I promise, this show is way better."

"So far, you've yet to disappoint me," I murmur, leaning forward and picking up my glass of wine. He keeps his gaze trained on me, smiling like the Cheshire cat, and then he focuses his attention on the TV screen.

And my ovaries are thankful...because it feels like I'm losing my mind when he's around.

TWO EPISODES LATER, I'm far from sober. This show is fantastic. Omar Sy makes it incredibly easy to fall in love with his character. His reactions are honest; I can feel every little emotion he's showing. Add in a gripping plot, and this is a real cocktail recipe for a successful show. Speaking of cocktails...

"Mind pouring me some wine?" I focus on Hunter's face as he starts the third episode. He glances at me and shakes his head. I knit my brows together. "Why not?"

"Because there's nothing left in the bottle," he snorts and pulls me closer, snaking a hand around my shoulders. "Plus, someone is already tipsy."

"You don't like me tipsy?" I ask, snuggling closer to him, not giving a damn about the wine or anything else.

"I like you tipsy when you're here with me, because I know nothing bad will happen to you. But I'm not a fan of anyone getting drunk in public. There are way too many bad people with sick intentions."

"Aw, you're so sweet," I purr, looking up at him. "You shouldn't worry about me. I know how to stand up for myself. Mom's string of boyfriends didn't really leave me any choice."

I don't even realize what I've said till I see his eyes darken and his smile slowly dissolve. "Your mom's string of boyfriends...did someone hurt you?"

"Hurt me?" I mumble.

"That's what I asked." His voice becomes chilly; his demand is noticeable. "Did someone hurt you?"

"No." I push myself away from him, all my playfulness disappearing. "All that is just my past."

"I've been taught that if you don't want to talk about what traumatized you, it means you're still holding on to the pain. It means you're far from moving on. It means the trauma still has power over your life and your actions. It means you live in fear," Hunter says harshly, and I feel angry tears form in my eyes. "Did someone hurt you, Piper?"

I take my phone from the couch and jump to my feet, grabbing my empty pizza box and wineglass from the table, and only then do I peer at him. "Thank you for dinner, Hunter."

Whirling around, I storm to the kitchen. I want to be back in my room, to hide under my goddamn blanket and just stay there till it's time to wake up. *That, Piper Meadow Evans, is exactly what happens when you don't watch your mouth.*

The empty box lands in the trash can, and I put my phone on the counter. I only have time to set my glass in the sink before I hear his footsteps behind me. I tense up; my muscles are so tight it's painful. Slowly, I lock eyes with Hunter. The sounds of the TV reach my ears, but it feels like I'm underwater.

I take a few steps forward, intending to leave the kitchen, but he blocks my way. His arms wrap around my waist, and before I know it, I'm sitting on the kitchen counter. He doesn't let go of me, just holds me firmly in place and stares me right in the eyes.

"Don't shut me out."

"Don't ask questions I don't want to answer," I counter, and I see the corners of his lips twitch into a smile. "No one hurt me, but my childhood was far from perfect. I'd prefer to forget about it."

"I want you to open up to me because I think it'll help you, not because I'm prying, Piper."

"I know," I sigh, as he glides his hands over my thighs.

"Then you should open up to me. Maybe not today, but at some point."

My poor damn pussy...it's fucking dripping already. Again. This man is dead set on sending me into orgasmic oblivion with his words

162

and his care. There's a very thin line between swooning and horny. I went from one to the other in a nanosecond.

"I will." I grip his tee in my hands and help him take it off. Roaming my hands over his broad shoulders and sculpted chest, I feel his every muscle, and my nipples pucker. He's so goddamn fine. "I want your cock inside me so much."

"I need you at my game, Piper. I don't want you to be in bed all day again," he murmurs, sneaking his hands under my tee and cupping my breasts. "Fuck, baby, your tits feel so perfect."

"Hunter..." I moan his name as his mouth lands on my neck, caressing it with his soft lips and his tongue. "Fuck me now. Please."

He groans when I lock my legs around his back, pressing my drenched pussy to his groin. His nostrils flare as the remains of his resistance leave his body. In the blink of an eye, he steps back and yanks off my leggings. He tosses them aside and pulls me to my feet. I don't ask questions, just let him take the lead, enjoying everything he's doing to me.

Hunter turns me around and pushes me facedown onto the kitchen countertop, pressing his hard-on against my ass. He gets rid of his shorts, sheaths his cock in a condom, and a moment later, he's deep inside me. I whimper, gripping the countertop. He's still fucking huge, and I'm still fucking sore. But I'm here for it. One hundred percent. The pleasure he gives me makes it all better.

"I've been thinking about your sweet pussy all day...I was pretty sure you'd had enough of me for a while," he growls, ramming into me from behind. "And look at you now –begging me to fuck you, bent over my fucking countertop, taking me fully...covering my dick with your juices..."

I close my eyes. The feeling of immense pleasure spreads through my veins and goes straight to my lower abdomen. Hunter grabs my hands and locks them behind my back with his hand. I stand on my tiptoes, because each time he slides deeper, I moan, unable to stand still. My hair falls in my eyes and sticks to my sweaty forehead. The sloppy sounds of our bodies joining together are the only thing I hear, and they make me a thousand times more sensitive. I'll be coming in no time, and he knows it.

"You're going to hold your orgasm, Piper." His fingers dig into my skin as a loud growl leaves his lips. "Do you hear me?"

"Yes." I'm breathless. My puckered nipples are rubbing against the kitchen counter, adding even more friction. My blurry vision makes it hard to concentrate.

The ringing of my phone comes so suddenly, we both freeze. I know that ringtone.

"It's your brother," I whisper.

"He probably knows you weren't feeling well and wants to check on you." Hunter slowly picks up the pace again, while my phone continues to buzz. Over and over and over.

"He won't stop calling until I answer," I mutter between two loud moans.

"Damn him." Hunter curses and reaches over to my phone. I expect him to give it to me, but I'm wrong. He presses my phone to his ear and answers without pulling out of me for even a second.

"Hey, Hayden. Yeah, she wasn't feeling well...Uh-huh...When Mom and Dad left, I went to check on her, and she was already asleep. Yeah...I decided not to wake her up...her presence doesn't...dammit..."

Hunter growls, feeling my walls squeeze his dick. My body spasms, and I clamp a hand over my mouth. I just came, listening to my boss talking to my best friend on my fucking phone.

"Sorry, I'm watching the La Liga game...and it's not good. Um, shit...her phone was in the kitchen...I heard it and decided to come... fuck!"

He slams his hips into mine at his own release, then continues pushing his length inside me, drawing out my orgasm.

"Sorry, Hayden...this game is fucking intense. I came into the kitchen, saw your phone number, and decided to answer...yeah, you can come over tomorrow morning. I'm sure she will be happy to see you...thanks, you too...bye."

He ends the call and tosses my phone onto the kitchen counter, then pulls out. I slowly turn around. My legs are wobbly, and my breathing is ragged.

"I don't remember telling you that you could come," he lectures me.

"You were too busy talking to your brother," I sass back, and he narrows his eyes. I'm playing a dangerous game...but I'm loving every second of it.

Hunter invades my personal space and puts his palm on my throat. He brings his lips to mine, and I feel my pussy twitch.

"Get your clothes. Go to your bedroom and wait for me on your fucking bed...with your legs spread wide and your fingers playing with your clit. I'm going to lick you dry, Piper." He slaps my tit, and I yelp, hissing between my teeth. "You have ten minutes."

He lets go of me and steps back. I bend down to take my clothes from the floor, and he slaps my ass hard. "For motivation."

"Asshole," I mutter and stomp out of the kitchen. The only thing I want is to be exactly where he told me to be: on my bed, with his head between my legs. He's my fucking addiction.

27
bonfire of jealousy

HUNTER

THE FIRST THING I SEE WHEN I OPEN MY EYES IS PIPER. OUR foreheads are almost touching. My hand is wrapped around her shoulder, keeping her close to my chest. My gaze roams over her face, taking in every little detail, and a smile crosses my lips. She's stunning, but what's more, she's incredibly sweet and kind. A real gem of a woman.

She stirs in her sleep, and I pull her closer to me. Hiding my nose in her hair, I inhale the sweet aroma of her shampoo. I don't want to leave this bed at all. Her skin is soft and warm, and I slowly let my hands travel down her sides. I could spend the entire day touching her, and it wouldn't be enough. She's like the most forbidden fruit, one I crave with all my soul. One I can't stay away from.

"We broke our rule." A quiet whisper brings me back to reality, and I focus my gaze on Piper. Her deep brown eyes are sleepy as she stares at me from under thick eyelashes.

I smirk, instantly realizing she's right. Last night, after I kept my promise and made her come all over my face and tongue, I told her we should get some sleep. Today is game day, and I needed to make sure I got enough sleep. I was going to leave her bed as soon as she fell asleep, but I ended up staying all night.

"We did. Do you regret it?"

"Are you joking?" She smiles, hiding her face in the crook of my neck. "I slept like a baby."

"Because I was here, or because I wore you out?" Hearing my question, Piper leans away and peers at me.

"Both."

I cup her cheek with my palm and bring my lips closer, kissing her sweetly. It feels blissful, slow, and erotic. There is no roughness, no desire to possess each other. It's aftercare, and I'm here for it. We kiss and kiss, and she slowly hooks her leg over my hip and straddles me, making me roll onto my back. She's completely naked, and my mouth instantly waters. Her round breasts are fucking perfection.

"What are your plans for tomorrow?" I ask when she places her hands on my chest.

"I'm going to go home tonight, because I promised to spend time with Riley," Piper murmurs, sliding her hands over my chest and caressing my skin. "I also have plans to hang out with Hade and the guys from the band. I want to introduce someone to Bo. Hopefully they'll be a match."

Bo? As in Hayden's drummer? The guy who left a hickey on her neck? Hell nah. I don't like that one bit.

"Doesn't he have a crush on you?" I ask.

Piper blinks, and her lips break into a smile. "Are you jealous?"

Instead of answering, I palm her tits and squeeze her nipples between my fingers. She moans, and her head tips back.

"Possessive. I don't like sharing what's mine."

"And I'm yours?" she whispers. I push myself to sit up, winding my hands around her waist. I take her nipple into my mouth and suck, drawing another loud moan from her parted lips.

"You sure are, Piper, and you better remember it."

Her hands fly to my head, and she hides her fingers in my hair while I swirl my tongue over her nipple. Her pussy is dripping as she rotates her hips, gliding it over my hard-on. Dammit, I need a fucking cold shower. Sometimes my rule—no sex before the game—sucks. But I'm not going to break it. I'll be too lazy if all my needs are satisfied, and today's game is more important than anything else.

She bends her head for a kiss, and at that moment the doorbell rings. Pure panic crosses her features as she scatters off my legs.

"It must be Hayden," Piper drawls.

Rolling my eyes, I stand up from her bed, quickly pull on my sweatpants, and grab my T-shirt from the floor. I glance at her over my shoulder. "Get dressed. I've got this."

I put on my tee on my way to the front door. I open it wide and see Hayden standing in front of me. A crooked smile plays on his lips as our eyes meet.

"I would've let myself in, but I forgot my keys at home," he says instead of a greeting. "Were you still in bed?"

"Good morning to you too, brother," I huff, stepping aside and letting him in. "I didn't think you'd be here so early."

Hayden halts in his tracks and gawks at me. "It's almost eleven."

"I know." *I don't.* "Well, I think Piper's still asleep. At least, I haven't seen her yet."

His face darkens. "Is she okay? Story told me Pip could barely walk yesterday."

"She didn't feel well, but hopefully she'll be okay today." I lift my eyebrow. "Do you want some coffee?"

"Definitely," he says with a smile, and we head into the kitchen.

HAYDEN and I are sitting at the table, drinking coffee and chatting about his classes, the band's rehearsals, and their upcoming shows. He asked me what game I was watching yesterday, and the only reason I didn't screw up was because of my love for Real Madrid. I know their schedule by heart, even when I don't watch them play. I also mentally pat myself on the back for cleaning up last night. He'll never know Piper and I watched something together.

Just as that thought crosses my mind, Piper slowly walks into the kitchen. She's wearing cotton shorts and a beige-pink tee, with her hair collected into a high ponytail. Cute and simple. Yet I want to see a different side of her. I want to see her dressed up...for me.

"Hayden?" She feigns surprise, coming closer and plopping down onto the chair next to my brother. "I didn't know you were coming by."

"If you weren't already asleep when I called, you would've known I was coming to check on you." Hayden slings a hand over her shoulders, pulling her to him for a kiss on her temple. "How do you feel?"

"Better," she murmurs, her gaze swimming to me for a brief moment. "I haven't slept that well in months."

"Good to know," he chuckles and moves away from her as I release the breath I was holding. "Thank God Hunter answered your phone yesterday, because I was gonna come over if I didn't hear from you. I was worried."

"Aw, you're too sweet," Piper says softly. "I was just exhausted, but I'm good now."

Another thirty minutes go by, and I go to my room. I need to take a shower and collect my things before I leave for the stadium. We already agreed Piper and Hayden will come to the game with Riley, and my parents will bring Story. I'm excited about today's match...but I'm buzzing when I think about the smile that will be on Story's face if our team wins. It'll be the highlight of my day for sure.

IT's the last twenty minutes of the second half, and it's tied. Two to two. My breathing is ragged; sweat drips down my forehead. I'm fucking furious. I scored ten minutes ago, but a lengthy VAR check adjudged me offside. Dammit. I want to win this game without it ending up in a penalty shootout.

I lick my lips and look up at the sky. This little pause is good for my nerves; I can start to calm my breathing. Every sport can be rough, and football isn't an exception. Our center back collided with the Nashville winger, who wanted to pass the ball. His leg connected with the winger's knee and it drew a gasp from the crowd when he fell, grasping his leg in pain. Thankfully, it wasn't serious, but we've still got at least a five-minute break. I'll need to use it to our advantage, because I don't want to let Story down. I promised her I'd do everything I could to win this game.

When the match resumes, Nashville's players attack. Their desire to win is just as strong as ours. No one wants to leave the pitch a loser. I keep my eye on the game, calculating chances to get the ball. And I finally see one.

It's a mistake young players often make. Sometimes, driven by their ego, they totally forget that football is a team sport. No one can play all positions. Eleven players should form a united whole, where every person knows what to do and is willing to assist any chance they get. That's how any team sport goes. Someone might be a fucking star who scores impossible goals, but once they forget there are other players on the team, they're doomed. If someone scores eight goals all by themselves, no one on their team will be happy for them. They'll think that person is a self-centered jerk.

I rush forward, stealing the ball from Nashville's forward and hurrying away from him. Jenner, our attacking midfielder, joins me, and I pass him the ball. It's the shortest exchange, and we are both running for our lives toward our opponent's net. I don't care if it's me or Jenner who scores—I just want LACFC to win. We see the opportunity, but then Nashville's fullback tries to steal the ball away from Jenner. A moment later, the ball lands right in front of me, and I go for it, kicking it into the low right corner of the net. Three–two.

My eyes land on Story as I run to the stands. She's jumping in the air with the biggest grin on her face. My teammates are running in my direction, so while I have time, I form a little heart with my fingers and show it to Story. There's no one in the world I love more than her. She's my everything, and that goal was for her. Only for her.

WHEN I HEAR the whistle that indicates the end of the game, I slump onto my ass and sit on the pitch. Not for long, because the guys quickly tackle me, celebrating our win. We won the Supporters' Shield today. The level of satisfaction I feel is enormous. Yes, we still have playoffs, but today—we're winners. We fucking did it.

The next forty minutes are a whirlwind. I spend about ten minutes answering reporters' questions and taking pictures. When I'm finally on my way to join my family, who are waiting for me at the edge of the pitch, Autumn Dunn stops right in front of me.

"Mr. Hale, do you have a moment?" She shoves her microphone in my face. "It won't take more than two minutes."

I glance over her shoulder, looking straight into the camera, and then I return my gaze to her. "Let's make it quick, Ms. Dunn."

"This was your first full game for LACFC, and, not surprisingly, you won. How do you feel about your time on the field?"

"I have the best teammates, and the level of understanding Coach was able to create between us is admirable. We did everything in our power to win, and now we're going into the playoffs as the Supporters' Shield winners."

"You were brilliant on the field, and your last goal was a masterpiece." She smiles, shifting a little. "Who did you dedicate it to? I think we all saw a little heart—"

"To my daughter. All my goals are dedicated to her. Just like the number on my jersey."

"Aw, that's very sweet of you." She bats her eyelashes at me, and I roll my eyes. I'm not subtle at all, but I don't care. "Thank you for your time, Mr. Hale. See you."

"Thanks. Bye." I skirt her and head to my family. When I'm almost there, I hear someone running after me. I look back and notice Vavro. He smiles as he lines up with me. "You did a great job, Marek."

"*You* did a great job, pushing my buttons and helping me improve my game." He nudges me with his shoulder. "You destroyed me during that practice, and I was hell-bent on not repeating that ever again. Thank you for that."

"Any time," I tell him, and he laughs.

"I hope the fuck not! I won't survive humiliation like that again, especially in front of my teammates." He sneaks a glance at me, eyeing me with curiosity. "I know it's early and we still have playoffs to win, but do you have any plans for the break before next season starts?"

Opening my school. But I don't say that aloud, just talk about my plans to go on vacation with Story. I haven't decided where yet. I just know I want to go somewhere with her...and maybe Piper. That way, my vacation will be a ten out of ten.

"Who is that?" Vavro asks as we reach the edge of the pitch.

"Who?"

"The girl near Story. Who is she?" I focus my gaze on Piper, and I instantly know my wish from this morning—to see her dressed up for me—has become a reality. Her white floral dress ends just above her knees, paired with high-heeled lavender sandals, and her long blond hair cascading down her shoulders makes her look absolutely stunning.

"That's Piper. She's Story's nanny."

Marek halts in his tracks and gapes at me. "Are you fucking serious?"

"Yeah, she's my brother's best friend. I've known her for years. What's wrong with that?"

"What's wrong with that?" He laughs, shaking his head and resuming his walk. "You have a gorgeous girl staying in your house, and it's the first time I've seen her! Is she single?"

Can I get away with punching him? Because my fucking knuckles are itching. She's mine. M-I-N-E, dammit. "She's my employee, Vavro. I have no clue what she does in her free time."

The lopsided grin on his face makes my eye twitch.

"Maybe soon her free time will be filled with me." He winks at me and hurries toward my family.

I ball my fists, following him with a forced smile on my face. Just this morning, my brother pissed me off with his touchy-feely attitude toward her, forming a fire in my chest. Now, seeing Vavro's gaze focused on Piper has turned that into a bonfire...a bonfire of fucking jealousy. She better not flirt back, I swear.

28
girl on fire

PIPER

"SOCCER IS MY NEW FAVORITE SPORT. IT'S JUST...IT'S SO, SO good. All the emotions, all the action. Everything," Riley murmurs, a dreamy smile on her face.

"And yet you never wanted to watch it with us before. What changed?" Hayden asks Riley as we wait for Hunter to join us at the edge of the field.

"It feels different when you're actually at the stadium. This atmosphere is contagious!" she exclaims. Thank God her crush on Hayden is over. It was ridiculous that she'd barely speak in his presence. She got over it pretty quickly, but he will always be her first unrequited love. Such an accomplishment. "Plus, Hunter is amazeballs."

Hade blinks and glances at me, knitting his brows together. I'll let him figure out on his own that Riley has a crush on his brother now. She told me the other day that she'd love for me to meet a man like Mr. Hale, because apparently men who love their kids are real husband material. I have no idea where it came from, but I agree. The way he loves Story? It's on another level.

Though waking up in bed with him, being pressed to his solid chest after he took care of my needs and lulled me to sleep by telling me about his years in Spain and in England...it feels like more than we agreed on. It feels deeper, more intimate, and it's starting to bother me a little. Not because I don't like it, but because I'm afraid I'm going to fall for him. This shit is scary, and I've yet to figure out how to stop it.

"I thought we were going to wait for Hunter in the locker room," Riley says, and I focus my attention on her.

Loud, uncontrollable cackles burst out of Hayden's mouth. "You're hilarious," he says between fits of laughter.

"What did I say? What's so funny?" She frowns.

"Who on Earth would let anyone inside the locker room? It's a freaking locker room. People get naked and—"

"Ew!" Riley slaps his hand and scrunches her nose in annoyance. "Can we not talk about naked men? I'm still a kid."

"I thought you were wiser now, *kid*," Hade teases, and her cheeks turn red.

I look away and notice Autumn Dunn approaching Hunter. Unease instantly worms its way into my veins, and Hayden and Riley's banter turns into white noise.

Their exchange is brief, and when he walks away she doesn't stay to watch him, just heads in the opposite direction with a cameraman in tow. I don't trust her, so I decide to keep my distance from Hunter and be incredibly polite and professional when others are around. I don't want anyone to think there's anything between us. I'm just his daughter's nanny, and he's my boss.

A player sidles up to Hunter, and they stroll toward us. I think the guy is LACFC's goalkeeper, but I'm not sure. A warm palm slips into my hand, and I look down to notice Story. She's beaming, and I can't help but smile back.

"Are you happy your daddy won?" I ask.

"Yes." She leans against me, pressing herself closer. "I was so nervous, and then he scored, and then his little heart...he did it for me because he promised to win this game."

"Your dad knows how to keep his promises," I tell her, thinking back to his promise to me. *Oh God*. I need to stop daydreaming about him all the damn time. A day off is exactly what I need to clear my head. "And I think you should tell him you want a cat."

"My birthday isn't until December, but you're right. I'll talk to him tonight," Story states, and I chuckle. The girl really knows how to get what she wants from her parents. "I can't wait for you to meet my mom. She's going to love you."

I highly doubt it. "I hope so."

Just then, someone stops in front of us, and I look up to meet a pair of crystal blue eyes. I blink. The intensity of his gaze sends shivers down my spine. He flashes me a lopsided grin and then crouches to Story. "Hey, little munchkin. How have you been?"

"Marek!" Story yelps, letting go of my hand and throwing herself at him. He catches her in his arms and stands up, whirling her around and making her giggle. Who is he? I shift my gaze and see Hunter talking to Hayden and his parents. Riley is sitting on the field, typing something on her phone. I look back at Story and this LACFC player just as he puts her on the ground. "You were amazing on the field."

"I could've done better." He taps his finger on her nose, sneaking a glance in my direction. Involuntary, my lips stretch into a smile. Well, he's kinda cute. "The second goal was totally my fault."

"No it was not." She stomps her foot on the ground and crosses her arms over her chest. "Dad always says that football is a team sport, and it's not your fault your teammates failed to stop your opponent."

"Your dad knows what he's talking about," he says. Then he looks at me. "Hey. I didn't see you here last game, so I thought I should take the chance and introduce myself. I'm Marek."

"It's nice to meet you, Marek. I'm Piper."

"She's my nanny." Story comes up to me and takes my hand in hers again. "And my best friend."

"You have a very beautiful best friend, Story." *Why the hell does my neck feel hot?* "Any chance—"

"You know, Marek, I don't think it's nice of you to hit on my nanny right in front of me." I've forgotten how to breathe and will die from lack of air in my lungs. This can't be happening. Did she really just say that? "Is that why you decided to talk to me?"

"No, of course not." *Very convincing, Marek. Try again.* "I'm just—"

"Is everything okay?" Hunter's deep voice goes from my ears to my toes, setting my body on fire.

"Marek tried to flirt with Piper." Story pouts, looking her dad in the eyes.

He shoots me a quick glance and kneels to her. "They both are adults, sweetie."

Excuse me? Here I am thinking he'd be jealous, but instead he says that? Ha! *Mr. Hale, you clearly have no idea who you're dealing with.*

"Your dad is right, Story. There's nothing wrong with Marek talking to me." I meet his gaze for a moment. His expression darkens instantly, and then he looks at Story. "Just...he shouldn't have made it so blatantly obvious."

"Sorry, Story, honestly," Marek mutters hoarsely. "I shouldn't have flirted with Piper when you were here. It was wrong of me. Sorry, Hunter."

"That's okay." Hunter bends down and takes Story in his arms. He bores his gaze into mine, looking expectant. "I'll go change, and then we're heading home. Do you need to get anything from your room, or are you planning to go straight home?"

"Hayden promised to give me and Riley a ride, so..." I hold his gaze and then sneak a glance in Marek's direction. Purposefully. It doesn't go unnoticed by Hunter. He narrows his eyes on me, clenching his jaw. "I'll be back on Monday morning, just like we agreed."

"Great," Hunter bites out. Then he shifts his gaze to his teammate and nods. Looking visibly pissed, he stomps away from us. *Well, Mr. Hale, this is all your fault. You should think more carefully about your words next time. This is just a little payback.*

I chat with Marek for a few more minutes but don't tell him anything personal. I joke around, and he shakes his head when he realizes I'm not going to give him my phone number.

"Hope to see you around," he tells me, stepping aside.

"You too." I smile and wave. "Bye, Marek."

"Bye, Piper," he says and heads into the locker room.

I watch him go, then edge to my sister. "Ready to go home?"

"Definitely." She stands up, and we saunter to the exit. I know we won't leave till Hunter comes out, so I'll have a chance to say bye to Story and her grandparents. Maybe her father too, but only if I feel like it.

I'M LYING on my bed with Riley. We're watching *Hocus Pocus*, eating gummy bears, and talking about her classes, her little dates with Josh, and my time with Story. I feel content and joyful. The atmosphere in this house is completely different from the way it was before. Wade makes our mom happy, and when she's happy...this place blossoms.

"Do you want something to drink?" Riley asks, standing up from my bed. I shake my head, and she pauses the movie on my laptop. I roll my eyes and watch her walk out of my room.

My phone buzzes. The second I see Hunter's name, my heartbeat accelerates. He didn't even look at me when we were leaving, only saying good-bye to Riley. What made him change his mind?

HUNTER HALE:

I've been thinking about going somewhere with Story once the playoffs are over.

ME:

Are you giving me a heads-up about days off? Isn't it too early?

HUNTER HALE:

No, I'm telling you to start thinking about what to pack.

He can't be serious, can he?

HUNTER HALE:

We're going to Spain, by the way.

By the way? Does he want me dead? I'm going to have a heart attack at twenty years old because of this man.

ME:

I thought you were angry with me.

HUNTER HALE:

I am.

I watch the three dots on my screen with my jaw hanging open. I didn't expect him to admit being jealous so quickly, but lately he's been full of surprises. And I'm all for it.

HUNTER HALE:

We'll discuss your punishment once you're back here on Monday. Brats like you deserve to be spanked.

I suck in a breath as Riley enters the room. Monday can't come soon enough.

29

simple intimacy

HUNTER

I'M SITTING IN THE LIVING ROOM WITH MY LAPTOP ON THE coffee table, staring at the screen without seeing anything. This isn't what I want. I'd hoped to open my school in January. Yet now my lawyer is telling me it can't happen any earlier than February. It's messing up all my plans and will make it almost impossible to do everything on time. I'm screwed.

I reach across the table, close my laptop, and lean back against the couch, shutting my eyes. I didn't sleep well last night, and I feel exhausted. And also incredibly stressed. I have no idea what I can do to make the process move along any faster. Or if I should do anything at all. Opening in February, three weeks before the first game of the season, when I'll be busy with constant practices? I wouldn't be able to dedicate even a single day to my school. It'd look like a half-assed attempt to do something great, while in reality it'd be absolute shit. Not how I envisioned it at all.

The sound of the door closing helps me find my way out of my thoughts. I open my eyes and sit up, anticipating seeing her for the first time since Friday. Without her, something is missing. She brings life to this house. Her sunshiny personality and her warmth fill even the darkest corners. I've never experienced anything like that at home, and it feels good. So good I don't even want her to leave on her days off. I want her to be here all the time...and it's the complete opposite of what I had in mind when we agreed on a casual relationship. A real recipe for disaster.

I hear her footsteps, and the next thing I know, our eyes meet. Her face lights up with a smile as she tucks strands of her hair behind her ears. "Hey, you."

"Hey." My gaze roams over her face and down her body. She's makeup free, and her long hair cascades down her shoulders. Her white dress with pink flowers accentuates every line of her perfect body, showing off her narrow waist. It ends just above her knees, making her legs look long. Piper is one of the most beautiful women I've ever seen in my life. It's effortless; it's just how she is. "How are you?"

"Good," she answers, sashaying into the room and stopping near the couch. I extend my hand to her, and she takes it, letting me haul her onto my lap. Her hands are on my shoulders, and I wrap my arms around her waist. I crack a smile, noticing a playful glint in her eyes. "How have you been?"

"I don't know. Everything is fine, but..." I look away, scrunching my nose. "It's nothing."

"It doesn't seem like nothing. Is there anything I can help you with?"

It might be nice to talk about my problems, especially to someone who won't judge me. "I got some news from my lawyer, and I feel lost."

"What happened?"

"I wanted to open a school for kids. To teach them to play football. To share my knowledge and encourage more people to fall in love with the game." I sigh, tightening my grip on her waist. "I've been super excited about it, and I'd hoped to use my break to prepare. Now? The timing sucks. I won't be able to do anything myself, and I hate it. There are basically two options. Either I proceed with my plan and open the school, hire people who will help me do things right...or

I postpone it, deal with everything without any rush, and open the school next year."

"I thought LACFC had their own academy." I nod, confirming her words. She's silent for a moment, and then she tilts her head. "If you want to coach kids, why don't you talk to them?"

"Because I want something of my own."

"I get it, but what if you use this setback in your favor? What if, instead of rushing things and letting someone else take your place, you coach kids at the LACFC Academy? In the meantime, you can get ready to open your own school, but without any stress. You can make sure everything is exactly how you want it." She speaks softly, her hands working magic on my shoulders. Why is she so fucking good at everything? "Right now, everyone sees you as a soccer legend, a great player. But do they know anything about Coach Hunter Hale? I highly doubt it."

"You kinda just boosted my ego and crushed it at the same time," I tell her, and she laughs heartily, adding more pressure as she continues to massage my shoulders.

"Sorry." Piper presses her forehead to mine, and my skin flames up in an instant. "I'm not an expert, obviously, but since I started working for you, I've gotten to know more about soccer. Not every great player can be a great coach, and not every great coach is a great player. The only one I can think of right now is Zinedine Zidane, but that's just because you talked my ear off with your stories about Real."

"Guilty," I breathe, my palms sliding down her hips. "What exactly do you think I should do?"

She sits up straight, putting her hands on my chest. "I think you should start by talking to LACFC to see if they're interested. You should be honest with them, don't hide the fact that you're planning to open your own school next year. Who knows, maybe they'll be interested in a collaboration? You'd be teaching younger kids, and they can go to their academy later. If they're talented enough, of course."

I blink. My head is spinning. "Can I say it again? I fucking love your brain."

"I love it when you praise me," Piper murmurs, her gaze darkening. "Makes me feel special."

"You are special." My voice is hoarse as I roughly grab the back of her neck. I bring our lips closer, kissing her. It's a knock-me-off-my-feet type of kiss, one that makes me lose my mind and forget where I am. Nothing matters except the person in my arms, except her lips moving with mine, except the emotions the kiss brings. Sometimes simple intimacy is the only thing I need to make me feel alive. "Wanna take a bath with me?"

"I need to pick up Story from school," she moans as I nibble on her skin.

"Not for three more hours. We have time."

"What about my punishment?" Piper wiggles on my lap, making me groan in her ear. She'll be the death of me, no fucking doubt.

"Tonight." My answer is curt as she leans away, her eyes sweeping over my face. "My mom is taking Story to the hairdresser, and they told me they want another sleepover. She'll go to school from my parents' house tomorrow." I take her with me as I stand up from the couch, and she locks her legs behind my back. "I was supposed to tell you not to come home today, but I'm too selfish for that. I hope you don't mind."

"Never," she whispers as I carry her upstairs.

"THAT'S GREAT," I tell my mom, pressing my phone to my ear. Standing in the kitchen with a steaming mug of coffee, I stare out the window. "The most important thing is she's happy with her new haircut."

"She's very happy. I'm sure you're going to like it too." Mom laughs, and I hear Story's excited chatter in the background. "She's talking to Amelia now. Your ex-wife is trying to figure out what to buy Story for her birthday."

"Story wants a cat," I mutter, taking a sip of my coffee. To say I was surprised when she told me that is an understatement. I have nothing against cats or dogs. I've just never had one, and I have no idea what to do with them. It's a whole new territory for me, and I'm as excited as I am scared.

"She wants a cat from you." Mom chuckles lightly. "I'm afraid if Amelia also gets her one, it'll drive you up the wall."

"I'm not that hopeless."

"You're not, sweetie. Plus, you have Piper, and I'm sure she'll be happy to help you. Speaking of which..." I pinch my brows together, setting my mug on the counter. "How come Amelia has never talked to Piper? I was sure you introduced them when you hired her."

I snicker, and my head tips back as I laugh. "Mom, I would've introduced them if my ex were interested in getting to know Story's nanny. All she wants to know is that she's treating Story right, nothing else."

"What can I say? Amelia never ceases to amaze me." Mom sighs. "Any fun plans for tonight?"

Fuck Piper till she passes out. "Not really. It's been a long day, and I just want to watch something and go to bed."

"Hunter, do you know why I've been having Story over so often?" The change in her tone is noticeable, and I frown.

"Because you want to spend more time with your granddaughter?" I ask, picking up my mug and taking a sip.

Mom laughs, and my lips break into a lopsided grin. I'm sure there's more to her logic than that, but it's fun to tease her. "That too, obviously. But I also want you to start living again. To go places, meet someone new, go on a date."

"Are you talking to my dad?" Story's voice rings out so suddenly, I choke on my coffee.

"Yes, honey. Why? Are you done talking to your mom?"

"Yes. Mom had to go," Story states, and I listen carefully. "And my dad doesn't need to go on a date. He already has everything he needs at home."

Right as she says it, Piper strolls into the kitchen, holding a box of donuts and a bottle of wine.

My mom says, "Sweetie, I'm sure—"

"My dad has Piper and me, and he doesn't need to go on a date."

"Aw, sweetheart, Piper is your nanny. She can't be your dad's girlfriend."

"I never said she could be his girlfriend, Granny." Is Story scolding my mom? It definitely feels like it. "You just don't get it."

"Mom?" I say, holding Piper's gaze. She sets the donuts and the wine on the counter and steps closer to me.

"Yes?"

"Can you please stop talking about my love life with my daughter? I don't appreciate it."

"Yes, sorry. It kinda got out of hand. I'll take her to school tomorrow morning, and then Piper can pick her up. Can you please call her? Or should I?" My mom's voice is uncertain. I'm sure Story's words destabilized her. Just like they did me.

"I'll tell her, don't worry." I put my mug on the counter and hook my hand around Piper's waist, pulling her to me. She smiles, pressing her hands to my chest.

"Good. Bye, Hunter."

"Bye, Mom."

I end the call and slide my phone into my pocket, holding Piper's gaze. She left right after she brought Story to her grandparents', saying she was happy to have another night off. I almost believed her...but I was sure she was craving my cock, the same way I want her pussy. My insatiable desire to have her has become hard to ignore. Not that I really try.

Piper is wearing yet another dress, but this one is way more revealing. A classic little black dress, and she's nailing it like the beauty she is. She collected her hair into a high ponytail, moistened her lips with some glossy lip balm, and added mascara to her eyelashes. She's all dressed up and just for me.

"Donuts and wine?"

"I wanted something sweet and something to drink." She nuzzles her nose in my neck, and I close my eyes, enjoying the feeling. "Will you drink with me?"

"You want me tipsy?" I joke as she sucks hard on my skin. Digging my fingers in her waist, I hiss through my teeth.

"I want you naked and balls deep inside me," Piper purrs, and my dick comes to life, wanting nothing more than to obey her. "And I want you to fulfill your promise...and punish me for my behavior."

"Oh, I will. Don't you worry." I spin her around, her back colliding with my chest. Pushing away her hair, I kiss her bare shoulder, feeling her tremble in my arms. "You'll be wetting my dick in no time, taking me in your tight pussy. But first..."

"Yeah?" A breathless whisper comes out of her mouth, and I smile.

"We're going to have dinner, drink wine, and watch something together." I sink my teeth into her collarbone, biting her slightly and drawing another moan out of her parted lips. "And then we'll go to my room, where you'll take off your clothes and prove to me what a good girl you are...always obedient and ready to do as I say."

"Oh God, yes..." She presses her butt to my groin, and I cup her breasts with my hands. *So fucking full.* "I'll do anything you want."

I smirk and lightly push her away, slapping her ass. "Go to the living room. Turn on the TV and find *Lupin*. I'll get our food."

Piper takes a few steps forward, grabs the bottle of wine, and then looks over her shoulder. "Yes, Daddy."

I blink, then blink again. My cock swells, begging me to send my plans flying out the window and go fuck her now.

"Careful with your words, baby. You don't want to get on my bad side."

"Who knows?" She heads out of the kitchen, swaying her hips and making me sweat. *Fuck.*

WE'RE SITTING in the living room, watching the last episode of season one. Piper leans her back on my chest, and my hand rests on her belly. She has a glass of wine in her hand, sipping on it from time to time, while my empty glass sits on the table. Whiskey is great, but I don't want to be drunk. Not with her.

"Did you talk to anyone from LACFC?" she asks suddenly, glancing over her shoulder.

"I did." The first thing I did when she left to pick up Story was call my rep. We talked things through, and then I called the team manager. I had no expectations, was just curious to know their thoughts. To my surprise, he was ecstatic to hear I wanted to try coaching. "I have a meeting with management on Wednesday. We're going to discuss my involvement in LACFC Academy and the plans for my school."

Piper sets her glass on the table and turns around to get a better look at my face. "What about your lawyer? What does he think?"

"Mr. Smith was more than happy to know I changed my mind and wasn't going to rush things," I say, and she smiles. "The team manager loved your idea. That my school could teach kids younger than eleven, and then the most talented could try out to join the Academy."

"Aw, I'm so glad I was able to help." Piper inches closer and presses her lips to mine for a kiss. I taste the wine on her tongue as I suck it into my mouth. She moans into our kiss, and I instantly know we're not going to finish the final episode tonight.

I break our kiss and stand up, looking down at her. "I'm going to clean up, while you…" She nods without taking her eyes off my face. "You're going to wait for me in my room. Fully dressed."

Piper frowns, knitting her brows together. "Okay."

I take our plates and glasses from the table and saunter into the kitchen. I can't stop smiling, remembering the puzzled look on her face. She has no idea what I've planned for her, and that feels even more exciting.

The second I step into my room and close the door, she stands up from my bed. I undress and climb on my bed, sitting comfortably with my back pressed to the headboard. I lock eyes with Piper and see her fiddling with the hem of her dress.

"Take your clothes off," I command, wrapping my hand around my cock and pumping it slowly.

Piper does as I tell her. She licks her lips and starts to undress. Taking a deep breath, I focus my attention on her face, banishing all other thoughts from my head. It's time to deliver her punishment.

"Get on all fours and crawl to me, baby."

30
kiss me, fuck me, hold me

HUNTER

PIPER'S EYES ROUND A LITTLE, AND SHE PARTS HER LIPS, looking at me in silence. I stroke my cock, holding her gaze. A taunting smile stretches across my face. Her chest rises and falls with her rapid breathing, and then she steps to my bed and climbs on it, getting on all fours.

Such a good fucking girl.

She inches closer, and I set my jaw hard, slowing down my movements. My cock trembles in anticipation. I've been with quite a few women, but this one...she's better than all of them. In everything. Piper is a new standard, and I'm one lucky bastard to have her all to myself.

I pat the covers by my side, and she crawls toward me, her eyes darting between my hand on my dick and my face. I extend my hand and cup her breast, massaging it gently and then sliding my fingers to her nipple. I squeeze it between my fingers and pull it down, making her whimper. She has very sensitive tits, moans any time I touch them. Once, she even came for a second time when I sucked her nipple into my mouth. I love discovering new things about her, and tonight I'm going to explore some of her limits.

"Open your mouth, baby," I say, putting my hand on her lower back and sliding it down to her ass. I press, urging her to move closer and give me a better view of her wet pussy.

Piper opens her mouth. I trace my thumb over her bottom lip, then slip it inside. Her velvety tongue curls around my finger as she sucks on it, hard. A low growl escapes my lips, making me lose my patience. I can't wait to be balls deep inside her, and yet I don't want to rush anything. I have the whole night ahead of me, and I'm going to enjoy every second with this beautiful girl.

"You're going to lean over," I whisper, her tongue still twirling around my thumb, "take my cock into your mouth, and suck me fucking dry."

She smiles at me when I take my finger out of her mouth. Just a heartbeat later, her lips are tight around my dick. My head tips back as I reach across her ass and slide my fingers down her pussy. *So fucking wet for me.* I tease her opening, my thumb rubbing her clit in slow circles. Piper moans, working her miraculous tongue on my dick, swirling it around my head and then licking the base of it. She sucks and nibbles, deepthroating me and gagging on my cock.

"You feel so good," she tells me, her hand wrapping around my dick. She starts jerking me off while taking my balls in her mouth. I set my legs wider, slipping two of my fingers inside her tight cunt. *Fucking heaven.*

Piper sucks my balls, pumping my cock faster with her hand. She rocks her hips back and forth, making me plunge my fingers deeper inside her. Her need for release is clear. So is her desire to make me come. I take my fingers out of her, quickly wet my thumb in my mouth, and slip two fingers back into her pussy. My thumb is pressing to her ass, and I start to massage it. Her body trembles under my touch, and she looks up to meet my gaze.

"Do you want me to stop?" I ask, and she shakes her head no as I add another finger inside her. "Then make me come, baby."

She lowers her lips to my dick, flicking her tongue up and down over my head, circling around it. I close my eyes; the pleasure builds up inside me. She sucks deeper and faster, her teeth occasionally grazing my skin. A gagging sound fills the room as I pump into her, my fingers coated in her juices. I've never been more turned on than I am right now. I lift my hips up and down, fucking her throat as my fingers move frantically inside her. She lets go of my cock, gasping for air as her walls close around my fingers. Piper comes, her legs wobbly, and she lowers her head again, taking my dick inside her mouth, high on her orgasm.

"Just like that, baby...just like that..." My thumb circles her clit. Shutting my eyes, I groan, and cum spills into her mouth. "Oh shit..."

Piper dries my balls, sucking me off till I feel numb. Hands down the best blow job of my life, no doubt about it. She sits up straight, her gaze burning into mine. I swallow hard, reaching over and brushing her hair from her face. "Come here." I gesture to the space between my legs, and she moves closer, settling in as I secure my hands around her. I nuzzle her neck with my nose as she sighs, leaning against my chest.

"For someone who wanted to punish me, you were rather gentle," she murmurs. I move my hands up, cupping her breasts. I rub her pebbled nipples between my fingers, tugging hard.

"Do you want to call it a night?" I ask, my lips seeking her earlobe and taking it into my mouth.

"Never," she breathes, wiggling her ass over my cock, slowly bringing it back to life.

"Good girl," I whisper. I lick the length of her neck, making her shudder. I glide my palm down to her belly button and lower, to her pussy. Pressing my fingers to her clit, I start gently massaging. Piper spreads her legs wider, and I take that as encouragement. I nibble on her skin. Her scent, lavender mixed with notes of vanilla, drives me wild. "I love seeing your body react to me."

"I want you to do whatever...Hunter," she rasps, clapping her hand over mine to stop me from touching her. I push her hand away, slipping my fingers down and deep inside her pussy. Her hips jerk forward; my name lingers on her lips. "Hunter, please..."

"Tell me what you want me to do to you." I fuck her with my

fingers as she rocks her hips, meeting me halfway. Such a greedy little pussy. "Tell me."

"I like it when you're rough with me..." She moans, becoming wetter with each stroke of my fingers. "I love it when you take me from behind, like that day when you fucked me in the kitchen..."

Smiling, I lightly slap her pussy. I don't want her to come just yet. I need her to tell me what else she wants, because let's be real—I'll do anything.

"What else?"

"I don't mind impact play..." Piper chokes on her words, voice hoarse and barely audible as I pick up the pace. "Once, my ex—"

That gets an immediate reaction from me. I grab her throat from behind, bringing my lips to her ear again. "Never talk to me about other men you've had sex with—ever." I tighten my grip and quicken my movements, going deeper and deeper until she fucking comes all over my fingers for the second time tonight.

I force her to look at me, still holding her throat in a lock. She's a stunner; I'll never get tired of admiring her beauty. Her hair sticks to her sweaty forehead. Her dilated pupils make her brown eyes darker than a starless night. Piper's gaze is heavy as she looks at me from under thick eyelashes, still riding the waves of her release. Her lips are begging for attention, and I don't want to deny what I love the most. Kissing her, devouring her, worshiping her. This girl has a power over me like no one else has ever had, and no matter how fucked-up it is... I'm all for it.

Inching closer, I cover her mouth with mine. Our lips are moving slowly, awakening even more feelings inside my chest. My cock is hard and my balls tight. I'm dying to fuck her. It's like I've been starving for months, and she's the most exquisite dish.

"I'm going to fuck you right now, exactly the way you want." I give her a quick peck on the lips, wrap my arms around her waist, and slowly turn us around. "Get on your knees and grab the headboard."

I move away, quickly reaching over to my bedside table and snatching a condom. I sheath my cock, watching her do as I told her.

A giddy smile crosses my face as I drag my eyes down her body. *She's mine.*

The words ring in my head, and my heartbeat grows faster. I can't allow myself to think like that. I can't give her false hope, because she has no future with me. And still, the beast in my chest wants to claim her, wants to make her mine, even if just for a little while.

I spread her legs wider and lean in. I tease her, rubbing my cock over her opening. I put one hand on her back, slide it lower, and force her shoulders down. Her face is in my pillows, and her ass is up in the air. Exactly as I want her. I smirk and slap her butt, making her whimper.

"You're not allowed to let go of the headboard, am I clear?" Piper nods. I collect her hair in my fist and pull her up. "Say it."

"Yes," she purrs, and even if I don't see her face, I know she's smiling.

Pushing my length inside her inch by inch, I grip her ass. It feels too good. She's warm and so fucking wet, making me lose my mind. I'm in no hurry, so I settle for a steady rhythm, letting her catch her breath and adjust to my girth until I'm all the way inside her. Our bodies slap against each other. This is how it should be.

"Do you want me to be gentle?" I taunt her.

"No. I want you to fuck me..." A quick pause as she glances at me over her shoulder. "I want you to fuck me like you own me."

Fuck. This girl makes me feel everything. She makes me feel seen and heard, makes me feel real, makes me feel like *me.*

"You said I might ruin you for all other men." I dig my fingers harder into her ass cheeks. "And that's exactly what I plan to do."

Thrusting harder, I make her moan louder. Then her breath hitches. My name is like a song spilling over her lips, the sound of her voice filling the space in my bedroom and painting it with the most vibrant colors. It brings my whole body to life, makes me feel things I thought were long gone. Things I never hoped to experience again... until her. Was I even living before I met her? Emotions spread through my body, wrenching my soul and twisting my mind. I'm losing my game if I even allow myself to think like that, but what if sometimes a game is worth losing?

"Oh God," she cries out as I slam inside her again, slapping her ass with each stroke. "I love your cock...I love your fucking cock, Hunter. Fuck me harder, please..."

That's enough. I grab her hands, tear them away from the headboard, and pull her to my chest. My palms are full of her tits as I pump into her. I let my hand slide down her clit, stimulating her and driving her insane. The bed is hitting the wall. Her whimpers and moans, my name on her tongue, and my groans all mix together as my release builds inside me. She rotates her hips, her hand reaching around my neck. She looks back at me, her eyes hooded with desire. She's levitating on the edge of her third orgasm. I see beads of sweat on her forehead and over her upper lip, and I dive in for a kiss, seizing her lips with mine.

Piper sucks on my tongue, her fingers threading through my hair. I fuck her deep and fast, knowing I won't last long. She comes first, fisting my hair and crying out my name, her whole body shaking with her orgasm. I close my eyes. The feeling of her walls tightening around my dick overwhelms me, and my own release takes over. Jesus Christ, it's a pure blessing.

I pull out and help her lie on her back. Then I get up from the bed and throw the condom into the trash can. Piper is stretched out on my bed, her chest rising and falling as she props herself up on her elbows, catching my gaze in the darkness of my room. A crooked smile ghosts over my lips as I lower myself down beside her. She turns onto her side, her gaze focused on me.

"I feel high," she confesses, and my brows pinch together. "I've never tried drugs. It's just...I feel like I'm in a different world because of you."

I laugh heartily, amusement loud in my voice. "I'm a fucking magician."

She swats my chest with her hand, giggling. "You make it sound cringe."

"I'm just stating the facts, baby." I turn onto my side to face her.

Cupping her cheek with my palm, I look her in the eyes. "How do you feel?"

"Exhausted, but in the most amazing way possible."

"I stretched your pussy damn good," I say, pride boosting my ego. Her eyes drop to my mouth, and all I want is to kiss her again. In the blink of an eye, I'm nibbling on her bottom lip. I'm not ready to go to sleep, and judging by the way she kisses me back...neither is she.

MY PHONE RINGS as I climb into my car. I sigh, picking it up from the passenger seat and seeing my mom's number. We already talked this morning, when she called to tell me Story was at school. Did something happen?

"Hey, Mom." I start the engine, ready to drive away from my house, my phone on speakerphone.

"Hey, Hunter. What are you up to?"

"Heading to the store. I ran out of Story's favorite cereal, and she refuses to eat anything else."

"Story is the cutest," she says softly. "Is she at dance class?"

"Yeah, Piper took her right from school."

"You're lucky to have Piper as Story's nanny. She's a gem." *She is.* "And she's actually the reason I'm calling you."

I instantly tense up; my grip on the steering wheel is hard. "Why?"

"Story told us about your plans to take her to Spain after the play-offs for a week or two. She said Piper would go with you, but...what if your father and I joined you instead? You could give her some time off. I'm sure she'd be more than happy for the opportunity to hang out with her friends, maybe meet someone." *Only if I lose my mind.* I'll never agree to that. "She's young, and your brother says she barely has time for him."

"You and Dad can join us, but Piper is coming too."

"It doesn't make any sense. I'm fully capable of looking after Story—"

"Piper is going with us," I bite out, sounding angrier than I intend to.

Mom is silent for a moment, and then she sighs. "I hope you're not doing what I think you're doing. I hope you're smarter than that." She exhales louder and adds, "Send me the details when you have them, so I can book our flight. Bye, Hunter."

"Bye." My jaw is clenched hard. This is not good, not good at all.

31
a villain

PIPER

At eight a.m., I stretch under the blanket. I slept like an angel, and now I feel rested and full of energy. Since we arrived in Minorca, I've barely done anything. This little vacation is a welcome break from my routine, and I'm trying to enjoy it to the fullest.

I toss the covers aside and walk to the floor-to-ceiling windows. The view is magnificent. The Mediterranean Sea is clearly visible from my room, and the blend of turquoise and azure hues makes it impossible to look away. The pines surrounding it only add to the picturesque and unique atmosphere. I've never been to Europe before, and I had no idea what to expect. Now? I'm in love. I'm enjoying every second of my time, not only because of the people I'm with, but because of my surroundings. Cala en Turqueta caught me off guard, and I won't be able to forget it anytime soon. If ever.

With a smile on my lips, I go to the bathroom. I hope I'm the first to wake up, because I want to cook breakfast for everyone. Willow has been doing it every morning since we got to this villa four days ago. I want to show my appreciation for Hale's family...and for Hunter especially. The man is so deep under my skin, there isn't a minute in which I'm not thinking about him. He's everywhere I go and everything I see. He's all I want, and I'm grateful his parents are with us. Or not. Sometimes I hate it. One stolen kiss in the middle of our first night is nothing compared to how much time we spend together at his house in LA. My need for him is only growing, just like my self-control is slowly disappearing.

Leaving my room, I go to the kitchen. The villa Hunter rented is quiet and peaceful, and I move as silently as possible. I don't want to wake anyone up. But the second I open the door, I know I'm too late. Willow is sitting at the table with a book in her hands and a plate of pancakes in front of her. Hesitating, I step into the room.

"Good morning, Piper." Willow puts her book on the table and takes her mug in her hands.

"Good morning." I come closer and lower myself onto the chair across from her. "I didn't think anyone would be up yet."

"I've always been an early riser, no matter where I go," she says, taking a sip. "I made coffee, if you want some. And pancakes. Go grab a mug and a plate so you can eat."

"Thank you." I stand up and quickly pour myself some coffee. The aroma is strong and awakening, but there's no cream and it tastes bitter. It's not how I usually take it. Not how Hunter loves it either. My stomach twists in annoyance with myself. Yes, my breakfast plan failed, but that doesn't mean I have to be a bitch about it. "Any plans for the day?" I ask.

"I don't know. Colin wants to visit Ciutadella, and I've been thinking about taking Story with us." She gives me a little smile as I sit down. "She's been spending way too much time with you on the beach. I want her to explore, to see the history of these old buildings and beautiful streets."

"Sounds good. I've been telling her the same. There's so much we haven't seen on the island, and we'll be leaving soon. If you need my help to convince her, I can do that with ease." I put three pancakes on my plate and dig in.

"That would be great. Thank you, Piper." Willow becomes serious in an instant. "I'm going to take this opportunity, since it's just us. I know there's something going on between you and my son."

Holding her gaze, I chew my pancake with intentional slowness. I don't show a single emotion, just keep my face straight. After swallowing my food, I pick up my coffee and take a sip.

"I'm his daughter's nanny."

She looks down for a moment, then looks back up at me. "Why is his daughter's nanny on vacation when she's clearly not needed?"

"I've been with Story—"

"I'm not saying you weren't with Story. I'm saying there are people here who can look after her, including her own dad. And yet, Hunter insisted on you coming to Spain." Willow sets her elbows on the table, leaning forward. "I'm not here to judge you, Piper. I've known you for a very long time, and I love you dearly. The only reason I decided to bring it up is because I don't want you to get hurt."

I've lost my appetite, and my mood has plummeted. "No one is going to get hurt."

"Piper," she sighs, "my son is not who you think he is. He's not built for marriage or a committed relationship. His whole world revolves around soccer and Story. There's no room for anyone else. Trust me."

"And yet, he was with his ex-wife for eight years."

"Do you think that was a happy relationship?"

I blink. A nauseating feeling forms in my chest. "I don't know."

"I do. The only reason they stayed together for so long is because they were both constantly on the road. A child will never be the glue that holds a family together, no matter how much their parents love them." Willow stands up and puts her mug into the dishwasher. Then she picks up her book and hovers over me. "Be careful with your heart, Piper."

She skirts me and heads to the door. I keep my mouth shut until it becomes impossible to stay silent.

"Hayden doesn't know."

Willow halts in her tracks, glancing at me. "I'm not going to tell him anything."

And then she's gone, leaving me alone in the suddenly cold kitchen. This isn't how I imagined starting my day. The worst thing?

The tiniest part of me thinks it's already too late. My heart is going to get hurt anyway.

"WHERE ARE WE GOING?" Story asks as we climb inside the car. I shrug, shaking my head. I have no clue, and I don't know why it's just us. "Daddy?"

"Do you remember Angelo?" Hunter looks at us over his shoulder, and Story nods. "We're going to dinner with him."

"Is Cissy here?" Her excitement is visible, while I'm fiddling with the skirt of my dress. Who the hell is Angelo?

"No, sweetie, it's just Angelo. He had a game, and took the ferry to come here."

"I love Cissy," Story whines. Then she turns to look at me. "Angelo is my dad's best friend. He's Atlético Madrid's goalkeeper... right?"

Hunter laughs, and for a moment our eyes lock. If he only knew how much I crave his touch, our intimacy...especially after my talk with his mom, but I prefer to keep things professional. For everyone's sake.

"Angelo is indeed my best friend, and he does play for Atlético. I didn't expect him to come, but I'm not surprised. The guy's determination is unmatched."

"Looks like you have a lot in common," I say, making Hunter snort. Shaking his head, he looks away and starts the engine. "Why did your parents stay home?"

"The trip to Ciutadella exhausted them both. Or maybe it was Story."

"Dad!" she yelps, folding her arms over her chest. "I didn't do anything."

I smile and relax into the seat, listening to their banter. I enjoy spending time with them. Their love for each other is overwhelming, and it makes me feel as if I belong, as if I'm a part of their little family...even if, in reality, I'm just the nanny.

A TALL GUY with jet-black hair stands up from his chair as soon as we enter the small, secluded restaurant. He has deep brown eyes, a little beard, and a radiant smile. His booming voice fills the whole space. "Hale!"

"*Hola*, Angelo," Hunter greets him, stepping closer and hugging him tightly. They talk briefly in Spanish, and I'm mesmerized listening to his voice. Deep and penetrating, incredibly melodic. Heat ignites in my lower abdomen, and I'm instantly back in his room, in his bed, our bodies tangled. My memories are flooding my mind, and my cheeks warm up. I shift, crossing my legs at my ankles. *Not the place for that, Piper.*

"Story, oh my God! Such a beautiful girl." Angelo steps aside and bends down to Story. She's smiling, letting him take her into his arms. "Cissy was asking about you. I promised to bring her with me next time."

"You should've brought her with you now. I love spending time with Cissy."

"I know, I know. We're going to visit you in LA as soon as the season is over. I can't wait to see your new home," he reassures her, and then shifts his gaze to me. Dilated pupils and a dropped jaw indicate his surprise, as if he's finally noticed me. "Hunter?"

"Oh, right. Angelo, this is Piper, Story's nanny."

"Story's nanny..." he echoes, glancing between me and Hunter. Setting Story on her feet, he steps to me and kisses me on both cheeks. "It's very nice to meet you, Piper. I've heard a lot about you, so consider me intrigued."

"It's very nice to meet you too," I murmur, smiling at him as he steps back. "I have no idea what you've heard about me."

"Only good things, don't worry." And again he glances to

Hunter. Does he know about us? Or is it just a suspicion? He keeps his gaze trained on me for a long minute, and then finally looks at Hunter. "Should we order something?"

"Definitely. I'm starving," Hunter says as we all take our seats at the table.

I'VE BEEN TEXTING with Riley, as she's preparing for a birthday party at her friend's house. It should be way easier, but my mind is occupied with all the information I gathered today. It's consuming and unsetting, and I'm having a hard time letting it go. I need Hunter.

A light knock on my door startles me, and my phone falls to the floor. "Come in."

The door opens, and Hunter enters my room. He leans against the doorframe, peering at me. "How are you?"

"Good."

"You looked pensive on the way home." He narrows his eyes. "Is something bothering you?"

I look back at him without saying anything, then pick up my phone. I stand up and come toward him, but I stop within arm's reach.

"I miss you."

Hunter rakes his gaze over my face, then pushes off the doorframe. He wraps his arm around my waist, pulling me to his chest. "I miss you too."

This thing between us...I don't know why I keep deluding myself. My heart is ready to jump out of my chest anytime he's near me. The butterflies in my stomach assault me when his hands touch my body. He's always on my mind and in my dreams. He takes up so much space in my heart, I genuinely wonder if anyone else will fit.

"Is Story asleep?"

"Yeah." He inches closer, his hot breath fanning over my face.

"What about your parents?" Their room is on the opposite side of the villa, so I have no idea if they're still up.

"Dad's in the living room. He's watching something." I pout, exhaling loudly in disappointment. "Piper..."

"It's nice here, but...I miss our time together."

His deep green eyes darken; his lips hover over mine. "If you only knew how much I want to kiss you, to rip this fucking dress off you and fuck you till you pass out..."

I put my hand on the back of his neck, pulling him to me for a kiss and silencing him. It's slow and gentle, because all I want is to savor the feeling, to enjoy another stolen moment.

Hunter presses me closer, deepening our kiss. The movements of his tongue grow demanding, daring. He wants more, and I know I won't say no to him. His hand slides down to my ass, and he lifts the skirt of my dress. A muffled groan scatters all over my lips when he abruptly steps back.

Opening my eyes, I look at him through clouded vision. It was the most honest truth in the world when I told him that I feel high when I'm with him. I don't want him to leave me alone. I don't want this night to end, and I'm done playing fair. Being a villain feels great... especially when I'm the one who will suffer in the end.

"Your mom thinks we have something going on," I mutter, watching him intently. To my surprise, he just shrugs. I open my mouth and then close it again, pinching my brows together. His reaction is pretty obvious. He knows what his mom thinks...and he doesn't care. But I want him to. I want him to care about it, about us. "She's afraid someone might get hurt."

Me. I'll be hurt when it's time to say good-bye.

Hunter continues watching me with a calm expression, making me lose my shit. Why is he so calm?

"Let's go for a ride," he says.

It's not a question. Not even a suggestion. It's a demand, and I obey. "Sure."

32
the sign of denial

HUNTER

PIPER PUTS ON HER LEATHER JACKET AND STROLLS TOWARD me. A smile curls my lips, and I don't even try to hide it. I miss my time with her, *our* time that we spent in my house. It's not even about the intimacy, because I don't think I've ever had so much sex in my life. It's about our talks, about me watching her read, about her watching me try to deal with school-related stuff—anything I do when she's around feels way better than when she's not. She fills my life with her affection, her kindness and care. And I can't get enough of it.

"What are you going to tell your dad if he sees us?" she asks.

"The truth."

"Don't you think—"

"Mom doesn't keep secrets from Dad," I point out. She gasps, her eyes rounding.

"Great." Piper folds her arms over her chest; her lips are pressed tightly together. She looks away and then sneaks a glance at me. "Why are you so calm?"

"Can we talk about it in the car?"

Piper doesn't answer, and it makes me realize her mood is drastically changing. And not in a good way. She's frustrated and annoyed, while I'm having a hard time figuring out why. Why should I care if my parents know about my relationship with her? Their opinion won't change my mind or my behavior.

"Piper?"

"Yes, we can talk about it in the car," she blurts, irritation rising in her voice.

I huff, opening my mouth to answer her, and that's when my father steps into view. He stops in his tracks, a mug pressed to his lips. Slowly lowering it, he looks between Piper and me. "Going somewhere?"

"We're going for a ride," I tell him, holding his gaze. "If Story wakes up, please call me, and we'll come back."

"Sure." Dad nods, focusing on Piper. He takes in her stance, her rigid posture, and frowns. "Is everything okay?"

She exhales harshly, boring her gaze into his. "Yes, we're just going for a ride. I haven't seen much of the city, and Hunter promised to show me around."

"The city is very beautiful, even in the dark. I'm sure you'll enjoy it." My father's face softens.

"I'm sure I will too," she says, resuming her walk. "Good night, Colin."

Piper opens the door and ambles outside, but my dad blocks my way.

"If you hurt her, no one is going to like it. Especially not Hayden," he says.

"You have no idea what you're talking about." I veer around him and head to the door.

"Quite the contrary, Son." I look over my shoulder, meeting his eyes. "You have no idea what *you're* talking about. You don't take a girl you're just using for sex on vacation with your family."

"Speaking from experience?" I smirk and close the door with a thud. He has no right to lecture me. Not after what he's done.

Piper is already by the car, standing with her arms crossed over her chest. She needs to drop this attitude and tell me what's wrong; I'm not a fucking mind reader.

"Ready to go?" I approach her, unlocking the car.

"Yes." She yanks the door open and slides inside. I close the door for her and go around to the driver's side, counting to ten and taking a few deep breaths. The last thing I need is to get into a fight with her over nothing.

I start the engine and drive away from the house. Piper is sitting quietly, looking ahead of her, not paying attention to our surroundings. I highly doubt she sees anything. Her gaze is glassy, and her fingers play with her butterfly pendant. She's lost in her thoughts, and I need her here with me.

"Piper, is something wrong?"

"Wrong?" She blinks and turns to face me. "What was rule number one?"

"It's a secret."

"How is it a secret if both of your parents know?"

"They aren't going to talk about it with anyone—not even with your best friend, if that's what you're worried about. Hayden won't know unless you tell him," I mutter, and she snorts.

"It's just sex. Why would I talk to him about it?"

I snap my head in her direction, slowing the car down. The way she says it...the tone of her voice implies the contrary. And that's bad.

"Piper, I couldn't care less about my parents knowing. I'm fully capable of making my own decisions, and I know what's right for me and what's not." I drive out toward the beach. There's a secluded area, and no one will bother us since it's close to midnight. The reason I'll always choose Minorca over Mallorca is simple: it's way less crowded, and much quieter. Exactly what I want for a vacation with Story.

"We should've set another rule. One neither of us thought of," I say.

"Which is?"

I don't answer her. I speed up, turn right, and drive straight for ten minutes. Piper keeps glancing at me, but it doesn't bother me. I know what I need to tell her, and it has the power to change everything. I've been honest with her from the start, and if things are different for her now, it's not my fault. I'm not leading anyone on.

Not anymore, at least. I know what might happen if I'm not clear enough. Being accused of things I haven't done and then having to lessen the damage isn't my favorite thing to do. Especially when Story's perception of me is at stake. I'll never risk that.

I stop the car and climb out. Then I head to the hood and sit on it. The Mediterranean Sea is calm, even if the weather is a bit windy. Nothing unusual for this time of the year. Moonlight casts long shadows, allowing me to see the waves crashing against the shore, and calming my nerves. I like Piper. I've never met anyone like her. I've never felt the way I feel around her. Does that change what I want for my future? Or where I see myself in five years or more? No.

"Why are we here?" Her voice is quiet as she joins me, stopping in front of me and blocking my view of the sea. My eyes roam over her face, my skin warming up from her beauty.

"Water always helps me clear my head. It's soothing. I don't know how to explain it better." Tucking a strand of hair behind her ear, Piper tries to suppress her smile but fails. She grins at me, stepping closer until she's between my legs. "What?"

"I feel the same way. Water has always had a calming effect on me," she confesses. I wrap my arms around her waist, pulling her closer. "I didn't think we had that in common."

"Neither did I." My hands slide down to her butt, and her gaze instantly darkens. The way we react to each other is out of this world.

"What rule did we forget to add?" Piper curls her hands around my neck, our noses nearly touching.

"If one of us starts to fall for the other, we need to stop. Immediately. That's a deal-breaker." She swallows nervously as I even my voice, making it sound emotionless. "Is this more than just sex for you?"

Moonlight reflects in her eyes as she stares at me. She's pensive. I don't see even a hint of the smile that was on her lips a moment ago. Taking a deep breath, she shrugs.

"No. It's just sex. You were more than clear when we made this agreement."

Searching her face, I know damn well she's lying to me. Her

expression speaks way louder than her words. It's the first sign of denial.

"Piper, I don't want you to get hurt."

She looks up at the sky, pouting. "What's wrong with your family? First your brother, then your mom, and now you. Why are you all so adamant I'll get hurt?"

Because my family knows me better than anyone, baby.

"My mother loves you, and she wants what's best for you—"

"And that's clearly not you. Exactly what your brother told me, almost word for word." She sighs and focuses her attention on me again. "I'm not going to get hurt, Hunter. Our agreement ends as soon as my contract is over. I'm okay with that. I promise."

Am I okay with that? The question appears in my mind out of nowhere, but as I let it sink in, goosebumps rise on my skin. We will go separate ways once she goes back to school. She'll be seeing other people...and just the thought of it makes me see red.

"That's good to hear," I say, ignoring the tsunami of emotions in my chest. "Your pussy is mine."

Piper leans closer to my face. "For now."

This girl...dammit. I twirl us around, lowering her onto the hood of the car. I bend down, and she hooks her legs behind my back. *Not just for fucking now.* An obsessive desire to have her crosses my mind. I'll deal with all that shit later. Right now, the only thing I want is to kiss her. Over and over again.

I smash my lips onto hers, and Piper opens her mouth for me, welcoming my tongue. The kiss is fiery and passionate; it's full of need and our longing for each other. She didn't lie when she said she missed me, and I didn't lie when I said I missed her too. Staying away from her when my parents or Story are around is hard, and I'm glad to finally be with her again. Even if it's just for a few hours.

I haul her to my chest, carry her to the car, and climb into the backseat with her. She's on my lap; my eyes are glued to her face. She takes off her leather jacket and tosses it aside. Pulling down her dress, she reveals her tits to me. I glance between her face and her pebbled nipples, my dick growing hard at once. Inching forward, I take her nipple into my mouth and suck.

"Fuck me, Hunter, please," she begs, digging her fingers into my hair.

"That's exactly what I'm planning to do, baby. My cock is lonely without your warm, tight pussy...and I'm going to fix that."

33
all the pretty words
PIPER

IS THIS MORE THAN JUST SEX FOR YOU? HIS QUESTION echoes in my head as Hunter's big hands massage my breasts. His touch is tender and full of need; his palms feel hot, setting my whole body on fire.

Is this more than just sex for you? It's way more than that. It has been for quite some time already...but I don't want him to end our arrangement. I know the consequences of an honest answer, and I'm too selfish for that. I want to enjoy my time with him for as long as I can. Even if my heart is at stake.

"Dammit, baby, if you only knew how much I missed this," Hunter murmurs, his tongue swirling around my nipple, his teeth grazing my sensitive skin. I moan, arching my back and rotating my hips, feeling his hard-on grow bigger. "Your tits are a fucking perfect fit for my hands. Everything about you is perfect."

Is this more than just sex for you, Hunter? The question is on the tip of my tongue, but I hold it back. It's not the time...and he's not a man to be pushed around. The second I demand answers, this will be over. I've learned that much about him. He needs to want this, to want us...and he's not there yet. If he'll ever be.

I help him take off his hoodie, then lean down and kiss his lips. Tasting him, savoring every single brush of our tongues. His cheeks are scruffy, making my skin tingle. I glide my pussy over his groin, and he grips my hips, holding me in place. A low growl springs from his mouth.

"I don't want to come in my pants, Piper." The warning in his voice sends shivers down my spine, and I'll be damned to say I don't want to challenge him.

"Then you better put your dick inside my pussy," I whisper, holding his heated gaze. Hunter narrows his eyes, his jaw set hard. I don't blink; anticipation is thrumming through my veins. Losing control isn't something he does often, but when it happens...our sex becomes wild. "Will you do that for me, Hunter?"

He grabs the back of my neck, forcing my forehead down to his. "I'll do anything for you, Piper."

Flipping us over, he lowers me onto the backseat. His dilated pupils make him absolutely irresistible. I'm falling for him harder than ever, just because he looks at me like that. As if I'm his entire world.

Hunter pats his pockets, frowning. "We have a problem."

I say on an exhale, "You don't have a condom."

"This little ride was spontaneous," he tells me, staying still between my legs. I lick my lips, my thoughts swirling, trying to remember what pills I packed for this trip. "Piper, I'm so—"

"You can come inside me." His face darkens, and the corners of his mouth drop. His reaction doesn't surprise me, even if I know most of the guys I've been with wouldn't have passed up this opportunity. "I have a morning-after pill."

He pinches his brows together, the wrinkles on his forehead deepening. "Are you sure?"

"I'm not trying to trap you, Hunter. I'll take it right in front of you as soon as we get back. I promise."

Silence settles between us as we continue to stare at one another. *His whole world revolves around soccer and Story. There is no room for anyone else.* Willow's words boom in my head, and my fingers fly to my pendant. Nervousness forms in the pit of my stomach; nausea washes over me.

"You sure about this?" His voice is just above a whisper, his eyes glued to my face.

"Yes." I slide my hands down and hike up the skirt of my dress. "I want your dick inside me so bad, Hunter."

His gaze roams over my exposed skin. A coy smile breaks out across his handsome face as he unzips his fly and pulls out his hard cock. "Whatever you want, baby."

Moving my panties aside, he teases my pussy with the head of his cock, slowly pushing it in and out, making me gasp anytime I feel empty. As he slides inside me to the hilt, a loud moan fills the car. Hunter fucks me slowly at first, then picks up the pace, holding my gaze the entire time.

"You feel so good," I whisper, my hand reaching down to my clit. I start circling my fingers over it.

My forehead is covered in sweat, and the windows have become foggy. The car rocks as he starts banging me harder. His grunts and my moans mixed with the sounds of waves crashing on the shore are the only things I hear. I'm chasing my orgasm, my fingers relentlessly massaging my clit.

"Harder," I beg, lifting my hips as he moves. Our bodies are slapping against each other. "Please, Hunter...harder."

He smirks, his hands wrapping around my ankles. The second he lifts my legs into the air and puts them on his shoulders, I whimper. He's so fucking deep...my vision blurs. His thrusts are rough, and I'm on the verge of my orgasm. Then Hunter slaps my tit, and my insides close around his dick at once. I come, his name on my lips, my body thrashing under him.

"Fuck...so fucking good..." he growls, smashing his hips into mine. "Who does your little cunt belong to?"

"You."

"Me," he states, and I feel him twitch inside me. He's coming hard and hot, eyes closed, mouth open. "Fucking mine."

"Yours," I tell him as he opens his eyes and peers down at me.

Hunter pulls out slowly, his gaze on my pussy. His breathing is ragged, and he suddenly starts smiling. "Who would've thought?"

"What?" I ask.

"My cum dripping out of you is the hottest thing I've ever seen. And I'm so fucking hard again...like I didn't just come inside you... fuck." His fingers are trembling when he pushes them inside my pussy. "It fucking belongs here...my cum belongs here."

My head bobs back as I try to bottle the feeling of immense, overwhelming pleasure. Not only because of the mind-blowing orgasm, but also because of the words he just said. They mean so much more than all his attempts to assure me that this doesn't mean anything to him.

All the pretty words he says make me fall harder for him.

Hunter slumps into the backseat, his jeans low at his knees. I sit up and crawl onto his lap, straddling him and taking his erect dick inside my pussy again. Sighing, I shut my eyes, my arms tight around his neck.

He brushes my hair out of my face, delicately tucking it behind my ears. "I'm so glad I decided to ask you to come with us," he says softly. "Even if we didn't sneak off to be alone, it still would've been perfect...I love watching you smile, listening to your laughter...seeing how much you love Story. Thank you, Piper."

"Thank you for inviting me." I roll my hips, and his eyes instantly fall closed.

"You fuck me so good," he confesses, winding his hands around my waist. Then he slides them down my ass and slaps my butt. I moan; my pussy tightens around his shaft. My eyelashes tremble as I ride his dick deep. One of his hands stays on my ass, pushing me to move faster, and the other wraps around my throat. I love it when he does that. It's the element of him being in control, even when I'm on top. Even when I'm the one who makes decisions, he guides me. I love being daddy's brat...but I'm hella certain I'd need to be wasted to call him that again.

I put my hands on his knees behind my back for better balance, bouncing up and down on his dick. Circling my hips, I deepen my movements as he adds more pressure, squeezing my throat. I smile; my eyes are trained on his face. He's the most gorgeous man I've ever seen, and it's still hard for me to accept that he wants me.

My moans change to whimpers when he slaps my ass with his free hand. Over and over again. I love how my pleasure combines with pain, how raw and real our sex is. He's dicking me down good, and I'm not sure there will ever be anyone better than him. I've lost count of the orgasms he has gifted me with, just like all the times his tenderness has sent my head spinning. This man is everything I never knew I wanted.

"Oh God, Hunter!" I cry out, moving my hips frantically as my pussy clenches around his dick. I'm in fucking heaven. The waves of my orgasm overtake my body, and my legs are quivering.

"Don't stop, baby…don't stop." His voice is hoarse, and his breathing is rapid. I wrap my arms around his neck, riding him as fast as possible, my body still high after my second release in a row. "Such a good fucking girl…"

His lips on mine silence our sounds as he comes. His hips move up and down when he shoots his cum inside me. Our kiss is full of passion, our tongues curling around each other. I don't want this night to end, not yet. It feels too good to be here with him, just the two of us.

Hunter leans away, cupping my face with his hands. "God, I have no words…anything I want to say feels like it's not enough," he murmurs, "because you deserve only the best. You deserve so much more than I can offer…"

I look him in the eyes, my lips curving into a smile. "I want what I want, Hunter, and it's to be in this car, on this beach in Spain, with you. Not anywhere else. Not with anyone else. With you."

He chuckles, drawing my face closer. My breath is fanning over his lips. "That's exactly where I want to be too…just here."

Sealing those words with yet another kiss, he takes away all the sounds around us, takes away all other thoughts. It's just us, and I'm happy to believe in that illusion for a few more hours.

"ARE YOU SURE YOU'RE OKAY?" Hunter asks, looking at me over his shoulder as he carries our suitcases into the house. I roll my eyes and tighten my grip on Story. She fell asleep on our way home from the airport, and I picked her up to bring her into the house. "She's pretty heavy."

"It's all good," I reassure him, following him closely.

Glancing to my right, I see Hayden's car parked in the driveway. I'm not surprised he decided to stop by. He was bombarding my phone every day with a thousand messages, demanding pictures of our time in Minorca. He wanted to know where we were, what we were doing, what places we were visiting. The guy is over the top, but I love him, so it didn't bother me.

"I should've known Hayden wouldn't stay away. Though I'm kinda baffled he didn't mention he would be here. I talked to him before we boarded our flight."

"That's how your brother is." I laugh under my breath, hoping I won't wake up Story.

"I probably need to get used to it." Hunter stops, opens the door, and lets me go inside first. "He's going to stick around forever."

"Brotherly love. What could be better?" I ask, turning around to see him close the door. Hunter sets down our suitcases and looks up, meeting my gaze for a brief second. Then his eyes dart to something behind me, and he immediately tenses up.

"How did you get in?" he demands, crossing his arms over his chest.

"Hey, I let us in." Hayden's voice sounds uncertain, and I slowly turn around to look at him, coming face-to-face with someone I've never met in person. Amelia Hale stands right in front of me, flashing her million-dollar smile. It's so sudden that I instantly look away, as if I'm afraid she's going to jinx me. Instead, I focus on Hayden. "Hey, Pip."

"Hey." I greet him in a barely audible voice, then take a deep breath and turn toward Hunter's ex-wife. "Um, hello, Ms. Hale."

Her light blue eyes sparkle as she looks me up and down. A knowing smirk forms on her puffy lips, and she arches her eyebrow at me. "You must be Piper. It's nice to finally meet you."

"You too," I mumble, shifting my hands a little. "I'll go put Story in her bed. Hopefully she'll sleep for a few more hours."

I start down the hallway, and Hayden jerks in my direction, following my every step. The atmosphere is heavy. The fact that Hunter hasn't said a single word gnaws at me, makes me feel weird. Did he know she would be here? I don't get it.

34
the house of exes

HUNTER

STAYING ROOTED TO THE SPOT, I GAPE AT MY EX. I HATE the fact that she showed up unannounced, and that Hayden let her in. It's my fucking house. He should've told me before bringing anyone here. It's that simple.

"Did you miss me, Hunter?" Amelia murmurs, smiling at me.

I scoff and stroll past her to the living room. "Not in a million years."

"Some things never change," she chuckles, following me, unbothered by my hostility. She knows she's not welcome here, and she doesn't care. Her question is nothing more than an attempt to taunt me.

Plopping down on the couch, I see her do the same. Amelia sits across from me, her light blue eyes glimmering with mischief. This woman loves playing on my nerves, and she's incredibly good at it. I think on some level that was what held us together for so long. I find it boring when my partner never challenges me, never puts up a good fight, and Amelia will never miss an opportunity to rile me up.

"What are you doing here?"

"Story's birthday is in ten days," she answers, hooking one leg over the other.

"And?"

"Did you think I'd come to LA for a day or two and leave as soon as her party is over?"

"Of course not. I just hoped you'd give me a heads-up instead of showing up on my doorstep as if it's the most natural thing to do."

"You're my daughter's father. It *is* the most natural thing to do, Hunter." Amelia speaks softly, her eyes roaming over my face. "I should've mentioned it when we talked last week, but...I thought surprising you and Story would be better. That way, I'd get your most honest reaction."

"Most honest? Did you want to confirm that you're the last person I want to see in my house?"

"Honey, you secretly love me, just admit it," she purrs. I focus my attention on her. She's wearing black sweatpants and a black hoodie, and she's wearing them well. Just like she does with the designer clothes she wears for her movie premieres. We've been through a lot of shit, said so many hurtful words to each other during our separation, but I'll never deny how beautiful she is.

"Love to hate you, maybe," I tell her, realizing I'm not angry with her anymore. There's no point in holding a grudge against Amelia. She always does what she wants, and I know that better than anyone. "How long have you been in LA?"

"My flight got in yesterday. I booked a hotel room since I knew you wouldn't be back till today." She shrugs, leaning back into the couch. "Then I remembered Hayden, and I called him. He picked me up and brought me here...maybe thirty minutes ago."

I sigh in relief, knowing she hasn't been here alone. "Good. Where are you staying?"

Amelia blinks, her eyebrows knitting together. "What do you mean? I only booked a hotel room for one night. I'm planning to stay with you and Story for the eleven days that I'm here. I miss Story, and I want to spend as much time with her as I can."

She's gotta be kidding me. I tsk, averting my gaze. Is that reasonable? Yes. Is it something Story will want? Yes. Is it something I want?

Hell no. She's going to mess up my whole routine, and I'm not even remotely happy about it.

"Hunter, I know you don't want me here, but..." She speaks quietly, and I look back at her. "Can't you deal with me for a few days? For Story's sake?"

I've been wondering when she was going to use Story to her advantage. She always does. She knows I'd do anything for Story. Including tolerating my ex's presence. "Fine. You can stay," I tell her. "Story will be happy to have you here. She misses you."

Amelia's face softens, and she beams at me. "Thank you, Hunter. I appreciate it."

"I hope you won't make me regret it."

"Who knows?" She laughs heartily. "What are our plans for tonight?"

"*Our* plans?" I ask, and Amelia nods. She's trapped me, and I didn't even notice it. "I think we should wait for Story to wake up. We can do whatever she's in the mood for."

"I'm sure she'd love to spend time with both of her parents. Maybe we can play Monopoly? Order some food?"

"Maybe." I smile back at her, mentally admitting defeat and not allowing myself to feel bad about it. I'm doing it for Story, and no one else. "We can—"

"Story is still asleep," Hayden announces, stepping into the living room. He heads to the couch and sits down beside me. He glances between Amelia and me, and then his face breaks into a huge grin. "I kinda expected shouting, maybe some broken furniture...but you're handling this divorced shit like real pros."

"We're better off divorced, that's all," Amelia chirps. "We don't have any lingering conflicts, nothing left unsaid. We're good. Right, Hunter?"

I hold her gaze, watching her intently. We're good for now, but it's not always like that. She knows what buttons to press to piss me off. "Yeah, we're good."

"So Amelia will be staying here? With you and Story?" Hayden looks at me with an arched eyebrow.

"Yes. It'll be better for Story."

"True. I thought that too." His smile grows bigger. "Piper will finally have time for me. She hasn't gone out in what feels like eternity."

The second he says it, it dawns on me. With Amelia in the house, there's no need for Piper to be here. I keep silent, my gaze glued to him. A shit ton of thoughts swirl in my head, and I don't like any of them.

"Yeah, she will…" I trail off, noticing Piper in the doorframe.

"I'm sorry to bother you," she mutters. "I'm not sure what to do… Hayden said I could take some time off, but I—"

"Story's mom will be staying here, so yeah," I say slowly, watching her pupils dilate. "You have eleven days off."

Piper steps back, straightens her spine, and flashes me a smile. "Sounds good. I'll go collect my things…"

"You should." My palms are sweating already. "I hope you'll come to Story's birthday party."

"I'd never disappoint her," she mumbles. *This isn't fucking good.*

"Well, I better go and help Pip." Hayden stands up. His gaze darts to Amelia, and then he focuses on me. "I'll leave you two alone. I'm sure you have things to discuss."

Things to discuss? The only person I want to talk to right now is Piper, but I can't do that. I don't need my ex-wife figuring out that I have something going on with Piper right off the bat. Amelia is way too smart, and I don't want to make it easy for her. I just hope Piper will understand my reasoning. It might backfire on me.

"Sure." I nod and look at my ex. "Will you help me make dinner?"

"Of course," she murmurs, standing up from the couch. "How about we go see what you have in the kitchen?"

"I was about to suggest the same." I stand up as well, casting another glance at Amelia. "Once Story wakes up, I can go to the store for anything we need. It'll give you two time to gossip without me around."

"Don't think we don't do that, Hunter," she says. "Story talks a lot, *about everything*."

ALL I'VE BEEN DOING the past five days is playing happy family with Amelia and Story. And I'm ready to climb the walls. The only thing that's keeping me sane is Story's smile. Otherwise, I would've flipped already.

"Hunter, can you please bring me a towel?" I meet Amelia's gaze. She puts her hands on the edge of the jacuzzi, smiling at me. Rolling my eyes, I walk back into the house.

God, I want a break from this shit.

Back outside, I find Amelia standing in front of the jacuzzi in her bikini. I sweep my gaze over her face and down her body. A year ago, I would've been hard just from the sight of her, even after our divorce. Now? It doesn't affect me in the slightest.

"Here," I say, extending the towel to her.

Amelia narrows her eyes. "Thanks."

"Why are you upset?" I fold my arms over my chest.

"I'm not used to you acting like this with me." Wrapping the towel around her body, she stomps toward the house.

"Don't you have a boyfriend, sweetie?" I follow her closely, a smirk playing on my face. I finally have the upper hand, and it brightens my mood. She's not the only one who knows how to play games.

"Derek isn't my boyfriend. You of all people should know better."

"Another PR stunt?"

"It's good for the movie. Helps create buzz, builds anticipation." She shrugs, climbing stairs as I follow her, step by step. "I don't want a relationship right now."

She looks over her shoulder, catching my gaze on her. Her lips curl into a smile, and the towel falls to the stairs. Stopping in her tracks, she unties her top and tosses it down as well. Slowly, Amelia turns around to face me, and my eyes zero in on her bare breasts.

Barely stopping myself from snorting out loud, I shake my head.

Her attempts to seduce me are adorable. I don't feel anything for her anymore, and it's time she understands it.

35
unbearable feeling
PIPER

"Mrs. Kennedy?" I press my phone to my ear as I stop at a traffic light.

"Piper, hey," Story's teacher greets me in a hushed voice. "I'm incredibly sorry for calling you, but I couldn't get ahold of Mr. Hale, so I thought I'd try you."

"That's totally fine. Is everything okay?"

"Story isn't feeling well, and I thought—"

"I'll be there in ten minutes. Don't worry." I end the call and toss my phone on the passenger seat.

Fifteen minutes later, I'm carrying Story to my car. She smiled when she saw me, but it was short-lived. She has a fever, and Mrs. Kennedy said she was throwing up. I put her in my car and quickly slide inside too.

"I missed you, Piper," Story mutters. I look at her in the rearview mirror.

"I missed you too, honey. How have you been? Having fun with your parents?"

"It's been good. Mom and Dad are getting along, and we spend a lot of time together. We were going to get a kitten for me tomorrow." She smiles weakly.

"I'm sure they'll take you once you're well," I reassure her, driving away from the school. "I'm glad your dad gave in and agreed to buy you a cat."

Story giggles quietly, shaking her head. "He didn't have a choice. Mom can be very persuasive."

I smile at her, but my chest is heavy. I'm not happy Hunter is spending time with his ex-wife. I hate that she's staying in his house... even if I understand why he's allowing it. The man will do anything for Story, and having her mom around is exactly what she needs. She loves Amelia, and they have a very strong bond, even if they live so far apart.

Shooing away all my worries, I clear my throat. "Have you decided what you want to name your cat?"

"No, I was hoping you'd help me...will you be at my birthday party?"

"I wouldn't miss it." I notice the tiniest smile light up her face. "Your uncle is planning something huge for you."

"I love Uncle Hayden. He's the best," Story murmurs, cocking an eyebrow at me. "Have you been spending time with him?"

"Well, he still has classes, so mostly I've been home with Riley. But he wants to hang out tomorrow."

"I hope you have tons of fun. You deserve it, Piper," she says. Then she presses her palm to her mouth. "I might throw up."

"That's okay. Use the plastic bag I gave you, and don't worry about anything." She nods, grips the bag, and just sits there with her mouth shut.

My poor little girl. I truly wish I could help her.

She spends the rest of our ride with her eyes closed, clutching the plastic bag to her chest.

I park in Hunter's driveway and take Story into my arms. She lowers her head onto my shoulder as I make her lock her legs behind my back. Her scorching forehead is pressed to my neck, and worry washes over me. She needs to see a doctor as soon as possible. I just hope her father is home. He'll know what to do.

Taking the keys from my pocket, I quickly open the door and walk inside. When I look up, my eyes land on Hunter and Amelia on the stairs. My cheeks heat up as soon as my mind registers what I'm seeing. The only clothes Story's mom has on are her swimsuit bottoms. Her hands are covering her full breasts.

"Sorry for barging in," I mutter as Amelia scurries up the stairs. "Story's teacher called me. She didn't feel well. And I was near the school, so..."

"What happened?" Hunter storms over to me. Deep wrinkles appear on his forehead.

"She has a fever." I let him take Story. "She's been throwing up. Looks like some sort of virus. It might be good to call her doctor."

"Of course. Thank you so much, Piper."

I nod, glancing at the stairs again. "I better go."

"Piper, it's not—"

"Story needs you, Hunter," I say through gritted teeth. Once I've closed the door in his face, I stomp away from the house.

I can't believe I let myself be so stupid.

In my car, the sounds of "Die For Me" fill the whole space. I turn up the volume. It's fitting, even if I'm being overly dramatic. Hunter doesn't owe me anything. We aren't together. We just fuck...and now he and his ex-wife fucked my mood up. I take a deep breath, let my shoulders relax, and drive away from his house. I'll text him later to ask about Story. The rest? I'm not interested.

"Why are we here?" I ask Hayden as we stroll into the nightclub hand in hand.

He glances at me. "Did you forget why people go to clubs?"

Laughing, I smack his shoulder. "I remember just fine. I'm surprised we're here alone. Where are the guys?"

"Well, Bo is with Jennie. Thanks to you, I barely see my drummer." I beam at him. The music becomes louder as we move further and further onto the dance floor. "All the other guys are here, waiting for us. They miss you, just like I do."

"Aw, who knew you were all such softies?"

"Pip, call my bandmates that again, and I'll make you pay for it. I mean it."

"Sounds promising," I tease him, wiggling my eyebrows. I wouldn't mind getting punished. A good spanking might help me get rid of that one image in my head. It's been haunting me since yesterday, and so far, nothing has helped me forget about it.

Hayden looks me up and down; a smile plays on his lips. "I love this side of you. When you're uninhibited and ready to have fun. I missed you."

"I missed you too," I confess, putting my head on his shoulder. "And I'm ready to let loose a little. I've been a good girl for far too long."

"I like the sound of that." Hade kisses my forehead, and I lean away, finally noticing the guys from his band. There are several girls at their table already. Some I've met before, some I haven't, but I don't let it bother me. I'm here to dance, drink, and have some fun. The rest doesn't matter.

Three hours later, I'm ready to scratch my eyes out. Hade's been making out with a girl for the last twenty minutes, and I want to gag. He's totally into her, and I'm having a hard time deciding what to do. I want to stay, but at the same time, I want to leave and go home. When her blond hair brushes my face again, I stand up.

"Pip?" Hayden finally breaks their kiss and stares at me wide-eyed.

"I'm going home. Have fun."

"Wait." He untangles himself from the girl and jumps to his feet, invading my personal space. "Why don't you stay?"

"Why should I? You've been busy—"

"I'm not busy."

"I think..." I sneak a glance in the girl's direction. "I don't think... um, *Sabrina* would agree with you."

"That's Stella." He laughs, instantly pissing me off.

"Bye." I twirl around, but he grabs my elbow and pulls me into his chest. "Let me go."

"Why?" he whispers in my ear, and my body goes rigid. I've never noticed it before, but his voice and his brother's are extremely similar. "You can stay and have fun instead of sulking."

"I'm not sulking, Hade." I slowly turn around. "I don't like being the third wheel."

He sighs, tugging on my elbow again. "I'm sorry, Pip. I should've realized. Do you want me to—"

"No. You look really into Stella. I don't want to ruin it for you." I take a step back, and he lets go of my arm. "I'm going home. It's for the best."

"I hate this. It's the first time in months when you're not busy, when Hunter isn't around, and I'm failing you."

"You're not failing me." I shake my head. My chest is heavy. He shouldn't have mentioned his brother. "We'll see each other soon. I'll be spending less time at Hunter's house since he has his break."

"Promise?" Hayden extends his pinkie to me.

I curl my own pinkie around his. "I promise."

He pulls me to him for a bear hug and then steps back. "You better be ready for Story's birthday. I plan to be super clingy and not let you out of my sight."

"Sounds scary." I giggle, waving to everyone at the table. "Bye, guys."

"Bye, Piper." The choir of voices makes me laugh as I make my way through the crowd.

Under other circumstances, I would've stayed. I would've found myself a guy and stayed. But tonight that's not possible, because I'm way too deep in my feelings for Hunter. Even if I hate his guts right now.

Outside the club, I take out my phone to call an Uber. I've just launched the app when a car stops in front of me. I look up, and my jaw drops.

The window rolls down, and my eyes meet Hunter's. "Need a ride?"

"What are you doing here?"

"Waiting to give you a ride home." He shrugs. "Get in."

I take a step back, narrowing my eyes. "No. I'll call an Uber."

"Get in the car, Piper."

I shake my head, focusing on my phone again. If he thinks I'm going to do—

"Get in the car, Piper, or I will drag you inside myself."

I glare at him, chewing on my bottom lip. I could make a scene. There would be a commotion, and Hayden would hear about it. He'd have questions. A lot of questions...and I'm not ready for that talk.

I scoff and get in the car. Fastening the seat belt, I look directly in front of me, not even glancing at Hunter.

"Whatever you want to say to me, I'm not interested."

He chuckles. "Good. I've got nothing to say to you anyway."

I scowl, balling my fists. Hunter drives away from the club as I slowly stew in my seat. What does he mean he has nothing to say to me? I need something to calm me down, because I'm risking making a scene for real.

"How is Story?" I ask, settling on the safest option.

"She's a little bit better. You were right; the doctor ran some tests and confirmed she has a virus," he says slowly. "She fell asleep, and I left. Amelia is looking after her."

Amelia...dammit, I hate that I care. "What did you tell your wife? Does she know where you were going?"

"My *ex*-wife," he corrects me. "I don't need to explain myself to her. I said I was going to meet a friend, and she didn't ask questions."

"A friend?"

"A friend," he repeats, and I turn my head to look at him. "Amelia and I are divorced, Piper. We don't tell each other what to do."

"You just sleep together."

Hunter gawks at me, and then bursts out laughing. "You're hilarious."

I set my jaw hard, my eyes narrowed to slits. "I saw you two on your way upstairs. She was wearing nothing but bikini bottoms. Do you think—"

"Do you think I want her, or anyone, after I've been with you?" he asks. "Amelia tried to seduce me. She was flirting with me—that's correct. But I couldn't care less about her. You're the only girl I want.

227

The only girl who gets my dick so hard it hurts. If you think I could be with anyone else after I've been with you, then I need to remind you who your pussy belongs to."

No sound leaves my parted lips as I gape at Hunter. My heartbeat is so loud in my ears, I don't hear anything else.

"How long were you waiting at the club?"

"Two hours," he says nonchalantly. "Hayden called me earlier to check on Story, and I asked about his plans. I knew where he was taking you."

"So you told your ex-wife you were going to meet a friend...at midnight?"

"Amelia never questions me, and the reasons she was flirting with me were superficial. She loves a good fuck, and she was hoping she'd get one with me. Nothing more."

He's so calm about it, while a green-eyed monster purrs in my chest. "How would you have felt if you'd seen me walking out of the club with someone?"

A smirk curves his lips as he pulls into my mom's neighborhood. He parks, unbuckles his seatbelt and mine, and then pulls me onto his lap. His hands immediately grab my ass in a firm grip.

"I would've seen red. I would've dragged you inside my car...and fucked you in the nearest parking lot."

"And how is that any different from what you're doing now?" I murmur. He lifts his hips, making me feel his hard dick.

"Now you're going to enjoy it," he states. His palm is on the back of my head, and he pulls my face toward him. Our eyes lock for a moment, and then I smash my lips onto his.

36
we all go a little mad sometimes

HUNTER

PIPER FORCES HER WAY INTO MY MOUTH, HER TONGUE slipping inside and tangling around mine. The kiss is wild as she lets her feelings overwhelm her. She sucks my tongue into her mouth, moaning against my lips. Her hands clutch my chest, fisting my hoodie. I drag one hand up her back and hide it in her hair, my fingers threading through her locks. She's so fucking sexy, I feel like I'm losing my mind any time I get to touch her. She's the only one who has this effect on me.

"I've been so angry with you," she coos as I help her take off her jacket and toss it aside. "So fucking angry, Hunter."

"Oh, baby, I know." I grab her hair in my fist, pulling her head so it bobs back. Then I press my lips to her throat. I lick and suck, teasing her skin with my tongue. When I reach her collarbone, I suck hard, leaving a big hickey. "I'm sorry for making you upset. The last thing I wanted was for you to see me with Amelia like that. You didn't deserve it, not a fucking second of it..."

I free her hair, and Piper cups my face with her hands, staring down at me. "Make sure to set boundaries...and make sure your ex-wife knows about them. I won't tolerate something like that again. Am I clear?"

My lips break into a smile. I've never seen this possessive side of her before. And it fucking turns me on.

"You're more than clear." I put my hands on her legs and slide them under her dress until I touch her panties. She's a fucking mess for me. "Fuck me, baby...ride my fucking dick like only you can."

"You have no idea what I'm going to do to you," she says breathlessly. She hoists herself up, hovering over me as I pull my dick out of my jeans. Taking a condom from my pocket, I tear the wrapper and cover my cock.

Piper lowers herself down, taking my dick inside her. I groan, enjoying the feeling of her warm pussy around me. *So fucking good.* She fucks me slowly, her hands winding around my neck. I fill my palms with her ass, deepening her movements. We maintain eye contact, and a smile ghosts over my lips. I've never been this comfortable with a woman during sex.

Watching her take me is one of my favorite things to do. Her emotions are written all over her face, and they are so easy to read. I have no doubt she loves our sex, and she has an orgasm every time. All the sounds she makes, her panting and deep sighs...I love it.

"Fuck, baby," I growl as she rotates her hips and speeds up her movements. "You feel so fucking good."

"Your dick makes me feel so full...so full, I'm ready to explode..."

Gliding my hands up her sides, I pull her dress down. Her breasts in a black lacy bra are the most beautiful things I've ever seen, but I love her bare tits even more.

"Oh God, Hunter," she whispers as I palm her breasts and lower her bra. I lean forward, kissing her puckered nipples and taking one into my mouth, grazing my teeth over it. "I'm so close...so close..."

Piper rides my cock, both hands on my chest. Her tits bounce in my face, and my mouth waters. She's fucking impeccable. I lift my hips to bury myself inside her. She fucks me slow, and my release builds inside me. I love being in control, always. But with her? I have no idea what's going on in my brain, but I'm ready to be on my fucking knees day and night if she says she wants it.

Her moans are loud, and the car rocks in time with her riding my dick. More and more, and I lose myself in her. No one exists in the world except us; no one matters except her. She's the only one I want...the only one who makes my heart beat faster, my dick harder, and my mind hazy. She feels so good in my arms that an idea pops into my head, one I haven't had in years.

What if I can have what I've craved for so long? What if—

"Oh my God," Piper gasps, ripping me out of my thoughts. Her insides tighten around my dick, and she comes with her mouth on mine. Ravishing her lips, I kiss her back, not allowing her to stop. She moves frantically, and my release swims from my head to my toes. I can't think about anything else anymore...only her.

"Will you stay with me a little bit longer?" I ask, gazing into her beautiful eyes.

Piper takes a deep breath, pressing her forehead to mine. "I'm not leaving this car without sucking you off, Mr. Hale."

"I love the sound of that."

"I'm sure you do," she purrs, kissing me slowly as I wrap my arms around her waist. "You love everything about me."

I lean away, holding her gaze. "I do. I love everything about you," I whisper, drawing her closer and covering her lips with mine.

"How was your night?" Amelia asks, pressing a mug to her lips. We're sitting in the kitchen. Story is still sound asleep in her room.

I shrug, taking a sip of my morning coffee. "Good."

"How was the sex?"

"Orgasmic."

Amelia snorts. "You never cease to amaze me, Hunter. I'm glad to know I was right about you."

"You thought I'd fuck someone as soon as our divorce finalized. It took me way longer," I tell her, "but now I realize that was a mistake. You were living your life to the fullest, while I was depriving myself of something I love."

"Sex?" Amelia smiles, setting her mug on the table. "Damn, Hale, you're something else. You wanted to get laid so badly you left the house in the middle of the night?"

"We all go a little mad sometimes, Amelia."

"We do." She stands up from the table and pats my back. "For the people we love."

Shaking my head, I stand up too. "You're making assumptions. As usual."

"There's something you always forget, Hunter." Amelia hands me her empty mug. "I *know* you."

"Because we spent eight years together?"

She sighs, looking me in the eyes. "No, honey, because we slept together. You're most vulnerable when you're on the edge of your release. Even if you don't want to admit it."

"DADDY!" Story squeals in delight, running over to me. I catch her in my arms and lift her up. "He's so beautiful."

"You like him?" I ask, smiling.

"He's the most beautiful kitten I've ever seen," she murmurs, pressing her palms to my cheeks. "You're the best."

"Just your dad?" Amelia steps into view with a little black kitten in her arms. His yellow eyes are focused on us.

"No, you too," Story says cheerfully. "I have the best mom and dad in the world."

"We're a work in progress, sweetie. We're still learning how to coexist," she mutters. "But for you? We'll move mountains. Together."

I lock eyes with her and nod. She's completely right. And it's been easier to deal with her. She doesn't irritate me like she used to. I'm calmer, and I'm even having fun spending time with her and Story—not something I expected to happen when I first agreed to let her stay here.

We spent most of the evening looking after Story's new kitten, playing with him and making sure he knows where his litterbox is. For some reason, Story says she doesn't know what to name him, that she needs time to figure it out.

I'm in the kitchen getting Story a glass of water when my phone dings. I pull it out of my pocket and run my fingers through my hair, my fingertips itching. I want to answer her...I do. But I also want to prove to myself that two days ago, in the car, when I told her I loved everything about her, was just a moment of weakness. A slipup.

PIPER:

Does Story like her new kitten?

Clenching my jaw, I swipe away her message and pocket my phone. I'll answer her later. Maybe tomorrow. Or maybe I can keep my distance till Story's birthday party. It's in two days, so I can talk to her then. Yeah, I totally can.

I pour some water into a glass and head back to the living room. I feel weird, but I decide to ignore it. As soon as she's back in my house, I'll figure out what it all means.

37
while i was away
PIPER

"I wanted to go all out for Story's birthday, but her parents said no," Hayden mutters as we stroll toward the house.

"She was really sick a few days ago." I shrug, pressing her gift to my chest.

"It was always supposed to be small," Riley says. I glance at her. "Story told me before you went to Spain that she only wanted her family...and us."

"You're part of the family, kid." Hayden leans forward to catch her gaze. "It's time you remember that."

"Really? Who is Piper married to? You or your brother?" She laughs, and my heart beats faster. Hunter hasn't spoken to me since he dropped me off at my mom's house four days ago. Not even a text. Total silence, and it makes my skin itch.

"You don't need marriage to create this kind of bond." Hayden meets my gaze and grins. I nod, grimacing, as if from sudden pain. I'm having a hard time returning his smile. I have no idea what would happen to our friendship if the truth about Hunter and me were to come out...or if things between us were to fall apart. Right now, the second option seems possible.

"Marriage still sounds better." Riley chuckles but instantly falls quiet once she catches me glaring at her. "Just kidding."

"Of course you are." Hayden snickers, knocking on the door. "Pip deserves the best."

"I love that you're so critical of yourself," Riley mumbles under her breath. "But who said Hunter isn't—"

"Can you two stop?" I snap. My neck is getting hot.

Hayden shoves his hands in his pockets, and Riley looks away, focusing on a bush near the porch. They are both pissing me off. My mood is already fucked-up enough. I don't need them riling me up.

A smiling Willow opens the door and lets us in. "You're right on time. Story's been asking about you."

"Sorry it took us so long," Hayden says, kissing his mom's cheek. "We needed to pick up this little monkey after her dance class."

"You're such an—" Riley says, and I clap a hand over her mouth.

Willow laughs, shaking her head. "Sweetheart, that's quite alright. My son deserves whatever name Riley wants to call him. She's far from a little monkey."

I give her an awkward grin and drop my hand from Riley's face. "It's still Story's birthday. I don't think she should hear words like that. Right, Riley?"

Her face turns red as she lowers her head. "Sorry. I should've thought about that."

I shift my gaze and peer at Hayden, as he's the one who started all this. He rolls his eyes, heaving a sigh. "I'm sorry too."

He's not, and he's not even hiding it. I'm not surprised, just disappointed. Lately, I've been thinking a lot, and I truly believe Hayden needs a reality check. He's been acting like a total douchebag and not bothering to say he's sorry, even when he knows he's in the wrong. Calling Riley a little monkey was definitely a joke, but his behavior afterward speaks for itself. He's used to getting away with everything, and I'm not okay with it.

"Everyone's in the living room. The birthday girl is playing Monopoly with her dad and granddad." Willow walks into the living room, and we all follow her after taking off our jackets. I hand our gift to Riley so she can carry it.

Stepping into the house, I'm cautious. I don't know what to

expect. The only thing I'm sure about is that I need to be professional. Willow and Colin might know about Hunter and me, but I don't want to add Hayden and Amelia to that group. And definitely not Story or Riley.

"Piper!" Story rushes over to me, ignoring everyone else. I kneel just in time to catch her in my arms, and she winds her hands around my neck. "I missed you so, so much."

"Me too, honey," I murmur, pressing her close to my chest. "How do you feel?"

"Good. Mom and Dad were with me, and I got better in no time." She leans away, studying my face. Her round eyes glimmer with warmth. "Come see my cat. I want you to help me name him."

"I was sure you already chose a name with your parents." Story shakes her head no, and my insides warm. The butterflies in my stomach do a happy dance. It means so much to me, I have trouble hiding it. "I'd be honored to help you name him."

She plants a kiss on my cheek, and I put her down. As I stand back up, I feel someone's gaze on me. I know it's Hunter's without even looking in his direction, and still I whip my head and lock eyes with him. He's sitting on the couch with his father. There's a little black kitten curled up on his lap, and he caresses its fur absentmindedly. I have so many questions for him, but I'm not sure I have the right to ask.

Playing with one of my curls, I look away and focus on Riley and Story. My sister hands over our gift, a little backpack full of puzzles, perfume, and a soft plush kitten, telling her she hopes all her birthday wishes come true. Riley kisses her cheek and stands up, sneaking a glance at me. I drape an arm over her shoulders and press her to my side.

"Thank you for coming with me," I whisper, and Riley snuggles into me, her nose in my curly hair. "It means so much."

"I wouldn't have missed it. I love Story."

I kiss her temple as we watch Hayden with Story. Willow is standing next to them, smiling. And then it hits me. In this idyllic picture, one person is absent. Where is Amelia?

As if on cue, she enters the room, holding a glass of wine. She's wearing a simple white dress, and her hair is in a high ponytail. Even so casual, she looks like the movie star she is. I shift uncomfortably as our gazes clash.

She sashays over, stopping in front of Riley and me. "I just realized we've never been properly introduced." Amelia extends her hand to me. "I'm Amelia."

"Piper. Nice to meet you." I shake her hand quickly and gesture to my sister. "This is my sister, Riley."

"It's nice to meet you, Riley," Amelia murmurs, bringing her eyes back to my face. "You have a very beautiful little sister. She'll be gorgeous once she's older, just like you."

"Um, thank you. Are you enjoying your time in LA?"

"I am. I like it here." She taps her fingertips on her wineglass. "Maybe I'll visit more often. I haven't decided yet."

"Story will be very happy if you do," I tell her, feeling someone's presence behind me. I glance over my shoulder and see Hunter's father approach.

"Should we sit down to eat? Lunch is getting cold," Colin says, wrapping an arm around Amelia's waist and ushering her toward the dining room.

My emotions are weird. I feel like a stranger in this house...and I've only been gone ten days. What else has changed while I was away?

I have a slight suspicion I won't like learning the answer to that question.

Exhaling harshly, I nudge Riley, and we stroll to the table. It's full of different dishes, and the smell is mouthwatering. But I'm not hungry; I feel nauseous. This little gathering is going to be much harder to survive than I thought.

TWO HOURS LATER, all I want to do is disappear. Not only from this house—but from the face of the freaking planet. I'm sitting between Hayden and Riley, and he has spent the whole time making fun of her with his silly jokes. They've been bickering for almost an hour already, and I haven't managed to stop it. No one else has any problem with it; everyone is laughing at their antics.

I caught Hunter's gaze on me once, but the moment was so fleeting I thought maybe it was an illusion. He ignored my texts for days, and now he's ignoring my presence. The only thing keeping me sane is the fact that he's been distant with his ex-wife too. He's all about Story, making sure she ate, talking to her, asking if she likes her birthday party. It does something to my lady parts. As usual. Even if I am mostly in the mood to strangle him.

Walking into the kitchen with a few empty plates, I almost stumble over Story's little kitten. I clumsily move around him, putting the plates on the counter. Bending down, I take him into my arms. I caress his fur, examine his little form, and smile. I know the name I want to suggest. It'll suit him perfectly.

"Do you like Story?" I ask, my fingers threading through his fur. Quiet purrs fill the room and make me smile. "I shouldn't have asked. She's impossible not to love. I'm sure you're having a lot of fun with her. The house is so big and so—"

"He mostly spends time with Hunter." A voice behind me startles me. I turn around and meet Amelia's eyes. "The little furball loves Story, but I highly doubt he sees her as his owner. He chose Hunter."

"Cats always choose the person who feeds them," I state, stepping aside to let her walk past me. She puts my empty plates into the dishwasher, along with the ones she brought.

"Maybe. I just know that cats are easy to satisfy." Amelia props herself on her elbow, leaning against the counter. "Not as easy as my ex, but you're managing pretty well."

"What do you mean?"

"Piper, I know what a sex-deprived Hunter Hale looks like. He hasn't looked that way for a while." She smiles, and it sends chills down my spine.

"You're making assumptions."

She tsks. The sound is loud and clear in the quiet of the kitchen.

"Listen, Piper, I have nothing against Hunter moving on. Even if it is with our kid's nanny. I know Story loves you, and that you love her in return." Amelia pushes herself off the counter. "The problem is him. I'm talking from experience. The man will never change, and I don't want Story to be disappointed and heartbroken again."

"You were together for eight years. Why do you—"

"He's not built for committed relationships. They scare him, and he pushes people away, hurting them to avoid hurting himself." Veering left, Amelia heads to the living room. I stay still, my fingers trembling as I hold the little kitten. Then she looks over her shoulder and meets my eyes. "Colin cheating on Willow ruined Hunter. The man is broken."

She walks away, and I find it hard to breathe.

Colin is a cheater?

38
spiraling

HUNTER

"ANY CHANCE YOU WANT TO PLAY SOMETHING ELSE?"
Amelia asks, lowering herself onto the couch beside Story. She jerks
her head no without even looking at her mom; her eyes are focused on
the board. "I should've known."

I sneak a glance at my Amelia, smirking to myself. She's pouting,
and her arms are crossed over her chest. She never wins at Monopoly,
and I'm not surprised she wanted to set the table instead of playing
with everyone. Riley and Story have more properties than Hayden
and me; they're almost neck and neck. They're competitive, but
they're also supportive of each other.

I look around the room. Where is Piper? I haven't seen her for a
while, not since we said good-bye to my parents. And that was an hour
ago. I try to focus on the game again, but I can't. I missed my turn
twice, and I lost all of my properties.

"It's definitely not your day, Hunter," Hayden teases, meeting my
gaze.

"I'm bankrupt." I shrug, stand up from the couch, and turn away
from Amelia. "Do any of you want some snacks? Drinks?"

Story and Riley look up at me and shake their heads. My brother
lifts his glass of whiskey, letting me know he's good.

I nod and head to the bathroom, using it as an excuse to go find Piper.

Ignoring her because my ex insinuated I'm in love with her? It's a mistake. She doesn't deserve that.

Once I'm out of my room, I go to the backyard. Piper is there, sitting on the sunbed. Story's little kitten is sleeping on her lap. She looks peaceful, staring off into the distance, her fingers playing with her little pendant. I come closer and sit down on the edge of the sunbed.

"You're not in the mood for Monopoly?" I ask, and she purses her lips.

My gaze coasts over her face and down her dress, and my throat tightens. Piper is breathtakingly beautiful. Her hair is in little curls pulled over one shoulder, and she's twirling it around her finger, letting it go and then twirling it again. Her deep turquoise dress, with its high neckline and long sleeves, makes it impossible not to notice her. She's all I want to look at...but I spent the whole day avoiding her.

"Did he follow you out here?" I nod to the kitten and hear nothing in return. "He spends most of his time with Story, but if he notices me on the couch or in my bed—he's instantly on my lap."

Piper keeps quiet. Her gaze is trained on the little terrace nearby. I've been giving her the silent treatment for four days. So afraid to show how much I care. I even asked my father to step in and distract her from Amelia instead of doing it myself. It's no surprise she has no desire to talk to me.

"Piper, I'm sorry. I should've answered your text, should've stayed in touch." The words rush out, and I feel like a little boy, nervous she'll leave before I get the chance to explain myself. "We had such a great time in my car, and—"

"You mean our sex was great, right?" she utters, her voice laced with anger. "You came for your fix, got it, and ghosted me. Left me on read for four days. Acted like I'm a stranger to you."

"It's not like that."

"That's the impression you gave me."

"I'm a jerk. I let Amelia's words get in my head and tried to prove her wrong. Hurting you in the process."

She smirks, shaking her head. "Looks like you're still not over her. Either way, I don't see any reason for you to believe whatever she said."

"She's manipulative."

"And you're gullible," she counters, looking me right in the eyes. I ball my fist and grit my teeth.

"Piper, you have no idea what you're talking about. She's an actress. A good one. She knows exactly what to say to rile you up." I hold her gaze. "You don't know how she—"

"Trust me, Hunter, I know how she is. We had a *lovely* talk in your kitchen."

My eyebrows draw together in confusion. I've been keeping an eye on Amelia, making sure she doesn't corner Piper. She was always on my radar, and I don't remember...*fuck*. Story went to her room to get her new favorite Elsa doll, and then she came back and asked me to help her find it. It took no more than five minutes.

"What did she say to you?" I ask.

"She's sure we're fucking," she replies with indifference, staring at me with a calm expression on her face. Then she snorts, a snide smile stretching across her lips. "And, surprisingly, just like your mom and your brother, Amelia believes you're going to hurt me, going to hurt Story in the process because we're so close. You're bad news, Hunter Hale."

My mouth hangs open as I gawk at Piper.

"Did Colin cheat on Willow?" she asks, and my blood boils. The vein in my neck bulges as I try to even out my breathing.

Jumping to my feet, I hover over Piper. The kitten startles; his fur puffs up. She grimaces, slowly wraps her hand around him, and lifts the skirt of her dress higher. He scratched her when I scared him, and a tiny streak of blood has appeared on her thigh.

"Fuck." Piper stands up and heads back into the house with the kitten pressed to her chest. I follow her, coming to an abrupt stop when she does.

Hayden leans against the doorframe. His hands are hidden in his pockets.

"How long have you been here?" I ask, stepping forward and lining up with Piper.

"For a minute or two," he answers, his eyes dashing between her and me. "You two looked kinda tense. What's going on?"

I'm fucking your best friend and have probably managed to fall for her. No big deal, obviously.

"The kitten scratched me." Piper pushes past him into the house.

Hayden and I just stand there in silence. I'm grateful for this moment to catch my breath, until—

"What do you want from Piper?"

"Excuse me?" I frown, my gaze clashing with Hayden's.

"You left the room and never came back. And then I found you sitting outside with her. A little too close for my fucking liking."

"We were talking," I state. "You're not her boyfriend."

"Because you are?" he demands, and I barely hold myself back from punching him. I don't want Story to remember her eighth birthday as the day when her dad and uncle got into a fistfight.

"She's Story's nanny. We've become close after spending so much time together, and I decided to check on her. Didn't I tell you to loosen up—"

"Fuck you, Hunter," Hayden spits, crossing his arms over his chest. "I'm just overprotective."

"You don't give her enough credit. She's fully capable of standing up for herself."

"She's always been there for everyone, especially her family, while no one but me was there for her. I just want her to be safe." He licks his lips.

I huff out a breath through my nostrils. "We were just talking, Hayden. I noticed she was gone and decided to look for her since I was losing anyway."

He nods. His shoulders slump, and a little grin plays at the corners of his mouth. "Story won. She's the monopolist."

"She sure is." I smile, gradually relaxing.

My talk with Piper won't be easy, but I'll explain everything to her. Just not tonight. Tonight, I'm going to talk to my ex...and she's going to regret meddling.

IT's quiet in the house. Story is already asleep with her kitten, who's curled into a ball on top of her blanket. Piper completely ignored me for the rest of the evening, focusing only on Story. They even made plans for next Monday, after Piper's week off. A huge weight left my shoulders when I heard that. I was afraid she'd quit.

Everyone left an hour ago, and now Amelia is sitting on the couch in the living room with a glass of wine. I plop down beside her.

"Who gave you the right to tell Piper anything about my father?"

"I thought she should know since it's the reason you're so opposed to the idea of a relationship." Amelia shrugs. "Anything else?"

"This is the last time I'll let you stay in my house. Your visit has messed up a lot for me."

Amelia watches me from under her lashes, then chuckles and stands up. "You're so wrong, Hunter Hale. I didn't mess up anything. It was all you."

"That's bullshit."

She snorts, bends down, and focuses her gaze on me. "Even before I got here, I knew you were fooling around with Piper. Our daughter talks a lot, Hunter, and she's sure her daddy is in love. Just like her nanny."

"She—"

"She told me how happy she was for you. How much she loves Piper, and how much she wants her to stay." Her lips twist into a scowl as her eyes roam over my face. "I wanted to make sure you were serious about her. To make sure Story wouldn't be heartbroken because her dad would screw up and Piper would leave. And you fucking failed."

What does she mean?

"I didn't fail," I insist.

Amelia takes a deep breath and continues with the tiniest shrug. "I noticed how you looked at her when you got home from Spain. How indifferent you were to me, even topless. I thought it was a good sign. That maybe you were changing...but you proved me wrong." She points her finger at me, straightening her back. "The second I said you were in love with her, you changed back into your old self. You're so afraid to admit your feelings, you'd rather ignore her."

"Were you snooping?"

"I didn't need to. I know you like the back of my hand." She steps back, bumping into the table. Her wineglass falls to the floor and breaks. Neither of us look at it, both too pissed to care. "If your actions and your fucking dick force Piper to leave and break Story's heart, I'll take her to London with me. And you'll be the one visiting us."

Amelia turns on her heels and storms out of the room. *What was that? She was testing me?* My vision blurs, and I hide my face in my hands. I'm spiraling...and it's not a good sign.

39
through his eyes
PIPER

THE FRONT DOOR OPENS, AND HUNTER'S GREEN EYES LAND on me. "Hey, come in."

He steps aside, and I walk into his house but stay near the front door.

"I wasn't sure if I should use my key. Didn't want to barge in without an invitation," I say.

"You're always welcome here," he tells me, pointing at my bag. "Can I?"

"It's fine." I shift, tilting my head. "I need to go to my room anyway since I have a few hours before I pick up Story."

He nods and slips his hands in his pockets. The look on his face is guarded, lips tight and eyes narrowed. "Can we talk after you unpack?"

"Is that necessary?" I drawl.

"I believe so."

I scoff, pinching my eyebrows together. "Okay. I need twenty minutes."

"I'll wait for you in the living room."

I feel his gaze on me as I head to my bedroom. Heaviness fills my chest. I've been trying to cool off, to not let it bother me, but I can't.

I'm not a doormat, but recently I've allowed myself to be treated like one. It needs to stop.

Hunter and I agreed to a casual relationship—no strings attached, no feelings. And yet, I fell in love with him. I want more. Not just because our sex is mind-blowing, but because I truly see how great we can be together. As partners, as friends, and even parents for Story. I want him to want me. To want us. And after that night in his car, I thought he wanted the same. Then he ghosted me.

I don't have a great track record when it comes to relationships, and I don't think he does either. But I'm willing to give him a chance. Put all of myself into this relationship and try to make it work.

While he acts as if it's better to cut all ties with me.

After I put my clothes back into the closet, I close the doors and step in front of the mirror. My hair is in a messy bun, and a few wild locks frame my face. I tuck them behind my ears and take a deep breath. I promised myself I'd give him a chance to explain and only then decide about my future.

In the living room, my eyes lock with Hunter's. He's sitting on the couch, and Story's kitten is lying on his lap. I try to suppress my smile, biting my inner cheek, but I immediately give up when the kitten sprawls out onto his back with his little paws in the air. It's way too adorable.

"You look cozy."

"I can't resist him." Hunter chuckles, lowering his gaze to the kitten as I come closer and sit beside him. "Any time I sit down, he's there, stretching his little paws, trying to get me to pick him up. I have no idea why he chose me."

"Animals are very intuitive. They can sense a good person from a mile away."

"Well, then I'm a good person. At least in this cat's opinion."

I roll my eyes, letting my shoulders slump when I lean against the couch. "What did you want to talk to me about?"

"Everything. I owe you an explanation."

"That's fair." I nod, pulling my legs up under my butt. As my eyes wander over the room, I feel conflicted. It's a sunny day, and the living room is decorated in bright colors, but the atmosphere is heavy. A dark and oppressive energy forms in the pit of my stomach, and I don't know what to think of it.

"There is a reason I told you I'd never get involved with anyone else at the start of our agreement. I'm not a cheater. Even when my marriage was slowly falling apart, I was never tempted. I would never risk Story's love, would never risk custody of my kid." He runs a hand over his face. "I'd never, ever cheat on a woman. I'd respect her way too much. I know what infidelity does to families. How it affects the kids. My own experience was traumatizing, and I'd never wish it on anyone else."

"Did Colin really cheat on Willow? How did that even happen?"

"Mom left the US for me. She was living in Spain with me, and then later with me and Hayden. She was happy, even if she had her hands full with both of us so far from home. While Dad...he was here, alone. Busy at work, barely going anywhere, cruising between our house and his office." He pauses, his fingers rapping on his thigh. "He was assigned to a project with his new colleague, Alice. The project was successful, and they went out to a bar to celebrate afterward. He fucked her after that little party...because he was drunk and lonely."

I grimace, my heart pummeling against my rib cage. "How did you find out?"

"We came home for Christmas. Mom found a bra in the dirty laundry."

"That's horrible." I wrinkle my nose. "How could he do that to Willow? How could he bring his mistress to his family's house? I would've been disgusted."

"That's why they sold the house."

"What?" I lean forward, my eyes searching his face.

"The house my parents live in right now isn't the house it happened in," Hunter says. "Mom gave him three months to sell the house, find a new one, and quit his job. He did what she asked him to do. She took Hayden and me back to Spain and arranged everything so I could live alone."

"So his infidelity..." I trail off, feeling so much pity for him.

"Is the reason Mom and Hayden returned to the US, and I was left on my own." He shrugs, focusing his gaze on something behind my back, his eyes glassy. "Mom forgave him. She found excuses. She said she had me and Hayden, but Dad was all alone. She even said it was her fault, that she didn't understand how lonely he was and how badly it was affecting him. The best evidence of gaslighting and manipulation."

"I don't know what to say," I quietly confess. "I never expected anything like that. I saw your hostility toward your father, but I never knew why. Hayden doesn't have a problem with Colin."

"Hayden doesn't know. Mom begged me to never tell him. He was too small." Hunter gives me a pointed look. My palms are sweating, and my stomach twirls and turns, nausea washing over me. "It was hard for me to move on. Their affair lasted four months. Who knows if he would've had the balls to stop it if Mom hadn't found out. That's not how a man should behave. I'm ashamed my own father treated my mom like that."

"Do you hate him?"

"Not anymore." Hunter shakes his head. "I forgave him, but I didn't forget. I know he did a lot for Mom to give him another chance. He proved himself to her and was a great father to Hayden. Just not to me."

I look at him, and I see myself through his deep green eyes. His gaze is warm and encompassing, just like his embrace. I feel good around him; I feel safe with him. He's like my own personal harbor, the place I want to return to. No matter the weather, no matter the hardships. It's a place I don't want to leave.

"Hunter." His name escapes my mouth, and my heart sinks to my feet. "I'm not bailing out of our agreement. I just need a little break. You ghosting me made me feel like a booty call, and this last time was too much."

He cups my cheek. The tenderness of his touch makes my knees weak. "I'm so sorry for making you feel like that. You're the most amazing thing that has happened to me in my entire life, and—"

Hunter stops, frowning as if he's realizing what he just said. I part my lips; my pulse is going insane. It's like we're back in his car and he's telling me that he loves everything about me.

I want him to want us. Simple as that.

"I—"

His phone buzzes, making me stutter. I close my mouth, watching as he picks it up from the couch. The more he stares at the screen, the angrier he looks. Eventually he grits his teeth and looks back up at me.

"I need to get going. I need to fix something."

Hunter stands up from the couch. His posture radiates cold rage. He runs a hand over his face, releasing a sharp breath. His grip on his phone is strong, his knuckles turning white. What could've happened for him to react like that?

"See you later, Piper." He storms down the hallway, and then he's gone. I don't remember ever seeing him so pissed. Something really bad must've happened. But what?

I'm on pins and needles, both excited and worried. I'm on my way to pick up Story. I missed my little girl so much, and I can't wait to spend time with her. But I also can't seem to stop thinking about her dad. I want to know what happened.

My phone dings as I park at Story's school. I pick it up from the passenger seat and see a message from Hayden.

HADE:

I have a gift for you

Three dots appear as he types his next message. I wait, curious to know what the gift is. Then a picture comes through, and I suddenly want to disappear.

It's a simple white coffee mug with a quote, one that's fully capable of ruining our friendship. *I sleep with my boss* is written in big, curving letters. *Fuck*.

ME:

How did you find out?

My phone dings a moment later, and a new picture pops up on my screen. It's a screenshot of an Instagram post from some gossip magazine. Hunter and I are kissing near his car in front of my mom's house. I read the caption, and slowly my breathing calms down. There's nothing about us having sex, only the mention of him giving his daughter's nanny a long good-night kiss.

Who would've said no to Hunter Hale kissing them good night?

HADE:

see you at our usual spot, tonight at seven

I take a deep breath and toss my phone back onto the passenger seat. There's nothing I can do to change what happened. It's time I face Hayden and tell him the truth. I just hope he cares enough to listen.

40
the end of us

SITTING IN MY CAR, I STARE AT THE OCEAN. IT'S CALM. Only tiny waves reach the beach, as if in slow motion. It has a soothing effect on me, and I'm beyond grateful for that. The state I'm in is close to hysteria. I'm anxious, and my heart is ready to jump out of my chest. The talk I'm about to have is scaring me to death. I don't want to lose Hayden. His friendship means the world to me.

I jump outside and shiver, the brisk wind enveloping my body. I put up my hood and pad to the ocean. Hayden is already there, sitting on the sand and staring out at the water. I lower myself beside him, focusing on the ocean too.

"Where is Story?" he asks in a low voice.

"With her dad. He got home forty minutes ago, and I told him I had something I needed to do."

Hunter looked exhausted when he came in, but I was too busy worrying about my talk with Hade to care what caused it. He didn't ask a single question when I said I was leaving, just nodded in agreement and told me he'd take care of Story himself.

Hayden squints at me, and I meet his gaze. "Don't you have anything to say?"

"Your brother and I sleep together. That's all."

Hade blinks, his gaze darting to the ocean and then back to me.

252

"Are you together? Or is it some kind of sick friends with benefits situation?"

"There's nothing sick about it." I fold my arms over my chest. "I like Hunter, and he likes me. Our agreement works perfectly for us."

"And how long have you been sleeping with him?"

"Two months." I take a deep breath. "I'm sorry I kept it to myself, but I truly don't think it concerns anyone else."

Hayden is silently seething. His nostrils flare as he clenches and unclenches his fists. His chest rises and falls, his eyes never leaving my face. He takes a long breath, and then he exhales loudly.

"Didn't I tell you Hunter is bad news?"

"You did. I don't agree."

"You don't know him—"

"I believe *you* don't know him. Hunter isn't who you think he is. If you spent as much time with him as I do, you'd see that," I counter. "He's kind and caring. And he's very intuitive when it comes to people. Hunter's been through a lot, but I highly doubt you know anything about it. It's not your fault, because he's obviously very reserved when it comes to others, but you don't have the right to judge him without knowing his side of the story."

Closing my mouth, I just look at Hayden. He stares at me without saying a word. My heart beats violently in my chest. He drops his gaze, his shoulders slumping. He threads his long fingers through his hair, looking anywhere but at me. Then he clears his throat.

"The way you talk about him proves it. You fell in love with him. You fucking love Hunter, and I'm sure you want to be with him." Hade licks his lips and swallows hard. "You're not wrong when you say I don't know a lot about him. But I know he'll never be with you. Sex, yes. But a relationship? No."

That's what Hunter told me too. I didn't have any illusions when our situationship started, because I didn't need more from him. I didn't want more. But that's changed. And I think it's changed for him too.

"For now, we're just enjoying our time together. Nothing—"

"Look me in the eye, Piper, and tell me you don't want to be with

Hunter. Tell me you don't love him. Tell me I'm wrong," Hayden demands, holding my gaze.

I purse my lips tightly, setting my jaw so hard my teeth hurt. "I can't."

Hade turns away, locking his hands behind his head. Then he watches me in silence, his eyes slowly narrowing to slits. He's lost in thought, and I'm scared to interrupt him.

"It needs to stop," he states, and I grimace.

"That's not for you to decide."

"It's for your own good," Hade says matter-of-factly. "He'll break your heart."

Leaving him will break my heart. When the thought crosses my mind, my eyes fill with tears.

"Everything is fine, Hayden. You haven't seen us together. You don't know—"

"Tell him you love him. Tell him you love him, and you'll see how quickly he kicks you out of his house."

"He won't. It would hurt Story."

"As if either of you thought about her when you started fucking. She'll be heartbroken anyway, because if you don't leave now, you'll leave once your contract is over. He'll never love you back, Piper. There's no room in his heart for anything except Story and soccer. The man doesn't even love his parents."

"He loves his mom!" I snap. The first tear slips out of my eye and slides down my cheek. "And he loves you, but you're too fucking self-centered to notice it."

"He couldn't care—"

"He *cares*, Hade." I wipe away another tear with the heel of my palm. "He's not the heartless jerk you try to portray him as."

Hayden runs a hand over his face, his green eyes stormy. "If he's not who I think he is, then tell him you love him. If you're right about him, you have nothing to lose."

"Why should I?"

"Because I said so," he hisses. "Tell him, or I'll do it myself."

My mouth hangs open as I gawk at him in disbelief. Is this really my best friend? The person who swore to help me? To always be by my side? This is not how friendship works. This is manipulation.

Standing up, I shake the sand off my jeans. I look down and hover over Hayden. He's my best friend...and my worst enemy at the same time.

"I'll let you know how it goes," I say and stroll toward my car. When I'm about to open the door, Hayden catches up to me.

He grabs my elbow and twirls me around. "Pip, I'm sorry if I'm too pushy...and too aggressive. I just really believe it's for the best. You'll thank me later."

Thank him later? Our friendship is done, at least until he knows how wrong he is.

I nod, pulling my elbow out of his grip. "Bye, Hayden."

"Bye, Piper." He frowns and steps back. "Call me later?"

I get in my car, start the engine, and only then look at Hade. My heart aches, because I know this is the end of our friendship. Whether it's just for now or for good will depend solely on him. He's the one ruining it right now.

"Good-bye, Hade," I whisper and drive away. Once I'm far enough from the beach, I let my tears flow.

WALKING INTO HUNTER'S HOUSE, I quietly close the door. I'm a mess, afraid to even look at myself in the mirror. At some point I couldn't even drive, so I pulled over in the parking lot of some restaurant and cried. I could've never imagined Hayden would act like that with me. He was always overprotective, and kinda nosy, but never like he was today.

"Hey." Hunter frowns once he sees me. "Is everything okay?"

"Yes." I nod, and then instantly jerk my head no. "No."

"Come here," he murmurs, and I drag my feet over to him. He wraps his strong arms around me, and I close my eyes, hiding my face in his chest. "Will you tell me what happened?"

"Yeah." I sniff. "Is Story already asleep?"

"I put her to bed an hour ago," he tells me, pulling away and taking my hand in his. "Let's go to the kitchen? I can make us some tea or coffee."

"Tea would be perfect."

"Anything you want," he says and kisses my forehead.

"WHERE DID YOU GO TODAY? You looked pissed after you read that text." I take a sip of chamomile tea.

"Autumn Dunn sent me a message. God knows how, but she got her hands on pictures of you and me kissing. She tried to blackmail me." I straighten my spine and look at him, forgetting how to breathe. "She got fired. Her boss didn't like what I showed him, and I made him listen to the recording of my conversation with her. Unfortunately, she wasn't the only one who knew about the pictures. They were live for a few hours, but they should've been deleted by now. At least from all major platforms. My lawyers are good at their job."

"Oh. You definitely know how to deal with all this stuff."

"It's called damage control." Hunter offers me a smile. "The last thing I want is paparazzi following our every step, trying to take pictures of us together, making up crazy stories. You don't need that stress in your life."

I know he means well, but after my conversation with Hayden, his words are too deep under my skin. They poison the blood in my veins, and I suddenly don't hear a thing. He doesn't want people to see us together because he doesn't want them to assume we're a couple. I'm a good fuck, but I'm not enough to be anything more than that.

"Hayden knows," I blurt, plunging my gaze into Hunter's. "He saw the pictures."

He pushes away from the table; his darkened gaze roams my face. "Did you see him?"

"Yes. He wanted to talk to me."

"And?" Hunter cocks an eyebrow at me, and I feel as if someone has their hands around my throat, strangling me. I'm struggling for air.

"He thinks we should stop."

Hunter's eyebrows pinch together. "He thinks he has the right to tell you what to do. Why?"

"He says it's for the best," I mutter under my breath. "He thinks you'll break my heart." I watch him intently, noticing as his face pales. "Because I'm in love with you."

"Piper..."

"I'm in love with you, Hunter. I know it's not what we agreed on, and trust me, I didn't expect it to happen. But I love you. I want us to try...I want you to want us to try."

My words drown in silence. He just keeps staring at me, not moving, not even blinking.

"Piper, I'm sorry." A sob bolts from my chest when he says it. "I think Hayden is right. We should stop."

I swallow the lump in my throat and set my mug on the table. "Okay."

"That's why I asked you in Spain if this was more than just sex for you. I didn't want you to get hurt...because that's what I always do to women. I hurt them." His words sound muffled, as if there's a wall separating us. "I was honest with you. It was always just sex. I don't want more."

I stand up in a daze, and he stands too. Our eyes lock as I take a step away from the table.

"Then it's the end," I say. "The end of us."

It's the only solution. The only one...even if it will break me into a billion pieces.

I look over my shoulder, raking my gaze over his face. His lips are pressed tightly together, and his eyes are narrowed. Hunter stands still, his hands hidden in his pockets.

"You'll need to find Story a new nanny. I can't work for you anymore," I whisper. "I'll take her to school tomorrow and bring her home later...and I'd like to talk to her. I want to tell her myself that I'm leaving. Please, can I tell her myself?"

"Piper, this is—"

"Can I tell her myself?" I ask, raising my voice. "I'll figure out what to say. Don't worry. She'll never know about us."

"You can talk to her."

Tears are stinging my eyes again. "Thanks. Good night, Hunter."

Without waiting for him to respond, I storm out of the kitchen, down the hallway, and straight to my room, tearing my clothes off once the door is closed. I amble into the bathroom, step into the shower, and stand under the pouring water. My tears are flowing, but I don't pay them any attention. My broken heart hurts so much it's blinding. I want it to stop.

41
know the enemy

HUNTER

I'M WIDE AWAKE. I CAN'T SEEM TO FALL ASLEEP. SHE'S JUST behind the wall, in another room, but it feels like she's miles away. *I want you to want us to try.* Her words are on repeat in my head. It's a never-ending loop, over and over, and it's all I can focus on. The pain in her eyes haunts me, making my skin sweaty and my veins throb. I broke her heart, and I don't even know what for.

All my life, I've been causing pain and heartbreak. The second a relationship became serious, I felt trapped, and I was out. I would focus on my career, refuse to even think about commitment. Women were distractions, and relationships were a nuisance I could easily avoid. I saw how my teammates would lose focus when they fell in love, how their game would fall slack when things were rough between them and their partners, how fucking terrible they were on the pitch after a breakup. I didn't want that. No-strings-attached relationships suited me well, and most of the girls I met were fine with it...at first. My situationships would get sidetracked, and they'd ask, *What are we?* Once that happened, I was up and gone.

My father's infidelity is partly to blame. I'd never cheat, but the fear of being cheated on is real. He was unfaithful because he was lonely, because Mom wasn't home. I was often on the road—barely home once championships started. The thought of coming home and seeing my woman with someone else was pervasive. No matter the reassurances, no matter how good my relationships were, I still expected them to cheat. It was a default assumption, one I made about every woman I was with.

When it became a huge problem, I finally decided to work on my issues. Two years in therapy helped me a ton.

After that, I was open to the idea of a relationship. That's when Amelia stepped into the picture. Dear God, how much I wanted us to work. I ignored everything that bothered me, convinced myself again and again that she was the one. Looking back, I don't regret my marriage. Because I got the experience, and because I have Story. She's the light in my darkness, the push that always keeps me going, my little princess. I'd build a whole damn castle if that's what she wants.

And yet, my divorce was the final nail in my coffin. I closed the relationship chapter of my life, decided to focus only on Story and football. Moving back to LA was supposed to help me with that. Then Piper walked into my house.

She's different from anyone I've ever been with. It's not about how she looks—it's what she makes me feel. She's nurturing and caring, loyal to a fault, and so kind. Everything in her is soft, her voice, her curves, her touch. She's warm, but her warmth isn't physical; it's the feeling she carries within herself. I'm aware of her wherever she is. Sometimes, even when I don't hear her move, I can still feel her. She filled this house with so much happiness and joy. At first, it felt foreign to me. It was empty without her, but now it's full. Full of laughter, conversation, and love. I feel complete with her around...and I just pushed her away. Ruined the best thing that has ever happened to me aside from Story. Wrecked it to the point where there's nothing left but ashes. Nothing left except the hole in my chest.

WHEN I HEARD the door close this morning, I didn't leave my room. I stayed in bed even after I knew she was back. Listening to her move around in her bedroom and knowing damn well she was packing her clothes. She only came back to me one day ago, but now she's leaving for good. All because I couldn't utter a word, couldn't tell her how much I love her.

I'm bad news. I can't give her what she needs. I always sabotage my life and my relationships. It won't change; it never does. I'm always the one to screw up and damage a good thing. Football and being Story's dad are the only things I know how to deal with. The only things I'm good at.

I get up from my bed, go to the shower, and stand under the cold water fully dressed. I want to shake off this feeling so bad, and yet I know I can't. Her talk with Story is approaching, and I have no idea if I'll be able to handle my kid's reaction.

AN EMPTY MUG sits in front of me as I stare off into the distance. Everything in my kitchen reminds me of her. How I was rude to her and she told me off, how I fucked her on the counter while talking to Hayden, how many laughs we shared cooking dinner, how many talks and stolen kisses this kitchen has witnessed. I run a hand over my face when I hear the front door open, and Story's voice follows.

"Daddy?"

Wetting my lips, I stand up from my chair. I go to the living room, and my eyes instantly find Piper. She's holding Story's kitten in her arms, caressing his fur. Her gaze is focused on the ground. She has makeup on, but it doesn't fool me. Her eyelids are puffy, and there are dark circles under her eyes. She's been crying.

"Yes, sweetheart." I force myself to look at Story, who's standing next to Piper. "How was your day?"

"It was good," she answers, coming closer. "I know what to name my kitten."

"What?"

"Binx. Like the black cat in *Hocus Pocus!*" Story's face lights up with a smile as she takes my hand in hers. "I watched it this Halloween with Piper, and when she reminded me about it today, I knew the name was perfect for him."

"The most important thing is that you like it. Hopefully he'll like it too," I say, ruffling her hair. "Do you have homework?"

"Piper promised to help me." Story gives me a cheeky wink and steps back. "I'll go change my clothes, then we can start."

"Okay." I watch her grab her backpack and head down the hallway. My gaze darts to Piper, and our eyes lock. She's looking at me from under her eyelashes, a little grimace on her face. "Piper—"

"I'll talk to her after homework," she mutters. "You can be there if you want. I figured out how to explain why I'm quitting."

"I'll still pay you for all the months—"

"Whatever," Piper says and leaves me alone in the living room.

"THERE'S something I need to tell you," Piper says quietly, sitting on Story's bed. I linger by the door. "And please know, I would never do this if I didn't have a very good reason."

Story frowns, her brows knitting together as she presses her book to her chest. "You're scaring me."

"Honey..." She falters, her voice trembling. "Sometimes circumstances get in the way of our plans, and we can't do anything about it. I've tried to find another solution, but unfortunately it's impossible. It's my last day here. I can't be your nanny anymore."

"No," Story breathes. Her eyes widen, and her mouth forms a little O. "No, Piper, please..."

"I'm so sorry, honey. I applied for an internship at a college in Nevada a while ago, and I honestly forgot all about it. If I knew I was going to be accepted beforehand, I would've made a different decision. But this is an opportunity I can't pass up. I'm so sorry."

Story's face contorts in pain, and she starts to cry. Soon she's sobbing and sniffling. Piper moves closer and hauls her to her chest, running her hands up and down her back. She whispers something in her ear and gently sways her from side to side. My heart is hurting, numbing all other feelings. This is all my fault.

"I would've never done this to you if I had a choice." She leans away, keeping her teary gaze on Story. "I love you, little girl. I love you so damn much. It hurts me to do this, but I have to."

"Will you...will you visit?" Story pleads.

"Not for a while. I'm leaving the city soon, and I won't be back until September." She tucks Story's hair behind her ears, gently brushing away her tears. "Once I'm back, I'll come see you. I promise."

Pushing myself off the doorframe, I go to the living room and plop down on the couch. I want to be anywhere but here. It's hard to breathe; my vision is blurry. I'm the culprit of my own pain. I hurt the people I love.

I don't know how long I sit there before I hear footsteps. When I walk out into the hallway, Piper is there with her belongings, and Story is standing with her back pressed to the wall. Her kitten is in her arms.

"Can I help you with anything?" I ask in a groggy voice.

Piper shoots me a look. "No, thank you, Hunter. I'm good."

"I'm going to miss you so much," Story whispers.

"Me too, sweetie. Call me whenever you want. I'll be happy to talk to you. Always."

They hug, and then Story rushes back to her bedroom. Piper wipes away her tears and picks up her bags from the floor.

"Piper, I'm so sorry it came to this," I mumble, my skin becoming hot.

"It's fine. I knew what I was getting myself into," she replies. She opens the door. "I cleaned my room up, and the keys are there, on the table."

"You shouldn't have—"

"I should, and I did." She glances at me over her shoulder. "Good-bye, Hunter."

So many different emotions overwhelm me. I should just tell her that I love her. Should own up to my feelings and confess, but I can't. It won't change anything.

"What are you going to do now? Any plans—"

"Nothing that concerns you," Piper answers and closes the door in my face.

I stand still, listening carefully. Once I hear her car drive away, I take a deep breath and go to Story's room.

"Hey, sweetheart." She's lying on her belly, her face hidden in her pillow. "I'm so sorry about this. I know you love Piper—"

Story sits up so abruptly I halt in my tracks. She glares at me; her eyes are shooting daggers. "I know *you* love Piper...and I know *you* made her leave."

"Story—"

"I hate you!" she yells, her face reddening. "I'm only eight, but I know I'm right. You love Piper, and you made her leave...it's all your fault! I hate you!"

Story falls back onto her bed, bawling and shaking from her tears. I stand in her room with my hands balled into fists. She's not wrong... and it makes me feel even worse than I already do.

I storm out of her room. Taking my phone out of my pocket, I quickly search for the number and dial it. I press my phone to my ear as soon as I hear Amelia's voice.

"Hey. Can you...can you please come back and take Story with you?"

Amelia sighs. "You screwed up, didn't you?"

"She said she hates me."

"She doesn't, but she's probably very angry with you," Amelia states, exhaling loudly. "I can be in LA in two days. Will you be able to deal with her till then?"

"Yes. Don't worry."

"Okay." She clears her throat. "You're such a fool, Hunter."

"Tell me something I don't know." I end the call.

I'm so much more than a fool. I'm my own worst enemy.

42
an eternity of misery

PIPER

A LIGHT KNOCK ON MY DOOR, AND MY MOM'S VOICE follows. "Can I come in?"

"Yeah," I answer, putting the book I'm reading down on my blanket.

Mom walks in carrying a tray with a piece of cheesecake and a mug of something steaming. She holds my gaze as she sets it down on my bed.

"You need to eat."

I snort, but I still take the plate and a small fork in my hands. "I didn't realize desserts count."

"Well, Wade's cheesecake is perfect, and he made it just for you. Riley told him it was your favorite." She smiles, lowering herself onto my bed. "Eat, Piper. I'm serious. No man is worth starving yourself to death."

"I'm not starving myself," I mutter as I take a little bite of cheesecake. My taste buds come to life, and I close my eyes, enjoying the delicious dessert. "And this is heaven."

"I'll pass the compliment along to the chef." Mom nudges me, her eyes roaming my face. She presses her palm to my cheek and caresses it lightly. "Is there anything I can do?"

I shake my head, pick up the mug, and take a sip. It's still strange to see how much she cares. How she willingly wants to spend time with Riley, and now me. To see how happy she is with Wade. They've been together since August. Now it's already the last week of December, and they're still happy. I don't see even a trace of my always-unhappy and ever-annoyed mother.

"I'm good."

"It's been two weeks, Piper. You don't leave the house unless Riley asks you to give her a ride. You barely leave your room. And all these books..." She waves her hand at my nightstand, at the pile of books on top of it. "How many have you read already?"

"Twelve." I shrug, taking another bite of cheesecake. "And there were two I didn't finish."

"A book a day," Mom says. "Your books won't mend your broken heart."

"I'm fine, Mom. I just need a bit more time to figure out what I want to do before school starts in September," I reassure her. "I want to go somewhere, to get out of this city and maybe even the state. I need a break from Los Angeles."

"Before you do, can you finally talk to Hade, please? He's been a pain in our asses since you came back home. He wants to know how you are, to take you out and have fun."

My fingers involuntarily fly to my neck, tracing my collarbone. I forgot my necklace with the little butterfly pendant at Hunter's house. I don't have the mental capacity to go get it. I might never.

"The guy is dense. I told him if he ever forced me to do something I didn't want to do, I'd block his number and unfriend him. He thought I was joking."

"He cares about you so much. He thinks he always knows what you need. And at some point he got a little overbearing," Mom says.

"I was used to talking about everything with him, even things he didn't need to know." I finish my coffee, washing down the last bite of cheesecake. "There were things I wanted to share with you, but you didn't really want to talk to me. Any time I tried to bring up something serious, you dismissed me. I didn't think you'd listen, so I always talked to Hayden."

She glances at me, then takes the tray of empty dishes from my bed and puts it on the floor. "Are we talking about all the times you tried to dig for information about your father?"

"I was a kid. I stopped asking when I was ten. I didn't think it was important anymore."

"Why?" Mom asks, and I shrug.

"If the man was never interested in me, why should I be interested in him? He isn't worthy of my time or attention." I meet her gaze, noticing her slightly narrowed eyes.

We sit in silence for a moment, and I allow myself to relax. If only she'd always been like this. My childhood would've been way different.

"Your father was my first love," she whispers. "It was a whirlwind romance, one I'd never experienced. Not before him, and not after. It was consuming and overwhelming, knocked us both off our feet. I was never loved like that again. Daniel was everything I ever wanted."

"What?" I clear my throat, my heart pounding. "What happened?"

"We'd been talking about marriage, you know. How many kids we wanted. How big our house would be." Mom takes a deep breath, putting her hands on her lap. "His parents had a little cabin, and we were always welcome there. I used to imagine going there with our kids when we were old. With our grandkids."

I can barely breathe, so afraid she'll backpedal. That she'll change her mind, just like she has a thousand times before.

"We got into a fight. It was incredibly insignificant, but we just couldn't agree on some detail about his birthday party, and it kept going and going. He slammed the car door in my face and left me standing in front of my apartment building. He went straight to the cabin." Mom wrings her hands, her veins bulging from how hard she squeezes. I cover them with my own, and she relaxes. The tiniest smile curls her lips for just a split second. "He was alone there, drinking and smoking. He fell asleep with a cigarette...burned the damned cabin to the ground. Two weeks after the funeral, I found out I was pregnant."

"Why didn't you tell me? What about his family? You said something about his parents—"

"They thought it was my fault. That I was to blame for him getting drunk and starting the fire. That if we hadn't gotten into a fight, he'd still be alive." She holds my gaze. "His father died of a heart attack a month later, and it broke his mother. She didn't even want to hear that I was pregnant. She called me a slut, ordered me to leave and never bother her again. I did as she asked. I packed my things, told my parents good-bye, and left Carson City. It was the best and worst decision I've ever made."

"Why the worst?" I ask, thinking back to my grandparents. We rarely visited them when I was small, stopped completely after Riley was born. They were helping Mom financially, but not with much else. The last time we went to visit was for my grandpa's funeral two years ago.

"If anyone ever tells you that raising a child alone is easy, punch them in the face. I was stuck-up. I thought I could pull it off. I failed. I was overwhelmed with my job, with looking after you. Things kept piling up and...I became so angry. At the world, at everyone who forgot that I lost someone I loved that night too, and I became distant with you. I was trying to find love again, hopping from one man to another, without realizing that everything I needed was waiting for me at home. You and Riley were all I needed, but I didn't realize it until you moved out and Wade came into my life. I was a horrible mother to you, Piper. I treated you like Riley's babysitter, didn't even think about how that must've been for you...to be a mom for your younger sister when you were still a child yourself. I was a joke of a mother, and I'm incredibly sorry for all the hurt I caused you. For all those years of not paying attention, of choosing men over my own kids. I'm sorry."

She sniffles, wiping tears I didn't even notice off my face. I take a deep breath and throw my arms around her, hiding my face in her hair. I cry, and she winds her arms around my waist. She tells me how much she loves me, how proud of me she is, and all I can think about is Story. And that makes me cry even harder.

I walked out of Hale's house two weeks ago, and there hasn't been a single day I didn't think about my little girl. I let her down, broke her heart and my own promise to her. I hate myself for that. I feel disgusted with myself. But I couldn't bear another day in his house. It was impossible.

I don't know how long Mom and I sit like that, but eventually my breathing calms down and I stop crying. I move away and even smile a little.

"Thank you for telling me. I needed that; I mean it. It'll help me move forward. There's nothing in the past now that's holding me back." I sigh and let my head fall against the headboard. "Now I need to figure out how to mend my broken heart. An eternity of misery doesn't sound appealing. Even books don't help anymore."

Mom pulls me to her side, and kisses my temple. "I actually like your idea about going somewhere. You need a change of scenery, and you have the money to pay for it. At least the man kept his promise and paid you everything you would've earned."

I blink, remembering that I have $135,000 in my account. He not only paid the rest of my salary; he tripled it.

"It's not your fault the man is a coward. You took the risk; you told him you were in love with him. He's chosen to live with regrets. And trust me, honey, it's the worst feeling ever to know what you could've had and lose everything because you weren't brave enough to go for it."

"He never loved me, Mom. He just needed a sex doll." I'm lying, to myself and to her. That wasn't the reason he invited me on that trip to Spain, but I want to believe it was. I want to believe him, to let myself be fooled by his lies. Because knowing that the man who loves me is giving up because of his fears and his past is way harder than suffering from unrequited love.

My mom shakes her head but doesn't say anything. We sit in silence, and then she starts smiling.

"Why don't you go to Carson City? You can always stay at your grandma's house. I'm sure she would welcome your company."

I already know this isn't a good idea. I'll be bored. I'll be at home all the time, or she'll judge me if I go out.

"Think about it, Piper. It might be exactly what you need," Mom murmurs, hugging me tighter.

What if she's right?

43

the months of solitude

HUNTER

"SO, HOW IS SCHOOL?" I HOLD MY PHONE BETWEEN MY shoulder and my ear as I put my oatmeal on the table. Then I set my phone on the table too, turn on my camera, and switch to video call. Story's smiling face pops up on my screen.

"School is good," Story replies, and shuffling sounds follow as she takes Binx into her arms. "Not as good as it was in LA, but I got used to it. Mrs. Clarke is very nice."

"That's great." I pick up my spoon, balling my fist around it. "Any plans for today?"

"Mom's out of town, so it depends on whether I'll be able to convince my nanny to watch something together."

"Are you okay staying with just your nanny?" I straighten my back and narrow my eyes. Amelia rehired Madeleine, the nanny who worked for us when Story was three years old. As far as I knew, my daughter was comfortable around her, and she didn't have anything bad to say about her. I took it as a good sign. I wasn't sure she'd accept anyone but Piper.

"Meddie is awesome. She's always kind to me and does the things I want to do. After I finish my homework, obviously." Story giggles, wrapping her fingers around her thin braid, and I lean back against the chair, the tension leaving my rigid muscles.

"How are you, Daddy? Aren't you lonely?"

I shake my head. "Of course I'm lonely, Story. Living in this house alone is a struggle, but I'm getting used to it. Thankfully, the regular season in March has a pretty tight schedule. I've spent most of my days at practice and games since we started training again in February. I'm only home to eat and sleep."

"It makes me sad for you." She sighs, letting her kitten jump onto her bed. "Isn't Uncle Hayden going to visit? He told me he was going to your place to hang out."

"He should be here in an hour."

"Good." She smiles. "Are you still planning to come visit me in April?"

"As if you had to ask. I miss you like crazy, princess. This house is not a home without you."

"And without Piper," Story points out, and I nod.

Without her, nothing feels the same, but I keep those thoughts to myself. I haven't seen Piper in three months, and with each day that passes she feels more and more like an illusion. One I wouldn't mind getting lost in, just to prolong the feeling of her in my arms, her scent on my sheets, her sweet, honeyed laugh filling this place.

"She's good, you know," she murmurs, flashing me a little smile. "She talks to me all the time."

"Lucky you," I say bitterly, putting my spoon down on the table. Piper doesn't talk to me or Hayden. She won't answer our calls or texts. And she doesn't answer my emails either. I don't know where she is. No one will tell me. And it fucking sucks. "Tell her..." I catch myself just in time and run a hand over my face. "Just tell her I'm happy for her wherever she is."

"Will do." Story glances over her phone, then peers at me. "I gotta go. It's time for dinner."

"Have a good meal, honey. I'm going to eat my breakfast."

"Love you, Daddy." She blows me a kiss and ends the call.

I tap my fingers on the table, staring in front of me. I zone out way too often lately, and I'm struggling to stay present. Only practice and games make me feel alive, make me feel the tiniest fraction of excitement. The rest of the time, I just exist. I'm like a machine, and my therapist says I need to break the spell. The problem? I can't. I need her, and I need Story. I need them both in this house, under this roof with me. But I have no idea how to find Piper, and I don't want to bring Story back without her here. She'll be unhappy.

With a sigh, I pull my oatmeal toward me and quickly finish it. Nothing tastes as delicious as Piper's cooking. Nothing makes me smile bigger than spending time with Story. If only I knew where to go; I would be on the way already. I would go anywhere to find her and bring her home. To beg her for forgiveness and tell her over and over how much I love her. I want everything with her, even the things I thought I couldn't have. If only I could find her...

"Hey." I look up and fix my gaze on Hayden, who's standing in the doorway. An awkward smile illuminates his face. "You didn't hear me knocking, so I let myself in. I hope that's okay."

"It is," I answer as he plops down onto a chair. "Rough morning?"

"I'm fucking spent. Rehearsal was shit. As usual." He stretches his legs out in front of him and threads his fingers through his bleached hair. I stand up, pour some coffee into two mugs and hand one to Hayden. He takes it and sips. "I think I need a break. I'm not in a good space, and I'm dragging everyone down. I can't write a single song, not even a line. The guys say they understand, and they're trying to reassure me. But I know I'm a failure."

"You just need to find your groove again. Your inspiration."

"Like I didn't know that," he snaps and sets his mug on the table. "I can't find my inspiration because my inspiration took off and left me."

"You're being dramatic, Hayden." I shake my head, gulping down my drink. "You're trying to put the blame on her. Again. If only you'd listened to me—"

"If only you didn't decide to fuck Piper, none of this would've happened," Hayden counters, and I glare at him.

"I love Piper, and if you hadn't intervened, she'd still be here," I retort, setting my jaw hard. "I would've had a chance to sort out my issues, and she would've stayed. With me."

He huffs, closing his eyes. He draws a long, deep breath, and then opens his eyes and focuses on me. "We're going in circles again. Any time we get together, we argue. And it's not fucking right. We should be working together."

"What do you suggest?" I ask, locking my hands behind my head. "I've been emailing her every day, but she doesn't answer. Her phone is off. She disabled her social media accounts, and the new one you found is private. How do you expect us to find her?"

"Talk to Riley. She likes you, I'm sure—"

"Riley told me I shouldn't worry about her sister. She's happy and loved, and doesn't have plans to return before the end of August."

"Well, at least she talks to you." He shrugs and takes a sip of his coffee. "I don't exist to Rye anymore."

"I wouldn't say we had a conversation." I laugh, and Hayden smiles too. The atmosphere slowly changes.

It's been like this for two months already. He comes over, and we talk, discuss all the places where Piper might be. Last week we went to Carson City because Hayden remembered that her grandmother lives there. It wasn't a completely useless trip—we found out she was there for a week back in January, but her grandma couldn't say anything about where she went after that.

"I'm still baffled Story refuses to tell you where Pip is," Hayden utters, bringing his drink to his lips and lowering it again. "I'm sure she knows."

"She knows, but she's not going to tell me. It's Piper's wish, and Story respects it. And so do I."

"So how do you expect to find her? Or did you decide to just wait for her to come back?" He scowls.

"I have a plan."

"And? Are you going to enlighten me?" Hayden asks, crossing his arms over his chest.

"Story loves Piper, but she also loves me. She misses me and wants to come back to the US. She'll tell me where Piper is, but only if I'm in London. I don't even try to talk to her about it on the phone. She instantly shuts me down and stops interacting," I explain, and his face lights up with a smile.

"You're a manipulator." He laughs heartily. "But I like it. All is fair in love and war."

These next two weeks before my visit to the UK will be torturous, but I need to get myself together and think positively. I know I'll be able to convince Story to tell me where Piper is. I just hope Piper is willing to listen...and that she's single. I won't give up on her again, but if I know she's in love and happy, I'll take a step back. I won't bother her.

Hayden and I spend the day together, watching hockey and talking. He ends up staying the night in my second guest room. He and I argue a lot, but at the same time we're very close. I never thought I'd be spending so much time with him, especially not because of Piper. She brought us closer without even knowing it.

So many things I want to tell her. So many things to murmur in her ear while caressing her beautiful body. I want everything with her, if only she'll let me. I'll make her the happiest girl in the world, shower her with my love and affection.

I've never loved anyone the way I love her.

Slipping under the covers, I glance at my nightstand. Her butterfly pendant necklace draws my attention. I found it in her room after she left. I keep it close, a little piece of her nearby even when she's out of my reach.

I sigh and pick up my phone. Quickly unlocking it, I launch Gmail and hit Compose. My finger hovers over the keyboard as I think about all the things I want to tell her. But then I settle for the simplest option.

To: piper.m.evans@gmail.com
I know you don't want to talk to me. I know you left for a reason,

and you have every right to hate me. But I love you, Piper...and I'll do absolutely anything for you to forgive me.

You're mine, and I'm yours. Forever.

I press Send and toss my phone on the nightstand. Two weeks. Two weeks and I'll know where to find her. Hopefully.

44

gone girl

HUNTER

"WELL, SHE'S FINALLY ASLEEP," AMELIA SAYS QUIETLY, slumping down on the couch. "I can barely stay awake. The flight was long and exhausting."

"You should've gone to bed. We can talk tomorrow."

She huffs. "We're going to talk now, Hunter. I wasn't even gone for a week, and you summoned me back because you want me to take Story to London. What happened?"

I press the palm of my hand to my mouth, staring in front of me. The past two days have been horrible. Story didn't want to talk to me, giving me only short yes and no answers when I asked her anything. She stayed in her room, even when my mom stopped by yesterday. She said she wasn't in the mood, scooped up her cat, and closed the door in my face.

"I screwed up."

"I know that already." Amelia chuckles, shaking her head. "I need more information, Hunter."

Sighing, I tell her everything from the start. And when I finally explain what happened two days ago, the room is full of deafening silence.

I lock eyes with Amelia. "Story won't be happy if she stays here. This *house will be a constant reminder of Piper, and I don't want that for her. She'll be better off with you."*

"What does she want? Did you ask her?"

"It's not up for discussion," I say sharply, narrowing my eyes. "I love Story more than anyone or anything in this world, and I don't want her to suffer because of my mistakes."

"But she already is, Hunter." Amelia speaks softly. "It's hard for her because she doesn't understand. She thought Piper was perfect for you, and she doesn't understand why you let her leave."

"I'm not capable—"

"Stop that!" She slaps my knee, knitting her brows together. "You just admitted you love her."

"I'll screw it up, and she'll hate me. And I can't even think about her hating me; I'd lose my goddamn mind." I hang my head low, staring at my feet. "Story needs to go with you. It's for the best."

Amelia is silent, but I feel her gaze on me. She doesn't move; only her fingers rap on her thigh. Then she lets out a long breath.

"I'll take Story with me, but only under one condition."

"Which is?"

"You're going to start therapy again. This"—she waves her hand in front of my face—"isn't you. You were ready to do anything to win my heart. You fought for me. For us. And now you're letting Piper go? This isn't you."

"I've never loved you—"

"The way you love Piper," Amelia finishes for me, her eyes narrowed to slits. "I'm aware, Hunter. Just like I'm aware of how much your insecurities are messing with your life. I can be a manipulative bitch, and some of my behavior further damaged your relationship with her, so I'm sorry for that. And I'm sorry for not realizing you needed help, and guidance. So please, Hunter, do me a favor and go back into therapy. You'll have a chance to win Piper back; I have no doubt about that. But you'll need to be okay—you need to learn to trust yourself. And you need to fucking get it into your thick skull that you're a great man, and you deserve to be loved and happy. Do we have a deal?"

I stare at her, my skin warming up. She's my ex-wife, and I'd be damned if I say our marriage wasn't bumpy. But right now, I'm reminded of how incredible she can be.

"You're pretty good at pep talk. Maybe I should hire you?" I tease her, and she breaks into laughter.

"Go to Hell, Hale." She stands up and towers over me, stifling a loud yawn. "Do we have a deal?"

"Yes. I'll go back to therapy. I was going to anyway. I owe it to Story."

"And Piper. If something is meant to be, it'll happen, Hale. And if she's meant to be yours, she'll be yours. You just need to make sure you don't screw it up again. And that's why, honey, you need to work on your issues."

I stand up. Amelia turns around and heads toward the hallway. I follow her, smiling to myself. Despite my shitty mood, she managed to make me smile. And what's more, we really talked to each other. It felt nice.

She steps onto the first stair, putting her hand on the railing. "Night, Hunter."

"Night, Amelia."

I slowly go to my room. It's time to let my mind rest. Getting Story ready to leave won't be easy.

My eyes snap open, and I look around to see people exiting the plane. Dammit. I didn't even notice I fell asleep, dreaming about my talk with Amelia. The conversation that pushed me back into therapy, that finally made things right between me and my ex-wife.

Grabbing my things, I zip up my leather jacket and rush to the exit. I put on my hat and pull it low over my face. People on the plane recognized me, but thankfully were respectful enough and didn't bother me.

I've seen the articles about me. They think I'm bored and want to return to the Premier League, especially because Story is here in London. In reality, all I want is to continue playing for the LACFC and preparing my school, which is set to open in September. This is something I'm passionate about, something I want to succeed. Something I desperately want Piper to know about. I want to thank her for listening to me that day and giving me advice. I already said it in one of my emails, but I want to thank her in person.

Outside the airport, I see the car I hired to pick me up. The driver helps me with my bags, and I slide inside, taking a deep breath. I miss Story so damn much. I can't wait to finally hug her. To listen to her stories, to spend time with her. I got permission to skip one game, as I plan to stay in London for two weeks.

My phone rings, and I quickly answer. Angelo's voice fills my ears.

"Hey, Hale. How have you been?"

"Hey, Russo. I'm fine. How are you?"

"I'm good. Buzzing for the Champions League game on Wednesday. You're coming, right? I saved a few seats for you and your family."

"If I miss it, you'll fucking eat me alive next time you see me," I mutter, and he bursts out laughing.

"Well, that's a little radical, even for me. I'd just stop answering your calls and pretend your pretentious ass doesn't exist anymore," he jokes.

"I already have Piper for that. So yeah, I'm good." I laugh, looking out the window at the traffic jam. "I'll come watch you play, don't worry."

"Good. Any news about your gone girl?"

"No, still nothing. I know she's good and happy, I just don't know where she is."

"That sucks, but I hope you'll get to see her again soon. And I hope she's still single." Angelo lowers his voice. "Seeing you so heart-broken in January wasn't fun at all. I don't want to repeat that experience."

"You have no idea how grateful I am that you came to visit me. I needed it."

He flew to LA right after New Year's, just to keep me company and talk. The amount of time I spent spilling my guts to him can only be compared to my sessions with my therapist. Angelo is the reason I was able to keep my shit together and not fall apart. I owe him for life.

"I know. But that's the reason we all need friends. Even loners like you."

"Even loners like me," I repeat. Then I change the subject, asking him about Luna and Cissy, about his parents and his upcoming games. This man's friendship is one of the best gifts my career has given me.

I RING the doorbell and shift my weight from one leg to the other. I'm nervous, and I don't even know why. They're waiting for me. When I talked to her last night, Story couldn't stop mentioning all the places she wants us to visit. Amelia is also in London, and she has a little break before the press tour of her upcoming movie starts. It's all good, and yet I can't stop myself from worrying about my plan to get Story to tell me where Piper is. If I fail, the only option is to wait for her to return in August. That shit is scaring me for real.

The door swings open, and my eyes land on Amelia. She's in light blue jeans and a knitted pink sweater. Her hair is cascading over her shoulders, a few locks framing her face. Her lips stretch into a smile as she lets me in.

"Hey, Hunter. I've been wondering when you were going to show up," she says, leaning against the door.

"I sent you my flight details. Didn't you get my message?" I ask, frowning and stepping inside.

"I did, but you're forgetting you're not in the US anymore. People know you here, and I thought maybe there would be paparazzi trying to get pictures of you, fans asking for your autograph." Amelia shrugs, slipping her hands in her pockets.

"The hat does wonders. No one recognized me when I was getting in the car."

She looks me up and down, scrutinizing me. "You look skinnier."

"I don't have much else to do but practice and play," I answer, picking up my suitcase. "The gym is the only place I go these days. I'm not skinnier, I'm leaner."

"Whatever you say, Hale." Amelia shakes her head, heading down the hallway. "Your room is on the first floor. I'll show you—"

"It was my house too, remember?"

Amelia looks at me over her shoulder. "I know, but I kinda like pushing your buttons. To see how long it'll take for me to piss you off."

"What a shocker," I say, and she giggles as we go down the hallway. "Where is Story?"

"She and Meddie went to pick up something delicious for dinner. They'll be back soon."

"*Meddie*? I get it when Story calls Madeleine 'Meddie,' but you?" We stop near the guest room, and I lift my eyebrow at Amelia. "I don't remember you being friendly with her back then."

"Story's nanny needs to be my ally if I want the atmosphere between her and our daughter to be amazing. So I'm trying to be an awesome boss, and so far, so good." She flashes me a smile and opens the door. "Make yourself at home. I'll be waiting in the kitchen."

I step inside and start to unpack my suitcase, putting my clothes in the closet. After a quick shower, I dry my hair and body with a towel.

Memories rush back, and I instantly see Amelia and me arguing about the design of our guest rooms. We ended up splitting them between us, and this one was completely decorated by me. Dark blue tiles and white bathroom countertops, with a single sink and a big round mirror. I loved it back then, and I still do. Just like the bedroom, with its dark blue, gray, and white colors. Comfortable and soothing.

I put on a white tee and gray sweatpants and thread my fingers through my hair, checking if it's dry enough. When I open the bedroom door, I hear Story's laughter, and then Amelia joins in. My lips involuntarily curl into a huge smile. I can't wait to see my little princess.

I saunter into the kitchen and stop abruptly. It's like I was just smacked in the face with a ball. Story is sitting at the table, and her mom is leaning on the kitchen counter with a glass of wine. They both peer at me, but all I see is her. Her long blond hair is in a loose ponytail, and she has bangs now. Her pink Minnie Mouse tee is long, covering her ass, and her long legs are in black jeans, crossed at her ankles. She holds my gaze, and I can't look away.

Piper is the most beautiful girl I've ever seen...and she's here, in London. In my ex-wife's house. She stands next to Amelia with a glass of wine in her hand.

What the actual fuck?

45
matchmakers
PIPER

THE LOOK ON HALE'S FACE IS PRICELESS. HIS EYEBROWS shoot up in surprise, his eyes wide and his lips parted. Hunter stands still, not blinking, not moving. His gaze is glued to me.

Amelia was totally right. He would've never guessed I was here. In London, with his daughter, in his ex-wife's house. *If you don't want the Hale brothers to bother you, you need to go somewhere they'd least expect. Come stay with Story and me. They won't be able to find you. Unless you want them to.* The woman is a genius.

Story sets her glass on the table, jumps to her feet, and rushes over to her dad. He catches her in his arms and only then breaks eye contact. Amelia chuckles beside me, hiding her smile behind the rim of her glass. I want to nudge her in the ribs, because it's not funny. I'm still not sure it's a good idea for me to stay here while he's visiting. It'll only complicate things, but what's done is done.

"I missed you so much," Story confesses, hugging her dad tightly and pressing her cheek to his. "I've been counting the days, crossing them off of my calendar every morning. I'm so happy you're here."

"Me too, princess." His deep voice sears my skin and goes straight to my heart. It's been four months since I've seen him in person.

Any time Story would FaceTime with her dad, I'd leave the room. Not because I was afraid he would see me, but because I didn't want to miss him. I didn't want to think about him. Most days, I hated him. For being a coward. For giving up on us. For sending Story away. For everything he'd been so afraid to tell me. And yet, there were days when I'd wake up remembering the weight of his body next to mine, the warmth of his skin. The feeling of his lips leaving trails of kisses all over my chest and down to my belly. Hearing his voice whisper all the sweet and filthy things he used to say to me. It was a game I couldn't win.

Heart games are always the worst.

"Want some wine, Hunter?" Amelia asks, and he glances between us, eyeing our glasses. He shakes his head. "Are you hungry?"

"Yes, I'd love to eat something. I only had breakfast today."

Story tugs on his hand and leads him to the table. I turn to my right, ready to busy myself, but Amelia beats me to it.

"You're not my servant, remember?" she asks, and I pout, unable to hide my disappointment. It's not about that. I just want to do something that'll help me avoid spending time with him. "Okay," Amelia huffs. "Can you help me with the salad?"

I smile at her, nodding. *Thank you.*

Amelia heats up the pasta we made yesterday, while I quickly cut up cherry tomatoes, cucumbers, and a green bell pepper. I toss in feta cheese and a few olives. I add olive oil and salt and pepper, mixing everything together for the perfect salad. So easy to make, and so delicious. I've become quite obsessed with European cuisine, trying different dishes all the time. I have no clue what I'm going to do once I get back to LA in August. It feels like a totally different world, one I don't really miss. Except for my family, of course.

I stay standing even after Amelia sets Hunter's plate on the table. She comes back to me, takes the salad bowl, and looks at me. There's no way I'm joining them at the table.

"Piper," she says sweetly.

"Amelia." I mimic her and press my glass to my lips, taking a sip. "I'm not hungry."

She holds my gaze, and then just rolls her eyes. I wouldn't be lying if I said we've become friends. She's kind and funny, but she can also be a total bitch if she thinks someone has wronged her. Her confidence is admirable, and I enjoy her company more than I could've imagined.

"Fine," she finally mutters and goes back to Hunter and Story, setting the bowl on the table. "Have a nice meal."

Hunter sits with his back to me; his body tenses up. He hesitates. His hand hovers over the fork. Before I can look away, he glances over his shoulder and meets my gaze.

"I don't bite, Piper."

Yeah, you just make my heart beat a mile a minute. Nothing to worry about.

I take a sip of my wine, lowering my glass a little. "I'm good."

His jaw ticks, and he returns his attention to his plate. I linger near the kitchen counter, toying with the stem of my wineglass. Story talks nonstop, dumping all her news on him at once. Amelia continues shifting her gaze between me and her ex-husband, lifting an eyebrow any time she catches my eye. I'm not joining them. But then, why am I here?

I gulp the rest of my wine, rinse my glass, and put it on the counter. Taking a step, I intend to leave the room, instantly drawing their attention. The Hale family peers at me, and my skin heats up. I should've stayed put.

"Piper, where are you going?" Story asks, a puzzled expression on her face.

"I'm going to my room. This is a great chance to get some reading done." I smile. "I don't want to bother you."

"You're not bothering anyone," Amelia says, the corners of her mouth trembling. "But if you leave, you will."

If someone had told me it's possible for an ex-wife to play matchmaker for her ex-husband, I would've laughed in their face. Not anymore, though. Now I know what she's trying to do, and I'm not a fan. Her manipulative side is the worst.

I smack my lips together and stomp to the table, plopping down on the chair beside Story. She sneaks a glance at me, a giddy smile on her face. Another matchmaker who dreams about me and her daddy becoming a family. I'm fucking doomed. I should've moved out for the next two weeks. I could've used the time to visit Ireland, or Portugal. Both countries sound amazing—a thousand times better than staying in the same house as Hunter motherfucking Hale.

"Where is Madeleine?" he asks and takes a bite of his pasta. Thankfully, he keeps his gaze trained on Amelia. "Did you ever hire her? Or was that all a lie from the start?"

"She was Story's nanny for two weeks," Amelia chirps and sips her wine. "I needed someone while we were waiting for Piper to arrive."

"Did you fly to London from Carson City?"

I blink, realizing he's addressing me. Then I frown. "How do you know about Carson City?"

"Hayden also tried to find you. And when he finally remembered you have a grandmother in Carson City, we went to visit her. She told us you'd been there for a week in January, but she had no idea where you went afterward," he explains, his eyes glimmering with warmth. He is clearly enjoying my shocked state, and the fact that I broke my silence. "Your family never told us where you were either." He looks between his ex and his daughter. "Just like mine."

"That was one of the conditions she had for agreeing to come." Amelia shrugs. "No one from the Hale family could know where she was."

"It was so exciting," Story announces, smiling from ear to ear. "I never thought I'd be able to keep a secret for that long. Especially from you!"

He swallows his food and peers at me again. "Why Meddie?"

I smirk and look away, not bothering to answer him.

"Piper's middle name is Meadow," Story says. "We thought it'd be funny to call her Meddie. You would've never guessed we meant Piper."

"Very funny," he says sarcastically, taking a spoonful of salad. "So you hired Piper—"

"I didn't," Amelia corrects him. "Piper isn't Story's nanny. She's my guest, but she helps me look after her."

Hunter watches her in silence, his eyebrows knit together. He puts his fork on the table with a tiny ding. "You're exploiting her? You don't pay her anything?"

Okay, I hate him. I hate him because he makes it really hard not to love him. He's aggravated and angry on my behalf, even if he shouldn't be. It's not what he thinks.

"You paid me more than enough. More than you should've. It made me feel weird," I tell him. "Amelia wanted to hire me and pay me a salary. I refused. It would've prolonged the process of me coming here. I don't pay for food. I don't pay utilities. I use Amelia's car when I need it. Everything's great."

Not to mention the number of times she's taken me shopping with her, the amount of new clothes she's bought me. Being sneaky and paying for everything while I wasn't looking. It bothered her that I was helping her with Story without compensation. But, truth be told, it was my pleasure. I wanted to be there for her. This escape from my life in LA was exactly what I needed.

"I still don't like it."

"No one asked you what you like or don't like," I point out, feeling my skin itching. "It was my decision, and I'm happy with it. That's the only thing that matters." I stand up and take a step back. "Sorry, Amelia. I'm going to my room." I ruffle Story's hair. "See you in the morning, sweetie."

I head to the second floor, straight to my room. I feel so conflicted it rips me apart.

Amelia told me he went back to therapy. She told me he loves me, that his fears and insecurities were what stopped him from confessing his feelings to me. She said he wants me back. But I...I don't know what I want.

Loving him feels right. It's sweet during the day and sweaty at night. It's full of sizzling hot passion and cute moments that melt my heart. His love is like the most pleasant day at the beach, warm and sunny, with a bit of wind to make the temperature bearable and soothing. Waves loving the shore, the lulling sound of the sea. It's all I want, but it also isn't.

His rejection was worse than any storm. Dark and destructive.

Picking me up and dumping me in the deepest water possible. A place that's really hard to get out of. After finding myself in the middle of the sea and collecting myself piece by piece, I finally feel like myself again. Only better. Strong and confident. And I know I deserve more than a man who hides me from the world. More than a man who would rather get rid of all signs of our relationship than own it and make me his. The Hunter Hale I know isn't like that.

He could be different now, after being in therapy. He could be ready to take the leap and make me his. But the truth is: it's not that simple anymore. Him saying "I love you" would've been enough then. Now, I need more. It's not about expensive gifts, it's not about the money I was tempted to send back, and it's not even about his words. It's about his actions. They always speak louder than words.

I slip under the covers, lying on my right side. I feel like a child again, wanting to hide from the world in the darkness and warmth of my blanket. I just need a moment. Just a few more seconds to compose myself. I suspected today would be tough, and it turned out even worse than I expected. I love him, but I'm not sure if I want to be with him. It makes me sad, and mad, and all sorts of feelings in between. I want to see if he's changed, and I want to keep him away from me.

The knock startles me. I didn't even notice I fell asleep. I toss the covers aside, grab my phone, and see it's just past ten p.m. Yawning, I walk over to the door and slowly open it. My gaze immediately clashes with Hunter's, shooing away my sleepy state.

He stands in front of me, hands hidden in his pockets. "Can we talk?"

I stare at him, not allowing myself to say even a word. Then I sigh and step aside, letting him in. The only thing I can do now is rip off the Band-Aid. That way, it won't hurt. At least, I hope it won't.

46
the biggest mistake

HUNTER

I just lost a bet. Amelia was sure Piper would let me in, but I was much more skeptical. How fucked-up is it that my ex-wife knows the woman I love better than I do? I truly hope I still have a chance to fix things and win her back. I need her in my life like I need fucking air.

I stop in the middle of her room. My hands are still in my pockets. She closes the door, edges to her bed, and sits down. I take a step forward and hesitate. Is it okay if I join her? What if my closeness freaks her out?

"You can sit, Hunter," she mutters in annoyance, reading my mind.

I give her a tiny smile and sit down beside her. "How are you?" I ask, and her eyebrows go up to her hairline. Her mouth forms a little O as her beautiful lips part. This simple question isn't something she expected.

"I'm good. I love my life here. I enjoy spending time with Story and Amelia. Everything's fine." She shrugs. "What about you? How is your school coming along?"

Licking my lips, I suddenly start sweating. I was right; she didn't read my emails.

"Things with my school are slowly moving in the right direction. As for the rest, unfortunately, I can't say I'm good, but I'm trying."

"I'm happy to know things with your school are good," she says, her eyes softening. "But what's wrong with the rest? Are there problems with the team? Or maybe Autumn Dunn?"

"No, everything is good with LACFC. We won all our games in March, so the team is on the roll. I haven't heard from Autumn Dunn since she was fired," I tell her and take a deep breath. "My house is too quiet without Story...and you. I prefer to practice and go to the gym —be literally anywhere but home."

Piper blinks and looks away. She loosens her ponytail, letting her hair cascade over her shoulders. I lean forward and rest my elbows on my knees, locking my hands in front of me. The urge to thread my fingers through her long locks is huge, but I'm doing everything I can to avoid it. I'm more than sure she wouldn't like that.

"You can't say things like that."

"I think I should," I reply. Her eyes narrow slightly. "There is no one to blame but me for how I feel. I'm just trying to be honest with you."

"Honest with me?" she asks. "Like you were honest when you told me we needed to break our agreement? Or when you completely disregarded me after I confessed my feelings to you?"

"That was the biggest mistake I've ever made. And I'm incredibly sorry about it."

"You being sorry won't change anything, Hunter. It's a little too late for that. We all have our limits, and I reached mine the day I left your house all those months ago," she exclaims, collecting her hair and starting to braid it. "I deserve better."

My heart's going insane. It beats loudly and violently, forbidding me from thinking straight. I lean back and turn to face her. "You deserve everything. The fucking world on a silver platter if that's what you—"

"I wanted to love and be loved in return, Hunter. Nothing else."

"I love you," I blurt and hold my breath. Her room is dim; only a bedside lamp illuminates the space. And yet I see how her face pales, and she lets go of her hair. "I should've said—"

"Hunter, stop. Please, stop." She jumps to her feet, hovering over me. Then she starts pacing, moving back and forth. "You have no right to come here and tell me you love me."

"I didn't know where you were because no one would talk to me about you. Except Hayden, but he's just like me—in total darkness."

"Hayden manipulated me into telling you about my feelings, even when I didn't want to do that. Unless he finally understands that what he did was wrong, I don't want to talk to him."

"He understands. If you give him a chance to explain himself, he'll make things right. He misses you, Piper. He can't even write new songs."

She balls her fists, her nostrils flaring. My words have the opposite effect from the one I'm hoping for. I'm pissing her off.

"Is that supposed to make me feel bad about my decision to leave?"

"No, of course not." I jump to my feet as well, halting her in her tracks. "I'm back in therapy, and things are honestly improving. I want to be the man who's worthy of your love, because you truly deserve the best in the world. You're kind and loyal; you're gorgeous, and your soul is beautiful. You're everything I want, and I'll do anything to prove it to you."

Piper folds her arms across her chest. She bites her bottom lip, her eyebrows etched in confusion. A long breath leaves her mouth, and her hands drop to her sides.

"Those are just words, Hunter," she whispers. "I loved you then, and I love you still...but I don't want to be with you. Not until I see that you've *really* changed."

All I hear is *I love you still*. It plays in my mind on repeat, making my head spin. She loves me. I have a chance to make things right, to make her mine forever.

"I desperately wanted to talk to you," I confess, stepping closer and cupping her face in my palms. "Your phone was off. Your family refused to tell me where you were...I felt low because I had so many things to tell you, but I couldn't." And then I remembered your email address."

Piper furrows her brow. "I haven't checked my email in months."

"I've been sending you an email every day. I think by today there must be around a hundred of them." I smile, caressing her cheek with my thumb, and she lets me. "Every single day without you has felt like torture. It's like I've been robbed of all my motivation, like I exist on the verge of total indifference. Just another day. Just another evening. Nothing makes sense without you."

"Hunter, I'm—"

I press my finger to her mouth, silencing her. "I should've never let you go. I should've never let you leave my house that day. And I should've never tried to hide our relationship, especially when I already knew I was in love with you." I drop one of my hands from her face and slip it around her waist. "My father's infidelity affected me way more than I ever admitted. It made it hard for me to trust. I always expected the worst, pushing women away, hurting them, just to avoid getting hurt myself. I was sure I'd hurt you...and you'd end up hating me. And even one single thought about that made me fucking feral. I couldn't stand the idea of you hating me. And I flipped when I realized I loved you."

"It hurt me more than you think," Piper whispers, her eyes locked on mine. "I knew you were in love with me...and yet you chose to let me walk away. You didn't fight for me, and you were so quick to erase any trace of us together...it made me feel like a whore."

"Never," I snap, louder than I expected. "You're my everything."

Piper swallows audibly and takes a step back. My hands drop from her sides, and my skin becomes cold.

"Your words aren't enough, Hunter. Not anymore."

My heart pummels so hard, I feel nauseous. I've had so many stressful situations throughout my life, so many crucial, high-stakes games. So many moments that determined who I am today, that helped me forge my personality and my beliefs. All that gets lost when she's not with me. When she stands just a little too far away from me, it feels as if she's on the other side of the world.

"I understand." I nod, taking a step back. "I know what I need to do."

She shrugs, avoiding looking me in the eye.

"There's a game in two days. Tottenham Hotspur versus Atlético Madrid. Angelo saved a few seats for my family. Will you go with me and Story?"

Her eyes sparkle, but she quickly covers it. "What about Amelia?"

I snort. I can't believe the love of my life is getting along with my ex. It feels surreal. "Amelia doesn't like going to the games. She'll want to stay home."

"She and I went to several games while you were in the US," she counters, and I snicker louder. "What's so funny?"

"I just still find it hard to believe that you were here all this time. With my ex and Story. Living in my house, going to the games."

Piper smiles, quickly masking it with a cough. "We even went to a game in Paris. PSG is a great team."

I arch an eyebrow. "Wanna bet?"

"Bet? With you? A professional soccer player?" I nod, and she bursts out laughing. "No thank you. I don't like losing."

You'll never lose. You deserve all the wins in the world.

"Will you go with me?" I ask, and she rolls her eyes.

"Sure. Angelo was incredibly nice to me in Spain. I'd love to cheer him on and return the favor."

"He'll appreciate it." I open the door and walk out of her room. Piper comes closer and lingers in the doorframe. I debate my next move for only a second. Then, inching forward, I press my lips to her forehead. "Night, Piper."

"Night, Hunter."

Things didn't go the way I planned, but they still turned out okay. My therapist would be proud. Today I did something incredibly important. I confessed my feelings to the woman I love, and I finally figured out what I need to do to make her stop doubting me. This game is going to be...eventful.

47

to make us public

PIPER

"WHY DON'T YOU WANT TO GO TO THE GAME TONIGHT?" I scrutinize Amelia as she sits on the couch beside me. "You love soccer —especially good soccer."

"I have some errands to run." She shrugs and takes a sip of her drink, cold water with a slice of lemon and some mint leaves.

"At eight p.m.?"

"My errands might or might not include running a bubble bath with some scented candles and a glass of wine." Amelia meets my gaze, barely hiding the mischievous glint in her eye. "Piper, stop worrying. It'll be good for you all to go to the game together."

"I'm not sure I want to go," I mutter, and she huffs loudly. She shifts, propping her head on her fist. "It feels way too...intimate, you know. Hunter, Story, and me. Like we're a family."

"Look, I get it, truly. I bet you're scared, and worried. And probably also confused." She gives me a gentle smile. "The guy you love showed up and confessed his feelings for you out of nowhere. Your reaction is valid. You were hurt, and you want reassurance. You want to be sure he's serious about you two, that he means what he says. But how will you know without giving him a chance?"

My shoulders slump, and I press my palms to my burning hot cheeks. She has a point, for sure, about everything. I told him words weren't enough, basically demanded action...and now I'm backtracking, trying to avoid him. As if hiding in my room will help me deal with my nervousness.

"I'm not being fair."

"You're definitely not, but at the same time...you're warming up to him. I saw you two talking yesterday in the kitchen. Laughing, joking. Flirting."

I open my mouth to argue, but she lifts an index finger in my face. "You were flirting, Piper. Stop denying the obvious."

"Fine. Maybe. I don't know..." I move my hands up, hiding them under my hair. Threading my fingers through my locks, I keep my eyes trained on Amelia. With a long sigh, I let my shoulders slump. "Why are you so supportive? He's your ex."

Amelia shakes her head, her brown hair veiling her shoulders. "He's the father of my daughter. And I want what's best for her." She reaches over and gently wraps her palm around my wrist, pulling one of my hands to her. "Hunter and I went through a lot of shit together. We said horrible, mean things to each other. We were never meant to be as a couple, but as parents? He's my ride or die when it comes to Story. I love him immensely for being such an incredible dad to our little girl. And I want what's best for him. And that's you."

I listen, feeling my heart hammer against my rib cage. My thoughts are in total disarray. We've had this talk before, but now I see things more clearly. Hunter is changing, evolving. He went back to therapy not just because Amelia told him to, but because he knew it was the right thing to do for Story...and for me.

"He was sending me emails...daily," I whisper. "I downloaded Gmail last night, and there are a hundred from him."

Amelia's eyes sparkle. "What did he say?"

I hesitate, twisting my fingers and avoiding looking at her. "I didn't open them."

"What? Why not?"

"Because...I'm afraid. Months ago, the amount of love I had for this man was endless. It was overwhelming, and it knocked me off my feet. It felt right. And then, he let me go...and my world crashed down. I don't want to go through that again. I want to make sure he's changed. Then I'll read his emails."

"Well, that's understandable, love. But I truly believe those emails could shake you to the core."

I roll my eyes, not even trying to hide my smile. "I hope in a good way."

Amelia winks at me and pats my hand again. "Tonight will be good, Piper. You won't regret going to the game."

"Are you hiding something from me?"

"Definitely not." Like I'm going to believe her.

"Where are Story and Hunter? Did he tell you where they went?" I ask.

"They had some errands to run." Amelia taunts me with another wink. "Well, that, and they needed some time alone. They missed each other."

"I have no doubt," I say. "I'm going back to my room. I want to read a little before I start getting ready. Do you need my help with anything?"

"Yes. I need you to get your ass out of here. Go to your room, enjoy some alone time. And get ready for the game. It'll be big."

"I don't—"

"Piper, you have no idea how popular Hunter is here. People know him, and they'll recognize him. Just get ready to be photographed." The back of my neck instantly flames up. "I can help you, if you want."

I hesitate, just for a moment, and then I nod. "Pretty please."

Amelia bursts out laughing and waves me off. "First just go to your room and rest. Everything will be great."

I smile timidly and head down the hallway. Hopefully I won't regret this. Fingers crossed, everything will be fine.

"So, what do you think?" Hunter asks, leaning down to my ear.

I sneak a glance, my eyes roaming the packed stadium. This isn't my first Tottenham game, so I just shrug, I'm not sure what he wants to hear. "It's...loud."

His brows pinch together for a second, and then he chuckles lightly. "It is loud." Hunter shakes his head, squinting at Story. She has her elbows on a little table, her chin nestled on her locked hands. Her gaze is glued to the field. "At least someone is excited."

"Hey!" I smack his shoulder. "I'm excited. It's my first Champions League game. Plus, I'm very curious to see Angelo play. I googled him, but seeing him play in person will be so much better."

"I didn't expect you to be such a fan of Angelo," Hunter teases me.

"I'm not a fan of Angelo. I'm not even cheering for Atlético tonight," I say pointedly. "I'll be happy with either team winning."

Plunging my lollipop back into my mouth, I look away from him and focus my attention on the field. It somehow helps with my nervousness—until Hunter decides to drape his arm over the back of my seat. My back is tingling, as if he's running his fingers up and down every nerve. I tense up and sneak a glance at him.

"You can't want *both* teams to win," he insists.

I pop my lollipop out of my mouth and give him a wicked smile. "Watch me."

His gaze darkens, and his fingers brush my shoulder. Narrowing my eyes slightly, I swirl my tongue over my lollipop. As slowly as possible. Hunter swallows hard, but no sound emerges. He licks his lips and inches over to my ear.

"That's the plan." My nipples pebble when I hear his words. Dammit. It's a good thing I'm wearing a leather jacket. I don't want him to know how much I crave his touch. How easy it is for him to turn me on. I'm still on the fence about whether I should give him a chance. "I can finally enjoy my favorite view in the world."

"Tottenham Hotspur Stadium?" I taunt.

His palm curls around my shoulder, and I'm losing it. "You."

My skin is scorching hot as I suck in a breath. I look around and notice curious gazes on us. Amelia chose a navy blue dress for me to wear. It ends a bit below my knees, and it fits perfectly. My hair is down; my blonde curls frame my face and highlight my cheekbones. I have nothing to worry about...and yet I'm ready to wave the white flag and leave. I bit off way more than I can chew when I agreed to come to the game with Hunter and Story.

"Daddy, can we see Angelo after the game?" Her voice is so sudden I almost jump in my seat. Hunter's hand drops off my shoulder as he faces Story. My shoulders slump, and I close my eyes, letting my breath even out. These mood swings are driving me wild.

"Mr. Hale! So, the rumor I heard at the beginning of the game turned out to be true." A guy with a broad smile approaches Hunter. Story and I linger behind him. "Did you come to see your old team play? Or..."

I look down at Story and smile. She beams at me, her fingers entwined with mine. She's cheerful, even if it's past her bedtime. I hope we can leave the stadium soon. Any time we mess with her routine, she has a hard time falling asleep.

The game ended in a draw, two to two. It was a nail-biting, heart-racing type of game. I enjoyed every second of it.

I'm lost in my thoughts, and a warm palm wraps around my wrist and brings me back to reality. But once I see a reporter smiling at me, I want to disappear. My gaze flicks to Hunter in a moment of sheer panic. I'm confused and nervous, but I let him pull me closer. Story also steps up to her dad, and the huge grin on her lips doesn't leave any doubt—she knows something I don't.

"So there's no chance you'll return to London? I'm sure Tottenham would be more than happy to have you back."

"I loved my time with Spurs, but I'm in a new chapter of my life. And I couldn't be more excited. LACFC is a great team, with players who get along, high-class management, and a very talented coach," Hunter replies, slowly wrapping his arm around my waist. "Plus, my school will be opening its doors in September, and who knows? Maybe in a few years there'll be more and more Americans playing in the Premier League and European championships."

The reporter's smile grows bigger as he sweeps his gaze over Hunter and then slides it to me. "I assume there's another new chapter in your life. A more personal one?"

Hunter glances at me, and my heart sinks to my feet. I wanted him to do something big. To acknowledge us publicly...but now I'm ready to throw up. This is a point of no return. A moment that will change everything.

"I really hope so," he murmurs, gazing at me lovingly. "I'm in love with an amazing woman, and I'd do anything to be worthy of her. "

Hunter presses his lips to my cheek, and my legs give out. The only reason I'm still standing is because his strong arm is holding me close. He confessed his feelings to me. He openly admitted to a reporter that he's in love with me. If this doesn't show me that he's not the same man I left, I have no idea what will.

I love Hunter Hale just as strongly as I loved him the day I walked out of his house. He loves me too, and he's ready to change his life for me. To change himself for me.

I need to read those emails.

48
do you remember our first time?

PIPER

THE DARKNESS OF MY BEDROOM IS SUFFOCATING. IT'S closing in on me, making me shiver though I'm not cold. My laptop is sitting on my bed, and its screen is the only thing illuminating the space. I keep staring at the unread emails as if it will miraculously solve my problems.

What problems, though?

Well, being in love with my best friend's brother might be considered a problem. Coupled with the fact that he confessed his feelings for me right in front of a reporter from a big sports channel. And now my face is everywhere, with headlines I would love to never see again. They're all surprisingly respectful, it's just the narrative I hate. A sexy twenty-year-old made a soccer star fall in love with her while nannying for his young daughter. It's frustrating. Especially since it's already all over the news in the US.

RYE:

OMG! OMG! OMG! Please tell me you forgave him?

RYE:

Piper, please. Hunter would be an incredible brother-in-law.

RYE:

> Pip? Did you black out? Why aren't you
> answering my texts?

Can I block her? My sister is so annoying. The way she instantly assumes Hunter and I will be together infuriates me. Wasn't she the one who told me the guy needs to grovel? That he needs to do something big to prove his love for me?

But he did. And I have a feeling his emails are the missing piece of the puzzle. I need to read them. It's the only thing that's stopping me from going to his room and telling him how much I missed him. How much I love him. I want to say all that while looking him in the eyes. In his deep green eyes with hints of blue. It's almost invisible, but when I look closely at his smile—it's all there.

I take a deep breath, click on the first email he sent me back in January, and start reading.

From: hunter.hale13@gmail.com

Hey Piper,

I'm probably the last person on the planet you want to hear from. You turning off your phone and your family not telling me where you are is the best evidence of that. And you're more than justified in your decision. I messed up. I watched the woman I love leave my house...and I did nothing to stop her. I let you leave while my heart was shattering into billions of tiny shards. Because I'm a coward. I broke your heart because I couldn't find the strength to tell you I'm in love with you.

I should've screamed my feelings for you at the top of my lungs...but I let silence win. I let my fears destroy me...and I wouldn't be surprised if you don't want to talk to me ever again.

I don't deserve you.

At least, this version of me doesn't.

I promise I'll do better. I know what I need to do to become worthy of you. I just hope I'll get a chance to show you.

Wherever you are, I hope you're happy. That's all I want for you. To be happy and loved.

Till next time,
Hunter

Closing my eyes, I try to steady my breath. I inhale and exhale until my heart starts to beat more calmly. Not the violent drum it was just a few minutes ago. That was only the first email. I still have so many to read.

Email after email, confession after confession. He tells me about his days, about his visits with his therapist, about his conversations with Story and how she refused to tell him where I was. My heart swoons and sings, and despite all the tears, I'm smiling. Hunter Hale has a way with words. I've read a lot of romance books, but his emails are everything. Maybe because they're written for me?

From: hunter.hale13@gmail.com

I don't think I've ever hated Valentine's Day more than I hate it now. Or I'm just sad and feeling pathetic because my girl got away from me. I deserved it, and I know it. But that doesn't make it any easier.

I miss you every fucking day. Your room doesn't smell like you anymore, and I'm mad at the cleaning lady I hired for ruining it. I swear I looked unhinged when I realized she cleaned your room too. She probably thinks I'm a jerk, and I deserve that too.

I'm sure you don't know it since you don't talk to Hayden either, but he and I are closer now. He comes over, and we talk. About life, about our plans for the future, and about you.

Hayden is a mess. And even if I do feel bad for him...I don't really feel that bad. He pushed you too far, even after I told him over and over again to back off and let you breathe. He should've never interfered. Some days he knows it, and some days he tries to put the blame on me. But I honestly don't care what he thinks. I'd do everything all over again, without the slightest hesitation. But this time, I wouldn't fuck up. I would never allow you to even think I didn't want to be with you. You're all I want. And I always will.

Story says you're happy, and you're loving your new place. I hope she's right.

I love you, Piper.

Hunter

Hayden and Hunter are close now? They finally had a chance to repair their relationship and become real brothers? Because of me? That's some of the best news ever. Something I never expected to happen, but I'm so happy it did. They always needed each other way more than they knew. And them finally bonding and becoming friends as well as brothers is priceless.

I wipe my tears away, sniffling. My smile grows bigger and bigger with each email I read. This man's dedication is admirable. Sending me an email every day without getting anything in response. Without knowing if I read it or not. Some are short, some are long. They are all incredibly moving. They make my heartbeat skyrocket.

From: hunter.hale13@gmail.com

Thank you. That's another thing I want to tell you when I'm looking you in the eyes. Not only that I love you, but also thank you.

Your advice about my school all those months ago is exactly the reason it will be open in September. With a fucking bang! The LACFC general manager was following the kids' practices with great interest, and now he wants to be a partner. He sees potential in my idea, and let me tell you...he almost choked on his coffee when I suggested preparing younger kids to later join the club's academy. He said I was a genius... but it's all you.

You helped me see things from another perspective, to clear my head of doubts and worries. You reminded me why I wanted to open my own academy in the first place. And why I wanted it to be on my terms.

You're brilliant, and I so want you to be mine. Damn, Piper, wherever you are, I truly hope I find you soon. Every new day without you feels like some kind of medieval torture. It's fucking terrible, but I need to bear it. It's my punishment for letting you go.

I love you more with each passing day. I can't believe it's March already. I'm nowhere near finding out where you are, but I'll keep trying. With Hayden's help.

Till next time,
Hunter

I cover my mouth with my palm. I'm no longer crying. My veins are warm, and my heart gallops. He's going to open his school in September, and I bet it'll be huge. With the LACFC's help, everyone will be bringing their kids. I can't believe he listened to me that day, that he did everything I suggested.

From: hunter.hale13@gmail.com

If there's anyone I miss as much as I miss you, it's Story. She's my little sunshine, my beautiful princess, and I'm unhappy without her. I talk to her on the phone and FaceTime whenever I can...but it's not enough. Even if I know I did the right thing asking Amelia to take her back to London.

She's with her mom, but I'm sure you know that. She says you two talk all the time. Can you believe I'm jealous of my own daughter? I'd do anything for a chance to talk to you. I kinda do with these emails...but it's April already, and I still don't know if you're getting these, if you're reading them. Or maybe you just delete them immediately.

I'm going to London tomorrow. Story is super excited, and so am I. I can't wait to spend time with her again, to learn about her routine, about her school and her new friends. And also...I hope she'll tell me where you are. There's a high chance she won't, but I need to try. I'm ready to fight for you. For us. For my family.

My therapist has helped me sort out my issues, and I feel like a new person. You deserve the whole world, and I finally know I can give you that. I can be your everything...and I desperately hope you want to be mine.

I love you, Piper.
Hope to see you soon.
Hunter

*I love you, Piper...*how is this possible? Hunter is my best friend's brother. Someone I barely saw when I was younger. Someone I knew nothing about. Someone who hired me to be his daughter's nanny. Someone who stole my heart all those months ago in his kitchen. The moment he set me on the countertop, I folded. Even if he acted like a douche after. I fell for him at that exact moment. I fell in love with a great man...and I'm so glad he came through. For me. He got into therapy and asked for help. He fought the demons of his past and the fears his father's infidelity sowed in his heart. He's a better man now...and I love him even more.

Hunter Hale is my end game. He's my happily ever after, and I'm not letting him go. I deserve the kind of love I read about in books, the kind I see in the movies. I deserve the world, and for me, Hunter is it. He's all I need now, all I will always need.

Closing my laptop, I quickly get up from my bed. Before I go see Hunter, I need to talk to someone else first. It's three a.m.—around seven p.m. in LA. Taking my phone from the covers, I find Hayden's number and dial.

"Hey," I say the second Hayden answers.

"Piper?" he asks hoarsely, and my heart squeezes. I've missed hearing his voice. I've missed him...despite everything that went wrong between us.

"Yeah, it's me. I thought I should—"

"I'm sorry, Piper. I'm so, so sorry," he rasps, silencing me. "I was such a fucking jerk to you, always thinking I knew what was best. Always treating you like you needed guidance and protection, while in reality you're a thousand times smarter than me. You see people for who they are, and I doubted your judgment. I robbed you and my brother of your happiness, pushing you to make a decision you weren't ready to make. I don't deserve your friendship; I never did."

I chuckle, wiping my tears with the heels of my palms. "And now you think you know what's best again. You were with me through thick and thin; there were days I wouldn't have made it through if it wasn't for you. I need my best friend, Hayden. I need you."

"Good Lord." He exhales loudly. "You really want to be friends with me? After everything—"

"I do...but on one condition."

"Anything you want."

"Promise you'll never meddle in my life again."

His laughter fills my ears, making me smile. "I swear. I'm miserable without you, and I'll do anything to earn back your friendship. You deserve the best best friend in the world...in addition to the best boyfriend in the world," he murmurs. "I saw the interview. You look good together, Pip."

"We do," I whisper.

"Are you happy with him?"

"You have no idea how much."

"Then I'm happy for you. That's the only thing that matters to me."

I grin. "Hade, do you mind if I call you tomorrow? I kinda need to talk to Hunter."

"*Talk.*" Hayden snorts. "Sure. I'll be waiting. We need to catch up."

"Talk to you tomorrow. Bye, Hade."

"Bye, Pip."

I end the call and quietly tiptoe out of my bedroom and down the stairs. Quickly, I knock on his door and wait. My heart is going berserk in my chest. What if he's so deep asleep he doesn't hear me? I lift my hand to knock again, but the door slowly cracks open. Hunter looks at me with one of his eyes half closed. He's sleepy, and he rubs his palm over his face, trying to hide his yawn.

"Piper? Is everything okay?"

I blink. So many thoughts are running through my head. I won't be going anywhere till Story's school year is over. That's something I know Amelia and Hunter discussed. It means I'll need to stay in London till July, away from the man I love and want to be with.

Am I nervous? Hell yes, I am. Do I think we will be alright? Absolutely.

Taking a deep breath, I step closer and wrap my arms around his neck. "I read your emails."

He sweeps me off my feet the very second the words leave my mouth. I hook my legs behind his back as he closes the door. His lips are on mine without any hesitation, taking my breath away. It feels like heaven. Everything about him is addicting, unraveling. He reads me with such ease, as if my thoughts are his own. As if there's nothing more important for him than to please me.

We land on his bed, his body blanketing mine with his warmth. He places one of his hands on the bed, balancing himself, as his lips leave a trail of hot, open-mouthed kisses on my throat. I moan, pleasure rippling through my veins. And yet, I stop him. I want him to hear me out.

"I love you," I tell him, and Hunter looks up, his eyes meeting mine. "And I want to be with you."

"Am I still dreaming?" he murmurs, caressing my skin. "If you only knew how much I've wanted to hear that. It feels better than I imagined."

I cup his face, my palms pressed to his scruffy cheeks. "Everything feels better with you." I sigh and go for it. "But I want us to take things slow. You'll go back to the US next week, and I'm staying here with Story till July. If I give in now, you'll be the only thing on my mind till I see you again...and I don't want it to be like that."

Hunter studies me with a light smile on his face. He leans down and plants a kiss on my nose. "Whatever you wish." He plops himself down on his back and pulls me close, until my head is on his chest. "So what does that mean then?"

"It means you're mine." A low chuckle vibrates under my ear. "And I'm yours. We're together."

"Story would love to know that."

"She'll be over the moon," I confirm smiling, and I hear him yawn again. We'll have time to talk about us, about things we both need to do. Now? I just want to cuddle with my man, to finally fall asleep with his body wrapped around mine once again. "Can I stay?"

"Did you even need to ask?" He kisses the top of my hair, hiding his face in it. "I just need to warn you—once I get my hands on you, you're not going to leave our bed until I say so. Am I clear?"

"Yes," I whisper, kissing his chest. "Do you remember our first time? In the shower?"

"How could I forget? I was a goner for you back in the club, but that shower? Fuck, baby, you've owned me ever since. Why do you ask?"

"Because I'm counting on you to make me pass out again when we finally get to that...and maybe more."

Hunter shifts, and I look up, meeting his gaze. So many emotions. Then he bends and kisses me again. "Whatever you wish, Piper." His whisper scatters all over my lips.

Falling asleep in his arms, I feel full and content. Hunter is my everything, and I can't wait to start our journey together. As a couple. As a family.

49
because i want it all

HUNTER

"YOU THINK SHE'S FORGIVEN ME? FOR REAL?" HAYDEN asks, sitting across from me in my kitchen. His palm is pressed to his forehead. He wears a worried expression on his face, and I'm enjoying it a bit too much. Letting him stew is one of the best paybacks I've come up with.

"Don't you talk to her all the time?" I gulp my coffee and set my empty mug on the table.

"Well, yeah..." He averts his gaze, his fingers rapping a nervous rhythm against his scalp. "But not in person, you know. She's coming home tonight, and I'm ready to fucking shit my pants. What if Pip doesn't want to be my best friend again?"

I roll my eyes. "She *is* your best friend. I think you won her over when you thoroughly apologized for your overprotective asshole behavior." I shrug, a smile peeking onto my lips. "And I think the song you wrote for her made a huge difference."

Hayden grins. "She sent me a video the other day. Pip and Story were dancing and singing 'Flawless' at the top of their lungs. It was precious."

Smirking, I stand up and edge to the dishwasher. "As long as you remember she has a good head on her shoulders, you're fine."

"As long as you two keep your hands to yourself around me." He gives me a pointed look, and I return a blank stare. "I-I didn't mean it in a bad way," he mutters. "I just need to get used to it."

"Piper is my girlfriend. She's going to live here with me and Story."

Hayden rubs the back of his neck. "Isn't she going back to college? I talked to her, and she has plans to enroll next semester."

"We'll figure it out," I say.

We need to be at the airport in two hours, and I still need to pick up Riley. She begged me to take her with me to meet her sister. I'm not sure the ride will be pleasant. She's still super hostile toward Hayden, and he tries to rile her up any chance he gets. I would've thought he liked her, but their five-year age gap makes that unlikely. So I've decided it's Hayden acting like a teenager, even if on paper he's a grown ass adult.

I STAND IN THE AIRPORT, my arms folded across my chest. Riley is bouncing on her heels and pacing back and forth, her eyes focused on the arrival gate. She's pissed at Hayden because of his jokes, so she's been silent for almost thirty minutes. She's ignoring me, too, because I refused to take sides.

When I feel someone's eyes on me, I tip my head. It's a tall, broad-shouldered guy with a ballcap shading his face. He takes a step forward, stops, shakes his head, and then goes for it, strolling toward us. The closer he gets, the easier it is for me to study him. He has a beard, and his eyes are deep brown. The guy is big and muscular, but I don't think I know him.

He steps closer, and a smile illuminates his face as he realizes I'm watching him.

"Hey. I'm incredibly sorry for bothering you...but I just can't help myself. Are you Hunter Hale?"

I turn to him and extend my hand. "Yup, that's me."

"Wow, I honestly never thought I'd get a chance to meet you in person." He shakes my hand, and my eyes drop to the tattoos on his hand. One is particularly entertaining—Winnie-the-Pooh is inked on his wrist. "I'm Colton."

"Oh my God." Riley's loud whisper makes me shift my gaze to her. She looks between me and this guy, her eyes wide like saucers. "You're Colton Thompson. The California Thunders center."

A hockey player? Well, now his appearance makes total sense. I watch hockey sometimes, but I don't know any of the players—unlike my brother. Hayden loves hockey, and the Thunders are his favorite team. He'd freak out knowing we met their center while he was buying coffee.

"What are you doing in LA?" I ask. "I thought you guys were based in San Jose."

"I promised to take my kid and my sister to Universal Studios months ago, and we finally got the chance to come. My family's here, and now I need to meet my little sis." He smiles, falling quiet for a moment. "I loved watching you play. And I was so damn proud! An American playing for my favorite team. What could be better?"

"Are we talking about Real?"

"Of course! Don't get me wrong; there are so many great teams in Europe, but Real Madrid is next level for me. I fell in love with them when I was a kid, and nothing's changed since."

We talk some more, about LACFC and the California Thunders. Riley not-so-subtly mentions she'd love to see Colton play in person, and with laughter he promises to arrange tickets for us once the season starts. The way she blushes is adorable.

"It was nice to meet you, Hunter. I'm going to get to one of your games while we're here," Colton says, taking a step back. "Bye, Riley."

He waves and walks away, and I focus my gaze on Riley. Her eyes are glued to the guy, and I chuckle.

"What?" she snaps.

"Nothing," I assure her and turn my head to the gate, just in time to see Story and Piper. They stroll hand in hand as Piper pushes their bags in front of them, and my whole body warms up. My girls. My future. My everything.

Story notices us and takes off running. I catch her in my arms, pressing her close to my chest. Inhaling her sweet scent, my lips curl into a huge smile. I'm so damn happy they're finally home. These last few months were hard, but they were also full of hope. I knew they'd be back, and now that they're finally here, my chest doesn't feel as tight. I can breathe freely and feel content. Everything is exactly as it should be.

"I DIDN'T EXPECT Story to go to your parents' just three days after our arrival," Piper says, popping a cherry in her mouth. She's sitting on the edge of the pool with her legs dangling in the water.

"Why?" I sit beside her and take a sip of my drink. It's past eight p.m., and we're finally alone. It feels like a blessing after three days of having our families constantly in our faces.

"We still have so many things to do: buy stuff for her room, make sure Binx gets used to this place again, and buy things for our bedroom," she lists, tucking one of her wild locks behind her ear. The rest of her hair is collected into a messy bun, and her sun-kissed skin is glowing.

I try hard to hide my smile but quickly fail. When my parents came to visit us two days ago, my mom spent an hour, if not more, apologizing for not believing in us. Later, in the kitchen, she asked if there was anything I needed her help with, and I asked her to take Story to their house for a sleepover. Why? Because I wanted to keep my promise to my girlfriend. And making her pass out from pleasure isn't really possible with Story sleeping just behind our bedroom wall.

"Why are you smiling?" Piper asks, fixing her necklace. Her fingers trail over her butterfly pendant. The smile on her face when I gave it back to her was priceless.

"Because I love spending time with you. Alone."

"You have me all to yourself every night," she murmurs, moving closer and leaning against me.

"I have no problem making you orgasm every night," I counter with a smile on my lips. "But I don't think I should be making you scream my name with Story in the house."

"Oh God," Piper groans and puts her head on my shoulder. "It was stupid of me to plan a quiet evening for us."

"We can still be quiet, if you want it that way." I smirk, wrapping my arm around her shoulders.

I bend down, tracing her bottom lip with my thumb. Her mouth pops open, and I slip my finger inside. Her tongue curls around it. The second I think I'm in control, she makes me realize I never was.

"Let's go back inside?" My voice cracks, thick with my desire for her.

She nods, and I drop my hands from her body. We stand up, and she takes a step away from me. It's the only thing she has time to do before I haul her to my chest. Piper winds her hands around my neck, her legs locked behind my back. Her chocolate brown eyes stare at me with such intensity, I feel pre-cum on my already hard cock. Waiting for her all these months, I missed sex and being intimate, but I wasn't tempted. Not even with my hand. All of me belongs to her, and I don't need anyone else.

We maintain eye contact as I carry her inside the house. Not a single word, not a single sound. Just our breathing and our heartbeats communicating on some totally different level. The understanding I have with Piper is out of this world. We talk, we plan, we give each other advice. We not only hear each other, we listen. And I know she'll never judge me, just like she'll never hear a critique from me, only guidance if I think things are going south. I'll never pressure her into anything, just like she always makes sure we're on the same page with our decisions. She's precious and all mine. So fucking mine, I feel like I'm ready to explode with my feelings for her.

"Any particular wishes, baby?" I ask, opening the door to our bedroom with my leg.

"I don't need you to be gentle with me," Piper purrs sweetly, hiding her fingers in my hair. "I want a rough and hard fuck—" She gasps as I press her back to the wall.

"Anything for you." A light kiss on her lips, and I put her down.

My hands roam over her narrow waist and down to her killer hips. Pushing down her bikini bottoms, I kneel and toss them aside as soon as she steps out of them. Piper spreads her legs, leaning back against the wall. I look up, and our gazes meet. She's watching me.

Her pussy is wet, and my mouth waters. Without any hesitation, I lift her leg and hook it over my shoulder, spreading her open. She jerks, and her eyes instantly snap closed once I flick my tongue over her clit. I smile to myself and ravish her little cunt with my tongue. I kiss and suck, licking and circling my tongue over her clit. Piper pants, her moans filling the room. She's not trying to hold back or keep her voice down. The house is ours for tonight, and I plan to make the most of it.

"Hunter..." She whispers my name, her fingers digging into my hair. She rocks her hips back and forth, riding my face. "You feel so good."

Nibbling on her clit, I draw a loud moan out of her, and she tugs harder on my hair. I hiss; her roughness makes me see stars, and my cock strains against my shorts. Plunging one of my fingers inside her pussy, I loudly suck on her clit, and her legs tremble. I push another finger inside her and slowly start pumping, moving my fingers in and out. My mouth never leaves her pussy as I lap my tongue over her clit.

Piper sucks in a breath and presses her palms against the wall. She's on the brink of her first orgasm, and there's nothing better than watching her come—on my tongue, with my fucking lips getting her off.

"I'm gonna come...right there...please, Hunter..." she moans. Her movements become erratic. A little more, and she's a goner. "Oh my God, Hunter..."

Standing up, I press my palm to her pussy and lightly slap it. Piper whimpers; her eyes are hooded as she licks her lips. I take a condom out of my pocket, push my shorts down, and kick them aside. Sheathing my cock, I step closer. My arms are around her waist, and I lift her, making her loop her legs around me.

Piper unties her bikini top and pushes her naked tits against my

chest. My hands lower, and I cup her ass. This girl and her charms...
dammit. My resolve disappears into an abyss, as if it wasn't there in
the first place. I position her for a better angle and slide my cock deep
inside her warm pussy.

Heaven. Fucking heaven.

She cups my face and presses her lips to mine as I fuck her slowly,
her back pressed against the wall. We kiss, our tongues playing with
each other. My skin is hot, and my veins feel like they're on fire. Every
emotion feels different around her, more heightened. It's like she's a
fucking energy drink, pumping through my blood and making me
feel unstoppable.

Loving her feels like the most natural thing in the world. Like the
rainbow that comes after the rain on a sunny day. It fills me with hope
and joy, spreads love throughout my body. Not loving her feels wrong.
As if a part of me went missing, and no one knows where to find it. I
have no desire to go back to how it was then, when I didn't have her in
my life.

My thrusts become rougher, and I grip her ass hard. I slam inside
her, going balls deep. Again and again. Piper chants my name; her eyes
are closed, and her tits bounce with each movement. She's so fucking
gorgeous, and she belongs to me. The thought settles in, and I know I
won't last long.

"Baby, are you close?" I ask, and she nods.

I cover her mouth with mine, drowning her moans and screams in
our kiss. She orgasms, her pussy squeezing my cock so hard I instantly
come too. I continue moving, prolonging the feeling of my release.
Her body is tense as she rocks on the waves of her orgasm, her fingers
threading through my hair.

Catching her gaze, I smile and amble to the table in the corner of
my room. With one hand, I push aside some documents and put
Piper on its surface. Mischief swims behind her irises as she trails a
manicured finger down my chest.

"Are we going to make it to bed tonight?" She arches an eyebrow,
making me snort.

"We have all night for that," I say, changing the condom and throwing the used one into the trash can.

"You'll not only need to fuck me, but also feed me," Piper murmurs, her hand draping around my waist.

"How about," I say, pulling her ass to the edge of the table, "I fuck your brains out one more time, and then we go to the kitchen. We can eat dinner and talk about your college arrangements."

Piper nods, her eyes sparkling. There is something on her mind for sure, because she keeps quiet, her palms pressed to my chest. I thrust my hips forward and start to move inside her again. I have no clue why I'm so hard so soon after my release, but with her it's my new reality. Not that I'm complaining, because I'll never say no to anything she wants. Because all I want is her.

epilogue

Two years later

piper

"Pip, do you have any plans for your birthday party?" Hayden asks, glancing at me. I shrug and scrunch my nose. The scent of cinnamon is too strong inside the café. "What's wrong?"

"Nothing," I huff and clear my throat. "I don't think I'm going to try their new latte. It's way too cinnamony."

Hade blinks, then raises one eyebrow. "What about your birthday? Or are you not in the mood for that either?"

"Story planned something for me with Hunter and Riley," I tell him, scanning the menu. Nothing seems too appealing, maybe some cheesecake. And a cappuccino. "But I'm not going to throw a party, if that's what you're asking."

"Since you and Hunter got together, you act like an old lady. You're always home. Always with your man. And it's been like that for two years."

"We have a lot of fun together. I don't need to go to a club or a bar. I have everything I need at home."

Hayden grabs my hand and examines it. "I don't see a wedding ring. Or even an engagement ring, for that matter."

I roll my eyes, pulling my hand from his grip. "Hade, the first year I was focusing on finishing my degree. I had a ton of classes since I was graduating a year early. Now I've started working at Story's school, and sometimes it's not easy. Spending time with Hunter and Story is exactly what I need to recharge my batteries. Or going shopping with Riley." I soften my voice as I put my head on his shoulder. "Or hanging out with you, when you're not busy with the band."

He stares at me from under furrowed eyebrows, but his eyes tell me he's not angry. He sighs and winds his hand around my waist. "Things are picking up for Sabotage, Pip. We're in talks to sign with a label, and if we do—we're going to hit the road. I'll miss you terribly, especially if I don't get a chance to properly celebrate your birthday. As you said, you've been working hard, and you deserve to let loose."

I know he means well, and a month ago I would've agreed to a giant party. But things have changed. "I'm in charge of a big event at school. And I'm also—"

"I still don't get why you need to work." He eyes me as if he's seeing me for the first time. "Hunter has—"

I scoff, catching my little butterfly pendant between my fingers and playing with it. "I don't *need* to work, but I want to. It's important to me."

Hayden studies me for another moment. Then he sighs and kisses my temple. "Fine. Just be happy, Pip. Okay?" I nod, cuddling closer to him as we order our coffee.

After a few hours with Hayden, I slide into my car. I'm exhausted. Lately every day has been a super busy, shit show, and I don't even know how that happened. I'm just glad I have my family in my corner. Without them, I would've fallen apart.

My phone buzzes, and I check my watch. A smile blooms on my face as I read a message from Amelia.

AMELIA:

Story told me your big news! I'm so happy
for you!

I grab my phone and text her back.

ME:

Story told me your big news too! When are we
going to meet him?

AMELIA:

Har har. Very funny. I have two weeks off in
August.

ME:

We'll be waiting...for you and your new boyfriend.

When I get a middle finger emoji in return, I laugh and start the engine. She's unbelievable, but her snark just makes me love her even more. I want her to be happy. So when Story told me about her mom's new guy, I was ecstatic. I truly hope she'll bring Matthew with her when she comes to visit. I'm certain her ex-husband and her new boyfriend will find things to talk about. They are both soccer players, after all.

I park the car in front of our house and jump out. My steps are light as I head to the front door. It swings open once I near it, and Story bursts outside, laughing. Her dad is running after her with a water gun. Does Hayden really think I need more fun in my life? This fun is the kind I love the most.

"Piper!" Story runs behind me, pressing her wet body against me. I straighten my back, gasping loudly from the contact. "Please, please, please, tell Daddy to stop."

"Hunter, please stop," I murmur, trying to fight my smile. His green eyes rake over my face, and his lips curl into a lopsided grin.

"Fine," he says, lowering the water gun. But the second Story steps to my left, he shoots water in her direction again. She squeals, and I break into giggles. I need to change my clothes, and then I can finally talk to Hunter. I have something I want to tell him.

SITTING ON THE COUCH, Story and I watch *Toy Story 4* for what feels like the millionth time. Binx is on her lap, purring so loudly I had to turn the volume up. Hunter walks out of the kitchen carrying a bowl of caramel popcorn. He comes closer, hands it to Story, and squeezes in beside me. His hand is instantly on my shoulder, cradling me to his chest.

Story sneaks a glance at her dad and then at me. I wink at her, and her face lights up with a smile. I let her and Riley know about my news, only because my mom suggested I ask for help from my two besties.

"Daddy, can you please pass me my flashlight pen? It's on the armrest closest to you."

"Sure." He reaches over, grabs the pen, and extends it to Story. She looks at him without saying anything, not taking the pen in her hand. "What's wrong? Did I..."

Hunter falls silent, finally realizing what he's holding. His eyes never leave the pregnancy test. Then he lifts his head, a smile blooming on his lips.

"Congratulations, Daddy!" Story shrieks, jumping to her feet and dancing. Her eyes are sparkling with warmth and excitement—it's the exact same look she had when I told her. She's perfect.

I swivel and peer at my boyfriend.

"How far along are you?" he asks.

"A month," I murmur.

"What about school? The principal loves you; I'm sure she'll be sad to see you go," Hunter points out, still smiling.

"I already talked to her, and she said we'd figure it out. She's happy for me."

Hunter watches me in silence, and then he jumps to his feet too. He grabs my hand and pulls me to follow him. We dance, laughing almost to tears. Our family already feels full, full of love and happiness. Full of understanding and appreciation. It's full of us, and I can't wait to bring another baby into the mix.

We'll do great. I have no doubt about it.

One year later

hunter

"Yes, your nephew is fine," I say, standing in the backyard, watching Story swim. "Yes, your niece is fine too. And your best friend ...actually, I think my wife is a little tired from all the sleepless nights."

"Can't you help her?" Hayden lowers his voice, becoming serious.

Sabotage's success turned him into someone I never expected. He gives all of himself to the band, to their fans, and they love the band in return. Grammy nominations will be announced in November, and everyone seems to believe that Hade will win a few. Only time will tell, but I'll be more than happy if that happens.

"I am helping her. Sometimes she's just too stubborn," I explain, my eyes narrowing on Piper, who's nursing our son, Hudson, in her arms.

She barely slept last night, and I'm determined to change that. I'm fully capable of giving him a bottle and putting him back to sleep myself. School and practice will never stop me from that.

After I hang up with Hayden, I scoot over to the pool, and Story swims toward me. She cocks an eyebrow as I bend down.

"Go inside, change your clothes. We'll be waiting for you in the living room," I whisper. She nods, her gaze darting to Piper and Hudson. "I want to cheer her up, what do you think?"

"I'm all in," she says and starts to swim to the pool ladder. Then she comes to a stop, and I look at her. "Riley says Piper needs to spend more time at the beach. It calms her down."

I smirk knowingly and shoo her inside. Once Story's in the house, I walk over to Piper and sit beside her on the sunbed. "Is he behaving?"

"Not really." She sighs as I take Hudson from her and press him to my chest.

He's four months old, but his hair is already long. Just like Story's was, with one exception—my son is blond. His big green eyes focus on me. My mom says he reminds her of both Hayden and me, while my mother-in-law is sure he looks just like Piper and Riley. He's the most beautiful little boy I've ever seen. Because he's mine.

"You need to rest, baby." I place a light kiss on her temple. "You're tired."

"Hunter, I just can't. You have practice every morning, and your school. I don't want to—"

I seize this moment and cover her lips with mine. A sweet little kiss, just to shut her up. Once I move away, her eyes snap open.

"I'm your husband, and I'm Hudson and Story's dad. And that's more important than being a football player or a coach. You're my family, and I want to help you with anything you need."

She sniffles, her eyes watering. "I love you so, so much," she confesses.

"I love you too, Piper." I nudge her with my shoulder. "Now go inside and get ready. Put on something nice and comfortable. We're going somewhere together. I'll look after Hudson. Go."

Piper smiles sheepishly, then nods and stands up. She wanders inside, and I lower my gaze to my son. The pacifier in his mouth moves relentlessly, and it makes me chuckle. We're not really letting him use it, but it helps a ton while he's teething.

"Buddy, you need to give your mom a break. She deserves it. She was up for three hours last night." My son listens to me carefully. Then the pacifier pops out of his mouth, and a toothless smile illuminates his face. He loves listening to my voice; Piper says I have a calming effect on him. And I love talking to him. It's the most precious thing, literally the highlight of my days. "I can't wait to see your first tooth. Who knows, maybe your uncle will get here just in time to see it."

I stand up from the sunbed and go into the house as well. I still need to prepare everything we need to take with us. I have the day off from practice, and things at school are running like clockwork. They don't need my supervision, but I still go there a few days a week, to make sure everything is exactly how it should be.

An hour later, I'm sitting on a blanket at the beach. My son is in his car seat, sound asleep. Piper and Story are playing with a Frisbee, laughing and chasing each other. They're having a ton of fun, while I juggle texting Amelia and Angelo. Both have news to share, and it makes my mood even better. My ex-wife is engaged to Matthew, a guy she's been dating for over a year now, and she's never been happier. They're discussing their wedding plans, and she wants to make sure we can all come. Angelo is finally going to be a dad to a boy, and he's over the moon. I'm also assuming he's pretty drunk, as his texts are becoming more and more ridiculous.

"What are you up to?" Piper plops down beside me, glancing at our sleeping son. She looks calm.

"Just texting with Angelo and Amelia."

I curl a hand around her shoulders and pull her to me. Piper settles between my legs with her back against my chest. We sit in silence, watching Story fly a kite. I hide my nose in Piper's hair, inhaling her familiar scent of lavender and vanilla.

"You know, before you and Story, I thought there was nothing I loved more than being at the beach alone," Piper mutters under her breath. She covers my hand on her belly with hers. "I was so wrong. There's nothing I love more than being at the beach with my family."

I reach over and tilt her face up to mine. We look at each other for a moment, and then I slowly kiss her. The murmur of the sea and Story's laughter surrounds us. It makes me feel full. Happy, content, and loved. I met my perfect match in Piper; I have beautiful children and a successful career. I have friends and a great relationship with my brother and my parents, including my dad. I was finally able to forgive him. I have it all, and I know she's the glue that holds my life together. She's the reason I'm so damn lucky.

She's my everything.

sin-bin excerpt

chapter 1 - fucker

ava

"Oh, Clay, yeah... Do that again... Oh, I'm gonna come... I'm gonna come... Clay, please..."

For the past thirty minutes, that's all I've heard. Moans, dirty talk, spanking, and more moans. Why can't she come already so I can finally get into my room and sleep? I literally hate my roommate.

It's my second week of college. Great Lake University in Michigan has a unique history, incredible professors, and it's the perfect place for me to focus on my communication and media major. It's not far from my hometown, so it's easy for me to visit my dad whenever I feel like it. I've been looking forward to spending time at GLU, studying and hanging out with my best friend, going to parties. I had it all figured out, and I was going to stick to my plan no matter what.

My roommate proved me wrong within hours. She's a nightmare.

Jordan Patterson is the type of girl who will chew you up and spit you out, and you won't even notice it. She's drop-dead gorgeous, but her personality is the biggest turnoff. As soon as she saw me coming, she scowled and loudly exclaimed that she definitely hadn't hit the roommate jackpot.

I thought the same, but I kept my words to myself.

I would've loved to live with my best friend, Layla Benson, but she's a year older than me, and this is her second year, so it's impossible. I got what I got, and I needed to get used to it, as my adviser said. I'd be curious to see her reaction if it were her sitting on the floor outside her room, waiting for her roommate to have an orgasm.

Please, Jordan, come already.

My phone dings with an incoming message, and I pick it up off the floor. I unlock it, see a text from my best friend, and instantly smile. Layla is my person, through and through. We have many similarities, but the one thing we don't have in common is our taste in boys.

Her family's house is across the street from mine, so I've known Layla all my life. We can call each other names, threaten to beat the living shit out of one another if one of us acts unreasonable or stupid. A few times, we've stopped talking altogether...but we're always there for each other, no matter what.

BESTIE:

How about shopping tomorrow?

ME:

All in. But only if I get some sleep.

BESTIE:

Meaning? You went back to your room almost an hour ago...

ME:

My roommate is having sex with someone named Clay.

BESTIE:

Gosh. She works fast.

ME:

Don't remind me. It got quieter, maybe they are done?

BESTIE:

Why don't you go inside? She needs to know it's not okay

ME:

Dunno.

I glance at the closed door. What if I open it and just go in? It's my room too, and I'm tired of waiting.

BESTIE:

Ava Mason, you're a badass. Why do you allow her to treat you like this?

I roll my eyes and rise to my feet. She isn't wrong. I've never let anyone treat me like this. Who does she think she is?

ME:

I'll text you later. I need to put someone in her place.

BESTIE:

That's my girl.

I laugh, shoving my phone into my purse. Then I square my shoulders and put the key into the lock. *It's do or die.*

I open the door and freeze straightaway. *What the hell?*

Jordan is totally naked, down on her knees, and giving head to a guy who's sitting in a chair. But that's not what blows me away. Another dude is on her bed, jerking off while watching his friend with my roommate. A nauscating feeling lodges in my throat. This can't be happening.

"You said your roommate left for the weekend." The voice of the guy in the chair is cold and distant, sending chills down my spine.

I don't see his face because the room is mostly dark, illuminated only by dimmed LED ceiling lights. The only detail I notice is his brown hair. He puts his hand on Jordan's head, keeping her in place. She gags on his cock, and uneasiness seeps into my veins.

What have I just dragged myself into?

Voices become louder; someone is coming down the hallway. *Shit.* It'd be the worst scenario ever to let someone see my roommate like this. No matter what I think of her, no one deserves that humiliation. I take a step forward and close the door with a thud. I look around without focusing on anything, crossing my arms over my chest and then dropping them to my sides. Still, I stay rooted to the spot.

"Want to join?" the guy from the bed asks me in a mocking voice.

It triggers me, boosting my confidence. I stomp in his direction, stop near the bed, and put my hands on my hips. "Get out."

His smirk fades away as he takes his palm off his dick. He stares into my eyes, but I just hold his gaze and say nothing.

"Girl, we were having fun with your roommate way before you got here. She told us you went home."

"I don't care when you got here. I don't care what she said about me. I want you out of my room. Now."

He frowns, hesitating. The slurping sounds become louder while I refuse to watch. One dick is enough for my colorful imagination for one day, especially one I never planned to see.

"If I knew you'd come in and ruin all the fun, I would've never even agreed to fuck this freshman." The guy stands up and heads for his clothes on the floor. He hurriedly puts his T-shirt and his pants on.

I observe him, trying to remember if I've seen him before. I bite my bottom lip in annoyance because nothing rings a bell. He's good-looking with auburn hair and yellowish-green eyes. His body speaks volumes about all the hard work he's clearly been doing in the gym. Is he from the hockey team? What if he knows my best friend's brother? With how often Layla hangs out with Drake, if this asshole is one of his teammates, I'm screwed.

The guy puts his sneakers on and straightens, looking over my shoulder at his friend. "Dude, are you done?"

"Almost." His voice changes, sounding a bit husky. And sexy. My eyes widen, and I inwardly curse myself. I have no idea what he looks like, and I think his voice is sexy? What's wrong with me?

The auburn-haired guy from the bed hides his hands in his pockets and shifts to look at me. "I'm Clay."

"Uh-huh."

"Not going to tell me your name, beautiful?" He beams, making me chuckle. He just had sex with my roommate. Does he really think I'd be interested?

"I don't think you deserve to know my name," I murmur, and his face lights up with a smile. I intrigue him, but ew—I can't even think about something happening between us.

"I'm a resourceful fella, and if you let me—"

"Not going to happen, Clay. Really." I speak softly.

"Shame." He shrugs. "I'll figure out your name with or without you telling me."

"Whatever." I let out a short laugh as I hear the sound of a zipper. Heavy steps follow, stopping right behind my back.

"You kinda ruined the moment," a voice rasps in my ear, its hot breath fanning over my skin.

I spin around and find myself right in front of him. I'm smaller than this guy. My eyes are at his chest, and I involuntarily look up to rake my gaze over him. I can't deny that he's stunning, but the look on his face makes me uncomfortable. So much arrogance and annoyance. A bad boy at his finest. The type I'm attracted to the most but prefer to run away from.

"You kinda ruined it yourself," I retort. "Get out. Both of you."

"No one tells me what to do." His stare darkens, and he frowns.

"Keep telling yourself that." I laugh, happy with my sassy response. I gradually relax, feeling more at ease, but it's short-lived.

He leans into my face. His deep brown eyes burn holes into me. "I hope I never see you around campus."

"Or what?"

His lips stretch into a big, radiant smile. "Or you'll regret coming inside this room while I was here."

"It's my room too, and it's not my fault she lied about my where-abouts." I grunt, narrowing my eyes. "Get out."

His pupils dilate, indicating his surprise. He didn't expect that kind of reaction from me. I bet he's used to people running for their lives when he looks at them that way. Not me. I don't care about this guy. I just want him gone. Period.

"Dude, come on. We have places to go. The night is young." Clay calls out to his friend, who keeps gaping at me in silence. It's ridiculous. He's not fucking royalty, yet he expects me to bow down to him. Suddenly, he inches toward my ear, and his lips graze my earlobe.

"I bet I can make you come in one minute. I can make you scream my name while you're riding my dick." He leans away, grinning like a fucking idiot while I feel my cheeks get warm. "But I won't. You're too fucking plain for that. Too simple."

"Fucker," I mutter, sucking in air. How dare he?

Without giving it any thought, I slap him across his face. So hard my palm stings. He fucking deserves it.

I don't even have time to blink before Clay walks around me, shielding me from his friend. "Colton," he says, as I take a few steps back. "Let's go. Okay?"

A second passes, then Colton pushes his friend away and storms to the door. He opens it, turns his head, and locks his gaze onto mine. "You just made a huge mistake."

"I don't see it that way." I put on a brave face, but my palms are sweating. Clay sighs, glances at me, and follows his friend out of the room. Then the door closes and they're both gone.

I take a deep breath and focus my attention on Jordan. She's silent, and it creeps me out. What's wrong with her? I edge closer to her and kneel. "You okay?"

Her mascara is smeared under her eyes, and her cheeks and neck are red. She stares off into the distance, then looks at me. "You ruined everything."

"What?"

"Those two...they're the most popular guys on campus. Girls dream about being with them, and I was lucky they both wanted to get laid tonight." Jordan peels her eyes away from my face. "Clay is good, but not exceptional. While Colton...he's a dreamboat. And when I finally get the chance to lay my hands on him, you decide to step in."

"You sucked him off," I mumble in annoyance. "Not sure he would've wanted to fuck you after his friend."

"I could've convinced him." she snaps, standing up and moving to put her clothes on.

I shake my head in disbelief. I don't know the guy; I just know the type. He would've never fucked her after his friend. A blow job was the only thing he was interested in. She should know better.

"I'm going to take a shower," she sneers through clenched teeth, then trudges to the door. But she stops in her tracks and looks at me over her shoulder. "Colton doesn't tolerate disrespect, Ava. Being his enemy will be extremely bad for your reputation."

"We'll see." I hold my chin up high, watching as she ambles out the door. I exhale loudly as soon as it closes.

I wipe off my makeup, comb my long brown hair, and braid it into a Dutch braid. I feel uneasy, but I try to brush off those thoughts. As soon as I'm in bed, I take out my phone and type a message to Layla.

ME:

I shooed the boys away. Already in bed. Shopping, here I come.

BESTIE:

Boys?

ME:

Clay and Colton.

BESTIE:

OMFG.

ME:

What the hell does that mean?

BESTIE:

Tell u more tomorrow.

ME:

Not fair.

I whine aloud, hiding under the blanket.

BESTIE:

Meet me at 11 a.m. near your dorm. Night.

I toss my phone on the nightstand and close my eyes. The image of that guy impetuously appears in my head. Memories of his severe glare send shivers down my spine. I shut my eyes tighter, erasing him from my mind. The last thing I want is to have nightmares because of that jerk.

I don't think love at first sight exists, but I believe in annoyed at first sight, and Colton is exactly that. He's obnoxious and self-centered, and I'll gladly keep my distance. He's bad news.

***

SIN-BIN is an enemies to lovers college romance, the first book of the Sinners on the Ice series. Available on Amazon, Kindle and in Kindle Unlimited.

barn burner excerpt

chapter 1 - snow queen

evangelina

I GLANCE AT THE CLOCK AND SMILE, SEEING MY ODDLY favorite numbers—12:12. I quickly close my eyes and make a wish for today to turn out well. It's a habit I've acquired over the years, allowing myself to believe in a little bit of magic. Even if it's more of an illusion. Magic has nothing to do with what people are capable of.

The second I let the time sink in, I curse. I'm running late. I have a meeting about my dessert shop's new menu in a little over an hour, and I still need to take Cooper out. He's been a good boy, waiting for me, but even his patience has its limits. For the past forty minutes, my Doberman pinscher has been following my every step, looking into my eyes with an absolutely miserable expression. As if I didn't take him for an hour-long walk this morning. This dog is a manipulative asshole...but I still love him.

I collect my hair into two Dutch braids and twirl around, checking out my outfit. I intend to get in a little run on the way, so I'm wearing a black sports bra and black leggings with red sneakers. Coop sits by the door, eyeing me warily, as if there's a chance I'd run away.

"Come on, Coop, let's go." I grab my keys and his leash from the table and reach for the front door. He always walks out of the house and waits for me, but not today.

As soon as I open the door, Cooper barrels downstairs. His loud barks echo on the street as he charges for the large-as-a-wall guy standing near my Lamborghini Aventador.

"What the hell? Get your fucking dog off me," the guy growls.

Cooper already has his paws on the man's chest, and he keeps baring his teeth, his ears drawn back. I stay planted on the porch, my mouth falling open. Rapidly blinking, I pinch my eyebrows together, and a trickle of sweat rolls down my back.

Oh my God, what am I doing?

I rush down the stairs, tripping over two at once. Then I seize Cooper by his collar and drag him away from the guy. I put the leash on my dog and take a step back. Palm pressed to my rib cage, I try to catch my breath and finally look at the man in front of me. He looks pale, and his dark brown eyes are shooting daggers at me from under etched brows.

"I'm so sor—"

"What the fuck is wrong with you?" he interrupts, making me shut my mouth. "Your dog could've bitten my leg off. Don't you know how to use a fucking leash?"

I made a mistake, and I acknowledge that. Apologizing is the least I can do, but this man won't even let me finish.

"Don't you know how to talk to a woman?" I hiss, furrowing my brow. My gaze roams over his face. I take in his eyes, his slightly crooked nose, and the noticeable stubble on his cheeks. He might be attractive, but he's incredibly far from what I consider my type. "My dog is—"

"Your fucking dog attacked me." The guy clenches his fists. His jaw clamps shut as he grinds his teeth.

If I wasn't so pissed, I'd be intimidated by him. A glance is enough to tell me he's into sports. This man might be an athlete, perhaps a football player like Dad, who's the only athlete I like. I'm not interested in the rest of them.

"I made a mistake letting Coop out of the house without a leash.

But I didn't know you'd be checking out my car. He's defending me," I say.

A door slams shut, startling me and making me take a few steps back. Two girls run down the stairs of the two-story house next door with the white facade and large windows. They're headed in our direction.

Did someone buy it?

"I was curious about your car, and I just wanted to have a look. I didn't expect to almost lose my leg in the process."

I blink. "A barking dog is not the same as a biting dog. Maybe try not to gawk at other people's cars next time to avoid problems."

"Avoid problems?" he mumbles, breathing heavily. A vein in his neck pulsates. One of the girls appears in front of him. I focus my attention on her and instantly see that it's Bella.

Eight months ago, when I moved to Santa Clara, Bella worked her magic on the interior design of my house. She's incredibly nice and sweet, and I like her despite the fact that her husband is the quarterback for the California Mustangs. Though Xander is kinda cool; he helped me when I was looking for a tattoo artist four months ago.

Okay, maybe not all athletes are so bad. Maybe I'm being a hypocrite.

"Hey, Eva." Bella steps closer to me and kisses my cheek. "How are you?"

Her familiar face is like an instant fix for my mood. I smile, feeling my muscles relax a little. "Hey, Bella. I was great until this little incident. Do you know this guy?"

"Of course. Drake is my client. He bought this house, and I'm helping him decorate it."

My smile slips away, and I absentmindedly touch my earring. "Is he my new neighbor?"

"Yup." The brunette who was silently standing beside the guy takes a step forward and extends her palm to me. "I'm Ava. It's nice to meet you."

"Eva. Evangelina." I quickly shake her hand and then let go, stepping back. Her eyes are glued to my face as she stares at me with curiosity. "It's nice to meet you too. Unlike this guy—"

"I did nothing wrong; it was your dog's fault. You shouldn't let him off the leash." His posture is still tense as he bombards me with accusations.

Sighing, I pull Cooper to my side because he's trying to get to Bella. I bet he can smell her dog, Milo, on her. "Listen, I didn't expect him to run at you like he did. He knows how to behave."

A moment passes; my eyes stay locked on this guy. He blinks and shakes his head, muttering, "Whatever."

He stomps to the BMW X6 parked near Bella's car and slams the door so hard Ava flinches. Someone definitely has a problem controlling his anger.

I return my gaze to Bella and Ava. "Sorry about that. He just pissed me off, yelling at me and not letting me apologize to him." Stepping back, I loosen Cooper's leash a little and squint at my watch. "I need to get going."

"Sure," Bella murmurs, hugging me briefly. "See you around, Eva."

"See you around," I tell her and focus my attention on Ava. She's gorgeous, and I'm sure I've never seen her with Bella before. If she's this guy's girlfriend, he should be more appreciative of her instead of acting like the biggest child on the planet. "Bye, Ava."

"Bye, Eva." She grins at me. My eyes linger on her face for a moment, then I quickly stroll away from my house with Cooper. I can't believe I wasted so much time on that rude guy.

***

I'm sitting on the couch in my living room, typing on my laptop, listening to my playlist on Spotify. It's Saturday night, and instead of going out, I stayed home to work. These calm evenings, when I do whatever I want without caring what others think, are exactly what I need.

I glance to my left and meet Cooper's eyes instantly. He's lying in his dog bed, chewing on a big bone I bought for him. Even if he didn't deserve it. No matter what I think about my new neighbor, the way my dog acted toward that dude was not acceptable. He didn't do anything to cause that level of aggression, and I feel puzzled. What the hell happened to Coop?

This guy doesn't look like Asher—the only person Cooper wasn't very fond of. He's more like my dad. Tall and muscular, a good six foot five inches. And Coop loves my father. At this point, I can only hope the situation won't repeat itself. There's no way I'll ever let him out of the house without a leash again.

My phone beeps with an incoming message, but I ignore it. I'm determined to finish the new marketing strategy for my dessert shop. A smile blossoms on my lips when I let my fantasies overwhelm my brain. So many ideas and so many plans. In moments like these, I'm happy I gave up being a runway model. This way, I have more time to myself...even if I loved being a part of the shows. Another huge thank-you to Asher—not. He's my biggest fuckup. If anyone from my family knew *everything* about my relationship with my ex-boyfriend... I'd be dead.

I blink and shake my head, refocusing on my laptop. What's wrong with me tonight? It's like I can't catch a break. I'm constantly switching from one thought to the other.

Getting up from the couch, I proceed to the kitchen. I open the fridge and take out a plate with the last piece of cheesecake I made two days ago. I've been experimenting with flavors, and I love how deliciously sweet this one turned out. Blueberries might not be my favorite, but in cheesecake? It's a ten out of ten. I can't wait to talk to Marcy about adding it to our menu.

I turn on the kettle and move around the kitchen, humming along with Taylor Swift. "Anti-Hero" is my own personal anthem, as my best friend, Nevaeh, said the second she heard me singing it. I'm the problem. Me and no one else. Who in their right mind would start a relationship with a guy knowing he's a cheater and a manipulator? Only Evangelina Jones. Next time I want to prove something to someone, I'll promise to prove it only to myself.

I refuse to ruin my life and body ever again.

Once I settle at the table with my mug of chamomile tea and plate of cheesecake, paws slap on the tile, and Cooper enters the room. I can't even eat in peace with him around.

"Bro, soon you're going to be bigger than the Titanic," I tell him as he comes to the table and sits near my chair, facing me. Cooper won't guilt-trip me into feeding him again. He already had his dinner.

I pop a piece of my cheesecake into my mouth and hear a loud sigh. Someone is definitely trying to get my attention. *Not going to happen, Coop.* With my one hundred and twenty-two pounds against his ninety-nine, he'll be walking me soon, not the other way around. And I hate not being in control.

Another loud exhale leaves my dog's mouth, and he lowers his head onto my lap as I take another bite of my cheesecake. Groaning, I look at him. "What?"

Ugh, Cooper, give me a break. This dog is going to be the death of me. I pat his head and slowly stand up. I step to the cupboard, get a few pumpkin dog biscuits, and offer them to him. He swallows them in the blink of an eye and tilts his head, as if asking me, *What else?* I go back to my seat and finish my cheesecake without paying any attention to Coop's gaze on me. I'm doing it for his own good. He should be grateful.

After I finish loading the dishwasher, I return to the living room with Cooper in tow. He saunters to his dog bed, where he continues to gnaw on his bone.

I should probably watch something, but my mood is all over the place. Debating my next steps, I stare at the ceiling. I reach for my phone, unlock it, and quickly dial Nevaeh's number. There's a good chance she's already clubbing somewhere since it's past nine, but I still want to try. I need company.

"Hey, Nev," I say as soon as she answers. "What's up? What are you doing tonight?"

"Hey, honey," she murmurs sweetly. "Pretty much nothing. I'm on my period, so I'm planning to watch something and cuddle in my bed."

"Do you want to do pretty much nothing with me?" I ask, and she laughs heartily.

"Sounds good. Be there in thirty. You better have something to drink."

"You bet I do."

"See you soon, Angie," she says and hangs up.

Later, I'm sitting on the couch with a bottle of rosé, two glasses, and a cheese plate with olives on the table. I hope it'll be enough for us.

Grabbing my phone from the table, I decide to check the time, and I see the unread message. I'd totally forgotten about it. As soon as I read it, anger fills every bone in my body. The fucker has no idea when to stop.

UNKNOWN NUMBER:

How is my Snow Queen doing? Any chance your heart is warming up to me again? I miss you, Eva.

A horde of goosebumps spreads across my skin, and I squirm. Asher makes me hate my name. Any time he's going through another phase, he crawls back. Begging for my attention, asking me to go on a date with him...or just fuck him wherever I want. I don't want any of it.

My third breakup with him left a dent in my confidence and ugly signs of his addiction on my body. I want him to leave me alone, but unfortunately, he doesn't seem to understand. For whatever reason, he believes I still have feelings for him...as if I love him because I'm single. Delusional motherfucker. He's my past, one I don't regret leaving behind at all. Asher needs a reality check.

I block yet another one of his phone numbers and toss my phone onto the table. The doorbell rings, and I push myself from the couch to the hallway. Opening the door, my eyes land on Nevaeh. She's wearing a baggy black hoodie and black sweatpants; her strawberry blonde hair is collected in two cute buns on top of her head. I step away, and she ambles into my house, giving me a loud smooch on the cheek along the way.

A bottle of Moët is the first thing I see when I lock the door and spin around. Nevaeh is grinning from ear to ear as she holds the bottle in front of her. "Will you get drunk with me tonight? Pretty please?"

"As if you had to ask," I reply, and she squeals, jumping into the air like a kid. Shaking my head, I follow Nevaeh into the living room. Now I'm more than sure this night is going to be amazing. Just like it always is when she's around.

**

BARN BURNER is a fake dating hockey romance, the second book of the Sinners on the Ice series. Available on Kindle, Amazon and in Kindle Unlimited.

breakaway excerpt

chapter 1 - it's nothing

One Year Ago

nevaeh

"Hey, Trav," I say, making sure the door of my apartment is locked. I press my phone to my ear. "Are you on your way?"

"Sorry, babe. I still have a ton of work to do. Release week is always crazy, and the testers found another bug just now. I need to fix it."

An exasperated breath springs out of my mouth, and I mask it with a cough. If I knew he wasn't going to join me, I wouldn't have agreed to go. I'm always happy to spend time with my best friend, but going to a club with her and her fake boyfriend is definitely not something I counted on.

"Any chance you can join me later?" I ask, descending the stairs. The click of my heels echoes on the stairwell.

"I'm not sure, Nev. No one is going to fix my code for me, and with the release on Monday, I have a pretty tight deadline. And–"

"Are you working overtime again?" I huff, tightening my grip around my phone.

"You moved our date twice last week, because you had to work overtime too. Have you heard me say anything? Writing the article about the art exhibition was important for you, and I knew it."

Sighing, I close my eyes for a second, admitting he's right. "Sorry, Trav. I know it's not your fault." I step to the front door and push it open, stepping onto the street. "See you tomorrow then? Maybe we can hang out at my place?"

"How about you come to my place after the club? Even if it's late. I miss you."

A smile lifts my lips, and warmth spreads through my body. Who knew that being stuck in an elevator could bring someone like Travis into my life? Definitely not me. It's too much like 'Serendipity' and I don't believe in fate. "Okay, I'll text you later," I murmur.

Once I finish the call, I shoot a quick text to my best friend. Just to let her know that I'll be third-wheeling with her and Drake.

ME:

I'll be at the club in 40. Alone. Travis is still at the office

ANGIE:

It sucks that he's busy, but don't worry, Drake says he can invite one of his teammates. You won't be alone with us

ME:

Tell your fake boyfriend I love him. He just saved me from being the third wheel

ANGIE:

'insert eyeroll emoji'

Chuckling, I shove my phone into my purse and notice my Uber parking near my apartment building. Well, I can only hope Drake's teammate is a nice guy, like him. I've hung out with my share of jocks when I was in high school and college, and I can say that those guys aren't my type. Too self-absorbed, and too cocky, not in the good way. In most cases I barely have anything in common with them. Spending the night with someone arrogant and self-centered would be a bummer.

***

"Nev, over here!" My best friend calls out to me from the entrance to the club.

Angie stands with Drake, his hand secured around her narrow waist. Her long brown hair streams down her slender shoulders. She's wearing a red dress highlighting her sun-kissed skin and her flawless body. Big and bulky, Drake hovers over her with his broad shoulders and six foot five frame. They are a picture perfect couple. She's the one who has always believed in magic, making a wish any time she sees 12:12, when she checks time. I'm not like her, but I'm literally ready to cross my fingers and even my toes for these two to finally get together officially. Them fake dating doesn't make any sense.

"Hey, lovebirds," I say with a smile, stopping in front of them. "Sorry if I made you wait. My Uber wasn't the fastest."

"Hey, Nev." Angie leans forward and plants a kiss on my cheek. "And you're fine, we got here five minutes ago."

"And we still need to wait for Roman," Drake announces, fixing his dark brown eyes on me. "Wanted to make sure you wouldn't feel left out without your boyfriend."

"So you set me up on a double date with your teammate? So I won't feel lonely without my boyfriend?" I tease, noticing his eyes rounding.

"What? No, I just thought—"

"Drake, I'm joking!" I giggle, glancing between him and my best friend. With how she chews on her bottom lip, I know she's trying to bottle up her laughter. "I love you two, but I'm glad I'm not going to spend the night feeling like I'm in the way."

"Never," Angie murmurs, glancing at something over my shoulder. "Hi, Roman."

Feeling someone's presence behind me, I turn my head and my gaze trails up a male's chest in a tight black tee until it clashes with eyes of a deep turquoise color. A mischief twinkles behind his irises and a coy smirk forms on his clean-shaven face. His eyes slide down my body, and my skin ignites. I'm suddenly feeling hot. The guy is easily the most handsome man I've ever seen, and it says a lot, considering I've been crushing on Chris Evans for years.

I blink, breaking the trance I've gotten myself into. Oh my God! Am I really salivating over a guy? Just because of his looks? *Don't you remember Kyle Edwards, Nevaeh?* A perfect picture look often hides the ugliest parts of people's souls.

Rolling my lips together, I look away and focus my attention on my best friend. Angie frowns, as her eyes roam over my face. The way I went from smiling to scowling didn't go unnoticed by her. Not that it surprises me. Since I met her on my first day in college, she's been the only person in my life who knows everything about me. Love, zero judgment and unconditional support – she gives me everything. And I love her in return just the same.

"Hey, Drake, Angie." The guy says, lining up with me. "Sorry, if I made you wait."

"Totally fine, man," Drake exclaims, shifting his gaze from this guy to me. "Roman, this is Nevaeh."

Glancing to my left, I crane my neck, so I can look him in the eyes. Even with my heels on, I barely reach his shoulder. He's probably a good six foot three, and for whatever reason it irritates me. Or is it his cocky grin as he studies me from under his thick eyelashes? It doesn't mean anything. I'm not going to be friends with this guy. It can be the first and the last time we see each other.

"Hey, Roman." I extend my hand to him. "I'm Nevaeh."

His gaze slips to my outstretched hand, then flashes back to my face. A slight tilt of his head, and he cradles my palm with his. My heartbeat goes pitter-patter and a breath gets stuck in my throat. Our eyes lock, and he gives my hand a firm handshake. His skin is warm, and calloused. A billion tingles spread through my body, my whole being vibrates from just his touch. It's so weird, it freaks me out. I force a smile on my face and pull my hand away.

"It's nice to meet you, Nevaeh," he murmurs, never averting his gaze.

I nod and look away, avoiding meeting Angie's eyes too. The last thing I need is for my best friend to start asking questions, when I have no idea what's going on with me myself.

"Should we head inside?" Drake asks, and relief washes over me. The crowded club is exactly what I need to pull myself together. I'm in a relationship, and that's all that matters.

***

"Do you need a refill?" Hearing the question, I squint at Roman. We've been at the club for three hours and are now sitting at the bar to catch our breaths. "Nevaeh?"

"No, I'm good," I tell him, returning my gaze to the dance floor. For the last five minutes I've been eyeing the crowd, where Angie and Drake disappeared. I don't know how I feel being left alone with Roman. The number of times he has made me laugh tonight is equal to the number of times I've wanted to strangle him.

"How long have you known Angie?" he asks, and I meet his gaze. A glass of whiskey in his hand, his blues glued to my face.

"Since our freshman year." I shrug, fingers drumming on the bar counter. "What about you? How long have you known Drake?"

"Well, we met on the ice before he joined the Thunders. Plus, his best friend, Colton Thompson, talked my ear off with stories about him. When Drake walked into the locker room last season, I felt like I had already known him for a very long time." He drawls, bringing his glass to his lips, and my eyes zero in on it. My mouth goes dry, and I pinch my brows together. *Please, not again.* "Your best friend and Drake look great together."

"He's helping her get rid of her ex. They're just fake dating." I mumble, noticing how his eyes widen. Oh my God! What am I doing? Angie's going to hate me. "Forget that, I'm full of shit."

Roman stares at me, the glass is still pressed to his lips. Then he lifts his shoulder and says, "*Horosho*[1]."

I sit up straighter and tilt my head to the side, watching him with my eyes narrowed. "You're Russian, right?"

A chuckle escapes his lips as he puts the glass down. "No."

"But that was Russian, the word you said...wasn't it?"

"It was," he deadpans.

"Then, how come you speak Russian, if you're not Russian?" I mutter, hooking one leg over the other to sit more comfortably.

"You do realize there are more countries where people speak Russian than just Russia, right?" Roman puts his elbow on the bar, propping his head on his fist.

"Duh, of course." I look away, not handling his taunting smile. Making a fool of myself in front of this guy becomes way too agitating. "Teach me something in Russian." I say, peering at him again.

"For example?"

"Teach me how to say thank you."

"That's easy. Spasibo[2]," Roman exclaims nonchalantly. "Do you want me to say it slower?"

"Spasibo," I repeat after him.

He continues staring at me, not saying even a single word. Just at that moment, Drake and Angie join us, glancing between Roman and me.

"You're saying it all wrong," he finally mutters, eyebrows pinched together.

Rolling my eyes, I exhale and say as slowly as possible. "Spasibo." I arch an eyebrow, crossing my arms over my chest. "What's wrong? I nailed it. Admit it."

His eyes slide to his teammate and my best friend, and then he brings his gaze back to me. "That time it was good, but you definitely need more practice."

My jaw unhinges, and my eyes are probably ready to pop out of their sockets. "You're..." I point my finger at Roman. "A jerk. That was my first time trying to say anything in Russian — of course I need more practice."

Not a care in his voice, he takes his glass from the counter. "Saying 'thank you' in Belarusian would've been way harder, doll."

"Doll?" I echo, snatching his drink and downing it in one go. "Buy yourself another one."

I snap my head in Angie's direction, calculating in my head how to tell her about my slip-up about the fake dating. Pulling her away from Drake and his insufferable teammate is my best shot. Without another thought, I jump off the barstool, wrap my hand around my best friend's wrist, and announce, "We're dancing."

Angie tries to argue, but I just drag her away, further into the crowd. Something about this guy makes me act stupid, and I need a break if I don't want to end the night doing something even more stupid. I've already made too many mistakes tonight.

"Nev, what's wrong?" my best friend asks, her deep green eyes warmly staring at me. I snake my hand around her waist, silently pushing her to start dancing. "Is it because we left you with Roman?"

"That's fine. Just..." I trail off, mulling my next words. "He was teasing me, and I let it slip that you and Drake are fake dating." Angie's mouth forms a little O, she blinks, her eyebrows etched together. "I'm so sorry."

She sighs. "It's fine. I'll talk to Drake. This whole fake dating is getting out of hand anyway. I should've never asked him to pretend–"

"Are you pretending?" I catch her off guard with my question, and can't help but smile, noticing a beam tugging at the corners of her mouth. "He's a great guy, Angie."

"I know," she murmurs, coasting her eyes over my face. "What do you think about Roman?"

The smile drops from my lips immediately. "He's okay. What should I think about him?"

"You've been acting kinda weird tonight, and I can't really put my finger on it, but I think it's because of him."

"I'm with Travis," I state, matter-of-factly. Not waiting for her next words, I wrap my arm around her waist and turn her around, pressing her back to my chest. "I'm happy."

Dancing with Angie, I try to push every single thought out of my mind. Memories about my time with Trav still reappear in my head, and suddenly I feel like the biggest liar on earth.

***

Heading toward the bar, I let my eyes roam over Roman. He sits with his back turned to me, a visible tension in his shoulders catches my attention. The rigged posture, his head hanging low is a significant difference from how he was with me, or even when we were all together. As if he's uncomfortable being here alone.

I swallow down my nerves, sliding my palms down the skirt of my dress, trying to straighten it. Once I'm just behind his back, I extend my palm and tap on his shoulder. Without any real reason for it, my fingers linger on his tee, feeling his tense muscles underneath it. Roman jerks in his seat, his head swiveling in my direction.

"Drake said you'd look after me," I mumble, pulling away my hand and climbing on the barstool beside him. "They left."

He scans me from my head to my toes, a glint in his eyes turning dark. The tip of his tongue slips out of his mouth and he slowly licks his lips. I watch him enchanted, the warmth unfurling in my lower abdomen. *The excitement. The longing. The craziest need.* I ball my fists on my lap, nails digging in my skin. What is so fucking special about this guy? I've never felt like this. It's just utterly wrong.

"Did you tell Angie about you blurting out her secret?" he asks, his voice deep and low. Even with the loudest music, I hear him clearly. As if he's whispering right into my ear.

"I did." I confirm. "Did you mention it to Drake?"

"I did." He nods, a smile lifting his lips. "I don't think they will be fake dating much longer. Those two are in love, it's clear to anyone around them. It's time they recognize it too."

Biting my bottom lip, I try to hide my smile but fail. With a big grin, I let my shoulders drop, the tension I felt disappearing. Lightness fills my every pore as I wave my hand to catch the bartender's attention. The guy beside me is not exactly who I thought he was, and maybe it was the reason I was so weird with him. That must be it.

"Do you want to hang out for a bit longer or you need to get back home?" I ask, realizing that even my heartbeat is calmer now. The lighting dynamically illuminates the place, an ever-changing spectrum dances to the rhythm. The music reverberates through my body.

Roman runs his fingers through his sandy blond hair, his eyes trained on me. "There's no one waiting for me at home," he tells me, just as the bartender joins us. "I can stay for a few more hours, if you're in."

I smile. "I'm in."

***

"Are you always such a gentleman?" I squint at Roman, as we make our way to the exit. His hand is on my lower back, guiding me forward and keeping me from swaying.

"I'm not a gentleman," he bites out curtly.

Stopping abruptly in the middle of the crowd, I make him halt in his tracks too. I half-turn to him, purposefully letting my eyes sweep over his body and up his face. The pulsating vein on his neck makes my breath hitch in my throat. I force myself to divert my attention. The second my gaze meets his, I smile despite the heat rekindling in my lower abdomen. "You are. You've been watching over me, making sure I always had a drink, waiting for me outside the bathroom."

Roman bends his head, pinning me with his stare. His turquoise eyes burn into mine. My chest rises and falls, and the rhythmic basses have nothing to do with how my body trembles.

"A man always keeps his word," he says and steps back, hiding his hands in his pockets. "Let's go."

Not sparing me even a glance, he turns on his heel, easily making his way through the crowd. I gawk at his back, as he moves further and further away from me. *Good job, Nevaeh.* Was it really that necessary to flirt with him *again*?

The last two hours that I spent in Roman's company were completely different from the moment I met him. All my awkwardness disappeared, and I was just myself. Flirty and easy-going. It

353

looked like he was in need of company, and my babbling provided that for him. Until he finally had enough of me ten minutes ago. I slap my cheeks with my palms slightly and follow after him.

Once outside, I lean my back against the wall and take a deep breath. Cool wind envelops my body and I shiver, noticing Roman moving toward me.

"Okay, I need you to tell me your address." He stops in front of me, a phone in his hand. "Nevaeh?"

I focus my blurry vision on him. The alcohol in my system is making my legs wobbly. "I'm not going home."

He sighs, pursing his lips tighter in annoyance. "Just give me an address, so I can order an Uber for us."

I click my tongue and tell him Travis' address, adding in the end. "I'm going to my boyfriend's."

Roman's blues find mine for a moment, and then he looks away. "Okay. I just want to make sure you make it home or to your boyfriend's place safely." He pockets his phone. "We're lucky, we don't need to wait long. Our car will be here in five minutes."

I push the strands of my hair off my face, tucking them behind my ears. "Why did you stay?"

"Because. It's nice to change the scenery from time to time," he replies, folding his arms over his chest. His tattoos on his right arm draw my attention, and I lean forward, trying to look closely.

He doesn't have any lines connecting his different tattoos in one ensemble. It's chaotic and kinda senseless: numbers, some words, a dreamcatcher, a bleeding heart. The second my gaze falls on one colorful tattoo, I reach my hand and touch his skin.

"SpongeBob," I mumble under my breath, lowering my head to get a closer look. There is a word written beneath it, but before I have a chance to figure it out, he steps back, arms dangling at his sides. "What's wrong?"

"Nothing," he states, holding my gaze. A deep scowl on his face screams otherwise. I should keep my mouth shut, yet curiosity gets the best of me.

"Do you love SpongeBob so much that you dedicated a tattoo—"

"It's just a tattoo." Roman glances over his shoulder, and I swear I hear him sigh in relief. "Our Uber is here." He turns his eyes on me, and I get literal chills running down my spine. The corners of his mouth drop, not even the tiniest shadow of a smile there. The heaviness of his stare makes my knees give out and I tumble forward, barely catching myself from face planting.

"You okay?" he asks, and I nod, beelining toward the car in silence. All I want is to get as far as possible from him. He gives me whiplash with his mood swings.

After thirty agonizing minutes in the car with the guy, who spent the whole ride texting with someone and ignoring my presence, I feel way more sober than I've been. The guilt for flirting with Roman gnaws at me, making me feel terrible about myself. Travis has always been nice to me, and he doesn't deserve his girlfriend hitting on another man the second he couldn't join me. It was disrespectful and stupid. I should know better.

The Uber stops in front of Travis' building, and I climb out of the car. I'm tempted to just slam the door and walk away, but his voice saying my name freezes me on the spot.

"Nevaeh?"

I bend my head, my eyes meeting his. "What?"

"Thank you for staying with me. You saved me from another night that I'd spend getting lost in my head."

"You're welcome." I shrug and take a step back. "Bye."

"I'll be seeing you." His soft murmur goes straight through me, the back of my neck feeling hot. Without another glance, I close the car door and hurry into the building.

Once I hear Travis' voice coming through the intercom, I relax. Everything that happened tonight stops mattering. A familiar comfort blankets me, and I feel at ease. I have no idea why I reacted the way I did to Roman, but if there is something I'm certain of - Travis makes me feel good. Whatever happened at the club is meaningless.

It's nothing.

***

**BREAKAWAY is an accidental marriage hockey romance, the
third book of the Sinners on the Ice series. Coming to KU,
Kindle and in paperback in Spring 2024.**

---

1. Хорошо - Horosho - Okay.
2. Спасибо - Spasibo - Thank you

acknowledgments

To *my husband and my son*, your love for football (aka soccer) is one of the reasons why I love this sport so much. And why I desperately wanted to write a book about a football player, planning the plot while watching my kid kicking the ball on the pitch.

To *Nicole*, thank you so much for always being there for me. For your love and support.

To *Alwyn*, thank you so much for your guidance and your support. I've learned so much from you, and I'll be forever grateful to you.

To my incredible beta-readers: *Jamie, Holly, Kasandra, Kelly, Kiki, Stacey, Stephanie,* and *Taniya*, thank you so much for your reactions, your feedback and suggestions! You helped me to make HALE better.

To *my editor Caroline*, thank you so much for your support and for perfecting Hunter and Piper's story.

To *my ARC readers*, thank you so much for taking time to read this angsty story. For your support and help with spreading the word about HALE.

To *my readers*, thank you so much for reading, for loving my characters, for recommending my books, for being with me on this eventful journey. It means everything to me.

also by anastasija white

SIN-BIN: An Enemies to Lovers College Hockey Romance

BARN BURNER: A Fake Dating Hockey Romance

HALE: A Single Dad Sports Romance

BREAKAWAY: An Accidental Marriage Hockey Romance (Spring, 2024)

POWER PLAY: A Second Chance Hockey Romance (Fall, 2024)

HADE: A Rockstar Romance (Winter, 2025)

DOMINIC: A Stepbrother Romance (TBD, 2025)

TURNOVER: A Forbidden Football Romance (Rules Duet, TBD 2025)

about the author

Anastasija is an indie author who spends her days creating swoon-worthy and steamy stories that will make your heart race. Her writing is filled with flawed and relatable characters that you'll find yourself rooting for. Whether you're in the mood for angsty drama or steamy romance, her stories take you on a rollercoaster ride of emotions with guaranteed happy endings.

When she's not writing, she loves to lose herself in reading books, rewatching her favorite tv-shows and spending time with her son. She loves traveling and exploring the world, and then including places she visited in her novels.

If you're a fan of romance that leaves you breathless and begging for more, Anastasija is the author for you. Connect with her on Instagram and TikTok, where she loves to hear from her readers and share sneak peeks of her books and upcoming projects.

Made in United States
North Haven, CT
21 June 2024